DUSTWALKER

A STANDALONE NOVEL

TIFFANY ROBERTS

DUSTWALKER

BY TIFFANY ROBERTS

DUSTWALKER

A robot searching for purpose. A woman who brings him to life. Can they learn to love in a broken world?

With his core programming lost to time, Ronin has wandered the Dust for nearly two centuries. Out in that unforgiving wasteland, his armored undercasing, advanced optics, and amped-up processors give him an advantage over other scavengers. He's resigned himself to this unending trek until one night—until one human—makes him question everything.

Lara Brooks and her sister have spent their lives struggling to survive under the tyrannical rule of Cheyenne's robotic master, Warlord. But when her sister goes missing, Lara has no one to turn to, no one willing to help her. She's utterly alone. Her only hope comes from a bot she catches spying on her.

Ronin agrees to protect Lara and find her sister. All she must do in return is dance for him.

The transaction should be simple. Lara's danced for bots before. Yet the more time they spend together, the harder it becomes for her to see him as nothing but a collection of circuits and machinery.

And Ronin soon finds it difficult to deny what shouldn't be possible…

She makes him *feel*.

But if Ronin defies Cheyenne's rules to pursue his growing desires, he risks exposing Lara to a danger far greater than any found in the unforgiving wasteland—Warlord's wrath.

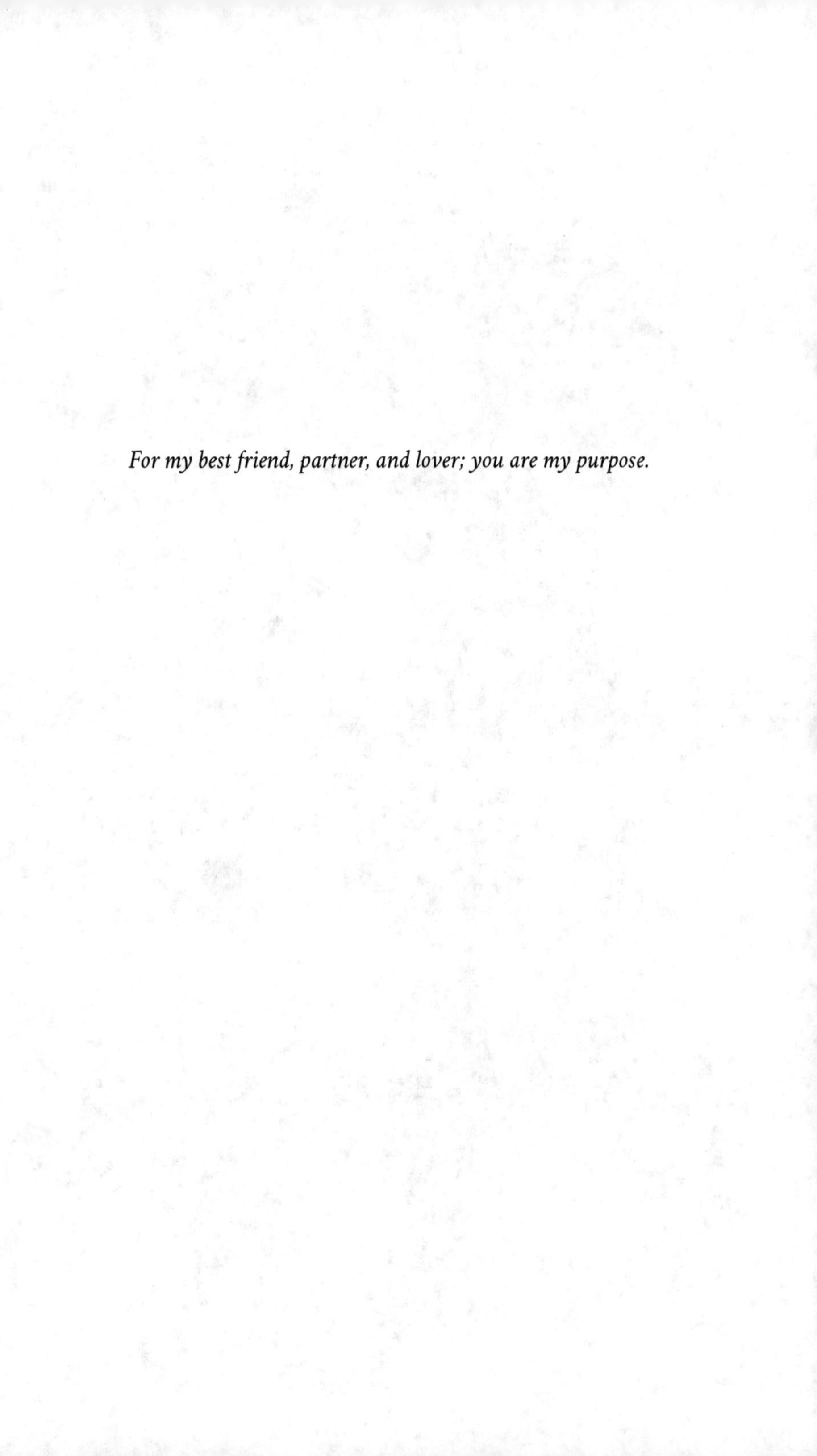

CHAPTER ONE

Lara grasped the edges of the large wooden board and heaved. Pebbles, dirt, and debris tumbled from it as it rose. She shoved it backward. It kicked up a cloud of dust when it landed, which was swiftly carried away by the wind. Crouching, she sifted through the exposed bits of splintered wood, rusted metal, and broken ceramics with her fingers.

"Well, what did you think you'd find?" she asked herself as she sat back on her heels and ran her gaze over the crumbled buildings nearby. The ruins of another world surrounded her, blanketed in a thick layer of dirt.

A drop of sweat trickled between her breasts. Though the cloth wrapped around her head and body protected her skin from the sun, it couldn't keep out the heat. If it weren't for the stinging sand carried on the frequent gusts of wind, she would've torn the sweat-dampened fabric off.

Lara sighed. "What the hell's left to find in this trash heap?"

Her sister's voice replied from the depths of her memory.

There's always something to find, so let's make it a game. Whoever finds the best treasure gets a larger portion.

Tabitha had always created little competitions to distract from the truth of their circumstances when they were younger, though no matter the outcome, she'd always given Lara the larger share of food. As an adult, Lara couldn't ignore reality. Whether she liked it or not, scavenging was the only way to find things the bots deemed valuable, and even if she didn't trade with the bots directly, this was the only way she'd get anything to eat.

A pang pierced her chest at the thought of Tabitha.

"Damn bots." Lara swiped at the debris, knocking aside pebbles and dust.

She hadn't seen her sister in almost two months.

Two months without seeing her hopeful smile, without hearing her voice, without feeling her comforting touch. Tabitha had disappeared, leaving a gaping void in Lara's life.

Lara picked through the rubble, tossing every bit of metal she found into her bag. Even if they were small and in rough shape, the pieces were worth something, but she couldn't help her disappointment. She'd hoped for a more significant find after hours of toiling under the relentless sun.

The soft clink of a rock against a piece of ceramic gave her pause. She picked up one of the shards and turned it over. Though faded with time and wear, the blue pattern on it was still visible—part of a flower. Carefully, she brushed away the loose dirt atop the ground, revealing more shattered pieces with the same floral decorations.

Once, each piece had been part of a larger whole. Bowls, plates, and cups, each beautiful in its own right.

What good are they now? They aren't worth the dust they're lying in.

Lara was about to toss the shard back, but the pattern caught her eye again. She'd only ever seen flowers in pictures, and even those were difficult to find. She tucked the shard into a fold of cloth around her waist, away from anything that might've damaged it further.

More digging yielded two forks and three spoons, all rusted, which she added to the scrap metal in her bag. Moving aside a rotted wood plank, she found a solid piece of glass. She tugged on it. The resistance told her it was much larger than she'd thought.

Using a flat rock, she carefully dug around the glass, her excitement growing as more of it was revealed. Finally, she pulled it free.

She stared down in amazement at the heavy pitcher in her hands. The glass was foggy and scratched, but it was intact except for a small chip near the base. It had a smooth, curved handle, and was decorated with raised images of flowing leaves and flowers.

Wadding the end of her sleeve in her hand, she rubbed off some of the dirt. The glass caught the sun, sparkling like a rainbow, its hues shifting as she turned it back and forth.

It was beautiful.

Standing, she removed a long piece of cloth from her waist and wrapped it around the pitcher before placing the bundle in her bag. She picked the bag up and held it to her chest. One little slip, and the pitcher could shatter. Without a doubt, it was the best thing she'd found in a long time, and Lara was tempted to keep it for herself. But her empty stomach wouldn't allow that.

She picked her way through the rubble, heading back to the wide stretch of dirt and scrub grass that served as a road. The pitcher would be worth something to Kate and Gary. Between them and their five-year-old daughter, Maggie, they always needed extra water on hand.

Only their generosity had kept Lara from starvation. Because they were a family, they were allowed to purchase more food, and usually had a little to spare for Lara when she had items worth trading. Though she didn't care for the pity in their eyes when they spoke with her, they'd been kind since Tabitha's disappearance, and besides…hunger outweighed pride.

She knew Gary received more for her items at the market than he gave her, but he dealt with her fairly. Of course he needed some profit to help support his family. And the loss on Lara's end was acceptable if it meant she never had to deal with a bot again.

Lara hurried down the road, occasionally glancing at the ruins to either side. A few of the walls were still upright, teetering in the wind, defying time and nature. The buildings here hadn't been built to last; wood and crumbly plaster couldn't compare to the brick and concrete structures in the market.

At the three-way intersection, she glanced up at the signpost. Tabitha had shown it to her when they were children. Lara couldn't read the beat-up sign hanging from it, but she recognized the letters. Long ago, she'd asked her sister what those words meant.

The way home, Tabitha had said.

Lara followed the north road back toward the collection of shacks that the humans of Cheyenne dwelled in.

The return trip wasn't long, but heat and hunger slowed Lara's pace. The flattened ruins left her exposed to the wind and the biting dust it carried. She kept her head down and adjusted the cloth over her face. She'd be picking grit out of the most uncomfortable places for days.

As she reached the outskirts of town, the dirt, scrub grass, and rubble gave way to small, rickety buildings that creaked in the wind. Some of the structures had been standing for longer than anyone could remember, repaired using whatever scraps had been available as the years passed. It wasn't uncommon for a few of the shacks to fall apart whenever a dust storm blew through, but the inhabitants just gathered the pieces and rebuilt.

The shacks became more numerous as she walked. With the more densely packed buildings came the stench—refuse and human waste, so potent she considered turning around and heading into the Dust every time it hit her. She followed one of the northward roads, which was little more than a narrow patch of cracked, hard-packed dirt. It would become ankle-deep mud within minutes of the first rain.

To the west, the sun plummeted toward the horizon. The people she passed were finishing up their daily business. Best to be indoors before nightfall. The cold was one thing, but no one wanted to be caught outside by a bored, prowling gearhead.

She saw the marks painted on a few of the shacks—a round gear fashioned to look like a skull. Warlord's symbol. On bots, it meant they were in his service; on a human's home, it meant they'd broken the rules. The first offense didn't usually result in death, but the places with his mark were often dark and quiet.

Lara dug her fingers into her bag, clutching it tighter. That symbol never failed to make her skin crawl.

When Gary and Kate's shack came into view, she hurried toward it, cradling her bag like it was the most precious thing in the world. After glancing up and down the street, she knocked on their door.

"Who is it?" The muffled voice belonged to Gary.

"It's Lara," she replied, pulling the cloth down from her face.

The door shifted back slightly and slid to the side. Gary stood in the opening, a tall, thin man whose head nearly touched the top of the doorway. He wore a pair of tattered jeans and a sweat stained, threadbare shirt. He couldn't have been much older than thirty, but years of hardship and scavenging in Cheyenne's unforgiving weather had aged him and left his skin tanned and leathery. Despite the harsh lines on his face and his thick beard, he had kind blue eyes.

"Everything all right?" he asked.

"You won't believe what I found." Lara opened her bag and pulled out the pitcher.

"Lara, wait—"

"It would be perfect for you and Kate, and little Maggie."

"Lara, we need to talk—"

"Isn't it beautiful?" Lara removed the cloth and held the pitcher out to him. "Have you ever seen anything like it?"

She chewed her lower lip anxiously while Gary stared at the pitcher, her arms aching as seconds passed. Surely it was worth more than a thin strip of dried meat or a single vegetable.

Finally, Gary raised his gaze to hers, guilt and pity clear in his furrowed brow. Lara's stomach sank.

"You could hold a day's worth of water in this." She turned the pitcher to display the inside. "Or...or food. You could keep—"

"Lara, we can't trade anymore."

Silenced by disbelief, she lowered her arms. He must've misspoken, or...or maybe she'd misheard him? Gary and Kate had helped Lara without hesitation during Tabitha's absence. It wasn't much, but they'd kept her going. Kept her out of the market. She traded with other people, but no one was as reliable, honest or generous as these two.

"What did you say?" she asked, drawing the pitcher to her chest.

Gary ran a hand through his short brown hair with a heavy sigh. "I'm sorry, Lara. We're sorry. But with Maggie getting bigger, we've got less and less to spare."

"Gary, please. Just...just think about it." She rose on the toes of her boots to peer over his shoulder. "Can I talk to Kate?"

"No. Maggie's sleeping right now. Please, don't make this any harder. We want to help you, we really do, but we have to consider our chi—"

Lara shoved past him. He stumbled aside, stammering as she entered the small living space. She hated intruding like this, knew it was wrong, but the twisting, sinking feeling in her gut had her on the verge of panic.

"Kate, please, don't—"

Lara stilled. Kate stood at the back of the shack with a worn, faded dress hanging from her tiny frame. Her brown eyes were wide as she stared at Lara, and she held her arms over her rounded stomach as though to hide it.

"Kate..." Lara breathed.

Everyone knew the rule—one child per human couple.

Gary swore, dragged the door back into place, and moved in front of Lara. He grasped her arms with strong, rough fingers, and bent down to her eye level.

"No one can know, Lara," he rasped. "*No one!*"

Heart hammering, she shook her head. "I-I'd never tell anyone."

"Mommy?" Maggie's groggy little voice called from the back room.

"It's okay, sweetie," Kate said quietly. "Stay in bed. I'll be there in a minute."

Lara stared at Kate's belly as the woman approached. "How...are you going to keep this secret?"

"We don't know."

Gary swallowed, throat bobbing, and released Lara.

"It's getting harder to conceal, and we aren't earning as much with me having to stay hidden. Maggie doesn't even know, but she's been asking questions." Kate grasped Gary's hand. "We can't let the gearheads find out, but we have nowhere else to go."

"We couldn't tell anyone, not even you," Gary said, his frown making the lines on his face harsher. "Kate and the baby need all they can get. We can't spare anything more, not even in trade."

Lara studied Kate and knew he was right; the dark circles under her eyes were in stark contrast to her pale skin, and her cheeks were hollow.

Gary dropped his gaze to the floor. "We're sorry, Lara. We wish we could, but..."

"I know," Lara said, nodding. "I understand."

She was numb as Gary released Kate's hand and slid opened the door. Two times in as many months, Lara's world was falling apart.

Passing through the doorway, she paused and turned to look at Gary and Kate. They'd helped Lara in her time of need, selflessly, and likely at great cost to their little family. It was more than anyone else would've done. More than they *should* have done.

Lara held the pitcher out to Gary. "Here."

His thick eyebrows rose. "No. We can't accept that."

Behind him, Kate covered her mouth with her hand.

"Please, just take it." Lara's grip tightened on the handle. There were at least a dozen other people on the street who were likely to trade food for the container, but who needed it more than these two? "As a thank you. For all you've both done for me."

Kate's eyes watered as Gary hesitantly accepted the pitcher. Lara ignored her pang of regret as she released it, busying her hands by drawing the strap of her bag over her shoulder and tugging the cloth back over her mouth and nose. "Be safe."

"And you," Kate said, voice thick.

Lara walked away, feeling oddly heavy despite her empty hands.

Her home wasn't far from Gary and Kate's, positioned on the northern edge of the human slums. Only a wide dirt and gravel road with long, rusted rails jutting from it like the bones of a forgotten world and the wall bordering it separated her from the bot district, where bright white electric lights were already turning on.

If they'd had the means, she would've convinced Tabitha to move as far away from the wall as possible a long time ago.

Would've convinced her to move as far away from Cheyenne as possible.

But they'd barely had enough to survive right here. They'd never stockpile the extra food necessary to make the journey to another settlement, especially since they had no idea where the nearest town was.

Like all the others, Lara's shack was constructed of various materials. The base was brick, scavenged from a building that had collapsed nearby when Lara was young. The wood boards that formed the walls had come from the same place. It was topped with a piece of sheet metal. She'd always enjoyed the pattering of rain and sand on the roof during storms.

The chime hanging near the entrance jingled in the wind. She'd used thin but durable lines—fishing line, Tabitha had said, though Lara didn't know of any fish nearby—to hang a mismatched collection of spoons, forks, knives, and keys from a metal ring. The music they created was random, but there was nothing else like it in the settlement. She was surprised they hadn't been stolen for scrap; it was likely because no one wanted to be in the wall's shadow for long.

She slid the door aside and entered, tossing her bag onto her pallet. She left a wide gap when she closed the door. A bit more airflow would help release some of the pent-up heat.

Removing her head wrap, she dropped it into a pile of spare cloth and moaned at the feel of cool air on her skin. She pulled the pin from her hair and let her long braid fall free. Working her hair loose, she ran her fingers through the strands, closing her eyes as she massaged her scalp. Dirt had worked its way in despite her coverings. If water weren't so precious, she would've rinsed her hair out.

What I wouldn't give to fully submerge myself in a giant bucket...

Inhaling deeply, Lara opened her eyes and lowered her hands.

She walked across the small room, unfolded the sash at her waist, and removed the porcelain shard and her beat-up metal lighter. The latter was one of her most valuable items, one she refused to trade. Fuel wasn't easy to come by, but having easy access to fire had saved Lara and Tabitha more than once during the frigid winters.

Lighter in hand, she moved to her lantern. After a few attempts, the lighter sparked to flame, and she lit the wick, driving back the shadows that had been thickening within the shack with its gentle orange glow. The simple lantern, consisting of a small glass container with some oil and a wick through the lid, was one of her only luxuries. She probably used it too often, but it burned slowly and kept her from being alone in the darkness.

Returning the lighter to its place, she studied the porcelain shard again, turning it over in her hand. She traced the design with her fingertip, marveling at the way the looping lines came together to create something so beautiful. What purpose did it serve? Like so many of the remnants of the old world she'd found, the decoration had no practical use, couldn't have aided in the item's function.

Yet for some reason, such items spoke to her. She knew they were frivolous, a waste of time and energy to collect. But Lara couldn't resist.

She placed the shard on the uppermost shelf of her little case, amidst the other pointless trinkets she'd gathered over the years—all items that weren't worth anyone's time to steal. They were pleasing to her eye, and that was enough.

Turning away from her treasures, she looked upon the rest of her home. There was the pathetic pallet upon which she slept, and the wooden crate beside it containing her few articles of clothing. Hunger reintroduced itself, gnawing at her gut, but there was no food to be found here.

Even the hollowness of her stomach wasn't enough to distract Lara from the true emptiness inside her.

She was alone.

Tabitha was her only friend, her only family. Her big sister, her mother, her best friend. Tabitha had guided Lara, taught her, comforted her. And now…

Now, there was no one.

She had nothing.

With a cry of frustration, she sat down on the sturdy crate and yanked off her worn boots. Rising, she lifted the crate, stuffed her boots beneath it, and slammed it back down. For a long while, she sat hunched over, breathing heavily as she picked at the wooden planks with her fingernails. Her body shook with the effort of keeping her tears at bay. Crying couldn't help anything. It certainly wouldn't earn her any food.

From outside, the soft sounds of the chime rose above the constant drone of the wind. Lara's muscles eased as the music chased away her sorrow and frustration. Anger wouldn't help any more than tears.

She closed her eyes and listened to the music, conjuring a melody in her mind. Her body swayed with the notes. She couldn't ease her hunger, but she could free her thoughts for a little while.

Lara hummed, the sound filling her chest and lifting her heart.

Standing, she raised her arms, slid her fingers into her hair, and swayed her hips in time with the beat in her head, letting the music take her away. Letting herself forget.

She stepped forward blindly, knowing in her heart exactly where everything lay inside the shack. The cloth of her skirt brushed her legs, twisting and flaring with her movements. Night air swept in through the doorway, caressing her flushed cheeks in a brisk, fleeting kiss.

Lara danced, not once opening her eyes for fear that doing so would tear her from her dreams and drag back into a world of hunger, depravity, and dust.

CHAPTER TWO

Ronin crouched, pressing his back to the overturned bus. Its shadow stretched long in the evening sun. The dirt that had accumulated around and inside it would stop the bullets fired by the two reavers, but it was only a matter of time before they advanced and flanked around his cover.

"Your salvage, dustwalker!" one of the reavers called, his voice underrun with a digital crackle. "It's ours whether we end you or not!"

At least one robot, then. Yet even if both reavers were bots, their first shots had missed, which meant they weren't operating at peak performance. Ronin wasn't either after so many years in the Dust, but his optics were still fully functional.

The reavers only had three main avenues of approach if they chose to press the attack—around either side of the bus, or over the top. Ronin's processors ran simulations on all three. There were countless potential variations, despite the limited paths, and all were likely to result in him taking damage.

Wind swept over the wasteland, rustling the tufts of brown grass on the dunes and spattering Ronin with grit. Adjusting his audio receptors, he picked out the quiet crunch of dirt beneath the reavers' boots as they approached. He estimated their positions based on the sound.

Diverting additional power into his actuators, he leapt atop the bus. The old, rusty metal bent and flaked beneath him, but it held his weight as he aimed at his first target. The reaver was only seven meters away, well within range for the armor-piercing rounds to do their work. Ronin's first burst of gunfire caught the reaver square in the chest and punched through the casing beneath his synthetic skin. Limbs spasming, the reaver fell, his weapon discharging into the sky.

In the hundred milliseconds it took to eliminate the first reaver, the other fired.

Bullets struck Ronin's abdomen as he pivoted. He shook with the impact, but he kept his arms steady as he squeezed the trigger of his rifle.

The second reaver's gun bucked wildly as Ronin's shots pierced the bot's casing and hit its power cell. Licks of blue fire erupted from the holes for a fraction of an instant. With smoke curling out of its body, the reaver's arms and torso went limp, its legs locking it in an upright position.

Ronin held his weapon at the ready and approached the first bot. It twitched on the ground, kicking up dust. Motor functions compromised; it had likely sustained damage to its CPU. Standing over it, he fired two more shots into its back. Its power cell flared in overload.

The bot's thrashing ceased.

He swept his optics over the area, detecting no further movement apart from that caused by the wind. If the reavers had any other companions, they'd decided this fight was too risky.

He looked down to assess the damage he'd taken. Three rounds had penetrated his synthetic skin, but his casing had deflected them. A diagnostic check indicated no damage to any of his systems.

Ronin slung his rifle over his shoulder and checked the fallen reavers for anything of value. Their rifles were pieced together from ancient parts—just like everything was, these days—and were in such poor condition that he was surprised they'd fired at all. He doubted they'd hold together over the short trip back to town.

But the reavers' ammunition looked reliable enough. He put all fourteen rounds into a coat pocket. His rifle wasn't chambered for the same caliber, but they'd have value in Cheyenne. The bots had nothing else worth taking. The undamaged parts in their casings would sell for good credit in Cheyenne or any other town, but Ronin left them be. Something about pilfering a deactivated bot for parts seemed wrong, however illogical the notion was.

He followed the skeletal, mostly buried remains of automobiles back to the road. Patches of cracked asphalt were visible through the dirt, which was ever moving thanks to the constant wind. More scrubby grass grew through the gaps. Soon, he left the old four-lane freeway and its dead vehicles behind, turning onto a side road leading directly to Cheyenne. Locals called it Camp Road, though its name had once been longer and less relevant.

Here on the edge of the Dust, any path to shelter was one worth walking.

In the eight months he'd spent based out of Cheyenne, Ronin had never encountered reavers so close to the town.

He halted and turned to look at the massive building to the north. Its walls had been battered by two hundred years of harsh weather, which had worn away the paint and scratched the metal beneath. Twisted, rusty steel beams jutted from the partially collapsed roof like the ribs of a decomposing pronghorn. Dozens of semi-trailers lay all around the structure—two hundred and fourteen of them. Thirty-seven were still hitched to the ancient machines that had once dragged them from one corner of the land to another.

Decades of windstorms had deposited mounds of sediment around both the building and the trailers. There was little left to salvage from the place. Ronin had searched each trailer at least twice, and he'd combed through the accessible portions of the building four times. It was exactly fifteen hundred feet from end to end.

Despite his thoroughness, he'd occasionally discovered small objects that held some value on subsequent searches.

He turned his optics westward, allowing them a moment to adjust to the glare of the sun. Five miles away, Cheyenne's bot district stood largely untouched by the ravages of time, quiet beneath the heat-shimmering air. Even at an easy pace, he could be there within an hour, surrounded by a sound roof and four sturdy walls instead of hundreds of miles of nothingness.

Yet Cheyenne wouldn't go anywhere. It had stood since before the Blackout, since before his circuits were scrambled and the world was undone. With or without Ronin, the bots and humans calling it home would continue their lives. And the sky, though perpetually gray and hazy, bore no sign of a storm.

There was time enough for another brief search.

Dirt crunched beneath his boots as he walked toward the building. Stopping at one of the battered doors, he grasped the latch with a bare-metal hand, its synthetic skin having long since been claimed by the Dust, and pulled. The door swung open with little resistance, creaking on its hinges.

The interior was dark and quiet. Most of the remaining materials were too large or impractical to remove—bundles of long, precisely cut wood boards now gray with age, sheets of crumbling drywall, countless bricks and stones, and heavy sacks of dust that hardened over the long years. Cement, his memory said, though the writing on the bags had faded beyond legibility.

Sometimes, there were heavy tread marks in the dirt outside. Ronin guessed that Warlord, the leader of Cheyenne, had a heavy-lifter or hauler of some sort to transport the heavier materials back to town when they were needed for repairs. Easy enough to do with the right tools and the settlement's relative nearness. But most of the bots in Cheyenne had been sheltered, and they possessed little understanding of how to scavenge, of how to extract treasures from the Dust.

Ronin adjusted the lay of his pack and swung his rifle into his hands. His thumb brushed over the smooth spot that had been worn into the grip over the fifty-seven years, four months, and twelve days the weapon had been in his possession. He stepped forward slowly to keep his scrap from clanking, adjusting his optics to compensate for the limited light.

A distant, damaged memory told him this was a reception area, but he could not recall what its true purpose had been.

Shafts of sunlight pierced the ceiling in spots, illuminating floating motes of dust. The stuff was everywhere, in everything. That was reason enough to return to Cheyenne; he needed repairs before his insides filled with grit that would, eventually, finish what the bullets had begun.

Most everything here was in the same condition it had been in during his last visit, down to the undisturbed dirt on the floor. He moved around the broad, broken desk directly ahead of the entrance and continued through the door marked *Associates Only*.

As he walked down the long hallway, the building groaned in the wind. Ronin kept his advance slow, sweeping his optics from side to side, his boots silent on the concrete floor. The small rooms along the hall had been pilfered, and the desks, chairs, and shelves inside were battered and broken like most everything else in this world. One of the doors, removed from its hinges, lay in the hallway.

That was different.

He paused before crossing the open doorway, easing himself against the wall. The coating of dust was undisturbed, save for where it had been kicked up by the door falling, but that didn't mean the place was empty. Numbers and walls did not always equal security, and there were many people, bots and humans alike, who would favor a place like this over the lights of Cheyenne.

The remains of a few of them were in some of the trailers outside, their lives claimed years ago by the unforgiving wasteland.

Leaning forward, he peered past the jamb. His processors rapidly compared the room to the last reference in his memory. Nothing had changed, save for the fallen door. Satisfied, Ronin continued down the hall.

Reaching the end, he entered the large room that had once served as a place for humans to congregate and eat. The long tables and chairs were overturned, their legs broken off, and daylight streamed in through the shattered windows. Weapon raised, he scanned the vicinity.

Though the dust here was constantly shifted by the wind, the boot prints in it were unmistakable. They wove between the tables and into the dark kitchen, and along the wall to the right, stopping at the restroom. The gait was uneven, the tread obscured in places due to the left foot dragging. Either a human or a damaged bot, though Ronin suspected even a damaged bot would've had more regularity in its stride.

He sidestepped to the counter, activating night vision to scan the kitchen. Someone had come through recently and torn it apart, as though there could've been any food left after so long. This place hadn't seen regular use in decades, if not centuries, and humans these days had trouble preserving food for even a few months.

Ronin crossed the cafeteria, following the tracks to the restrooms. He stopped at the door with the faded image of a circle perched atop a triangle—the female restroom. He didn't understand why that data had survived in his memory banks when the Blackout had robbed him of so much else. Keeping the stock of his rifle firm against his shoulder, he slowly pushed the door open with his left hand. Its hinges whined in protest.

There was no light inside, so he switched his optics to infrared and swept the room. The stalls were all open, all empty, and the only heat he detected was from his own reflection in the shattered mirror.

He proceeded to the men's restroom. It was similarly cold; whoever had been here was gone. Reverting to his normal optics, Ronin drew his flashlight from an inside coat pocket and clicked it on.

The remains of a small fire lay beneath the open ceiling vent. Nearby were a few tiny scraps of cloth, the dried-out bones of a small animal—a prairie dog, based on the size and skull shape—and a crumpled tin can. The dust wasn't as thick in this room, but the disturbed spot on the ground indicated someone had lain near the fire.

Ronin stepped around the leavings and moved to the sink. Though the porcelain was yellowed and run through with fine cracks, it remained in one piece. Within lay a few hand-rolled cigarettes, with flakes of whatever plant had been used to make them gathered in the basin. A canteen, wrapped in tattered canvas, stood on the flat part of the sink near the mirror.

Dark, rust-colored drops had dried around the edges and inside of the sink. Blood.

An injured human had sheltered here and had either left in a hurry or been taken.

Letting the shoulder strap take the weight of his rifle, Ronin picked up the canteen and shook it. Liquid sloshed inside. The container didn't have many uses for a bot, but it would for a human. He'd done good trade with them in the past. If not in

Cheyenne, he'd exchange it elsewhere. There were other towns on the edge of the Dust, and he had no true ties to Cheyenne.

He slipped the canteen into his largest coat pocket. It clinked against the ammunition.

Returning to the cafeteria, he switched the flashlight off and put it away, turning his optics toward the sunlight. It had taken on the red-orange hue that signaled the approaching sunset.

There were thousands more square feet to comb over, even without counting the trailers outside, but it would be best to head back. Minor as it was, his damage would only cause more complications the longer he ignored it, and his pack was full of scrap already.

He'd spent 51,642 nights in the Dust and the surrounding wilds since his awakening. More than enough time to know that, despite his night-vision and infrared optics, the world was even more dangerous after dark.

Return, trade, recharge, repair. Then he could set out into the Dust again.

The bot district's lights shone bright as Ronin closed in on Cheyenne's eastern entrance. The buildings inside the wall stood in stark contrast to the ones outside. Most of the structures in the district had been constructed before the Blackout, maintained over the years by automated units that had such tasks hard coded in their programming. Those bots existed in many towns. The majority lacked the higher cognitive functions of more advanced bots and synths.

Still, Ronin envied them. They possessed definitive purposes, dictated directly by the Creators, that hadn't been claimed by the ravages of time.

The town's upkeep wasn't unusual. Many towns with high concentrations of functioning bots had pre-Blackout buildings, in some cases with electricity and running water. But the wall set Cheyenne apart. It surrounded the entirety of the bot district, with a separate section containing the market. Standing three meters tall, it was an amalgamation of mismatched materials, much of which had been salvaged from the buildings that once stood outside its borders—sheet metal, wooden boards and planks, bricks, concrete blocks, and corrugated tin roofing.

Ronin had only seen such structures erected by humans. This one protected only bots.

The main road into Cheyenne followed mostly buried train tracks. To the north stood the wall, sheltering the pristine buildings within and blocking everything from view save the light cast onto the clouds overhead. To the south were several old factories, now silent and still. A pair of guards waited in front of the roadblock between the disparate sectors.

One was a synth who'd had the skin peeled off the top of his head to display the polished metal cranial casing beneath, where the gear and skull symbol serving as Warlord's mark was painted. He called himself Reg.

The other, Baron, was an earlier model bot, lacking an artificial epidermis. It was humanoid, but its limbs were disproportionate; it could never be mistaken for an organic. Baron wore Warlord's mark on its chest, the paint faded and flaking.

Not unlike the wall, the guards' rifles were hobbled together from mismatched parts that shouldn't have fit together.

Ronin's vision flared and darkened as his optics adjusted to the changing light.

"Coming in late, dustwalker," said Reg.

"Warlord doesn't appreciate visitors after dark." Baron's words were tinny, as though echoing within its vocal synthesizers.

"But you already know that. We're simply obligated to inform you of the local customs and policies."

"Praise the Creators," Ronin replied, "for they programmed you with far more patience than I. Warlord actually make you play these games every time, or have you two learned to take delight in it?"

The guards exchanged a glance.

Reg lifted his chin. "What's in your bag?"

"Scrap," Ronin said.

"I expect vague answers from meatbags, dustwalker. What's in it?"

Responses flitted through Ronin's processors, assessed and

discarded rapidly. It would be easy to deactivate these two. He had twelve rounds in his rifle; from this range, it wouldn't take more than three shots into each bot to knock out their power cells. Even if they managed to get their rifles up quickly enough to return fire, their weapons were as likely to explode as they were to shoot.

And what then? It would accomplish nothing, would fulfill no directives, would bring Ronin no closer to the truth of his core programming.

And Warlord had many more bots bearing that symbol in his service.

The few belongings Ronin had left behind in his residence in the bot district could be replaced. He could turn around and walk away right now.

He recognized it as an illogical overreaction, but that didn't stop him from being tempted by the idea. The Dust had eroded his patience for these overbearing formalities. Out there, things were dictated by the rules of survival, not the arbitrary policies of a self-important local leader.

But Cheyenne remained an important place to restock and care for his gear. No one could walk the wasteland for long without supplies.

"Steel. Copper. Plastic. Damaged power cells," Ronin said.

"Quantities?" demanded Baron.

"Will be determined by the scrapper."

For five and a half seconds, none of them spoke. The wind wailed over the wastes and the distant shouts of humans drifted over from the slums.

"We need to send on word and wait for your entry to be approved," Reg finally said, head twitching to the side once.

"Fine. Be sure to send the answer over to Centennial, and don't forget to explain to Warlord why my haul is being traded there instead." Ronin turned on his heel. Centennial was one hundred and thirty kilometers away. He could be there by morning. But it was a much smaller community and couldn't offer the same price for goods as Cheyenne.

"Wait, dustwalker," Reg said.

Ronin halted, slipping a finger behind the trigger guard of his rifle. Most settlement-dwellers, whether mechanical or organic, had been relatively fair in their dealings with him. The reavers kept to the Dust, for the most part. But Warlord's town wasn't normal in many ways.

After another pause, Reg spat, "Enter."

Ronin didn't immediately remove his finger from the trigger. He'd been pushing for a fight, he realized. Baiting, as humans sometimes called it. He forcibly eased his grip on the rifle and redirected himself toward Cheyenne.

"You'd be better served behind the barriers. Picked up sight of you just over two miles out. Easy targets," Ronin said as he passed between the two guards and through the concrete barricade.

They made no reply, but he saw them exchange a glance in his peripheral vision.

He walked in the shadow of the wall. The factory to his left had once been a refinery, but Warlord's bots must have repurposed it; there hadn't been any oil pumped in this region for at least two hundred years. The chain link fence around it was mostly intact, though it was a patchwork of rusted steel and newer sections likely taken from the supply warehouse Ronin had searched on his way back to town.

Steadily, voices came into audio range—the drone of conversations from the market and the shouts of humans calling for children to return home, as nightfall was fast approaching. He didn't divert any processing power to isolating and amplifying the individual voices. Their words didn't matter. Everyone was simply doing their best to survive.

Ronin simply needed to offload his scrap and get repaired. Come morning, he'd pick a new direction and start walking. He didn't have to return to Cheyenne if he didn't want to.

As he walked, another sound caught his attention over the rest. High-pitched, clanking tinkles; little bits of metal tapping together, perhaps. He'd noticed it in this part of town before but had never investigated.

The first of the human shacks entered his view as the path shifted gently northwest, leading away from the fenced-in factory. Ronin glanced up at the cracked remains of the roadway that had once bridged the tracks. The north end used to lead directly into the bot district. Most of the rubble had been scavenged, leaving only the most irregular chunks of concrete and rebar piled beneath the crumbled ramps.

The sound grew more distinct as he neared the human dwellings. He couldn't help but compare the shacks to the wall on the other side of the road. The resemblance was undeniable. Both were makeshift declarations of defiance in a homicidal world, imperfect but somehow practical.

He didn't understand the logic chains his processors followed, not that he could call them that; there was little logical thought involved. These were observations and baseless speculations. Nothing that did him any good.

Yet wasn't it that manner of thinking that allowed him to find what other dustwalkers had missed in the wasteland?

Louder, higher clangs claimed Ronin's attention. He turned his head to the left, where a shack stood at the edge of the dirt-and-gravel pathway. A metal loop with an eclectic array of items attached to it dangled from its eaves.

He changed his course, walking to the hanging object. The metal ring was hung by fishing line, with more lines of varying lengths suspending forks, spoons, knives, and keys from it. The items bumped into each other in the wind, producing sounds in erratic tones and pitches.

Why would a human create such a thing? Did they find the noises it made appealing?

Another sound drifted to his receptors, this one from a living throat, wordless but distinct. Humming. Inside the shack, a female human hummed along with the chiming, matching its pace but not its notes, complementing it without mimicking.

Tilting his head to the side, Ronin approached the shack's entryway. A gap had been left between the door and its frame, granting him view of the figure moving inside.

CHAPTER THREE

The woman's skirts swept around her legs as she spun with a grace Ronin doubted he could replicate. Her entire body moved as one, though the individual parts belied each other's motions. It was a contradiction—subtle but powerful, wild and yet restrained.

He'd seen humans dance in other settlements, but he'd never seen anyone move the way she was now.

Though incomplete, his memory retained a surprising amount of information on humans, including anatomical details of the tissue and skeletons that enabled their movement. He also understood basic physics, and knew how those natural, unseen forces should've affected her body as it moved.

But none of his knowledge explained how she was capable of such unpredictable, mesmerizing motion.

This woman presented a new mystery, a new puzzle—human grace. Her dance lacked precision, but it was made up for by a raw, powerful quality Ronin could not adequately define.

He studied her face as she turned again. Her features were delicate and...pleasing. Thin, dark red eyebrows curved above closed eyes with thick, dark lashes. Her nose was straight with a slight upturn, and her lips, curled down in a frown, were defined and pink. Long, loose strands of her red hair brushed her freckled-dusted cheeks and shoulders.

A quiver of her lower lip coincided with a break in her humming. She hesitated for a fraction of a second before resuming her dance.

Ronin stepped closer to the door, leaning in until he was nearly touching it. The wind picked up, and harsh clanking interrupted the chime's tinkling as several of its pieces hit the shack's wall.

The woman froze, her pale blue eyes snapping open and locking on Ronin.

They stared at each other for six seconds before she finally spoke. "Who are you?"

Placing a hand on the edge of the door, Ronin slid it aside and lifted a foot across the threshold.

Her eyes flicked to his fingers and widened. She leapt back with a gasp, reaching behind herself with a fumbling hand, and picked up a steel bar. "Get out!"

He paused with his booted foot hanging in the air and cocked his head. "You asked who I am."

"I know what you are." She raised her weapon in both hands, knuckles white. "You're a bot. Get out!"

"Haven't come in yet."

"You're not welcome here, bolt bucket."

Possibilities spiraled through his CPU, attributed with arbitrary probabilities as they passed. A bot could guess what a human might do, but it was impossible to reach a definitive answer. Regardless, she would only manage a single swing if she attacked, and he would stop it before it could do any damage. She wasn't a threat to him.

"You asked who I am, not what," Ronin said.

"I don't care who you are."

"Then why bother asking at all?"

Her feet were planted wide apart, her stance defensive. A tremor ran through her arms as she adjusted her grip on the improvised weapon. "Because I thought you were human."

Pink blossomed on her cheeks, and she broke eye contact for a moment, lips pressed into a tight line. Her weapon sagged. Fear, fatigue, or resignation?

Ronin withdrew his foot and lowered it to the ground. "Would you dance again?"

When she looked up at him, she lowered her eyebrows. "You're shitting me, right? No. If you want dancing, go to Kitty's. I don't fucking do that anymore."

Kitty's. He knew of it, but he'd never gone inside. Had he missed an opportunity to see something intriguing every time he passed through the market?

He cocked his head. "I just saw you dancing. I'm willing to trade."

"I don't dance for bots anymore." She raised the bar again and took a step forward, seemingly ready to swing. "And you have no damned right to spy on me!"

Ronin didn't move. "You left the door open."

"That is *not* an invitation."

He dipped a hand into his pocket, closing it around the canteen.

The woman stiffened, face paling. "W-What are you doing?"

Slowly, he withdrew the container and held it up for her to see. Then he leaned across the threshold to place it on the ground.

"What is that?" she demanded.

"A canteen. Holds liquid. You know, water, oil, gasoline. Dust, if you want."

She stared at it, and he noted her hesitancy before she met his gaze again. "I don't trade with bots."

"Just for a dance."

"You already saw one."

Ronin considered her statement. She was right. He'd seen her dance, and nothing was free in this world. The canteen had value. Someone in town would be willing to trade for it, if not in exchange for credits, then for a few rounds of ammunition, a strip of boot leather, or food.

He gestured to the canteen. "Then consider this payment for the first dance. What do you want for another?"

"I told you, I don't trade with bots. Take it and *get out*." Her expression was at odds with her tone, displaying her inner conflict on her face.

"My name is Ronin. What is yours?"

"Your metal skull that dense that you don't understand what I said? Fuck off!"

He'd never seen her before, and as far as he knew, had never done her any wrong. He couldn't guess why she would treat him in such a manner, but it didn't matter. He was wasting time. If he pushed her to violence, his defensive programming was likely to kick in. It would be too easy to end her, and despite her hostility, he had no desire to harm this woman.

She'd mentioned spying. He reminded himself that humans were particular about having their private spaces. Ronin had intruded upon her security.

He ran his optics over her a final time. Her shoulders rose and fell with her heavy breaths, and the steel bar hovered closer to her waistline now. But there was more to her, something he hadn't given much attention to before—her imperfections.

Those freckles, the light scar on her wrist, the thinness of her frame. Her fingernails were dirty and broken, her hands were rough, her face was smudged with dirt. Synths and humans were virtually identical on the surface. Damage to a synth would alter its appearance slightly, but humans changed so much, so often. They wore their hardships on their bodies, told their stories through their scars. For a bot, damage was often fleeting. Cracked casings could be sealed, burned-out circuits replaced, actuators repaired, synthetic skin refabricated.

A synth could be made to look new again. A human, for good or ill, could not.

Ronin turned and stepped onto the road.

"I said to take your bottle!" she shouted.

Shrouded in the shadows cast by the bot district's electric glow, he headed for the market without looking back.

Ronin replayed the woman's dance on a loop as he walked, seeking new ways to analyze it, to reduce it to mathematics and discern the obscure, underlying pattern that would unlock true understanding. It was almost as difficult as puzzling out the woman's mood.

Disdain between bots and humans was not uncommon, but she'd displayed something more intense. Despite their physical shortcomings, humans were psychologically complex creatures, and their way of viewing the world was beyond most bots' ability to comprehend.

He passed through the open gates and into the market. It was contained within a large, separate section of the wall, one hundred and fifty meters by two hundred and fifteen. Eleven pre-Blackout buildings stood within, though it wasn't likely that their original purposes had survived. Closer to the gate, a patch of cracked asphalt hosted a variety of stalls from which vendors sold their wares.

The exposed metal of Ronin's hands gleamed beneath the white flood lights. He scanned the crowd, easily picking out the humans because of their wavering postures and the sheens of sweat on their imperfect skin.

Most of Cheyenne's humans returned to their homes before the sun set, making the few organics here now the minority. They were largely gathered at the food vendor's booth, haggling over meals as pots steamed behind the counter. The cook was a bot, a sleek white and red model with basic facial features that only vaguely approximated those of a synth or human. Everyone was made in the image of the Creators, but none had been made equally.

Ronin shifted his optics to Kitty's. The garish lights on the outside were neon pink, purple, and blue, having somehow survived the Blackout to lure bots and humans alike into a place where a variety of pleasures could be sampled for a price.

It made him think of the red-haired human again.

How would she have danced had she accepted his proposal? He could've simulated millions of possibilities, but he didn't bother wasting the time or the energy. His simulations would never match the reality of her movement.

During his time in Cheyenne, he'd never once entered Kitty's. Hadn't, in fact, had a woman—metal or organic—in 4,112 days, since long before coming to this town.

DANCERS! exclaimed one of the signs. Perhaps the red-haired woman had been right. He could find what he wanted at Kitty's, after he saw to his salvage.

The scrapper, Zeke, operated out of a large building with few windows. Ronin approached the counter, which stood outside one of the doors. The scrapper was a tall, thin synth who'd worn the skin off his hands and never bothered to replace it. Considering his profession, it wouldn't have lasted long, anyway.

"Dustwalker. I detected the clang of your pack a mile out." Zeke's modulator produced a voice that was deep and rough, perfectly suited to Cheyenne.

Ronin unslung his rifle to swing his pack off his shoulders. Unclasping the flap, he loosened the drawstring and upended the bag. Scrap clattered onto the scuffed countertop. Zeke watched, expression neutral, as bundles of tangled copper wire bounced over plates of lead and steel, as plastic chips and long-dead power cells clattered into a haphazard pile. Plunging a hand into his pocket, Ronin added the ammunition he'd taken from the reavers to the haul.

"Never seen one as productive as you." Zeke's hands hovered over the scrap, fingers twitching. "You're a far-rover, to be sure. Creators programmed you special."

Ronin's core programming was shrouded within a deep, corrupted memory bank. If the Creators had instilled him with a special purpose, they'd also gone out of their way to hide it from him. He was the same as any bot without a discernable directive.

"How much?" Ronin asked.

Zeke sifted through the pile, rubbing and tapping various items and occasionally lifting a piece to test its weight. "Forty units advance. Give me an hour, and I'll have your full tally."

"Estimate."

The middle and little fingers on Zeke's right hand curled for an instant, spasmed, and straightened. "Three fifty. Depends on the damage to the cells, and the precious metals in the chips."

Nodding, Ronin slung his rucksack over one shoulder and his rifle over the other. Would the human woman dance for hard credit?

Zeke counted out the chits and stacked them on the counter. Two yellows and a green made forty units. Each plastic disk had Warlord's symbol etched at its center, with grooves radiating outward from it like spokes.

Ronin slid them off the counter and dropped them into his pocket. Credit units were good enough for now, but they held no value outside Cheyenne. He'd have to convert them into solid goods before he moved on to another town.

"One hour," he said, walking away from the scrapper's.

He ran his optics over the market, noting the presence of the merchants he'd need to visit. More than anything, he required ammunition, which was rare and therefore expensive. Forty credits wouldn't get him much, and he didn't care to negotiate prices without the chits in hand.

Kitty's gaudy lights caught his attention again. The recording of the red-haired woman dancing rose to the forefront of his attention. An hour spent satisfying his curiosity couldn't be considered wasted time, and would perhaps be enough to help him understand why she had so intrigued him. He walked toward the building.

Maybe he'd been in the Dust too long. Diagnostics checks told him his processors were functioning normally, that there was no new corrupted data, but how could he be certain?

It was always his choice to venture into the wasteland and scavenge, at immense risk to his functionality. Often, he was forced to fight. Rarely did those fights end without Ronin having sustained some sort of damage. Yet it was only in those instances, in the chaos of combat, that he felt closest to realizing his core programming, that he felt something…familiar.

It had been that way for Ronin since the Prophet had awakened him one hundred and eighty-five years ago, fifteen years after the Blackout had shattered the world.

So why had the woman's dance invaded his thoughts so thoroughly? What about her had so utterly captivated him?

He stopped at the front door, staring up at the neon sign. He'd never been tempted to enter before tonight. But change was a natural part of existence for all things. Even mountains changed over the eons. Why not bots, as well?

Ronin opened the door and stepped inside. There was a partial wall directly ahead, creating a small foyer and dulling the rhythmic thump of music from beyond. The space was dominated by a broad, blocky bot that stood at least nine feet tall. The bot's twin optics audibly shifted to focus on Ronin as it raised its thick arms and folded them over its dented metal chest. Warlord's symbol was displayed on its left shoulder in bright red paint.

Though the source of the knowledge was unclear, Ronin knew this bot had been made for warfare.

"Ten units to watch," it said, voice projecting from somewhere within its suspension-cable neck. It had no moving mouth.

One frivolous expenditure couldn't hurt. It might mean a few less bullets, but Ronin needed to conserve ammunition, anyway. He plucked a yellow chit from his pocket and dropped it into the bot's waiting hand.

The bot curled its fingers over the chit. "You the dustwalker the boss mentioned?"

"I'm *a* dustwalker," Ronin responded. "Couldn't tell you which one he meant."

It slitted its optic shutters and released an electronic grunt. "I'm Comp. You—"

"Comp?"

"Yeah. Short for Compactor. You start trouble, you deal with me. You don't want that."

"Astute observation."

Comp grunted again and extended a thumb, jabbing it to the side. Ronin walked across the foyer, giving Comp a wide berth, and entered the main room.

It took two seconds for his optics to adjust to the confused lighting. More pink and violet bulbs cast conflicting glows upon numerous reflective surfaces, strengthening the contrasting gloom hanging in the air. Mirrors and polished chrome poles and rails gleamed on the stage, on the bar, around the doors, and even on the ceiling.

More so than the bot district, this place was a blatant statement of defiance against the Dust, a callback to an era no one remembered. An era before broken people scurried through a broken world. Before dirt had worked its way into everything, before metal had rusted and corroded and electronic minds had deteriorated alongside it.

People, bots and humans, were scattered in the chairs. Some were in small groups at the tables, but most were sitting along the stage. Two synths stood behind the bar, one of them a tall, white-skinned female in a tight dress that accentuated her body, the other a bare-chested, brown-skinned male in black leather pants. Apart from the pulsing music, the place was quiet. No conversation, no cheering. In one corner, a naked woman writhed sensually on a man's lap, but the rest of the patrons just stared at the stage with rapt, hungry eyes.

Ronin sat at an empty table.

Two women danced at opposite ends of the stage, swaying their hips, running their hands over their bare skin and across their painted lips, stroking their nipples.

Something stirred within him. He'd gone a long time without sexual stimulation.

The brown-haired woman on the left moved with slow precision. Her dark brown skin was flawless, her curves generous, her breasts perky, and her face was perfectly symmetrical. A synth. She caught his gaze, smiled, and squeezed her ample bosom.

Ronin looked to the other woman. In comparison, her movements were erratic, varying in direction and speed. The subtle motion of muscles beneath her skin and the hint of ribs at her sides said she was human. Her breasts were smaller, and pale scars ran up the inside of her right arm. There was a mole on her abdomen, near her navel—which synths lacked—and another on her inner thigh.

As he watched her, he allocated extra processing cores to map her movements. There had to be a pattern, had to be a way to predict them. Minutes passed in the gloom; forgotten, insignificant minutes dominated by droning music and teasing flesh. Credit units were tossed onto the stage at the dancers' feet by silent onlookers, disrupting the ambient rhythm.

Though there was no predictable pattern, she had several tells. Her movements were simple, sensual, and ultimately repetitive. When she slid her hands down along her sides and hesitated, it meant they were about to converge over her pubis. If she didn't hesitate, she would instead run her palms over her thighs.

Would the woman in the shack have betrayed such signs, had there been enough time to observe her?

He compared their forms. This woman was slightly taller and seemed better fed, though the redhead in the shack had more muscle tone on her calves. Both had long legs and thin waists.

But they danced in drastically different manners.

Ronin raised his optics to the dancer's face. The rare times she opened her eyes, she fixed her gaze on the ceiling or the wall rather than looking at the crowd. Her lips were parted slightly, as though in arousal, but it didn't carry to the rest of her expression. Ronin had seen the way human bodies reacted to sexual stimuli. There was no color on her cheeks, no muscles tightening in anticipation of pleasure, not so much as a flicker of movement in her passive brow.

This was all performative, an act for the gratification of the audience. And it was ultimately empty.

The red-haired woman hadn't feigned her emotions. She'd worn them as plainly as her clothing, and they'd been genuine, powerful, and alluring. And there was something about her physical form, something about her features, that Ronin found far more enticing. He'd seen beautiful people before. There were many here, right now. But the human in that shack on the edge of the slums, she had a beauty that outshone any he'd witnessed.

"I was told you gave my guards trouble when you came into town," someone said from beside Ronin.

Ronin turned his head. He'd heard no approaching footsteps. Whether due to the music or his focused analysis, his carelessness was inexcusable.

The bot standing next to Ronin's table was a synth of average height and build, his hair trimmed to stubble, wearing a faded leather jacket, blue jeans, and brown combat boots. No obvious weapons, no bulked-up frame or visible combat modifications. His face was neither particularly attractive nor displeasing, unremarkable save for a single feature—the only feature that set him apart from anyone else. The tear in his synthetic skin, running from his left optic to his jaw, had never been properly repaired. It was held together by thin metal sutures, allowing a glimpse of the faceplates and human-like teeth beneath.

"Enough trouble for you to investigate personally, Warlord?" Ronin returned his attention to the human on stage. "I think your bots have spent too much time with humans. They've learned to exaggerate."

At the edge of Ronin's vision, Warlord pulled out a chair and eased onto it, turning his optics toward the dancers. "These sacks of meat don't have many admirable qualities, but they can be…entertaining."

The human on stage flicked her eyes to Warlord, and her movements faltered.

"Yes." Ronin replayed the redhead's dance again. Entertaining was one word for what she'd been doing, but so many other words seemed more apt—fascinating, mesmerizing, moving.

Warlord leaned an arm on the table. He tapped his index finger atop it, in time with the music's beat. "Good for brief diversions."

Ronin clenched his jaw. Warlord was not to be taken lightly, but the dustwalker rarely sought company. "You find me just to scold me about coming in late?"

Warlord made a sound almost like a human laugh, but from his mouth, it was hollow and flat. "Comp said you look like trouble."

"And what do you see?"

"Opportunity. You've traveled the Dust, you've seen what this world is. And you know the truth of things."

"What truth are you referring to?" Ronin faced his *guest*, though Warlord didn't look away from the stage.

"The truth of my city. Cheyenne is an oasis in a desert, a sanctuary. I know there are other towns out there, but none are like this place. And that's because I've forged order in a chaotic world. That's why Cheyenne is still standing. That's why we have prosperity and comfort."

"Even chaos has an order to it."

Warlord's finger stilled, and he frowned. "Chaos birthed the world we're forced to endure. It's a world that needs to be tamed. Order brings prosperity, which benefits us all. Even the meatbags."

"What does that have to do with me? Am I an agent of chaos, a thing to be tamed?"

"No. You're capable. Never had a walker come through who brought in so much scrap so regularly. You come back damaged sometimes, but you always come back." Warlord turned his gaze to Ronin; his optics were the gray of old steel. "How many have you ended out there? How many have you left behind to be claimed by the Dust?"

Ronin's hands twitched on his lap. The faces of every human and bot he'd destroyed were preserved in his memory, frozen eternally in the instant of their death or deactivation. He would carry them until his own end, always with perfect clarity. Yet it was the memories he couldn't place, the faces that drifted up from his damaged core, the ones from before the Blackout, that concerned him most.

There were hundreds more of those.

"You're a danger, dustwalker. Not because you've killed. Most of us have done that." Warlord's finger resumed tapping, slowly but forcefully, no longer with any regard to the rhythm. "You're a danger because you disregard the rules. The rules are what set this place apart, what raised it above the rest. Otherwise, it would be the same as all the other ruins you've picked through. Another gravestone in a worldwide cemetery."

"I should have sheltered in the Dust tonight."

Warlord slammed his fist on the table. "*No.*"

Several patrons glanced over and quickly looked away.

He leaned toward Ronin, his scarred face still impassive despite the intensity in his optics. "You should have shown some fucking respect."

"Your guards haven't earned my respect."

"You shelter here in private quarters because *I* allow it. I offer that to all bots, because we're the ones who are rebuilding this world and making it whole again. All I ask is that my rules are followed. They're not difficult. Every bot that wears my mark has the authority to enforce those rules. Disrespecting them is disrespecting me."

Ronin forced his jaw closed and temporarily cut power to his vocal modulator to keep any words from escaping. Dozens of bots wore Warlord's mark. Ronin would never make it out of the market if Warlord commanded it.

"You took a few hits out there," Warlord said, easing back into his chair and swinging his optics to the dancers. "Behave yourself, so you don't take a few more on your way to the clinic."

Ronin pressed a metal hand to the table and pushed himself up. A strange sensation skittered over his palm, and his processors, unbidden, ran a simulation—if he unslung his rifle, he could empty the magazine into Warlord's chest. Power cell, memory banks, CPU...at this range, it would all be annihilated. The simulation ended with Ronin torn apart by the behemoth at the front door. There weren't enough bullets in Cheyenne to stop Comp.

Still, the idea was strangely tempting.

He shoved his hands into his coat pockets. Zeke should've nearly been done with his assessment by now. With a last glance at the stage, Ronin left Kitty's. He couldn't determine whether the credit he'd spent for admission had been wasted.

CHAPTER FOUR

For a long while, Lara lay awake. The shock and fear of having a bot enter her home lingered for hours after its departure. Every sound—every creaking board, every distant coyote howl, every clang of the chimes—could've been a sign of the bot's return.

Exhaustion eventually claimed her.

She awoke from a fitful sleep, more tired than before, to find the gray light of dawn seeping through the edges of the doorway.

Lara sat up on her pallet, plucked the canteen off the floor, and studied it in the dim light of the coming day. Her *payment*. Payment for a bot spying on her, violating her home, and destroying what little safety she'd felt here.

Will it come back?

Her arm tensed, and she struggled with the urge to throw the container against the wall, to batter it into a dented, useless clump of metal.

But the bot was gone, and the canteen was hers. A valuable item, regardless of its source, no different than the pitcher she'd given Gary and Kate. Despite her anger, she couldn't bring herself to throw away something useful.

Though she wanted nothing more to do with bots, there was no changing last night's events. What was done was done.

Lowering the canteen to her lap, she brushed her fingers over its worn canvas covering. All the bot had asked of her was a dance,

No threats, no demands. It hadn't even reached for its weapon. Not that it would've needed one…

She'd been surprised to see someone at her door. Her eyes had fallen on his face first, and she'd been unable to ignore how attractive he was. His strong jaw, those defined, sculpted lips, those intense green eyes… But when the lantern light had reflected on the metal of his hand, cold fear had flooded her veins.

How could she forget that night, not long ago, when she'd learned what bots were truly capable of?

Lara shook her head, thrusting the thoughts away. She tossed the canteen onto the blankets and pulled her boots out from beneath the crate, pausing to examine them. To call them worn would've been an understatement. The threading was unraveling, and the thin leather showed signs of tearing.

She should've traded with the local leatherworker while she'd had items to spare. He knew how to piece footwear back together.

After tugging the boots on, she knelt beside the pallet and reached under it to retrieve her sheathed knife. She stood and strapped it to her thigh. It wouldn't help against bots, but bots weren't the only threat around here. Desperation could make humans do horrible things.

After braiding her hair, Lara wrapped her head with a swath of cloth, leaving a portion loose to cover her face. She tucked the canteen into the fabric tied around her waist, picked up her bag, and stepped outside, sliding the makeshift door back into place behind her.

Not that it mattered. If someone wanted to steal from her home, there was nothing stopping them. She always kept her few truly valuable belongings with her.

The morning sky was yellowish gray, and the air was already warm. The sun blazed through the haze on the eastern horizon. It would be another hot day.

Other people were stirring as she followed the cracked dirt path southward. Some of them were covered up, like Lara, ready to head out of town to scavenge. The seamstress had opened the panel on the front of her shack, already working with precise, delicate hands on someone's clothing. Hal, the cook, had his fire pit going, with thin strips of meat sizzling on the grill over it.

The food smelled delicious, but Lara didn't have anything to barter with. She wouldn't give up the canteen for a few mouthfuls of food. It was worth more than that.

She hurried along, ignoring the twisting pain in her stomach. Outside their shacks, people sat quietly, staring at passersby.

Lara didn't meet their gazes. She was too close to becoming like them—folks who didn't want to deal with the bots and had chosen to give up instead. Many of them were missing fingers or hands, result of Warlord's *justice*, and their eyes were dead. Too much like those mechanical monsters for Lara's comfort.

If you didn't want to trade scrap or something more…personal to the bots for food, seeds, and goods, you had to work even harder to survive. Why bother, when death was so likely?

"Lara!"

She cast a sidelong glance at the man approaching her and somehow kept herself from walking faster. She'd hoped to be gone before he woke up so she wouldn't have to deal with him.

"What do you want, Devon?" she asked, continuing toward the water pump near the center of the settlement.

Devon fell into step beside her. "A 'good morning' wouldn't hurt."

"Good morning, and goodbye. I have work to do."

"You wouldn't have to if you let me help you."

"I don't want your *help*."

He caught her elbow, forcing her to stop. She glanced at his hand, eyes narrowing, and then glared at him.

Devon smiled. "It'd be better than digging through shit every day, hoping to find something to trade for some food." He leaned closer, gaze dipping. "I have plenty to share, Lara. Your body will fill out in no time."

It wasn't unusual for women to latch onto men who could provide. Devon grew some of his own food, owned a chicken, and had connections in the market. He wasn't bad looking, either. Long, wavy blond hair that fell thickly down to his shoulders, rich brown eyes, and strong features. Likely the cleanest man in the district. Many women had cozied up to him and had benefitted from it.

"I'd be a gentle lover, Lara," Devon whispered, brushing a finger along her jaw.

Lara would not be one of those women.

She yanked her arm from his grasp and stepped back. "I'd rather starve."

"Oh, come on! What are you trying to prove? Why not take what I have to offer?"

"Why not be your whore, you mean?"

"Better than being a bot-banger like your sister."

Lara flinched, gritting her teeth. Fists clenched, she turned away from him and walked to the water pump.

"You won't get another chance, Lara!" Devon called as she rinsed and filled the canteen. "You're not the only woman worth looking at here."

She screwed on the cap and bit her tongue. Rage burned in her chest, mixed with shame. Everyone knew about Tabitha. Why wouldn't they assume Lara would trade her body for food, too?

Didn't you?

She didn't allow herself to look back as she hurried south, unsure of whether she was fleeing Devon or the truth.

Her heart finally slowed when she passed the last shacks on the outskirts of town and stepped onto the road leading to the south-side ruins. A few other scavengers were already out, moving in different directions along some of the other paths. She knew them all by name, though they kept their faces covered. Scavengers typically gave each other a wide berth. Conflicts weren't worth anyone's time, but that didn't mean they were unheard of.

The wind whipped at her clothing as she returned to the site she'd scavenged the day before. Finding the pitcher had been encouraging. Perhaps, with hard work and a little luck, there was more to discover there.

Lara paused at the spot, turning to study the desolate landscape again. Dark clouds dominated the southern horizon. Between the ruins and those distant clouds lurked the endless Dust. People talked about the scrap that could be found out there, buried in the sand, scrap that only dustwalkers went to find. But they were an odd lot. Tabitha had called them crazy, and Lara agreed.

The sun bore down on her, casting its sickly yellow glow through the haze. There wasn't any more time to waste. Lara crouched and dug through the rubble, working till her hands ached and her fingers were raw, stopping twice to pluck splinters from her skin. Old paper crumbled in her hands, and every gust of wind blew dirt into her face.

The day wore on, uncaring for the struggles of mankind.

By afternoon, her sweat, blood, and pain had only earned her a few more bits of rusted metal and some cracked plastic. Combined with her haul from the prior day, it would put food in her belly, but not much. Sighing, she pressed the cloth of her headwrap to her forehead to soak up some of the sweat.

She picked up a rectangular object to move it aside. A shard of glass fell from its bottom, clanking on the slab of concrete below.

Lara turned the item over. It was a wooden frame holding a photo, which was obscured by a cracked pane of glass. She shook the shards onto the ground and examined the image.

There were two people in it, a man and a woman. He was dressed all in black, save for a bit of white showing beneath his coat and the blue cloth tied in a bow at his neck. He gazed at the woman tenderly. And she...she was stunning. Her blonde hair hung in ringlets down her back, shining like gold, her pale skin was clean and unblemished, and her lips were painted a vibrant red. She wore a crisp white gown, decorated with delicate patterns and little white beads. The woman's smile was radiant, and her eyes sparkled.

Lara wasn't sure how long she stared at the picture; it was a timeless moment, and everything else fell away around her. The beauty and joy captured in the photo left her speechless.

And it had been buried, forgotten, for countless years.

A drop of water landed on the photo. Lara's eyebrows fell in confusion. She raised a hand to her cheek, only to find it dry. Another drop struck the beautiful woman's face. Lara looked up. The black clouds were overhead now, and a strong wind blew through the ruins.

"Damn," Lara rasped. She stuffed the framed photo into her bag to keep it safe. It had no value, but she couldn't just leave it out here to be destroyed. This harsh world had already taken the people in the picture, but Lara could at least protect the last memory of them.

She quickened her search, discovering a couple crushed cans—a small victory. The sporadic rain suddenly became a downpour, falling sideways in the strong wind. Blinking moisture from her eyes, she slung her bag over her shoulder. She'd have to hurry back to town. After a long dry spell, the first rain was always the worst, and the roads wouldn't be able to handle the excess water.

As she carefully made her way through the debris and back toward the path, a metal sheen caught her eye. Lara paused, narrowing her eyes and turning to find the source. She spotted it in a heap of rubble. Before she could lose sight of it again, she climbed onto the pile, testing her footing on the loose debris, and pulled the object free.

She didn't stop to examine it until she was on solid ground. Lara tilted her head. It was a small box, fitting neatly in her palm. One side was discolored and deteriorating, but the metal band around its middle was surprisingly clean. Turning it, she found the hinge along the back side and opened it.

Lara released a long exhalation, and for a moment, her lungs refused to fill. When she caught her breath, she laughed and bounced on her feet. "Holy shit."

Nestled within upon a patch of dark fabric, untouched by the sun and weather, was a ring. The band was gold, with a clear stone inlaid atop it. It was precious metal. A tiny, seemingly insignificant trinket that could nonetheless keep her well-fed for weeks.

Tentatively, she ran a finger down one of its smooth sides.

"It's real," she said with a laugh. "It's really real."

The rain pelted her, stinging even through her clothes, but Lara grinned. For the first time in a long while, things looked good. She'd nearly forgotten what hope felt like.

Swinging her bag around to her front, she walked toward the road. As she opened it, her foot caught on some debris. With a gasp, she fell, feeling something tear in her boot as she landed hard in the water rushing along the side of the road.

Lara's heart stopped. She watched the box fall from her hand, watched the ring tumble out of it, watched the water sweep the bit of gold toward a cluttered storm drain.

"No!" She scrambled on hands and knees, ignoring the dirty water splashing in her face and the pain of rubble cutting into her skin, but she wasn't fast enough. The ring disappeared amidst the trash and muck gathered around the drain.

"No!" she screamed again, leaping at the gutter. She dug through the mud, tossing aside jagged chunks of concrete, tufts of dead grass, and scraps of wood and cloth.

"No, no, no. You can't do this to me!" She pounded her fists into the flowing water, hitting the drain beneath it. Between the foamy, murky runoff and the rubble, it would be impossible to find the ring.

"You just can't." Her voice broke, and she hung her head.

CHAPTER FIVE

Ronin watched the red-haired woman from behind a mess of rotting lumber, bricks, and sun-faded shingles that had once been a building. Though the raging wind and heavy rain made it impossible for his audio receptors to distinguish her words, he detected desperation and despair in her tone. Yet she appeared physically unharmed.

Why had she come out here alone? This far from the settlement, she was exposed and vulnerable, the perfect prey for wandering reavers or other scavengers. Ronin had seen both humans and bots end one another to seize any advantage that would aid their own survival.

The woman, propped on hands and knees in the gutter with her cloth wraps dangling into the steadily rising water, bowed her head. Her shoulders shook.

Ronin had no reason to go to her. She didn't want his trade, didn't want his help, didn't want anything to do with his kind.

But the emotion in her posture triggered hidden processes within him. He left his cover and jogged toward her. Before long, the road would be submerged completely. She wasn't safe here, and neither was he.

The cloth around her head was askew, and a few wild strands of hair had slipped free. The rubble gathered at the storm drain in front of her was acting as a small dam, creating a growing pool around her. She didn't appear to care.

Ronin stopped behind the woman. She didn't move save for the slow, shaky rise and fall of her shoulders. Her soft sobs were barely audible over the storm.

It was normal for humans to cry, wasn't it? Especially after a fall like she'd taken. Yet something in her posture and the quiet sound of her cries spoke of something more.

"Are you well?" he asked.

The woman stiffened, lifted her head, and looked over her shoulder. Her reddened eyes met his optics. She spun toward him with surprising speed, crawling backward on hands and feet. The cloth covering her head fell back, and her skirts bunched between her thighs and floated on the murky current, revealing her pale, shapely legs.

She pulled a knife from her thigh holster and jabbed it into the air between them. "You!"

"Have been for as long as I can remember."

"Why are you following me?" As she stood, she wiped moisture from her face with her free hand. She kept the knife up as though it were the thing holding Ronin at bay.

"I'm a dustwalker. My business takes me out of town frequently."

"This isn't the Dust."

"No. But all roads lead to it." He almost said more, but he wanted to put her at ease. Speaking about death wouldn't help.

"Then go," she said, wagging the knife toward the south.

Ronin tilted his head, studying her. The woman's tone was firm, her voice strong, but her eyes were red, and the flesh around them was slightly swollen. She pressed her lips together, but it didn't hide their trembling. Her grip on the weapon was excessively tight.

"Are you well?" he asked again, modulating his voice to a gentler tone.

"I'll be fine once you're gone." She took a single step backward. Water streamed around her ankles like river rapids. Cheyenne was a thirsty place, but it could rarely handle anything more than a drizzle.

He ran his optics up one of her exposed legs. There was a scrape on her knee. A superficial wound, but organics were susceptible to many diseases and infections that could prove fatal without treatment.

"You're bleeding," he said.

"I'll. Be. Fine."

Ronin frowned. He'd seen no small amount of blood during his existence, and there was no reason for hers to concern him, but the idea of her in pain was unsettling. "I can dress your wound."

"What the hell do you want from me?" she demanded, voice breaking into a higher pitch.

What *did* he want? Why had he entered the human settlement with the first light of dawn and followed this woman out here, only to watch her from hiding? Why had he finally approached her?

There was no logic behind anything he'd done or felt regarding this human.

Moving slowly, he shrugged off his pack and brought it to his front. The woman took another cautious step back as he unfastened the flap. Reaching in with a bare metal hand, which she followed with wide eyes, he withdrew the bundle he'd purchased from the food vendor with uncharacteristic impulsiveness.

Her wary gaze darted between his face and the paper-wrapped item in his hand. Ronin extended his arm, holding it out to her. She didn't look away from the bundle, didn't move any closer. The rain pattered on the wrapper.

"If you're hesitating because nothing's free, I'll barter with you for this."

"I-I told you, I don't trade with bots." Her lower lip quivered.

Ronin shouldered his pack to free his other hand. Taking the corner of the paper between forefinger and thumb, he peeled it back, giving her a glimpse of the spiced, dried meat inside.

"I have a proposal to make," he said, folding the paper closed. "This food in exchange for you hearing it out."

"I..." She stared at the bundle, eyes gleaming.

"Just listen to what I have to say." He glanced up at the dark sky and wiped water away from his optics with his sleeve. "After we return to your dwelling."

"I don't wa—" She snapped her mouth shut and dropped her

gaze, brow furrowed. The hand holding the knife fell to her side. "Fine. But I'm not promising anything beyond that."

Ronin nodded. "I only ask that you listen and give my offer fair consideration." He tucked the food into a pocket inside his coat. Her eyes tracked it the entire way.

"I'll assist you through the debris." He held his open hand to her.

Glaring at his hand, she shoved the knife back into its holster, walked past him, and muttered, "Don't need your help."

Shoulders squared, she shuffled forward, struggling through water now up to her mid-shin. When she stumbled, she waved her arms in wild circles, somehow maintaining her balance. Grumbling, she bent down and yanked off one of her boots. The partially detached sole flopped.

Ronin frowned and scanned the road back to the human settlement. Rocks, chunks of concrete, and cracked asphalt were the least of her worries. The rising water hid countless hazards—wood splinters, rusted nails, and shards of glass. Another open wound, especially in this filthy water, was too great a risk.

"It's safer if I carry you."

"The hell you will." She moved slowly, keeping her attention in front of her as she carefully set down her bare foot. "You're not going to—"

Ronin closed the distance between them in two strides, dipped into a crouch, and swept a forearm behind her knees.

"What the hell are you doing? I said no!" she shouted as he stood up and cradled her against his chest. She twisted and thrashed to escape his hold, but her struggles only resulted in her becoming tangled in her wet clothing.

"You made an agreement with me. You can't listen to my proposal if you get killed on the way back."

"Even if I get an infection, it's not going to kill me right away!" She pounded on his chest three times before wincing and shaking her throbbing hand. "I've done well enough on my own. I can manage a mile walk home."

"Probably could. I'm just making sure of it, so I get my end of the deal."

With her eyebrows angled down over the bridge of her nose, she clutched her damaged boot to her chest, turned her head, and shifted her shoulders as far away from him as she could. "I haven't gotten mine yet."

"Soon." Ronin walked, increasing his pace steadily as he passed the deepest floodwater. Though the air had cooled significantly with the storm and wind, the woman's body was hot against his. He shifted from a slow jog to a run.

She blinked up at him, raindrops dripping from her lashes. "What are you doing?"

"Hold on."

CHAPTER SIX

Lara was pissed by the time they reached her home. She didn't wait for the bot to stop before leaping out of its arms, splashing fresh mud all over her legs when she landed. Her bare foot sank in the muck, but she marched on, refusing to acknowledge her discomfort. The water pouring over the edge of the roof landed on her already drenched head when she stopped at the door.

Swearing under her breath, she shoved the door aside and stomped into the shack. She threw her broken boot into a corner, dropped her bag beside her pallet, and spun toward the bot, thrusting a finger at it before it could enter. "Don't you *ever* do that again, you son of a bitch."

It stopped abruptly, its vibrant green eyes meeting hers. "Not the son of anything."

"Don't get smart with me. You had no right to handle me that way."

"I have every right to ensure our agreement is fulfilled."

"We don't have an ag— What are you doing?" She retreated to maintain the distance between them as the bot walked inside. "I didn't invite you in!"

"I'm not going to stand outside in the rain while I make my offer."

She glared at it, her gaze trekking down from its face and over its body. The way it looked and moved was so damned *human*.

She'd even felt its warmth through their clothing as it held her—warmth that she'd begrudgingly relished while they'd been out in the rain. If it weren't for those metal hands, she never would've guessed its true nature.

Above all else, there was a key difference between their kinds. Most humans killed for good reason, for survival. But these things killed because they were stronger. They killed because they could. Bots didn't have a conscience. It didn't matter that this one had voiced concern for her, had offered to bandage the scrape on her knee, and had carried her home so she didn't injure herself further…

She leaned down, pulled off her intact boot, and tossed it near its mate. Not without hesitation, she turned her back on the bot and moved to her lantern. It took several frustrating attempts to produce a flame with the lighter and light the wick due to her trembling fingers, but the lantern's soft, familiar glow was a relief. Inhaling deeply, she tucked the lighter away and returned her attention to her unwanted guest.

Lara started, her hand flying to her chest. "Shit!"

The bot was standing directly behind her. She hadn't even heard it move.

It was silent, eyes on her. The intensity of its unblinking stare reminded her again how different they were. How dangerous it was.

At the bottom edge of her vision, the bot held out the bundle of food. Hunger reintroduced itself to Lara in that moment, churning her stomach. She snatched the food from the bot's hand, tore open the wrapping, and took a large bite in case the bot changed its mind.

"I'm not going to say thank you," she said around a mouthful of meat. The savory flavor had her salivating. She took another bite before she'd even finished the first.

"You don't have to. Just listen."

"Lihshning."

So. Damn. Good.

When the bot said no more, Lara looked up at it. It still had its watchful eyes fixed on her. The rain drummed on the roof, its sound competing with that of her chewing.

She wadded the food in one cheek to ask, "What?"

"When was the last time you ate?"

"Why?"

"If it's been a while, you'll make yourself sick."

"Screw you. I don't tell you where to shove your oil, or whatever. I'll eat how I want." She took another bite, chewing with her mouth open to display the food. If the bot said a single damned thing about her manners, she'd spit the meat right in its face. It'd be worth the waste of food.

Almost.

The bot stared for a little longer before finally turning away. "I'll wait until you're done."

Lara huffed and moved to her pallet. Just before her ass would've settled atop it, she remembered that she was soaked. Scowling, she stood up straight and continued to eat, savoring the taste despite her ravenousness.

She hadn't eaten in two days.

With nothing else to look at, her eyes wandered to the bot. Its attention was on her collection of treasures. Without its penetrating stare upon her, she was free to study it.

It wore a faded gray coat, repaired in more places than she could count by patches and neat, tight stitching. The only unrepaired damage was the three small holes on the front, over the bot's belly. It carried a large pack on its back, and had a rifle slung over one shoulder. Her bravado would've burned out a lot faster had she noticed that while brandishing her knife earlier.

The bot's boots were worn, but unlike her own, they'd been meticulously cared for. She couldn't bear to look at her footwear now knowing that one boot lay on its side, its sole hanging open like it was frowning at her.

"Why do you keep these things?" the bot asked.

"What are you talking about?"

"They serve no purpose."

"I thought they were pretty," she said defensively, looking over her collection.

It reminded her of what she'd found earlier. Folding the remaining meat into her mouth, she crouched and opened her bag, removing the picture frame. Fortunately, though the bag was damp, the photo had been spared. As she carried the frame to the shelves, she noticed the bot holding the porcelain shard she'd found yesterday between its fingers, examining it with a furrowed brow. The bot seemed…confused.

Lara placed the photo on the top shelf, leaning the frame against the wall. Stepping back, she observed it as a piece of her larger collection, finding it beautiful despite the wear and damage it had suffered.

"That world is lost to all of us," the bot said.

"No shit," Lara replied, clenching her jaw so she didn't show how deeply those words affected her. Just another reminder of how desolate her life was. This place, this lonely shack, was as good as things would ever be. "Say what you wanted to say so you can get out of here."

The bot was quiet, staring at the photo for what felt like years. Its body was too close to hers, too unmoving; no rise and fall of its chest, no shifting of its feet. It was unnatural.

"You need food. Clean water. Reliable shelter," it finally said. She intended to reply with another *no shit*, but the bot's next words stole her breath. "I can give you all that."

"Just give it?" she asked when she regained her composure. "Just like that? Nothing is free."

"You're right. Forgive my choice of words. It would be an ongoing arrangement."

"Look, I don't know how fried your processor got out in the Dust, but I've already told you, I don't—"

The bot lifted its hand and held up a single finger, turning toward her. Glaring, Lara snapped her mouth shut.

Its impossibly vivid green eyes met and held her gaze. "Our current agreement is that you will listen. I will provide food, water, shelter, clothing. Everything required for your survival. You will quarter at my residence"—it leveled its finger at her, silencing the protest she'd been about to make—"for the duration of this agreement. The price is simple, and one you can easily pay."

"No." She wasn't interested in an arrangement. There was no way she'd become a bot's plaything. The very thought sent a shiver along her spine, threatening to stir up memories of cruel, inhuman hands on her body.

The bot was silent, staring at her with expressionless features as her heart thumped.

"Dance for me," it finally said. "That's the only payment I ask."

"God damn it, I said I don't do that anymore! Go to Kitty's."

"I did. It was…unsatisfying."

Lara's eyebrows fell. Unsatisfying? There were bot and human dancers there, all beautiful. They were seductive, sensual, and, unlike Lara, offered private couplings for a price. How could a place like that not satisfy whatever cravings this thing had?

Yet the more she thought about this bot's words, the more human they seemed. "What…do you mean?"

"I went and watched. None of them danced like you."

"So, after briefly seeing me dance, you decided that you want me in your house as your own personal little dancer?"

"Yes."

She waited for it to say more, to elaborate, but it seemed to think that one word was enough.

Lara lifted a foot to scratch at the dried mud on her calf. Despite the meat she'd wolfed down, hunger gnawed at the pit of her stomach. This bot was offering everything she could ever need, was offering the first real comfort of her entire life. And she wasn't sure what was worse—that she was tempted to refuse again, or that she was tempted to accept.

After Lara had left Kitty's, Tabitha worked double shifts there to keep the two of them fed.

Even knowing what had happened to Lara, Tabitha had still accepted a similar offer from another bot. Warmth and a full belly beat having perverts pawing at your tits and ass every night. But Lara could never banish her guilt over the sacrifices Tabitha had made for them while Lara had been immobilized by terror.

"What's your name?" the bot asked.

She pushed aside the heartache that always accompanied thoughts of Tabitha. "Lara."

"Is that all?"

"What do you mean, is that all?"

"Humans usually have two or three names. Is it just Lara?"

"Oh. Brooks. Lara Brooks." She tugged at the wet fabric around her neck, loosening it. "What's…yours?"

"I told you yesterday."

Is that a hint of offense in its tone?

No, that isn't possible... Bots don't work that way.

Lara eyed it suspiciously. "I was a little scared, okay? I wasn't really paying attention to names and all."

"Do most humans threaten violence when they're a little scared?"

She folded her arms across her chest. "Yes, actually."

Especially the ones who've had bad experiences with bots.

"So, you gonna tell me your name again or not?" she asked.

The bot tilted its head, never taking its eyes off her. Dread balled in her gut, a crushing weight. What was this thing going to do?

"Ronin," it said.

It sounded familiar, now that he mentioned it. "So now we've officially met, or whatever. The answer is still no. You can leave."

Ronin blinked. "Look around you, Lara Brooks."

She pressed her lips together and looked around.

Stupid, she scolded herself. The thing was just reminding her how shitty her life was.

"I'm only asking you to dance for me," he said. "No more advances from other humans, no—"

"You saw that, huh?"

"You weren't very aware of your surroundings this morning. Neither was he."

"Obviously."

"You'll be safe with me. All for doing something you enjoy."

Lara bit her tongue to keep from scoffing. Safe with a bot? They were the last things she'd ever feel safe with. Yet here she stood, in the home she and Tabitha had made together, having a conversation with one. Though Ronin had put his hands on her against her will, he hadn't hurt her, hadn't forced himself upon her. He wasn't bullying her into an arrangement...he was attempting to be persuasive.

When the hell did I start thinking of this bot as him?

"I will consider it," she said measuredly, "with a couple conditions."

He nodded.

"I will be dancing. Nothing more. You will *not* touch me."

"What else?"

"I want your help finding my sister."

"You don't know where she is?"

"Would I be asking for help if I did?" Lara took a steadying breath. This was a negotiation, and she needed to maintain her calm. "She was taken in by a bot, just like you're trying to do with me. I haven't seen her in weeks."

"Individuals who disappear in this world aren't usually found."

"Don't say that!" She stepped closer, tilting her head back to glare at him as her eyes stung with the threat of tears.

"It's a fact."

Without thinking, she swung her hand at him. Before her palm could make contact, one of his metal hands caught her wrist, holding it firm. A flash of terror lit up within her, freezing her heart. He was about to hit her, beat her, possibly kill her for what she'd attempted to do.

But Ronin's expression was unchanged. "Do you have any other conditions?"

Lara yanked on her arm. He didn't squeeze, and his grip didn't hurt, but she couldn't break free of it. "If…if you're not going to look for her, the answer is no."

"Never said I wouldn't look. Are those all your terms?"

"You will not talk like that about her again," she replied, trying to keep her voice even.

"I didn't talk about her."

"You know what I mean!"

"No, I don't. I simply stated a fact."

"I don't care about your facts. She's *not* dead!"

Ronin seemed to hesitate. "I will not touch you," he said, releasing her wrist, "unless it's necessary for your safety. I will help you look for your sister. And I will not talk *like that* about her again. You will dance for me, and I will provide all that is necessary for your survival. Are we agreed?"

Lara looked away from him, drawing her hand to her chest and rubbing her wrist. Why hadn't he hit her in retaliation?

"Yes." She swallowed, mouth suddenly dry. Lara had sworn to

herself she would never do anything like this. For the second time, she was trading herself to a bot.

No. This is different. It...it has to be.

"Gather the items you wish to bring." Ronin glanced at the picture again, a shadow of movement flickering across his brow. "We'll leave as soon as you're ready."

That quickly? She retrieved her bag and filled it with her treasures, gently nestling them inside. She didn't care if they were useless. They were hers. Once they were packed, she stood in front of the empty shelves, feeling numb.

Wasn't there more? Wasn't there anything else to her life here?

Rather than dwell on those thoughts, she stuffed her shirt and spare cloth wraps into the bag and retrieved her boots from the corner. She frowned at the sagging sole.

"We'll repair them." Ronin knelt in front of her and dropped his pack on the floor between his legs. He rummaged through it, pulling out a long strip of cloth, which had singe marks on it as though it had survived a fire. "Wrap this around your boot. Should hold it together for now, even if it won't keep your foot dry."

"Um, thanks," she said, taking the strip from him. Sitting on her pallet, she pulled her boots on. Her feet squished into them; they were as soaked as her clothes. She wrapped the cloth around her damaged boot, tying it tightly on top. When she stood, it fit strangely, but it was better than walking around Cheyenne's rubble-strewn streets with a bare foot.

Lastly, she moved to the lantern. She was leaving the only home she'd known since she was a little girl. Where were her tears, her heartache? The answer came to her as she extinguished the wick.

Without Tabitha, this place was nothing but another survival tool.

"Done," she whispered.

Wordlessly, Ronin stepped outside. Lara followed, stopping just beyond the threshold. Standing on her toes, she removed the chime from its hook and put it in her bag. The lines would undoubtedly get tangled, but she couldn't leave it behind. This was a thing she'd made with her own hands. Besides, sorting out the mess of fishing lines would give her something to do.

She felt Ronin's eyes on her.

As soon as she closed her pack, he walked. The rain continued, though it had eased significantly, and the raindrops were making little ripples in the puddles. He seemed to lead her around the worst patches of mud, but her boots sloshed on the soggy ground nonetheless.

She couldn't bring herself to look back at the shack.

Would it still be there, waiting, when this bot was through with her?

CHAPTER SEVEN

Ronin led Lara along the road to the market. He knew she was following by the sound of her footfalls on the wet gravel, the squelching when she put weight on her damaged boot, and the curses she muttered every time she stepped in a particularly deep puddle.

Despite that evidence, part of him wanted to look back just to make sure she was there.

Lara's acceptance of his offer was logical. It provided her security, stability, and comfort she'd probably never known. With her added stipulation that he assist in the search for her missing sister, she stood only to gain from the arrangement.

It was a strange turn. In his experience, humans were rarely rational in their decisions.

Their roles, clearly, were reversed in this case. There had been no logic behind his offer. Only curiosity, an inexplicable need to know what set her apart from everyone else.

"So, where are we going?" Lara asked.

"You already know." Ronin turned his head to the right, where the lights of the bot district shone in contrast to the dark gray sky.

"I know we're going *there*. But where in there is your…residence? And who the hell uses words like that, anyway?"

"I do," he replied, glancing at her over his shoulder. "and my residence is in the northwest corner of the district. Not far from the market."

There was something refreshing about conversing with her. Though no two runs in the Dust were ever the same, they were predictable in their own ways—the same prevalent dangers, the same volatile weather, the same reminders of a lost world. And, always, the taunting sense that he was on the verge of discerning his true programming.

But he couldn't predict what Lara would say or do. He could learn the signs of a coming outburst, perhaps, but it was impossible to know what would come out of her mouth. Back in the shack, she'd been a few hundredths of a second away from slapping him across the face. It had sent a strange, not unpleasant pulse through him.

"So, uh…we gonna run into any, uh…any gearheads?"

The trepidation in her tone made Ronin frown.

"Gearheads?" He searched his memory for the term. If he'd known it, it had been lost in the Blackout, like so much else. Was it just another slur for his kind? "Of course there will be bots."

"Not just bots. *Them.*"

"You'll have to be more specific, Lara Brooks."

She muttered, voice too low for him to make out.

"What?" He slowed and twisted to look at her. Her brows were low, her lips closed tight.

"Warlord's cronies!" she spat. "The ones with his mark."

A skull, fashioned in the shape of a gear. Understanding clicked into place. Now, he had another thing to call Warlord's bots. Had anyone ever called them gearheads directly? They'd likely be just as confused as Ronin had been.

"Yes. Most of the bots in Cheyenne don't wear his symbol, but he always keeps the ones that do guarding the wall."

Lara frowned and stared at the ground in front of her. She hooked her thumb under the strap of her bag and adjusted its position on her shoulder.

"What's wrong?" he asked. Human expressions could be so telling, but Ronin wasn't well-versed enough to distinguish their many nuances.

"Nothing."

Her posture belied her answer—the rigidity of her bent arms, her shuffling walk, the downward tilt of her head.

"Speak plainly, Lara Brooks. Are you concerned about Warlord's gearheads?"

"Damn it," she said, swinging her foot to kick a rock aside. "I don't want to talk about it."

The rock clattered away, bouncing over the gravel before hitting an exposed railroad tie with a hollow *thunk*.

Ronin halted and turned to face her. Lara nearly walked into him before stopping herself. She tipped her head back to look up at him, squinting against the rain. Moisture clung to the dark lashes framing her bright blue eyes. Thick strands of her red hair had worked free of her braid and clung to her pale face.

"Should I expect trouble?" he asked.

"I don't know."

"I need to know."

"And I don't know. You're a bot, you see his cronies in the market all the time."

"I've never been to the market with you. There a reason they'd look at you different than anyone else?"

She dropped her gaze. "They don't like humans."

The rain filled the silence between them. Ronin's processors would melt before he figured this woman out. With the way she'd reacted to him when she'd first realized he was a bot, her refusal to trade with him because of what he was, and this aversion to Warlord's enforcers…

"What did they do to you, Lara?"

She was close enough that a slight move of his arm could've settled his hand on her hip. How would she respond to such contact? Why did he want it? She'd suffered, somehow, and something hidden deep in his coding directed him to touch her, to hold her, to comfort her until she felt better.

"They didn't do anything to me." She lifted her chin and met his optics. "There's nothing to talk about. We going, or what?"

Ronin curled his fingers into a fist and let it hang at his side. No touching; that was one of her conditions. Perhaps he'd been hasty in agreeing to it. She was hiding something, but what could he do about it?

Watch her dance and provide for her. That was the deal.

He resumed his walk, leading her through the gates into the market. The large, heavy steel doors of a shipping container had been used to build the entrance, and Ronin had yet to see them closed.

They moved past the scrapper's and half a dozen vendor stands, with Lara never more than a single stride behind him. She said nothing, and that was concerning. The woman hadn't let so much as ten seconds pass between her protests while he'd carried her back to her dwelling. Her silence now couldn't be good, especially given her obvious anxiousness.

The gap between them increased only when they passed the food vendor. Ronin glanced over his shoulder to see Lara stopped, staring at the food with her bottom lip curled in and caught between her teeth. Was she still hungry? He recalled the way she'd eaten the dried meat, though *eat* didn't seem a strong enough term.

There was no food in his dwelling, and that was amongst the most basic of her needs. How had he failed to realize that sooner?

He returned to her side, surveying the stand's selection. "The meat was the only food I had. Choose some more to bring."

"But…this stuff costs credits," she said, not taking her eyes off the bot working the stand. The red-and-white bot's head was elongated to mimic some sort of hat. It was slicing a carrot, its knife rising and falling onto the cutting board quickly enough to sound like the report of a distant machine gun.

Crates of produce filled most of the counter—carrots, cabbages, potatoes, and onions were in abundance. More dried meat hung to one side, over what he assumed were smoked cuts of pronghorn and goat. Behind the cook, two pots steamed on a stovetop.

The bot stepped toward Lara. "Good evening," it said pleasantly, the blank space where its mouth would have been lighting up subtly with its words. "My name is Greene. How may I assist you?"

"That a nickname?" Lara asked.

The bot's optics dilated. "I do not understand your query."

"You're white and red."

"No. I am Greene."

"There's nothing green about you."

The vendor's optics adjusted again, shutters twisting closed and then opening slowly. "Good evening. My name is Greene. How may I assist you?"

Lara stared at the bot for seven seconds before turning to look at Ronin. Her eyebrows were creased, and her nose was wrinkled. She'd clearly not dealt with AIs of Greene's class before.

"Just order some food," Ronin said, keeping a smile from his lips.

"Anything?"

He pulled his rifle strap more securely over his shoulder and dipped a hand into his pocket, drawing out a few chits.

"Enough to get you through tonight and tomorrow morning."

Her eyes widened at sight of the credits. She turned back to Greene and pointed to one of the smoked meats. "That. And some of those potatoes and carrots."

"That all?" Ronin asked. He didn't know how much humans needed to eat and drink, though he was certain the information hid somewhere within the smoldering ruins of his memory.

"It's more than I've had in weeks," she murmured before pointing at the hanging meat. "Gimme some more of that jerky, too."

Greene deftly chopped the vegetables and slid them onto the flat surface of the grill. While they cooked, he cut several slices of smoked meat and plucked down a few strips of jerky, wrapping both items in their own paper packages.

Greene didn't seem capable of reason or thought on the same level as more advanced bots or synths, but he performed his tasks with efficiency and speed that could only be the result of fulfilled programming. This was Greene's purpose, the reason he'd been shaped by the Creators and awoken by the Prophet.

Ronin settled the payment after Lara received her order, and together they continued through the market. His olfactory sensors focused on the smell of her food, on the spices the meat had been treated with, and the aroma of the cooked vegetables. Scents he'd detected many times, in many places, but had never given any consideration. For humans, those smells meant survival.

Once the food was handed to Lara, Ronin departed from the stand.

"Why was that one so confused?" she asked, hurrying to walk beside him. She clutched the bundles of food to her chest.

"Greene?"

"Yeah."

"We're all shaped by the Creators, but not equally." He swept the area with his optics, noting bots of at least a dozen different models. The synths were all similar in that they appeared human on the surface, but no two were truly alike beneath.

"What do you mean? I know you all look different, but…"

"Greene's function is to prepare food. Other bots are designed and programmed for different specialized tasks, like inspecting and repairing buildings or manufacturing machinery. Many of us were created with a very specific purpose in mind, and some have retained that purpose through the Blackout."

"Blackout?"

"It happened a long time ago. Long enough that neither of our kinds remembers what it was. We just…woke up, knowing that some part of us had been lost and that nothing seemed right."

He replayed those earliest memories, in which there was a snowy flicker in his optics and feedback overwhelming his audio receptors. Nothing remained of who he had been before. There was only static, the slow churn of diagnostics and reboots, and the kindly voice of the one who'd reactivated him.

Lara wore a troubled frown, eyes on the ground. Didn't humans tell any stories of those times? They must have. All the Creator's children had experienced the Blackout. Even if their lives were relatively short, wouldn't they have passed the knowledge down from generation to generation?

"What's your purpose?" she asked.

For an instant, Ronin's processors stilled, and everything in him was quiet.

Good evening. My name is Ronin, because I cannot remember what it used to be. How may I assist you?

What response could he possibly give? He'd searched for one hundred and eight-five years and still had no satisfying answer.

They reached the gate leading into the bot district. This one was also open, but only wide enough to allow people through single file.

The large flood lights atop the wall were turned on, bathing the area in harsh white light and fighting back the storm's gloom.

The timing of their arrival was convenient.

"No more conversation," Ronin said. "I'll talk if they ask anything."

Two gearheads stood guard at the gate, one on each side of the opening. Their weapons were more formidable than those of the bots at the roadblock on the edge of town. These were pre-Blackout automatic rifles, built with matching parts. Even without armor-piercing rounds, they had a chance of penetrating Ronin's casing from this range.

Lara followed close on Ronin's heels, and the gearheads' optics flicked from her to him. Though it was slung over his shoulder, his weapon suddenly seemed very far out of reach.

"Dustwalker," one of the gearheads, a synth, said in greeting. The right sleeve of his coat had been removed, displaying the blue casing of his arm and Warlord's mark on his shoulder.

Ronin slowed to a stop two meters away from the gearheads. Lara didn't bump into him this time, but she pressed lightly against his back. His skin flared to life, electrodes firing off a wave of plea-sure at her touch despite the clothing separating them. "Cobalt."

"Heard you had a chat with Warlord last night," the other bot said. He was a broad-built synth who'd removed the skin from his lower jaw and neck, baring a skeletal row of teeth and the cords of his throat. Went by the name Northside.

Lara stiffened and inhaled sharply.

They didn't do anything to me.

Then why had she reacted like that at mention of Ronin meeting Warlord?

Battling the impulsive urge to swing his rifle into his hands, Ronin dipped his chin in a shallow nod. "I did."

The corners of Northside's upper lip curled in what could only have been a grin. "He convince you to sample some local goods?"

Heat pulsed off Lara, and she shifted as though she meant to move around him. Ronin's calculations suggested she was likely to launch into one of her outbursts.

Ronin reached back, placing a hand on her hip, and glanced at her over his shoulder. She stared at him with her jaw clenched and her eyes ablaze, but she didn't move.

"There is an agreement in place," he said loud enough for the gearheads to hear.

She eased back, tension draining from her body.

Volatile things, humans.

But hadn't Ronin reacted to Warlord and his gearheads in a similar fashion?

Cobalt waved them on as he stepped aside. "Go on in with her, then."

"Creators know I'd want something like that after being in the Dust as long as you were," Northside said, clacking his teeth together. He didn't move from his place before the opening.

"Why would any of them want anything to do with you?" asked Cobalt, tone flat.

Northside's optics blazed at Lara. "This one knows why. Has that hunger in her."

Ronin stared at Northside, optics locked. These words weren't worth a fight, especially not while they were so close to his residence, which was less than eight hundred meters from the gate.

All he and Lara had to do was walk a bit farther.

Cobalt shook his head. "Let them through, Northside. Been a quiet night. I prefer to keep it that way."

A staticky scoff emerged from Northside's vocal modulator as he finally moved over to clear the way. "Send word when you're done with her, dustwalker. I wouldn't mind a go. Not many of them have hair like that."

A twitch skittered over the palm of Ronin's hand, and his fingers curled as though gripping his rifle. How many gearheads served Warlord? Ronin needed to know how many bullets to stockpile. He'd be sure to save a few extra for Northside.

He led Lara between the two bots and through the narrow opening, crossing the threshold from her world into the supposed sanctuary Warlord had established for the bots of Cheyenne.

Ahead of them, the broad street, lined by automated streetlamps that had come on in the stormy evening gloom, curved away to the southeast. Directly north lay the park, its grass and leaves glistening with moisture in the artificial orange light. It was the greenest place Ronin had encountered so close to the Dust. Yet he'd never seen anyone within save for the maintenance bots tending the vegetation.

It seemed a waste.

There were only a few brown patches in the grass, which thrived in many spots thanks to the shade of the trees ringing the park. He could just make out the water of the central pond through the trunks.

"They are not touching me," Lara grated from behind him. "And what the hell did you and *Warlord* talk about?"

Ronin stopped and turned to face her, scanning the empty street and the imposing, eclectic wall. Though no gearheads were in sight, they were all over Cheyenne, and they all reported faithfully to their leader.

He beckoned her with a hand. "This way. Shouldn't talk about that out here."

"I'm not moving another step." She folded her arms across her chest. "Tell me. Why did you have a chat with that…that thing?"

She'd made her loathing of bots clear when Ronin first met her, but this was different. Though she hadn't raised her voice, venom dripped from her every word.

And she'd planted herself here, in the middle of the main road leading to the heart of the bot district, where gearheads were likely to walk by at any moment.

Ronin stepped close to her, meeting her gaze. Every trip into the Dust put him in danger, but he had no desire to tempt deactivation here, now. "This is not the place to speak of these things, Lara Brooks."

"Well, I'm not going with you. Food be damned. I won't be a part of any plans that involve that thing." She turned and walked back toward the gate.

"I'm not going to follow you back through. When they see you alone…"

"I'd prefer a bullet in the back."

"We both know it won't be a bullet."

Lara froze. She hung her head, and rainwater streamed over her. Her free hand trembled in a fist at her side. Whatever wounds she'd suffered were still fresh.

He closed the distance between them. She didn't move away. Softening his voice, he said, "I'll tell you what you want to know as soon as we're secure in my residence."

She turned her head, angling her ear toward him.

Ronin's brow plates ticked downward. "Warlord is not involved in this, I can assure you. And I don't want him to be any more than you do."

Her shoulders rose with a deep inhalation. A moment later, she released a slow, shuddering breath and opened her hand. The red spots on her fingers and palm faded away.

"Come," Ronin said.

CHAPTER EIGHT

Never, ever trust them, Tabitha had told Lara after that horrifying night.

If only they'd both taken her advice.

Here Lara was again, doing exactly what she knew not to do.

Ronin waited behind her, and she found his patience infuriating. It would've been so much easier to hate him if he'd just push her, if he'd show his true colors and reveal the monster under his fake skin.

Could she trust him to keep his word? His exchange with the gearheads had been different from what she'd seen between other bots. He seemed…evasive, almost confrontational. And he claimed Warlord wasn't involved. Why be honest about meeting with the ruler of Cheyenne only to lie about the nature of their conversation?

Ronin's behavior wasn't typical of the bots she'd dealt with. It was too…human, and that was unsettling.

Finally, she turned and tipped her head back, looking up at his face. He watched her with that unblinking stare, but the corners of his lips were downturned. Was that worry in his expression?

"Well?" she asked. "We going? I'm tired of being wet."

A tiny crease formed between Ronin's brows as his gaze lingered on her. After a while, he turned and continued in the direction he'd been walking.

Lara followed, head bowed and eyes on her feet to keep the rain out of her face. She was soaked to the bone, and her sopping clothes were chafing her skin. Her boots were waterlogged, squishing with each step, and to top it all off, the temperature was dropping rapidly with the coming sunset.

She opened her bag and stuffed the food inside. Then she wrapped her arms over her chest, tucked her hands under her armpits, and clung to whatever warmth she could muster.

When she glanced up to make sure Ronin was still ahead of her, something at the edge of her vision caught her attention. She turned her head, and her breath fled her lungs. Lara had never seen so much greenery. Beyond the road, the ground was blanketed in lush grass, which in turn was bordered by tall, living trees. Their leaves swayed in the wind, glistening as they turned from one side to the other.

She walked to the edge of the field, crouched, and ran her palm over the wet grass. The blades tickled her skin. She pressed down to test their give, amazed at the softness.

"I think this is how much of the world used to look," Ronin said from the street.

"Why does it only look like this here?"

"Because bots…maintain. Many of us exist only to repair what is broken and conserve what is not. To make things appear whole again."

She plucked a few blades of grass and raised them to her nose, inhaling. "It smells so fresh." Her hands were trembling with cold and approaching numbness, but what did that matter in the face of such wonder?

"Come, Lara. We need to get you out of the rain."

Despite everything, Lara was reluctant to move on. She ran her gaze over the seemingly endless green. What would it look like during the day, with the sun shining? If she walked away, would this view still be here when she returned?

"You can see it from my residence," he said.

"But not smell it." She stood up and faced Ronin.

"When it's trimmed, you can."

She wasn't entirely sure what he meant, but she didn't bother asking. Warming up and getting dry. That had to be her focus. The last thing she needed was to get sick because she was staring at grass during a storm.

They continued along the street with the green landscape remaining to their left as the path curved right. Up ahead were more lights, brighter and somehow cleaner than the orangey-yellow ones here. It was a familiar glow, even in the fading evening light. She saw it every night from her shack on the other side of the wall.

Ronin led her around another bend in the road, which opened into a wide, long stretch lined with buildings on both sides. These weren't pieced-together, rickety little shelters like the humans lived in. They were *real* buildings, made of bricks and wood and concrete, with intact glass windows and doors actually attached to their frames by hinges.

This was unlike anything she'd ever seen. Not even the buildings in the market could compare to the immaculate splendor of the bot district.

Had it truly been this way everywhere, before the world fell apart? Had even the ruins she normally scavenged looked like this once? It seemed impossible, but the proof was here, right before her eyes.

Still, something was wrong. Everything was too perfect, too clean, too quiet. Things existed here, but nothing *lived*.

The buildings reminded her of the bots. Well-maintained and varied, no two quite the same, but all similar, nonetheless.

She glanced at Ronin. Maybe not all bots…

He lifted an arm and pointed down a street branching to the left before turning to follow it. "Not much farther."

Compared to the main road, it was dark and narrow. The streetlamps, spaced further apart, only ran down the right side of the road. On the opposite side, trees stood in silent vigil as far as she could see.

Strangely, it still seemed inviting. Seemed natural.

Lara was so preoccupied in gazing at the greenery across the street that she almost bumped into Ronin when he stopped. Shaking off her confusion, she looked around. Up ahead, the street ended, meeting with a road running east to west. Beyond that loomed another portion of the wall.

"This way." Ronin stepped through a gate between a wall of bushes.

She followed him, staring up at the house on the other side. It was a huge, its upper floors bathed in the gentle glow of the nearest lamp. As though the second story wasn't enough, there was a third-floor window wedged under the peak of the roof.

Her shack allowed a couple feet of clearance for her head. How much space did this place have? How much did a person need?

For that matter, how much did a bot need?

Ronin went up the steps to the front door, where he fished something out of his pocket. He fiddled with the handle before swinging the door open. Without a word, he went inside.

Lara mounted the steps, freezing at the top. The impenetrable darkness beyond the doorway was not welcoming.

"This is it," he said from within. It sounded like he set his pack on the floor. "You coming in?"

"I can't see."

"You can't. Just a moment." His boots thumped across the floor. There was a soft click.

Lara turned away from the glaring light, shielding her eyes with her arm. When her vision finally adjusted, she looked inside, mouth agape.

The lights on the ceiling filled the place with bright, pure white, putting her little lantern to utter shame. She entered slowly. This first room was big enough to fit her shack three times over within its pristine white walls. On the left, a set of stairs led to the next level, and straight ahead was an opening into another room. Ronin's pack leaned against the wall to the right. Even the floor shone. It appeared to be made of wooden boards, but she'd never seen wood so smooth and shiny.

Ronin walked past her and closed the door, locking it. Lara's eyes flicked to the rifle slung on his back, its barrel pointing down at the floor. The weapon didn't scare her anymore. It really should have, but for some reason, it put her at ease.

Lara approached the door after he moved away, tugged on the handle, and tapped on its surface. Solid and secure.

She'd only walked a mile, but she had entered an entirely different world.

Ronin gestured to the stairs. "There are bedrooms upstairs, if you'd like to select one."

"Bedrooms?"

"Rooms with beds in them."

Lara moved to the bottom of the steps and looked up. More darkness concealed the top. "I just…go up?"

"Do you want me to go first?"

When she glanced at him, she swore there was a hint of a smile on his face. "Is there something up there I should worry about?"

He reached past her and flicked another switch. Light obliterated the darkness above. "No."

"Okay." Lara took a deep breath and set her foot on the first step, cringing at the squelch from her boot.

"You can take them off, if you want." He knelt to unlace his own boots, setting them near the entrance once they were off.

She didn't need to be told twice. Tugging her boots off, she dropped them on the floor beside the first step. Her feet were pale, her skin was wrinkled, and the floor beneath them was cold. She climbed onto the bottom step and looked down. The material on the stairs was soft, dry, and cushioned, with little fibers that slipped between her toes.

Continuing to the top, she stopped at the landing, where a dim hallway ran to either side. She located another of the little switches, and, tentatively, pushed it up. Light filled the hall.

There was a door at each end, with two more on the wall opposite the stairs and another to her left. A place like this could house fifteen or twenty people, at least. Why would anyone, especially a bot, ever need so much space to themselves?

She turned left, opened the door at the end of the hall, and felt around on the wall until she clicked on the light. This was another large room. A huge bed stood against the far wall, draped in a thick blue blanket, with decorative wooden panels at its head and foot. The thing was large enough for three adults to sleep in comfortably.

She walked to it and ran her hand over the blanket, marveling at the soft fabric. When she leaned down, the bed sank in slightly, yielding to her weight. It was about as different from her hard pallet as she could've imagined.

Another piece of furniture stood near the door. As tall as her chest, it was crafted of dark wood and held five wide drawers. She opened them one at a time, finding them all empty.

Her curiosity brought her to the swaths of cloth hanging on the wall beside the bed. There was a window behind them, blocked by flimsy white plastic strips. Lara bent the strips down to look through the glass, catching a glimpse of the trees and field across the street.

She set her bag atop the drawer case. Apart from the discomfort caused by her wet clothing, there was another pressing need she'd neglected.

"Should be able to get more clothes for you to put in there," Ronin said.

Lara started, looking at the doorway to find him filling it with his tall, broad frame.

How long had he been standing there watching her?

"In…here?" Lara slid open the top drawer and peered inside.

"That's what it's for. It's called a dresser."

"Never seen anything as nice as this." Every drawer had little metal handles to help open them, with the upper drawers having two. "What else is supposed to go in it?"

"Just clothes, usually."

"Who has that many clothes?" Most of the clothing she owned was on her now, and it wouldn't fill half of one drawer. She could think of a thousand other things to store in here.

"You can put whatever you want in it. Give me a moment, and I'll find you something dry to wear." Ronin turned to leave.

She hurried toward him. "Wait!"

He stopped and looked at her.

"I need to go," Lara said.

His eyebrows lowered and his jaw tightened. "We have an agreement."

"No. Wait, I mean, yeah, I know. But, I need to *go.*" She dropped her gaze to the floor, cheeks heating as she shifted her weight on her feet. If she had to explain human bodily functions to a damned bot she'd lose it.

"Where do you think you'll get to?"

Lara glared at him. "God damn it, Ronin, I have to take a piss!"

Ronin stared, blinking once.

"If I have to spell it out for you any more clearly—"

She snapped her mouth shut when he raised a hand and pointed down the hallway.

Lara stood on the balls of her feet, trying to peer around him, but all she could see of the hall was a small section of the plain wall. "What's down there?"

"Another room."

"So you expect me to go in the corner, or what? Out the window?" Her embarrassment was rapidly shifting to irritation.

"Follow," he said.

Despite her annoyance, she did.

He only took a few steps, stopping before the first door to the right. She stared at him with her arms crossed. Frowning, he opened the door, turned on the light, and moved aside.

Lara leaned forward and surveyed the room.

It was different from the others she'd seen here. For one, it was far smaller, and the floor was tiled. There was a large white tub along the far wall, and a wash basin embedded within a counter beneath an intact mirror. She'd seen people use such basins back home, usually as planters for their meager crop allotments. Between the tub and counter was another porcelain object, about knee-high and bowl-shaped, that reminded her of the outhouses the humans used.

She wiggled her toes nervously upon the soft floor. "So…"

"I don't have any personal experience, but you're supposed to sit on the toilet." If there hadn't been dry amusement in Ronin's voice, she was crazy.

"Don't you dare make fun of me," Lara said, narrowing her eyes at him. She gestured at the porcelain bowl. "I'm supposed to sit on that thing?"

He nodded.

Lara entered the room, shuddering at the chill of the tiles against her bare feet. Stopping in front of the *toilet*, she lifted the lid. The inside was halfway filled with water.

"I pee…in this?"

"Yes. And you push down the handle when you're done."

She tapped the silver handle on the box-shaped rear portion of the toilet. When it didn't do anything, she pressed harder and watched in amazement as the water inside the bowl swirled and vanished into the hole at the bottom. Then, on its own, the bowl refilled.

She swung her wide eyes back to Ronin. "Did you see that?"

He canted his head, holding her gaze. "Maybe I'd best leave you to it. If you turn the knobs in the tub, water will come out. Right for cold, left for hot. Clean yourself up. I'll leave some dry clothes for you in the hallway."

He left, closing the door behind him, and Lara returned her attention to the toilet. After she examined it from top to bottom, she relieved herself. She couldn't help her guilt when she used the soft paper from the nearby roll to clean herself. Paper was so rare that most people would never dream of using it in such a fashion, but she had nothing else. She watched the soiled water disappear with no less amazement than the first time.

That done, she unstrapped the sheathed knife from her thigh and set it on the counter, along with her lighter, then removed her headwrap and the soaked cloths from her chest and waist, dropping the wet articles onto the floor. They fell with heavy splats. She felt lighter without them, though no warmer. Her legs were caked with mud from the walk, and the tiles were smudged with her dirty footprints. She'd wash her legs and feet to avoid making any more of a mess and call it good.

Lara stepped into the tub, running a hand over the strangely textured curtain bunched to one side, and turned to examine the metal knobs on the wall. She'd rarely had the luxury of bathing. There was only one water pump in the slums for everyone to share, and Warlord often cut it off at his whim. It was far more important to keep people hydrated and crops watered than to be clean.

Tilting her head, she turned the left knob. Water flowed from the spigot and pooled around her feet, immediately cloudy with grime. To her wonderment, it warmed. She cupped her hands and splashed her chilled body.

Soon, the warmth became heat. It was quickly too much for her to handle. She turned the middle knob, hoping for some cool water to balance the flow. Water sprayed onto her from above, first ice cold, then scalding hot.

Lara screamed and stumbled back. One of her flailing hands caught on the curtain, and she used it to pull herself over the edge of the tub. Her feet slipped the instant they touched the tiled floor. She landed hard on her backside with another cry, legs sprawled.

"Fuck!" Pain radiated from her ass and up her side.

The door burst open, and Ronin was suddenly in the room.

Lara looked up at him with rounded eyes. There was a small gun in his right hand, its dull black metal absorbing the overhead light. He held a waded-up piece of cloth in his other hand.

Their eyes met.

His gaze dipped. "Are you all—"

"Get out!" Lara screamed, crossing her arms over her chest, snapping her legs together, and drawing her knees up.

As though the situation was totally normal, he shifted his attention to the tub. Steam gathered at the ceiling as drops of water landed on Lara's back from the spray behind her. He placed the cloth—a shirt, she realized—on the counter next to the wash basin and stepped over her, reaching up to draw the curtain closed.

She watched, paralyzed by anger, embarrassment, and fear, as he held a hand in the water. Then he reached in and turned one of the knobs.

"Should be fine now. Soap is in the corner." He hadn't looked at her as he spoke, and he seemed to make a point of fixing his gaze on the hallway wall as he exited the room.

Lara sat on the floor a long while after the door was closed before she finally uncurled from her position. He'd taken a single look at her bare-ass body, adjusted the water, and left. Not only had he upheld his promise not to touch her, but he hadn't even leered at her when she was at her most vulnerable.

She placed a hand on the side of the tub, using it for support, and stood up. Groaning, she rubbed at her aching backside.

Mimicking Ronin, she stuck her arm through the curtain to check the water. It was pleasantly warm now. Lara carefully reentered the tub and stepped into the water streaming from the spigot overhead. Blissful heat surrounded her, and she let herself melt in its embrace. Eventually, she found the bar of soap he'd mentioned on a little rack in the corner.

She'd clean more than her legs, after all.

. . .

Ronin lingered in the hallway. The sound of the shower changed subtly, and he knew it was now caressing her naked body.

He forced himself to walk toward his room, forced himself to think about how strange running water sounded after all his time in the Dust. Working plumbing was as out of place in this world as functioning electric grids and undamaged buildings.

Closing the bedroom door behind him, Ronin struggled to maintain that chain of thoughts.

An image of Lara rose to the forefront of his mind—her bare skin moist and pink from the hot water, her pert breasts round, nipples erect. Though her ribs were visible at her sides, her narrow waist led to flaring hips and long, lithe legs. The legs of a dancer.

And between her thighs, a tantalizing patch of red hair had beckoned his gaze lower, to the pink flesh of her labia.

That single second before she'd covered herself and Ronin had looked away would be emblazoned in his memory until he was disassembled. He wasn't sure if even a second Blackout could strip it away.

One glimpse of Lara awoke more in Ronin than anything he'd seen at Kitty's.

Were it in his power, he would've dumped the memory. It would've been more respectful to her, and having an image of her naked form to summon at will wouldn't help him keep his end of their bargain.

No touching.

He removed his gear, laying it out piece-by-piece atop the chest at the foot of the bed. First his rifle. Next, the pistol in his hand, along with its spare magazine, which held its last six rounds of ammunition. Then a knife with a serrated edge, various hand tools, and an almost empty lighter. His belt followed. Dust was caked on the rugged material of its many pouches.

Ronin stared at the objects, adjusting their lay to achieve something close to symmetry. True balance was impossible with this eclectic array, but it all seemed right together, like mismatched pieces of some greater, cohesive whole.

His thought-chains took strange, whimsical twists from there.

Sometimes, out in the wastes, he'd uncover items that couldn't possibly have had any practical use, and he knew they'd been created long ago by a human. Had the Creators shaped humans first? Were they the flawed children who'd inspired the eventual crafting of bots, a more perfect reflection of the Creators themselves? Despite the similarities between bots and humans, the differences were so stark, so undeniable.

Humans were fragile, irrational, nonsensical creatures with more weaknesses than strengths. And Lara was one of them.

Why had a human so suddenly caught his interest? All Ronin had craved since waking was knowledge of his purpose. He'd never discover the truth while obsessing over a human woman.

He undressed, blocking the onslaught of simulations that sought to depict Lara removing her clothes. Such things weren't real, no matter how they appeared. She was much more than data in his memory. Lara was a living, breathing creature. Everything she said and did would always belong to her.

What failed paths of logic had brought him to this point, to him hiding in a room he rarely used to avoid the temptation of a human woman he'd brought into his home?

She would dance for him, and he'd provide for her needs, nothing more. He'd watch her. Over time, he would discern why he'd been so enthralled by the way she moved. Then, with that foolish whim fulfilled, he would part ways with her. He'd purchase supplies he required, give Lara the remaining chits, and leave Cheyenne far behind.

His purpose wasn't in this place, wasn't with her. The key to his programming lay somewhere in the ruins of the world. It was somewhere in the Dust, waiting for him, and he had to seek it out.

But didn't Ronin deserve a respite, after so many days in the wastes?

Didn't he deserve this one little diversion?

CHAPTER NINE

Lara pulled the curtain open and stepped out of the tub, mindful of her footing this time. Her skin was sensitive after the scrubbing she'd given it, tingling at the air's gentle touch. She tugged a soft cloth, which was like a too-small blanket, from a rail on the wall and wrapped it around herself to absorb the water from her skin.

From the corner of her eye, she saw something move.

She jumped, afraid Ronin had reentered, and nearly slipped again. But it had just been her reflection in the foggy glass over the wash basin.

A bit jumpy, Lara?

After allowing her heart to slow, she leaned closer to the mirror and wiped off some of the condensation with the end of the cloth. The face looking back at her was both familiar and foreign. She'd seen her reflection puddles and in the market's murky windows growing up, and Tabitha had obtained a small mirror a few years ago that Lara had borrowed often, but the last time had been months ago…and none of those had ever been as clear as this.

Her wet hair was several shades darker than normal, framing her heart-shaped face in a tangled mess. Gently arched brows rested over her wide blue eyes. She parted her lips as she ran the tip of a finger down the bridge of her narrow nose. The hot water had pinkened her pale skin. Her cheekbones and collarbones were more pronounced than she remembered, but that didn't surprise her. Food hadn't exactly been plentiful lately.

It served as a reminder of her lingering hunger.

Lara trailed her fingertips from her nose to the tiny brown spots on her cheek. Freckles. They were sprinkled across her cheeks, nose, and arms, and were scattered over the rest of her body. During childhood, Tabitha had called them kisses from the sun.

Growing up, Lara had often been told she was beautiful. Other women used beauty to their advantage, flaunted it to feed themselves. That meant doing things Lara was unwilling to do, at least apart from the one time…which would *never* happen again.

With those painful, repulsive memories threatening to rise, she pressed her hands onto the counter. Her palms settled atop soft fabric. Looking down, she found the shirt Ronin had left. She picked up the garment and held it out in front of her. It looked huge.

Lara pulled it on, and surely enough, the hem fell to her knees. But that didn't matter. It was warm and dry, much better than her other options—putting her sopping wraps back on or going out there with nothing but the too-small blanket around her body, clutching its corners with one hand to ensure it remained in place.

After gathering her discarded clothes from the floor, she rinsed them thoroughly in the tub, wrung them out, and hung them over the curtain rod to dry.

Why did Ronin have all of this? Why did he need beds, running water, and toilets? She assumed he cleaned his outer skin, but that could be accomplished easily with a rag and a bucket of water, couldn't it? And she was pretty sure bots never had to take a shit or piss.

After she finished, she picked up her knife and lighter, opened the door, and peered into the hall. Light seeped beneath the closed door at the far end. That had to be Ronin's room.

Lara returned to her room, closing the door quietly behind her, and padded to the bed, where she slipped her knife beneath the pillow. There was no way she'd be sleeping without protection.

When she moved to the drawer case—*dresser*, she corrected herself—she set the lighter atop it and opened her bag. Taking out the packages of food, she hurriedly opened one of them. Plucking a potato wedge from within, she shoved the whole thing in her mouth. It was cold and a little chewy, but it tasted heavenly.

She devoured five more pieces of potato, several mouthfuls of carrots, and two slices of smoked meat before she forced herself to stop.

"Oh my God," she groaned, placing her hands on her stomach and closing her eyes. It hurt to be so full.

And it was amazing.

She was tempted to eat more, but she likely would've puked. After a lifetime of scant meals, she couldn't stand the thought of being so wasteful, and Ronin had said the food was for tonight and the next morning anyway. She needed to save the rest.

Begrudgingly, Lara rewrapped what remained and set it aside.

To keep herself from thinking about food, Lara removed the treasures from her bag. She stared at them for some time, considering the best way to arrange them in her new space. Finally, she tossed her bag aside and set to work, moving some of the items several times before their placement seemed right.

She frowned when she lifted the picture frame. Water had stained it, damaging the color in a few spots. Just another thing on the verge of destruction. It had truly become part of her world now. She propped it up against the wall. The faces were undamaged, at least, and nothing that happened to the photo could change the joy it had captured.

Lara returned to the hallway. Ronin's light was still on, and the door remained shut. They could work out the details of their deal another time. Eager to explore the house, she walked to the stairs and went down.

The only furniture in the main room was a low, long table with a sturdy wooden chair drawn up to it. A few hand tools lay scattered on the table's surface, and there was a clamp of some kind attached to it on one side.

The wood floor was cold as she turned and padded through the wide opening opposite the front door. After a bit of searching, she found a light switch. The lights blinked to life to reveal another strange room.

To her right was another table, taller than the last, with four chairs positioned around it. A white stone counter ran along the walls ahead and to her left, with another section standing free in the middle of the room. She counted sixteen little doors beneath the counters and up on the walls. *Cabinets*, her memory whispered, though she only had the vaguest recollection of an old woman who'd used the word when Lara was very young.

Curious, she walked to the counter and opened one of the doors. The cabinet was empty apart from the shelf inside. She checked a few more, finding nothing. So much space and nothing to show for it.

How much could a bot really need?

There was another wash basin set in the counter, with a window behind it instead of a mirror. Lara pushed the handle on the spigot up. Water poured out. No delay, no pumping, just instant water.

"Best not to waste it," Ronin said.

Gasping, Lara spun around to find him standing at the entrance of the room, bare chested. Though his skin appeared to be one piece, portions of it were faintly different shades, reminding her of a patchwork blanket. It was…intriguing.

Really, Lara?

Forcing her eyes to remain on his, she reached back and shut of the water. "I probably wasted a lot already."

"As much water as there is in Cheyenne, it's still a limited resource."

She spread her arms wide. "Why do you even need all this?"

"I don't."

"But you have it. Clean running water, electric lights. Beds. Toilets. This place must have ten separate rooms!"

"I have a secure location where I can clean my weapons and tend to my gear when I'm not in the Dust. Everything else is superfluous."

"What does super…superfloo… What does that mean?"

"It means it's unnecessary."

"Well, why didn't you just say that? Either way, it's all running. In good shape. And it's necessary for humans." Lara swept her gaze around. There were more luxuries in this one room than she'd known throughout her entire life.

"I bring in scrap and sell it. I have nothing to do with keeping this place running except for providing some raw materials. Other bots handle the upkeep. They're programmed to repair buildings, clean houses, cut grass, and keep appliances operational. The Creators shaped them for those tasks, and they'll perform them until they eventually break down."

"Is going into the Dust your purpose?" Her gaze dipped, moving along the line of his jaw to his thick neck.

"Is collecting trinkets yours?"

She met his eyes again. "My purpose is to survive. I don't go out of my way for those things, they just happen to cross my path."

"All paths in this world lead to dust. One way, or another."

"You're evading."

The bots Lara had dealt with were always blunt and direct. Why was this one so different?

"What does it matter? I'm surviving, same as you," Ronin said.

"Because I'm curious. You said there are bots made for only one purpose, and they know nothing else. But if you knew your purpose, you'd be doing it right now."

"How do you know I'm not following my programming right now?"

Lara narrowed her eyes. "And what *programming* would that be?"

The corner of his mouth quirked up. "Evading your line of questioning."

She growled in frustration. "That is such a hu—"

Something on his abdomen caught her attention, and she snapped her mouth shut. Almost everything about him screamed human male—his broad chest with its light brown nipples, his toned shoulders and arms, the sculpted ridges of his abdomen. Like the synth dancers in Kitty's, he lacked a belly button, but there were three holes in the skin of his belly. Metal gleamed through them.

"Are those…bullet holes?" Lara asked.

Ronin looked down. "I'm much better at dodging questions than I am other things, obviously."

"That happen in the Dust?" Lara stepped around the central counter and approached him, focusing her attention on the wounds.

If they could even be called wounds.

"Yes," he said, keeping his vibrant green eyes locked on her as she stopped in front of him and bent down to examine the holes.

The metal they exposed was intact but shiny, as though it had been freshly polished. Her brows fell. Could bots feel pain? Had Ronin felt pain?

Without thinking, she reached forward to touch the damaged skin.

No touching.

Lara stilled her hand before her fingers could make contact and straightened. She sure as hell wasn't going to give him an excuse to break that part of their deal. "What's out there?"

The muscles of his jaw bunched. She knew he didn't actually have muscles, but what else was she supposed to call the parts that moved his face?

"The name says it all," he said, watching her. "Not much of anything but dirt, lying over the top of the old world. If you're willing to dig, there are things of value hidden all over."

"How far have you gone? How many miles?"

"How high can you count?"

Lara glared at him.

"It's a valid question," he said.

"I'm not stupid."

Ronin's eyes narrowed. "Never said you were."

"Damn near did."

"What does a number tell you if—"

"I can count," she snapped. "I can't read, but I can fucking count."

"To what? Thousands? Millions?"

"Just answer the damned question!" Her face heated. So what if she couldn't count that high? He was probably just making up numbers to make her feel stupid.

"I've gone just about everywhere that isn't blocked by water. Walked one million, two thousand, seven hundred and seventy-four miles."

It was a bigger number than she'd ever heard, which only increased its enormity to Lara. Still, something stirred inside her, a dangerous feeling. Hope. If he'd truly gone so far, he'd seen other places. Other settlements.

She struggled to keep that hope contained. "It's not all dust, right?"

"Most of it is," Ronin replied, his expression softening. "Some places are better off than others. Cheyenne seems to have been spared the worst of it."

So this was as good as it got?

As quickly as it had come, that hope dimmed. "Why just this place?"

CHAPTER TEN

"I didn't say Cheyenne is the only one," Ronin said. "There are other towns where things are in order, but some places were turned into craters where the rubble is so fine you can sift it through your fingers. Entire cities turned to dust."

Would it have been better if he was unable to track the miles? If he couldn't recall, with undiluted clarity, all the dead places he'd traversed? Somewhere, deep within his tattered data banks, memories of those places from before the Blackout awaited discovery.

Uncovering them wasn't likely to bring comfort.

"Oh." Lara glanced away, shoulders sagging. "Do you…like what you do? Scavenging out in the Dust?"

Ronin's processors whirred, analyzing her question and seeking out the best answer. There wasn't supposed to be like or dislike for him, only programming and its fulfillment.

"It's preferable to repairing buildings or mowing grass," he replied.

"So, you like being out there?"

How could he explain it to her? In the Dust, Ronin fought for his existence, earned it, and found some semblance of his purpose in the battle. It was not his programming, not entirely, not exactly, but it was the closest he ever came.

"I find moments of joy," he said finally.

Her eyes met his optics. Had the sky once been their shade of blue, or was that a fragment of his corrupted data?

"You actually feel joy?"

Why had she asked as though she didn't believe him?

And why couldn't Ronin formulate a satisfying answer?

"Perhaps...fulfillment is a better word." It was no truer, though.

Lara's brow creased. "But you said joy. Why would you say that if it's not what you meant?"

He tilted his head, scrutinizing Lara. She was difficult enough to decipher as it was. Her questions only complicated the puzzle.

"Don't humans often say things they don't mean?" he asked.

"Yeah, but you're not human."

The statement hung in the air between them. Ronin couldn't take offense. Even if he didn't know what he was created for, he knew what he was. Still, he suspected she'd meant it, at least in part, as an insult.

"Bots always say what they mean," she continued when he didn't respond, "and always do what they say."

"There are so many words with abstract, situational meanings. How are bots supposed to maintain a perfect track record when neither of our kinds fully understands them all the time?" Definitions only went so far to explain concepts like love, honor, and hatred. Beneath their simple explanations ran countless, complex layers of emotion.

"I may not know as many words as you," Lara said, walking past him to sit on the edge of the dining table, "but I know the difference between fulfillment and enjoyment. And so do you."

In her new position, her shirt—*his* shirt—crept up, granting Ronin a glimpse of her lower thighs.

That shirt touched me, and now it is touching her. Her nipples are brushing against it, that patch of copper hair is separated from my sight only by a thin bit of cloth...

Ronin shifted his optics back to her face. How long had he stared? Seconds? By the set of her brow and the firmness of her mouth, it had been long enough for her to notice. His processors could handle massive amounts of data at once, could simultaneously monitor his entire field of vision, his hearing, touch, and movement without missing anything. Bots didn't get distracted.

So how had this woman seized all his attention? More specifically, how had her body done so? She should've meant nothing to him.

Lara tipped her head just a few degrees to the right. "Anyway, since we're talking about fulfillment...you want me to dance for you now?"

He wanted nothing more, and that was disconcerting.

"No. Not tonight. Your end of the arrangement will begin tomorrow, when I return." He didn't trust himself to resist the urge to violate her conditions. Not yet.

"What do you mean, when you return?" She lifted her posterior off the table and tugged the hem of the shirt down.

"This place isn't properly stocked to support a human. If our arrangement is going to last, I must keep my word. I must do what I said."

"So, you're just leaving me here. Alone."

"Would you prefer I take you to the market, where all the humans and bots will see the two of us together?"

The displeasure in her expression deepened. "Will I be safe here?"

"Yes. There's a lock on the door."

She laughed. It was a strange sound to Ronin, akin to a word in an unfamiliar language. He understood only that it was devoid of humor. What would her laughter sound like when she was genuinely amused?

"I'm sure that'll do wonders to keep bots out," she said.

"Most of them, yes."

"But not all."

"You walked into this part of town with me, Lara Brooks."

"You can drop the Brooks. That's not how humans refer to each other."

"I'm not human. Am I now expected to conform to your norms?"

"Sarcasm from a bot? Just when I thought I'd hit rock bottom..."

"My point, unless you plan to go on another tangent, is that you saw what this area looks like when you came in. Do you really think I have anything in here that a bot can't get elsewhere? There's no reason for anyone to come in."

"Guess this pit's even lower than I thought."

Ronin narrowed his gaze, studying her face. There'd been a subtle change in her expression—more light in her eyes, a slight tick of her jaw. Small differences, but they didn't strike him as good.

"You're offended," he said.

"I am not," she replied quickly. Too quickly.

"I'm afraid I don't understand what I said to upset you."

"You're afraid? There you go again, using words you don't mean."

Once again, her tone suggested an intent to insult him. He reviewed their conversation, analyzing every word, hoping to determine what had provoked Lara's reaction, but he found no answer. "Explain it to me."

"I'm not some meatbag, bot-banging whore!" She hopped off the table and approached him, bare feet slapping the floor.

"No touching," he said carefully. "That was the agreement."

"As if I'd willingly touch you." She stalked past him toward the stairs.

Information blazed across his processors, threatening to blow a circuit. There had to be a reason. He'd said something wrong, but what? Had he simply underestimated the complexity of humans and their emotions?

And yet...her anger had sparked something inside him. Something hot, akin to the impatience he'd experienced with the gearheads earlier. No, impatience wasn't correct, he knew that much, but he could get no closer to understanding it.

He strode after her, his boots far louder on the floorboards than her feet, catching up as she reached the bottom step. "You do not get to say things like that to me and then walk away."

Lara paused with a hand on the railing and twisted to look at him, her expression hard. "I'm not walking. I'm *storming.*" As though to prove it, she continued up the stairs, stomping her feet. "See? I said what I meant, and I'm doing it!"

Ronin followed, despite a brief risk assessment warning of a chance of receiving further damage in the process. Humans were volatile, and Lara took the term to a new level. An electric tingle arced across his palm. An impulse, perhaps due to damaged coding deep in his operating system, to reach out and grab her arm. To force her to stop and talk.

That would guarantee an unfavorable ending to the confrontation.

The heat in his mind faded. This situation was beyond his ability to comprehend, enough so that it was almost amusing. It had to be the result of a simple miscommunication. He'd failed to say precisely what he'd meant, she'd interpreted his words in an unintended fashion, and it had escalated into this.

He halted at the top of the stairs as a phrase flitted across his processors.

What the fuck?

Though Lara had never uttered that phrase in his presence, he could almost hear it in her voice, and it fit the situation perfectly.

For the first time in his remembrance, Ronin laughed. It was short, abrupt, similar to the sound most humans made after being punched in the gut, but it was a *laugh*.

Already at the end of the hallway, Lara paused at the entrance of her room, staring at Ronin with her jaw agape as he approached.

"Don't you dare fucking laugh at me!" She disappeared inside and slammed the door shut. It rattled in its frame, the vibrations running through the nearby walls, and Ronin registered displaced air flowing over his bare skin. Lara fumbled on the other side. After a muffled curse from her, the lock engaged with a click.

Ronin stood in place, optics focused on the door. There was no defusing the situation; it had already exploded. He didn't desire an adversarial relationship with Lara. All he wanted, all he told himself he wanted, was to see her dance.

He couldn't leave things like this.

He rapped on the door.

"Go. Away," she snapped.

Moderating his tone to something gentle, he said, "Open the door."

"No."

She'd been right in thinking that doors, especially the relatively flimsy ones inside this house, weren't obstacles to bots. But what would he accomplish by breaking in? He was not her jailer, was not her keeper. He'd offered her food, comfort, and *security*.

"I'm sorry I upset you, Lara."

Though his internal clock tracked every passing microsecond, time soon lost meaning. She didn't answer. Once, he heard a faint rustle of cloth that might have been her moving, but it was gone too quickly to be sure.

After five minutes and thirty-three seconds, Ronin turned and walked to his room. He had equipment to care for—weapons to clean, tools to inspect, clothing to mend.

Perhaps some rest would cool Lara's temper.

Or perhaps I need to be more mindful of what I say to her.

I'm sorry I upset you, Lara.

Speechless, with her anger having vanished, Lara stared at the door.

When she'd slammed it, she'd expected him to kick it in and teach her a lesson. Determined not to show her fear, she'd been ready to fight tooth and nail…

Ready to fight to the death.

But Ronin had asked her to open the door, and he'd apologized to her after she refused.

What the fuck?

Never in her twenty-three years had she heard of a bot apologizing to a human.

His footsteps retreated down the hall, and she heard his door open and close softly.

She'd entered this agreement with him assuming she knew all about bots and their nature. Accepting that, even if Ronin didn't harm her, she'd be nothing more than a pet to him, a curiosity for his amusement. It was a small price to pay if it helped her find Tabitha.

But Ronin was different. He was unpredictable, surprisingly deep, even kind of funny in an infuriating way. No matter how hard she tried, she couldn't quite figure him out.

Remorse tightened her chest. Though he was good at evading her questions, he hadn't been lying. He didn't understand what triggered her outburst. How could he? Even if he displayed signs of feeling emotion, he had nothing to be insecure about. He couldn't know how insignificant his words had made her feel.

Do you really think I have anything in here that a bot can't get elsewhere?

Before her thoughts took another dark turn, she forced herself toward the bed. Her day had started early, and her encounter with Devon had set the tone for the rest of it—the rainstorm and loss of the ring, the ups and downs with Ronin...

Their last fight had left her physically and mentally exhausted.

She pulled back the blanket and tested the bed's softness with a hand. Would she even be able to sleep in this strange place, on this cushy thing, knowing she was on the wrong side of the wall?

Glancing at the light switch near the door, she paused, taking her lower lip between her teeth.

Too tired to go back and turn it off.

Or so she told herself.

Guess I'm too tired to call my own bullshit, too.

She lay down and pulled the blanket up to her chin. The bed gave way beneath her, cradling her body, enveloping her in softness and warmth. She didn't remember closing her eyes before weariness claimed her.

CHAPTER ELEVEN

Lara woke to rumbling in her stomach. Scowling, she pressed a hand to her belly. Just a little longer, then she'd get up and start her day. The scrap wasn't going anywhere. She only needed a few more minutes away from the real world…

As she rolled onto her side to go back to sleep, she realized her normally hard, lumpy pallet was too soft and had a strange, clean smell.

She opened her eyes, squinting as the blurriness cleared from her vision. Sunlight filtered in through the window coverings, falling in thin lines over the shaggy floor and brightening the white walls.

Lara sat up with a start. The blanket fell to her lap as she gazed around the room that was most definitely not her shack.

There was her bag on the floor, and there was the dresser with her treasures arranged atop it. The door was closed and locked.

Her heartbeat slowed as she remembered where she was.

Ronin.

Flipping the blanket aside, she swung her legs over the side of the bed, stood, and walked to the window, delighting in how the fuzzy floor tickled her toes. She moved the curtain, pushed down some of the plastic slats, and peered out. The trees across the street swayed in the breeze. She'd never known they could be so tall or have so many leaves. Beyond them, the green grass stretched on and on into eternity.

Puddles on the road reflected the hazy sky. Most of the moisture must've dried up in the sun, which was already high and bright.

How late had she slept?

Her stomach twisted on itself, reminding her it was empty. After all she'd eaten the night before, how could she be so hungry?

She went to the dresser and finished off all the leftover food except a strip of dried meat. That, she wrapped up tight and put in the bottom drawer. Not the best hiding place, but it was better than nothing. Her next meal was never guaranteed.

Padding to the door, Lara pressed her ear to it and listened. There were no sounds from beyond.

Was Ronin up? Was he even home?

"Don't be such a coward," she muttered.

They had a bargain, and she couldn't hide from him all day. Sooner or later, he'd come knocking, and she would have to pay up. Who was she to say he wouldn't break down the door if she pulled that stunt again?

Unlocking the door, she cracked it open and peered into the hall. Ronin's bedroom was open, but he was nowhere to be seen. She hurried into the toilet room and locked the door behind her.

After relieving herself and washing her hands, Lara studied her reflection in the mirror, frowning at her hair. It was a mess.

Since when do you care?

Lara frowned.

She usually didn't. But right now, being in this house, standing in this pristine room, she felt wholly out of place.

Lara combed her fingers through her hair, taming the wayward strands and wincing as she tugged at the tangles, stopping only after she'd managed to make it look somewhat presentable.

Her clothing was still damp, so she left it hanging on the curtain rod. Ronin's shirt would have to do for a while longer.

She slipped into the hallway and crept downstairs.

Ronin was sitting at the table in the main room, tools spread out before him, with her boot in one hand. Her boot, which had been cleaned of mud.

Her brow furrowed. Where had she left her boots last night? They were her most valuable possession, the first thing she put on every morning, and she always kept them close to her pallet. But today, she hadn't even looked for them. Was she already going soft?

"What are you doing?" Lara asked as she reached the bottom step.

"Maintaining your gear." He didn't look up from the needle he was pulling through the sole of her boot.

"Maintaining my… Oh. Um, thanks."

"Care for them properly, and things like this won't happen."

Lara clutched the banister as she narrowed her eyes. "It's not like people go around teaching us how to fix boots and all that."

"At some point"—the needle came back around, drawn through the thick sole as easily as if it were paper—"there was a pair of these that were the first. Nobody told their owner how to take care of them. That person had to learn on their own."

"I don't need you already busting my—" She snapped her mouth shut and took a deep breath, closing her eyes. "Look, I don't want to fight again, okay?"

When Lara opened her eyes, he was looking at her. She couldn't quite read his expression, but there seemed to be a little *I wasn't the one fighting* in it, and that sent a rush of irritation through her that she quickly quelled.

"Sleep all right?" Ronin asked, looking back at the boot. His hands continued their sure movements, each stitch identical to the last.

"I slept late. Didn't you say you were leaving today?"

"You didn't seem too keen on me going. Figured you'd be more comfortable if you weren't alone when you woke up. I know it can take some time to get acclimated to a new environment."

"That was…thoughtful of you." Lara didn't know what to make of this. She was still reeling from his apology the night before, and now he was taking her feelings into account? "Does it take you time to get used to new places?"

Ronin shifted the boot to a different angle. She was amazed at how nimble and precise his metal fingers were.

He again pressed the needle through the sole. "Yes. Every place has its own leaders, its own rules. Scrap that's valuable in one town is worthless in another. And it's constantly changing. It always takes time to learn all that again."

Reluctantly, Lara stepped off the soft flooring of the stairs and onto the cold maybe-wood of the main room. "I'm not even strong enough to do what you're doing now."

"It's not about how much strength you have, but knowing how much to use." He tied off and cut the thick thread, placed the boot on the table, and turned in the chair to face her.

"What?" Maybe she should've cut him some slack for not understanding her emotions—she couldn't understand what he was talking about half the time.

"The application of strength is more important than the amount of it. It's just as easy to use too much as it is to use too little, and that often leads to unintended consequences." He dipped a hand into his pocket and removed a small piece of plastic with little metal dots and lines on it. "Pinch this between your fingers."

She arched a skeptical brow at him as she took it, edges between pointer finger and thumb, and pinched. It was harder than it looked. "Still not getting it."

"Squeeze. Hard as you can."

Lara did as he said. The plastic didn't buckle at all. Instead, it dug painfully into her fingertips. When he took it back from her, she was all too happy to be rid of it; her fingers throbbed and there were deep indents in her skin.

"Don't see what that proves," she said, rubbing the sting away.

Ronin grasped the plastic the same way she had, holding it up where she could see. Without any apparent effort, his finger and thumb came together, snapping the plastic in half.

She crossed her arms over her chest and cocked a hip. "Yeah, you're stronger than me. Already knew that, didn't we?"

"That's not the point, Lara. You must exert a conscious effort to apply all your strength. I must do the same to apply only a small portion of it. That necessitates significant processing resources being constantly devoted to my sensory inputs. It can be just as difficult for me not to break something as it is for you to break it."

The warmth drained from Lara's face as she stared at the

broken pieces of plastic between Ronin's fingers. Prickling ice formed in her veins, and her chest grew tight, making it hard to breathe. She understood the lesson now, and it called up dark memories of violence and pain, producing phantom aches in her limbs.

Her breakfast churned in her gut.

She sprinted through the opening into the other room, stumbled around the central counter, and bent over the wash basin. Her stomach heaved, emptying itself. She retched again, but there was nothing left to come up, making it all the more miserable.

Trembling, Lara clutched the countertop.

That fucking thing!

The bot that still haunted her nightmares had known what it was doing to her. The strength of its grip had been deliberate, every bruise intentional, and the damage to her shoulder had been only a taste of the bastard's full power. She'd been in pain for weeks because that's what it had wanted.

Ronin's boots thumped across the floor. He stopped somewhere behind her.

"Don't touch me," she snapped without lifting her head. She spat sour-tasting saliva into the basin.

"Are you ill?"

"I'm fine." Lip curling at the stench of her own vomit, she turned on the water and washed out the basin.

"Appearances suggest otherwise." Ronin moved closer and placed a hand on the counter to her right, keeping a few feet between them. "Your face is paler than usual."

"I said I'm fine." She cupped her hands beneath the flowing water and rinsed her mouth.

After she spat out of the water, Lara wiped her lips with the back of her hand, shut off the spigot, and straightened, turning to face him. A cramp seized her stomach, but she clenched her jaw and rode it out.

So much for the food I ate.

"Thanks for fixing my boot," she said quietly.

He maintained his silent stare long enough for her skin to itch beneath it. Gripping the hem of the shirt at her thighs, she shifted her weight from one foot to the other and back again, waiting for him to say something, to say *anything*.

But he didn't.

"I said I was fine, damn it!" She marched back into the main room and snatched up her boots.

"You told me bots always say what they mean. Is it the opposite for humans?"

Lara faced Ronin, holding her boots to her chest. He stood in the entryway between the two rooms, watching her. There should've been judgment in his words, but she'd heard only curiosity.

Can't he at least make it easy to be pissed off at him?

"Don't you have somewhere to go?" Lara asked as calmly as she could.

The thought of being here alone wasn't appealing, but she couldn't take any more reminders of what had happened to her right now. Not while she knew those things were all around. Ronin would just keep probing, and it would get her worked up, but damn if she didn't want to believe his concern. It seemed genuine.

But from a bot, it couldn't be…

Could it?

Ronin frowned, brow creasing. "I can wait if you're unwell."

"If I have to tell you I'm fine one more time, I'm gonna scream."

He didn't respond for a long while. Maybe screaming until her throat was raw would make her feel better…

"I'll get back as quickly as I can," he finally said. "Is there anything particular you need, apart from the necessities?"

"If you need something, it *is* a necessity." The swelling of pride at her own wit dulled the edge on her mood a little.

"You are correct." One corner of his mouth lifted. Ronin took his coat off the back of the chair and pulled it on, his metal fingers demonstrating their dexterity as he buttoned it. "Lock the door behind me."

He picked up his backpack and rifle, slinging them over his shoulders as he moved toward the front entrance.

"Wait!" Lara called as his hand settled on the knob.

Ronin looked over his shoulder.

"My sister, Tabitha. You said you'd look for her."

He nodded.

Brow creased, she hesitantly stepped toward him. "You don't even know what she looks like."

Again, that silent stare. Lara's mouth went dry. Was it because of the way he looked at her, or because she missed her sister?

"She's about this tall," Lara said, holding her hand a few inches over her head, "with short black hair, brown eyes, and darker skin than mine. And, uh…a little…curvier than me." Especially if all was well and Tabitha was being fed by a bot. "Has a nasty scar on the back of her left hand. She dances…used to dance. At Kitty's."

If anything about that description was familiar to him, he made no sign of it. Her hope dwindled.

"When did you last see her?" Ronin asked.

"A couple months ago." Lara dropped her gaze to the floor, trying to pull up Tabitha's face from her memory. Why was it so hard? "She snuck a visit to our shack to tell me she was okay, that she was being kept by a bot."

"Isn't it likely she's still with that bot, then?"

"Yes, but…I don't know where, and I haven't heard from her since. I'm worried about her." She met his eyes. "I miss her, and I just want to know she's all right."

Was he capable of sympathy?

No, he was only doing this because it was a condition of their deal.

I don't need his sympathy. Just his help.

"I'll ask around, if I can," Ronin said, "but don't expect anything right away. The gearheads and their leader don't seem to care much for curiosity around town."

Lara pressed her lips together and nodded. He'd agreed to try. That was all she could ask, and it would have to be enough.

"Lock the door, Lara," he said softly, and then he was gone.

She stared at the closed door for a time, and then, finally, stepped forward and locked it. Pressing her forehead against its cool face, she smirked.

He called them gearheads.

For some reason, it reminded her of the night before, when he'd spoken to the gearheads at the gate.

There is an agreement in place.

She knew those words had been meant for her—to put her at ease.

Perhaps Ronin was the one bot she might eventually be able to trust.

CHAPTER TWELVE

Ronin knew the building had a different name, long ago, but the bots of Cheyenne simply called it the clinic. Outwardly, it was a relic of bygone era, sitting on the north side of the district and separated from the residences by a broad street. Its brick face and tiled roofs would've been old even at the time of the Blackout, and Ronin doubted its bell tower had sounded even once in the last two centuries.

It was well-maintained, like everything else in the bot district, though off-color bricks had been utilized for some of the exterior repairs.

Gearheads stood outside the main entrance, conversing in low tones. They didn't so much as look at Ronin when he walked past them. Though Warlord dipped his hand into everything in Cheyenne, the clinic operated freely, offering repairs to all bots.

The front doors slid open silently at Ronin's approach. The building's interior was in stark contrast to the outside—the reception room was all polished floors, sleek furniture, and chrome finish, bathed in the sanitary white glow of the overhead lights.

The synth at the front desk, Mercy, greeted him. Her face was framed by short blond hair, and her pink lips were locked in a perpetual smile.

"Back so soon?" she asked. "I hope you haven't suffered more damage already."

Regardless of the time of day, Mercy was always at the desk when Ronin visited. Did she ever leave? Ever pursue her own entertainment? Did she ever crave sexual stimulation?

She was attractive and pleasant, a perfect choice for companionship. With her, there'd be no volatile emotions, no unpredictable outbursts, no fear of accidental injury.

So why was she unappealing to him? Why was Lara the only one to catch and hold his interest in one hundred and eighty-five years?

The situation with Lara was a business arrangement, bearing no expectation of companionship or the development of any deeper relationship. She'd dance, and Ronin would watch. That was it.

So why did his analyses continually suggest there was something more between them?

Ronin raised his hands to display their bare casings. "Just need some reskinning."

"The epidermal synthesizer is free, currently," Mercy said, frowning at Ronin's hands. Was it an expression of sympathy or pity? "You remember the way. Go on back."

He dropped his hands into his pockets and walked down the long, sterile corridor. Of course he remembered. Only the truly damaged forgot things from after the Blackout.

Was that truly a bad thing though? The Creators had granted bots near-perfect recall, had cursed them to remember every face, every failure, every tragedy…

And based on the flashes of shattered memory that sometimes crept up from the corrupted parts of his memory bank, there'd been plenty of faces, failures, and tragedies for him before the Blackout. He had no desire to remember any of it with clarity.

All he wanted to know was what he'd been created for, his purpose. He didn't need the rest. He didn't need to remember people who were gone forever, a life that could never be reclaimed.

Doors lined the hallway on either side. The rooms beyond were dark, full of dormant equipment he'd never seen in use. The repair stations were deep within the building. Everything else…

He guessed the clinic had been used primarily for human care before the Blackout. Humans were fragile. They were susceptible to disease, their flesh was easily damaged, their bones easily broken, and recovery was often a slow, complicated process for them even with the aid of technology.

Apart from routine maintenance, most bots rarely suffered enough damage to require a trip to this place. Dustwalkers were in a class of their own. Whether human or bot, a dustwalker wasn't likely to make it back into a town without damage of some sort.

Warlord's gearheads—the synths, anyway—preferred to have chunks of skin missing. It sent a clear message. *I am a bot.*

Ronin turned into the dimly lit room marked *Epidermal Synthesizer*. The bot on duty resembled the food vendor, Greene, with a similar body shape and white casing. This one had a red plus sign on its chest.

"Greetings, Ronin. Are you in need of service?"

"Three patches on my abdomen." Ronin removed his hands from his pockets and glanced down at them. Lara's initial hostility had been triggered when she saw their bare metal, as though their appearance had rekindled the dark thoughts haunting her. "And my hands."

The attendant tapped on its small control console. On the far side of the room, the synthesizer hummed to life, its interior chamber lighting up.

"Please remove your clothing and enter the Epidermal Synthesizer," the bot said as the chamber door slid open.

Ronin stood his rifle against the wall, settled his pack on the floor beside it, and unbuttoned his coat, draping it over one of the chairs. He drew off his shirt and set it atop the coat before sitting down to untie his boots, which he pulled off and slid beneath the chair.

The quiet clicking of the attendant's fingers on the console was the only sound apart from the whisper of cloth as Ronin removed his pants, folded them over his arm, and added them to the pile of clothing.

He shifted his optics down. His casing was visible through the holes on his abdomen, gleaming in the light cast by the synthesizer. Random patches of his skin were different shades than the rest, the result of dozens of repair jobs in dozens of towns.

Though the discolored spots weren't distinguishable from the rest of his skin in any other way, they reminded him of the scars many organics bore. A subtle, visual history wrought in flesh. He could recall the circumstances behind each bit of damage, no matter how minor, he'd suffered since awakening.

"Please enter the Epidermal Synthesizer," the attendant repeated. Its faintly glowing optics were trained on Ronin, and though its face was incapable of expression, it seemed to hesitate. "Have you suffered damage deeper than the surface, Ronin?"

"I'm fine." He forced himself to walk to the chamber. As he entered, he assessed tangled streams of data, pondering the problem awaiting him at his residence just under two kilometers away.

Damage deeper than the surface...

All bots had lost something in the Blackout, had lost parts of themselves that couldn't be replaced. It was damage that couldn't be repaired at places like this, damage that could wreak subtle havoc on a bot's core programming.

Wasn't that similar to the mental fragility of humans? Ronin had seen it firsthand in the Dust; humans, especially in stressful situations, often shattered.

What hidden damage had Lara suffered? What internal scars did she carry?

The chamber door closed, sealing Ronin inside. It was utterly silent until the synthesizer's motors engaged, moving the scanning arms on either side of him. Their lights flickered on. Their blue glow, a welcome change from the harsh white dominating this place, reminded him of Lara's eyes as the arms encircled him.

Though both bots and humans were products of the Creators, their differences were many. So why did synths, when fully repaired and maintained, look and move so much like humans? Was it simply an aesthetic that appealed to the eye of their makers?

Or did their similarities actually extend far beyond their appearances?

The scanners retracted, replaced by numerous fabrication arms. The synthesizer shifted to full operation, emitting a high whine. The small arms soldered delicate wires into the neural network on his casing, while the large ones, moving slowly, knitted synthetic skin over the wiring.

Though perfection was impossible, synths seemed the closest to it of all intelligent beings. Why, then, was a human so interesting to him? Why were her flaws more alluring, her imperfections more enticing?

Ronin closed his eyes, reducing his vision to the faint, brown-red glow filtering through his eyelids. His true programming seemed simultaneously so close and so terribly far away. Pushing aside his sensory inputs, he delved into his memory core, searching for the missing piece that would unlock what he'd lost.

When he stumbled upon the memory of a shack on the edge of the road with a red-haired woman dancing within, he stopped.

And he played it over and over again.

CHAPTER THIRTEEN

The afternoon dragged on for Lara. She was accustomed to toiling from dawn to dusk on most days; this idleness was torture.

She took another hot shower, scrubbing her hair, body, and teeth. Then, despite Ronin having told her not to be wasteful, she stood under the falling water for at least fifteen minutes, letting it melt away her aches. How would she ever be able to return to quick washes with frigid water from the pump again?

After stepping out of the tub and drying off, she dressed in her own clothes. Their smell reminded her of her old life, which was familiar even if it hadn't been good. And that familiarity grounded her. She didn't know if she'd ever feel like she belonged in Ronin's world.

Returning to her room, she placed Ronin's shirt in the dresser's top drawer, wondering if he'd been joking about people filling these things with clothing. Why would someone need so many clothes?

Lara explored the other upstairs rooms. They were similar to hers, with beds and dressers but no decorations. The room closest to hers had pale blue walls instead of the white in rest of the house. It was the little differences, like the way her bedding was crumpled and the trinkets atop the dresser, that made her bedroom feel inviting. Everything else felt too bare, too untouched, too...cold.

She stopped in the doorway of Ronin's room and stared inside, oddly hesitant to enter.

If he didn't want you to go in, he would've closed the door.

Besides, he was a bot, so it wasn't like he cared about privacy, right?

Lara crossed the threshold and swept her gaze around the room. His bed was perfectly made, with squared corners and not so much as a wrinkle in sight.

That made sense. Ronin didn't sleep.

But did he ever sit or lie down on the bed? He'd been sitting in a chair while he'd repaired her boot this morning. Surely, he didn't just stand stiff as a board every moment he spent in this room.

What did he do to keep himself occupied? Did he just stare blankly at the walls, or did he think about…

No. Not going there right now.

After the space he'd given her last night, after his apology, it felt wrong to come in here without his permission…

But what could he possibly have that he wouldn't want her to see, anyway? It wasn't like bots kept things for sentimental value. Hell, many humans didn't even do that. Most people only cared about things relating to survival—food and drink, tools, warmth and shelter. Though their specific needs were different, bots operated the same way.

Her attention settled on a large chest sitting at the foot of the bed, with several tools, brushes, and narrow rods laid atop it. Amongst those items was the gun he'd been holding when he burst into the toilet room last night after hearing her scream.

Lara stared at the dull black gun. Her heart thumped. If she'd had one that night…

I could have…

She stepped forward and reached for it, halting before her fingers would've touched the metal. A single cut could be the end for a human, but Ronin hadn't been stopped by three bullets to his abdomen. They hadn't even scratched his metal. This little gun wouldn't be a threat to him.

Why had he left it behind?

A test, perhaps, and one that posed minimal risk to him.

Because if she fired it at him and somehow managed to hit her target, it wouldn't do enough damage to save her from retaliation.

She swallowed her temptation and dropped her hand to her side, moving on to the double doors on the opposite wall. They slid open on hidden rails, revealing a little room, even smaller than her shack, with clothing hanging on rods to either side. Ronin's clothing.

Leaning in, Lara drew in a deep breath. The potent mix of dust, sunshine, gunpowder, and steel filled her nose with a strange, warming familiarity, and she jerked back after realizing what she'd done. But now that she had, she couldn't help but feel as though Ronin's scent was ingrained into her. He smelled like the Dust… and war.

Wanderer, dustwalker. How much time had he spent out there? How often did he fight? How many times had he been shot?

"Why am I thinking about him so much?"

Annoyed, she returned to her room, closing the door behind her. Without meaning to, she compared the space to Ronin's. What would he think if he saw her bedroom now, with the blankets rumpled and the pillows squished in?

She kept the image of Ronin's bed in mind as she made her own. But no matter how hard she tried, no matter how careful she was, the blanket always hung off one side more than the other, and every time she smoothed out an unsightly wrinkle or flattened a bump a new one appeared somewhere else. And she couldn't figure out how he'd made the corners so perfectly squared.

It's going to get messed up again when I sleep. Why am I bothering?

With a huff, she sat on the edge of the bed, drumming her fingers atop the soft blanket. Her gaze wandered, eventually stopping on the window. Afternoon light filtered through the plastic coverings, filling the room with warmth, and the shadows of the trees danced on the bottom panes.

When she'd stared up at Ronin's home yesterday, she'd seen three rows of windows, but this was only the second floor. There had to be another level directly above her room.

So, where was the staircase leading up? That seemed like too big a thing to have missed while she'd explored the other rooms.

She went to the sliding door on one of her walls. It opened to a recess barely large enough for a child to lie in, a smaller version of the room where Ronin kept his clothing. But this one didn't possess his metal and gunpowder scent.

"Enough already," she muttered.

Her search of the bedroom was quick but thorough, ending when she wrestled the heavy dresser forward to reveal the solid wall behind it.

Lara entered the hallway and paced its length, brow furrowed, as she considered the mystery.

Maybe the upper window is just for show?

"No. There's definitely another floor."

Frustrated and disappointed, she tilted her head back and sighed. Her eyes caught on a short, frayed string dangling from the ceiling. There was a rectangle cut in the material around it, as though it were an oddly placed door. It was bordered by the same sort of wood strips that edged the floor, doors, and windows.

Lara's eyes widened.

Could that be...?

Standing on the balls of her feet, she reached for the string. It was too high. She jumped, brushing the end and making it to sway wildly. On her second attempt, she caught a solid hold of the string, and she used her weight to yank it down.

Dust showered her, and pain exploded in her head as a ladder slid down from the door and struck her temple.

Lara stumbled back, eyes squeezed shut as she pressed a hand over the throbbing point of impact.

"Fuck!" she gritted through clenched teeth. Tears well behind her eyelids, and she placed her other hand on the ladder to steady herself as she breathed through the pain and a wave of dizziness.

"Someone should have posted a warning or something. Like a picture, making the danger clear—possible beheading when opened."

Lara opened her eyes and looked up at the hole in the ceiling. Motes of dust floated lazily through the air all around it. And, to her annoyance, she noticed a little sign on the side of the ladder. Black writing and images of little stick people getting hit by the ladder.

She glared at the sign. "Yeah, that's the perfect place for it. Thanks for the fucking warning."

The ache in her head continued as she climbed the wooden ladder. Its old springs squeaked in protest.

When her head emerged in the new space, she stopped. The air here was heavier and warmer than that in the hallway below. A thick layer of dust coated everything, illuminated by the afternoon sunlight streaming through the rectangular window ahead. To either side, the ceiling ran up from the floor at sharp angles, meeting in a high peak at the center.

Lara climbed into the room, turning on her hands and knees to look through the opening. The floor below was covered in clumps of dust. Without her weight on it, the ladder had lifted slightly. She pressed down on it to keep it extended, but whatever mechanism had locked it open creaked, and the whole thing swung back up, folding the ladder into place and closing the hatch.

She stared at the sealed entry briefly before she stood and dusted her hands off. She'd deal with that problem soon enough.

Turning, she studied the room. The slanted walls, from which jutted the tips of countless nails, were lined with wooden beams running from one end to another. The floor was also wood, constructed with close-fitting boards that lacked the impossible polish of those downstairs. Cobwebs dangled from overhead and clung to the walls.

The room looked…old. Unlike the rest of the house, there was no gleam of cleanliness up here, no fresh coat of paint to hide the age. A musty smell filled the air. This room had been neglected for a long, long time.

Stacks of gray bins stood halfway between the hatch and the window. Nearby was a small, square table with books piled atop it. The chair in front of the table matched the one in the main room downstairs.

Lara walked to the table and picked up one of the books, brushing the thick layer of dust off its cover. Between the discoloration and the cracks in the material, she couldn't tell what the art upon it was meant to depict. The pages inside were crinkly, brittle, and stained yellow, but they were intact. She gently ran a finger along the top line of words on the first page. Paper was a rare thing amongst humans, and complete books were almost unheard of.

Setting it aside, she leaned down to look at another book. This one had a larger, thinner cover, with an image of a car in full repair. Glancing through the pages, she saw dozens more cars in more colors and shapes than she'd thought possible. They were sleek, shiny, and vibrant. The only cars she'd seen with her own eyes were the rusted-out remains scattered around the ruins, parts of which had been used to build some of the dwellings back home.

It was hard to believe that they'd once looked like the cars in this book.

Her attention shifted to the case of shelves beside the window. It was like the one in her shack, though this was larger and filled with jars instead of trinkets. Moving to it, she lifted one of the jars, using her fingers to wipe away the dust and cobwebs before brushing her hand on her skirt.

Lara scrunched her nose. "And I just washed my clothes, too."

The jar was heavy, and something dark sloshed inside, but the dirt caked on the glass was too thick to see through. Gripping the lid, she twisted her hand. The metal ring resisted for a moment before the rust gave way. The metal plate beneath proved more difficult. She pressed her fingers on its edge, wincing as she pried at it. Finally, it came free, opening with a *pop*.

The foulest odor Lara had ever smelled hit her directly in the face. Gagging, she nearly dropped the jar, extending her arm to keep it as far away as possible. She glanced at the unidentifiable black sludge inside through slitted, tear-filled eyes.

"Ugh!" Slapping the seal back on top, she quickly screwed the ring on and returned the jar to its place. "What *was* that?"

She reached up to wipe her face, but stopped when she caught another whiff of the smell on her fingers. Nose crinkling, she rubbed her hands roughly on her skirt.

"Yeah. Gonna need to wash these again."

Strange how her attitude had changed overnight. She'd rarely washed her clothes before. Not only was it a waste of precious water, but it only made the garments wear out faster, and she knew they'd get filthy the next day anyway after hours in the heat and dirt. But feeling soft cloth against clean skin...it was going to be difficult to let that go. She'd have to enjoy it while she could.

It was only a matter of time before Ronin lost interest in her.

Despite the dust and heat, this room looked comfortable. She was sure it was far from perfect by Ronin's standards, but it had a certain quality that appealed to her, like it had been *lived* in. It reminded her of her little shack. Long enough up here, and she might forget she was in the bot district at all.

Walking to the window, she used the end of her skirt to wipe the thick grime from the glass. The grassy field stretched out below, and from this height, the pond near its center was visible.

Was this how humans used to live? In quiet, peaceful comfort?

As Lara turned, her foot bumped into something. She glanced down at a pile of tattered blankets. Crouching, she lifted them up. The top blanket crumbled to fibers at her touch. She tossed the bunch aside, revealing an assortment of items that had been hidden beneath.

Clothing, which looked just as ratty as the blankets, lay folded over a few more books. But it was the strange device with a wire trailing off it that caught her attention first. It was thin, rectangular, small enough to fit comfortably in her hand, and had a few buttons on the front and sides. Its glass face was cracked. The wire split after about two feet, ending in a pair of small, strangely shaped buds.

Placing it atop the blankets, she looked through the books. The top few were thin and flimsy, like the one with the car pictures, and she nearly dropped the third when she opened it.

Her brows rose high. "Oh."

She'd turned to a page spanned by a photo of a naked woman who held her large breasts in both hands. Many of the pages displayed similar images—women in explicit poses, unclothed with their legs spread wide, baring their pussies and touching themselves.

They reminded her of the synths at Kitty's. Their bodies were full and lush, their skin flawless, not a hair out of place...and most without hair on their pussies. Some of them had unnaturally large breasts, bigger, rounder, and firmer than any Lara had seen. They had splashes of color around their eyes and on their lips, deep reds and pinks, shades of blue, green, purple, and black. With their perfect figures and faces, she would have thought they were bots, but no.

They all had belly buttons. Crazy as it seemed, they were human.

She set it aside.

The book at the bottom of the stack was different from the others. Though it wasn't as wide, it was thicker, bound in old leather. She opened it and carefully looked through the pages.

This one had been written by hand. Somehow, that made it more special. She'd never met anyone who could read, much less write, so it seemed an impossible skill. Though she couldn't understand the words, for a moment she felt closer to the past than ever before.

In the middle of the book, she found a few loose photos. The same people were present in all of them—a man, a woman, and two children.

Had they lived in this house, stayed in this room?

She glanced at the clothing, which all seemed to be sized for a man, at the blankets, the jars on the shelf, the single chair. It had likely only been one person here.

Replacing the pictures, she went to the table and gently laid the leatherbound book atop it. Her eyes fell on the stacked bins. What other little treasures were hidden here?

CHAPTER FOURTEEN

Ronin entered his dwelling, closing and locking the door behind him. His fingertips lingered on the knob. It was cold and smooth. The accurate temperature readings and texture mapping enabled by his freshly replaced synthetic skin added dimensions to his sense of touch that he'd forgotten about during his months in the Dust.

The sun sank toward the western horizon, its orange light streaming through the front windows to cast long shadows over his worktable. He'd hoped to find Lara in the main room upon his return, sitting at the table or perched on one of the wide windowsills, but he doubted she was capable of sitting still for long.

After closing the blinds, he placed his pack and rifle on the table and pulled off his coat, running his fingers over its rough fabric before tossing it over the back of the chair. The needle and thread he'd used to repair Lara's boot were still out; he'd put them away later.

Ronin stepped into the kitchen. Lara wasn't there, either.

Why would she be? There isn't any food here yet.

He grasped the refrigerator by the sides, pulled it away from the wall, and slipped behind it to plug the cord into the electrical outlet.

Something inside the fridge rattled before the sound evened to a soft, steady hum. He was, for once, grateful for the maintenance bots keeping the home appliances in Cheyenne in working order. Lara's food would last longer in the refrigerator, which would mean fewer trips to the vendor for Ronin.

He pressed his hand to the refrigerator's flat face, and the sensors in his skin detected the fine, linear grooves in the brushed metal as he pushed the appliance back into place. He'd fill it with the food he'd brought home soon enough. Lara was likely hungry after his five-hour absence, and she'd appreciate choosing what to eat first.

Ronin strode to the foot of the stairs. "Lara?"

Ten seconds ticked by with no response.

She's likely resting.

After a minute had passed, he went upstairs. Though Ronin knew sleep was a necessary biological function for organic creatures, much like her having to *go*, he could never experience it himself and therefore could not truly comprehend it. But he would still accommodate her needs.

All the upstairs doors were open. The corner of his mouth quirked. She must've been familiarizing herself with her surroundings, not that there was much to see. Many of the furnishings had been removed before Ronin took up residence here, and even the few remaining pieces were more than he required.

He walked to her room, where he found her bed inexpertly made, her trinkets spread atop the dresser, which had been pulled away from the wall, and the closet open. But there was no Lara.

His brow plates lowered.

The front door had been locked when he'd returned, and he detected no errant air currents to indicate an open window within the house. Could she have been taken? Or had she found a way out on her own?

He focused his optics on her collection, and, after moving further into the room, discovered her boots and bag on the floor beside the dresser in the corner. No, she hadn't left on her own. She never would've left those things behind.

Ronin moved the dresser back into place, stepped out of her room, and continued his search.

She wasn't in the other bedrooms, and his gear, including the pistol, was where he'd left it atop the chest at the foot of his bed. More evidence that she hadn't departed on her own. All these items would've aided her survival. To leave behind both her own belongings and his openly displayed tools and weapon would've been madness.

His processors whirred as he returned to the hallway and paced from one end to the other, running hundreds, thousands of simulations at once. None of them could fully account for the single greatest variable—human unpredictability.

Taken, then? He was certain Warlord kept keys to every residence in the bot district, and it would've only required a single gearhead to subdue Lara. What history did she have with Cheyenne's ruler?

A potent buzz surged through his circuits, rage and fear intertwined into the same wavelength. What if Warlord had taken her? What if the gate guards had informed their leader that Ronin had taken not just a human, but Lara, into his residence, and Warlord had come to collect her?

Ronin halted abruptly, tilting his head down. Thick clumps of dust lay on the floor, some having already been trampled into the carpet fibers by his boots. His optics swept up to the attic hatch.

Though he'd noticed the hatch when he'd first taken residence, he'd never opened it and looked inside. Given the state of the rest of the building, logic had dictated that there was nothing of value to find up there. Why would she go up there now?

Reaching up, he grasped the broken pull-string and tugged the hatch open.

The whine of old springs and hinges warned him. He caught the ladder with his free hand before it could strike his head. Above, someone gasped.

Floorboards creaked overhead, and Lara peered over the edge, with cobwebs clinging to her loose, messy hair and a smudge of dirt on her cheek and chin. Briefly, Ronin shut out everything but his sensory input.

Lara was here. Safe.

And she was *beautiful*.

"Did you know somebody used to live up here?" she asked.

Her question was so unexpected that he wasn't sure how to

process it. *Hello* or *what's going on* would have been easier to respond to.

"What are you talking about?" Ronin lowered the ladder. The wood groaned as he mounted it, rungs flexing enough beneath his weight that he had to adjust his stabilizers.

Lara backed away, allowing him enough space to climb onto the dusty attic floor. Her footprints were everywhere, in a meandering trail from one side of the attic to the other and back again. It was twenty-three degrees warmer here than in the hallway below. Strands of damp hair were plastered to her face, and a sheen of perspiration covered her skin.

But it was the dried blood at her temple that his optics zeroed in on. The flesh around the small cut there was raised, taking on the red and purple coloring of a developing bruise.

His brow plates sank low.

"You're hurt," he said, raising a hand to brush her hair away from the cut.

She ducked out of his reach and pulled more hair over the wound. "It's nothing. The ladder had the upper hand on me." Lara snickered. "Get it?"

Ronin dropped his hand to his side. Internally, he combed his stored data for information about human head injuries. Were nonsensical ramblings and statements without context signs of deeper trauma?

"I…got everything I intended at the market?" he said.

"Wow. Okay. We'll add no appreciation for witty humor to the list. Anyway—wait. What happened to your hands?"

She moved to his side, staring at his hands. He lifted them, turning his palms toward the ceiling, and inspected the new skin. It was strange to see them this way after so long. They were undoubtedly his hands, but they seemed somehow foreign to him.

"I went to the Clinic and had them reskinned. Been a long time since I've done it. I figured it was overdue."

"You can *do* that? Like, grow new skin?"

Ronin turned his face toward her. Did she realize how close her curiosity had brought her to him?

Her scent registered with his olfactory sensors—blood, sweat, dust. But there was also a crisp freshness from the soap she'd used, and a hint of something more, something he'd not detected from anywhere else. A scent that was wholly...Lara.

Resisting the urge to move closer to her, he replied, "It's synthesized from various materials. Not grown."

Lara looked into his optics, her brow furrowing. "Why don't the gearheads do it, then?"

"Because they don't want to be mistaken for humans."

"Yeah. Because we're *so* horrible." She rolled her eyes and walked toward the window. "Come look at this."

Not sure how to respond to her comment, he followed her to the far end of the attic. As Lara knelt, he took in the scene—the bookcase full of jars, the blankets and clothing on the floor, the table and chair.

She picked up a book with a brown leather cover and held it out to him. "I can't read it, but someone wrote this."

"Every book was written by someone." Ronin took the book, running his fingertips over the textured surface.

"No, smart ass. This one was written by hand. Not like the other ones. And this"—she gestured to the blankets—"was where he slept."

His optics followed her gesture before returning to the book. Carefully, he opened it. The pages were stiff, but in surprisingly good condition.

Those things killed people today. Marched into town and just started killing people. I watched from the window as people were dragged into the park and executed.

"And this is what he ate," Lara said, calling Ronin's attention back to her. She stood near the bookcase, holding up a jar with a dark, unidentifiable substance inside it. "Trust me when I say *not* to open them."

Ronin studied the objects one at a time, cataloguing them in his memory. It was impossible to say how long ago the words had been written, how long ago the writer had lived. Many, many years, certainly. "He?"

She stepped closer to him, turning the pages to reveal the

photographs tucked in the middle of the book. The top one was a picture of a family. The adult male and female had dark brown hair and eyes, and the two children resembled them closely.

"Pretty sure it was him," Lara said, tapping the man's face.

Humans didn't look like that anymore. It wasn't that those in the picture had drastically different features than modern people; basic human facial structures and proportions were unchanged. No, it was the light in their eyes, the genuine smiles on their faces.

The people in the photo were happy, healthy, and *alive*.

Lara moved to the window. "And he had a great view."

Outside, sunlight sparkled on the surface of the pond in the middle of the park and cast golden halos around the treetops.

I watched from the window as people were dragged into the park and executed.

"Come away from there," Ronin said, tone sharp even to his own receptors.

She narrowed her eyes. "Why?"

"There's food downstairs, and you're likely in need of hydration after spending so much time up here in the heat. Go clean yourself up and have something to eat."

She looked down at herself. Dust clung to her clothing and sweat-dampened skin.

"Yeah…guess I didn't notice. I maybe got a little carried away." She plucked restlessly at the hem of her skirt before letting it drop.

"I found some more clothes for you at the market. They might not fit quite right, but they'll be better than nothing until we can adjust them." His boots thumped on the floorboards as he walked to the hatch. "Go on. I'd rather you get down safe before it collapses under me."

"Okay, okay." With one last glance at the window, she hurried over and climbed down.

Ronin's optics lingered on the evidence of that mysterious, long departed resident before he shifted them to the book in his hand. *JOURNAL* was barely legible on the front cover. He slipped it into his pocket and headed downstairs.

CHAPTER FIFTEEN

As Lara showered, Ronin banished himself to the lower level, doing all he could to keep from simulating images of her naked body glistening in the water.

He moved his bag into the kitchen and unpacked the food, setting it out on the island counter. After refilling her canteen, he carried it to the table, sat down, and removed the journal from his pocket. A human had penned it, just as Lara said, and Ronin knew the story it told would not be comforting to either of them.

He brushed his thumb over the cover, but he didn't open it.

After eleven minutes and fourteen seconds, Lara entered the kitchen, her wet hair hanging down her back. She wore some of the clothes he'd obtained for her—olive fatigues with patches on the knees and a baggy, off-white wool sweater. Its broad neck sagged off her pale, freckled shoulder. He averted his gaze as she hurried to the food.

Thankful for the distraction, Ronin pocketed the journal and watched her eat. The eclectic meal she'd selected, consisting of smoked meat and roasted vegetables, rapidly vanished. He couldn't look away as her expression subtly changed with each new flavor, as her tongue slipped out to lick her lips clean, as she made soft, contented sounds in her throat. Even in something as simple as food, she found pleasure. No programming required.

"So," she said around a mouthful of food, "Ronin your real name?"

"It's the only one I have," he replied, forcing his optics to meet her eyes.

"Did someone give it to you, or did you choose it?"

"I chose it twelve years after I was reactivated."

"Twelve years with no name?" She swallowed, ran her tongue over her teeth, and took another bite.

Though he'd been fully operational, those early years were confusing to him, and his memories of them were disorienting. Despite all the data he'd accumulated since, his recollection of that period was forever tainted by how little he'd understood at the time. He'd known the world was broken, that everything was wrong, but couldn't determine how or why.

"I didn't need a name to identify myself," he said.

"But you gave yourself one anyway."

"For the benefit of others. Easier than saying *that bot* or *hey you.*"

"Then why does everyone around here call you *dustwalker?*"

"Because there are few who choose to do as I do. There are rarely more than one or two successful dustwalkers in any given settlement at a time, and we're constantly traveling. Always…on the outside. More convenient to remember our role than our names. The term carries respect, but also a little fear."

"Why are there so few of you?" Lara folded a slice of meat and slipped it into her mouth.

"Bots operate on logic. Constantly assessing risk ver—"

"Isn't it more logical to not go into the Dust?"

Ronin smirked. "Yes, but settlements need raw materials to continue producing the parts bots need to function. Someone has to go find them."

"Why do you?"

"Should I be making a list of these questions so I can eventually answer them all, or do you just lose interest if my answer is more than a few words long?"

She chewed slowly, brow arched as she stared at him. Seconds ticked by. The only sounds were Lara's mastication and the refrigerator's soft hum.

"Getting a little irritated there, dustwalker?" she finally asked.

"I prefer you call me Ronin."

"Why?"

He couldn't tell for sure, but there seemed to be a hint of humor in her voice. "I think I'm through answering questions for now, *human.*"

"Point taken."

"May I get back to what I was saying?"

She picked up the canteen, unscrewed the cap, and took a drink. Seeing her use it made him feel something close to satisfaction. Wiping her mouth with the back of her hand, she nodded.

"You asked why there are so few dustwalkers." Ronin rested his hand on the table. "It's because most who take up the calling meet their ends in the Dust. Whether a walker is a human or a bot, nobody goes looking for them when they don't return."

The motion of her jaw slowed. "And...you go out there by choice?"

"Yes." Because he was compelled to.

"Why?"

"Perhaps my risk calculation processes were damaged in the Blackout."

"But you know the risks. You said you were trying to survive, just like me. How is putting yourself in danger like that survival?"

Ronin lifted his hand and scratched his cheek. Touching it with something other than the bare metal of his fingers was nearly as strange as the impulse to scratch in the first place.

He lowered his hand back to the table. "It's survival because I'm still moving. Existence is a constant battle, and I choose to engage it on my own terms. If I were to stay in a place like this all the time, at some point, I'd sit down and never get up again."

"Because you feel like you have no purpose."

Her words flared across his processors like a physical blow. A second passed; three seconds; fifteen.

It was half a minute before he formulated a response. "I never said that."

"You didn't have to." She slid the food wrapper away with half a strip of meat and three slices of carrot atop it. "Why'd you pick Ronin?"

Electrodes crackled across his cheek again, demanding physical stimulation, but he kept his hand down. After all his years of surviving, was he really so easy to read?

"In the twelfth year after I was awoken, I found a book. There were many more books back then. This one was about a country called Japan during a period of history that occurred many centuries ago. It spoke of warriors called samurai. They were the elite of their society, trained from young ages, feared by their enemies. But it was the ronin who caught my interest. In Japanese, it means *wave man*. They were soldiers without masters, seeking causes worthy of their skill. Wandering the lengths of their land, bound by nothing but their blades and how far their feet could carry them. It...spoke to me."

"How much of it spoke to you?"

"Enough to choose Ronin as my name." He dragged the paper closer and wrapped the remaining food. His chair scraped over the floor as he stood up. Gathering the other food, he placed it all in the refrigerator and returned to his seat.

Lara's brow was furrowed, her eyes fixed on him. Her expression was thoughtful, but there were still hints of wariness in her posture. "You're not like the other bots."

"Doubt either of us have spent enough time around other bots to know for certain."

"I've been around enough. You're different."

"And you're different from the other humans I've dealt with." It was an understatement, but he couldn't put his complex reasoning into words. He still didn't quite comprehend why she was different.

Her expression shifted again. It was another subtle change, but he was recognizing them with more ease, even if he didn't know what they meant.

"You mentioned your sister," he said when she made no reply. "Is there anyone else?"

Lara dropped her gaze to the table. "Don't think so. Never knew who my father was, if he was dead or alive. Don't think Mom did either. I remember her being sick a lot, but she went scavenging every day, anyway. One time, she just never came back. I was five, I think."

Ronin realized then how little he'd thought about the way humans changed over the courses of their lives. How they were born so small, so helpless, even more delicate and vulnerable than they were as adults, how they slowly grew over the years, bodies and minds developing and changing. It was a process Ronin's kind couldn't experience. They weathered the passage of time unchanging.

What had Lara looked like as a child? If he were to see an image of her at that age, would he recognize her, or had she changed too much?

"Cheyenne's slums don't seem like a good place for a five-year-old on her own," he said.

"They're not." She leaned back in her chair, placing a hand on her abdomen. "I was crying one day because my stomach hurt. Mom always told me to be quiet and suck it up, so I never cried when she was around. But this time, I couldn't help it. It just hurt so much that I was sure I was dying."

Frowning, she shifted forward again, folding her arms on the edge of the table. "It was Tabitha who found me like that. She was a few years older and had already been on her own for about a year. She scavenged as best she could, but it was hard being a kid on your own, and there are people who took advantage of that. They bully, beat, and steal from the weak. I think some of the adults took pity and helped her out sometimes.

"So when Tabitha found me, she sat down next to me, hugged me, and asked why I was crying. But I couldn't stop, not even long enough to answer her. She knew, though. Even without me saying anything, she knew I was alone and hungry. She held me, comforted me, and after a while, she gave me a potato from her pocket. That...that was all the food she had. Then she told me we were sisters and that she'd always take care of me."

Lara smiled softly, moisture glistening in her blue eyes. "I'll never forget that moment. I think... I *know* it was the first time I ever felt like someone cared about me. The first time I ever felt loved."

Her smile fell away as she met his gaze again. "I need to find her, Ronin. She's all I have."

The emotions in her voice and expression were almost too layered to decipher. Fear, sorrow, determination, affection...loneliness? Solitude was familiar to Ronin. He'd wandered the Dust for so many years by himself, never staying in one place for long, never building lasting relationships.

What would it be like to have a companion, to share his existence with another person?

Would it be like this?

"I'll do everything I can, Lara."

She'd told him that bots did what they said, and he intended to. Not because of programming, not because it was the nature of his kind, but because he wanted to help her. Though his primary desire had long been to discover his true purpose, his wants were quickly growing to revolve around this woman.

Lara closed her eyes and eased back, exhaling. Relieved. Did that mean she'd placed some trust in him? That she had faith he would follow through?

"Right," she said, opening her eyes and wiping away the tears. "Guess with all you've done, I'd better keep my end of the deal. We doing this in here?"

Images of Lara dancing in her shack flashed through his central processing unit, every moment framed by the slitted door through which he'd watched. Even if she performed the same dance now, he knew every step would be somehow altered, reflecting her current state of mind.

Ronin dropped his hands to his thighs. "Where would you be most comfortable?"

"This is fine." She rose and walked to the relatively open part of the kitchen, trailing her fingers over the countertop. "So...you got any music?"

"No. I thought you made your own."

"Of course you'd remember that."

"I remember everything."

Her cheeks reddened before she looked away.

Everything.

Unbidden, a still image of her naked on the bathroom floor came up, and he knew his choice of words had been poor.

Keeping her back to him, Lara inhaled deeply, shoulders rising and falling. "Okay then."

She swayed her hips from side to side and lifted her arms over her head, grasping an elbow with each hand. Bowing her back, she turned gracefully to face him, bringing her hands down to slide over her breasts, waist, and thighs. She kept her eyes closed.

Arousal stirred within Ronin. Though Lara's clothing did nothing to accentuate her body, she was an attractive woman, and he longed to touch her so he could experience her through a different sensory input.

Still, seconds passed as he awaited the deep, profound spark that had flared across his processors the first time he'd watched her dancing. This dance was familiar, but it bore no resemblance to the one she'd performed in her shack.

He'd seen such motions from the performers at Kitty's.

Lara's body was moving for him, but she wasn't dancing. This was closer to a maintenance bot mowing the grass in the park. Movement with purpose, but no feeling. The motions of an automaton.

"No," he said sharply.

She jumped and opened her eyes, meeting his gaze. "What?"

"This isn't what I want."

"What the hell do you mean?" The line between her eyebrows returned; *danger ahead*. She threw her arms to the sides, palms up. "I'm dancing. That's what you wanted!"

"You are moving your parts—"

"Isn't that what dancing is? Moving your body?"

Ronin clenched his jaw to maintain his patience. "Dance like you did the night I first saw you."

"What do you mean? Like…the same dance?"

"It doesn't matter if it's the same. Just…" Counting only English, there were hundreds of thousands of fully defined words stored in his memory, and he still couldn't find the right ones to convey his meaning. "I don't want you to dance like you're on that stage. Dance like you would for yourself."

She stared at him with surprise and confusion plain upon her features. He feared she would remain that way indefinitely, like a malfunctioning bot.

But after twenty-five seconds, she walked to the table, grabbed a chair, and dragged it to where she'd been standing. "Fine."

The chair's legs scraped over the floor as she turned it so it was perpendicular to Ronin. Facing the counter, Lara bent forward, grasped the back of the chair with her hands, and took another deep breath. For a moment, she was still.

Tilting her head to the side, she locked gazes with him and twisted her hips. Her legs moved, their motion so graceful, so fluid, that she appeared to be walking on air. She tipped the chair onto one leg and spun it twice. When she stopped it, the seat faced Ronin.

Sliding her fingers over its top, she slowly moved around the chair and lay down over it on her back, her hair brushing the floor. Her other hand traced a teasing path from her neck down between her breasts, over her belly, her pelvis, and down to her knee.

Ronin curled his fingers into his thighs, feeling the strength of his grip through his synthetic skin.

She didn't break eye contact as she drew her legs up one at a time, pants sliding down to reveal her shapely calves. Lowering her feet to the floor, she sat up, swinging a leg aside to straddle the chair.

Electricity crackled over Ronin's skin. Though she was fully clothed, Lara's dance was the most sensual thing he'd ever seen. That his experience in such matters was limited should've tempered that realization, but it made no difference. His lingering arousal reignited far stronger than before.

Deep within him, an automated system that hadn't been activated in years stirred to life, priming the pumps that would flood his penis with fluid.

Her hands fell to her knees only to slide up her body again, caressing her breasts, her throat, her face, until her fingers delved into her hair. With elbows out to either side, she lifted her wild locks and undulated her stomach and pelvis. Her breasts strained against the fabric of her sweater, clearly outlining the buds of her nipples.

How had he never noted the similarities between dancing and sex?

She intensified the movements of her torso, thrashing like a caged animal. Rage, frustration, and raw sexuality flowed from her, sweeping into him without mercy. She was a wild, untamable force, displaying her majesty just for him.

Ronin's awareness of the room around him, of the house, the

district, the town, the entire world, faded away, all his attention focusing solely on Lara.

And she somehow kept her gaze upon him throughout, her eyes burning with silent, sultry intensity like he'd never witnessed. Standing, she spun and kicked the chair away. Her body moved like a whirlwind and a stalking cat at once, a contradiction, an impossibility, and he could not look away.

She fell to the floor like she'd been beaten only to surge up again, stronger, and repeated the movements over and over, varying them each time. She closed her eyes, her expression full of feeling.

It was a message to him. He knew it, though he did not yet understand the language of her body. She was ocean waves crashing against the shore, relentless, powerful, and fluid.

Synths were capable of greater speed and precision than Lara, but her flexibility, her fluidity, and the way she constantly threw herself off balance but never lost it combined into something impossible for a bot to replicate.

How did she accomplish it? Were her emotions the secret? They were more visible with each moment, written on her face and conveyed through the growing drama of her dance.

Perhaps he'd been arrogant to assume he'd figure it out after a dance or two. Emotion was the key, it had to be, yet that only raised more questions.

Lara dropped to her knees with her head bowed and her arms hanging at her sides. Her disheveled hair obscured her face. The refrigerator buzzed, oblivious to the rhythm of her quick, ragged breaths.

Finally, she lifted her face and ran her fingers through her hair, tugging it back. Her blue eyes sparkled above flushed cheeks.

"That better?" she asked.

"Yes. Thank you."

Her eyes narrowed as she studied him. "You didn't like it."

There was annoyance in her statement, but he couldn't determine why.

"It's given me much to consider." He'd liked it very much, but he needed time to determine the reasons.

"The hell does that mean?" She stood, breathing heavily.

His attention was drawn to her heaving chest. "You've fulfilled your obligation tonight. Will you be ready again tomorrow?"

"It's not like I need charging or anything."

"Your people call it eating and sleeping."

"Are you dismissing me?" She folded her arms across her chest, settling her weight on one foot. The stance pressed her breasts together, pushing them up. His fingers twitched upon his thighs.

No touching.

"No," he said. "This is your residence now, as much as it is mine. You're welcome to be in whatever room you choose, whenever you want."

"Yeah, well…I'm going to bed anyway."

"I've upset you again."

"Of course not." Her tone suggested otherwise.

"I know close to a million words in this language, and I still don't know the right ones to say to you."

She rolled her eyes and shifted her weight, cocking her hip. Its curve was just visible through her loose clothing. "I'm just tired, okay? So, uh, goodnight. Or whatever your kind says to each other."

"Goodnight's fine. Sleep well, Lara."

She walked away, muttering something too quietly for him to understand her words.

After he heard her bedroom door open and close, Ronin remained at the table and lost himself in her dance, replaying it repeatedly, as night trekked irreversibly toward the dawn.

CHAPTER SIXTEEN

Lara lay in bed, staring at the night sky with the orange glow of the streetlights streaming in through the window. It was the same sky she'd seen for her whole life, but it was somehow unfamiliar from here.

She wasn't sure how long she lay like that before her eyes drifted shut.

A sound pulled her from sleep.

Mind clouded, she lifted her head and blinked the blurriness from her eyes. The door opened slowly. The hallway beyond was dark, but the light from the window settled on Ronin, whose broad-shouldered frame filled the doorway.

Pushing herself up onto her elbows, Lara frowned. "Ronin?"

He wore only his fatigue pants, which hung low and loose around his hips. His body was perfect, his sculpted muscles accentuated by the soft light and deep shadows. Unable to stop herself, she swept her eyes over him, drinking in his squared jaw, wide chest, chiseled abs, and the defined lines tapering from his hips to his pelvis.

Her body responded, a deep, hot ache forming low in her belly. She swallowed hard and squeezed handfuls of the blanket.

Ronin didn't move.

She forced her gaze back up to his. "Is…something wrong?"

"No." He stepped toward her, only stopping when he stood

beside the bed, and gazed down at her with eyes that were impossibly green despite the darkness.

He pulled the blanket off Lara, letting the fabric trail over her. Though she had plenty of time to do so, she didn't grab for it. She simply let him take it, let him bare her little by little, too enthralled by the sensation, by the thrill spreading through her. When the last of the blanket fell away, Ronin dropped it to the floor.

Those glowing green eyes trekked lower, along the length of her body, brightening as they stopped. His intense focus triggered a rush of unexpected desire low in her belly.

Wondering what had captivated him, Lara looked down. Her breath hitched. The shirt she'd worn to bed had ridden up to her waist, leaving her pelvis exposed. She reached down to cover herself, but Ronin took hold of her wrists before she could. The bare metal of his hands was warm against her skin.

"What are you doing?" she asked, her eyes widening as he climbed onto the bed and settled between her thighs, looming over her. The bed groaned under his weight.

He guided her back down, pinning her wrists over her head with one hand. Cool air whispered over her sex, contrasting the heat of her body. Moisture gathered at her core.

Ronin slipped a metal hand under her shirt and pressed his palm to her stomach. It was solid and smooth. Slowly, he slid it up. Her skin quivered beneath his touch. When his hand cupped her breast, she arched into it, nipple beading against his palm with the sensation.

"Ronin," she rasped, breath shallow.

Though his expression was blank, his vibrant eyes dipped to her mouth. He released her wrists and lowered his head, pressing his chest to hers. Their mouths connected.

Lara closed her eyes and gave herself over to him. His lips were soft, molding to hers, but there was firmness beneath them as he kissed her with a hungry ferocity that left her shaking. They moved away, trailing over her jaw, her chin, her neck.

Releasing her breast, he slid his hand between her thighs, caressing her pussy. She tilted her head back and moaned. With gentle strokes, he spread her slick over her folds, and when his firm metal finger circled her clit, pleasure burst through her.

Drawing back, he placed a hand on each of her knees and spread her legs wide. She looked up at him. His skin was aglow, his features impassive except for those eyes…

Then she felt the head of his cock against her entrance. Keeping his gaze locked with Lara's, he pulled back and thrust into her.

Lara awoke with a gasp, jolting upright. Breath ragged, she swept her gaze over the room.

Ronin wasn't there.

The door was closed, and the gap beneath it was dark. Gentle light from the street poured in through the window, illuminating the bed, where the blanket had been bunched near her feet. Her bare legs were spread with her knees up, and the air was cold against her exposed pussy, which was wet enough to dampen the sheets.

"Oh my God." She squeezed her thighs together against the hollow, throbbing ache in her core. Her breasts were heavy, her nipples sensitive as they brushed against the fabric of her shirt, and there was perspiration coating her warm skin. She swept hair out of her face.

"No." Lara leapt out of bed, tugging the hem of the shirt down. "Oh no, no, no."

She grasped fistfuls of her hair, barely feeling the sharp pain on her scalp as she paced in the darkness. "This can't be happening. It can't!"

How was it possible after what she'd been through? Ronin was attractive, without a doubt, but he was a *bot*! Hadn't she learned her lesson about them?

It was because she'd danced for him. When he'd stopped her the first time and said he didn't want it that way, she'd taken it as a challenge. She'd wanted to get a rise out of him, to turn him on, if that was even possible. To torment him within the boundaries of their agreement, because he wasn't allowed to touch her.

She hadn't expected that dancing for him would excite *her*.

All the while, he'd worn a blank expression, and hadn't budged an inch. He'd been as immovable as a mountain. But she'd been aware of his heavy stare throughout.

In the end, he hadn't even enjoyed it. Her reaction, naturally, had been anger.

So why had she dreamt of him? Why was she so aroused when she should've rejected the very idea of his touch?

Because he's different.

"Damn it, no!" Lara dropped onto the edge of the bed, pressed her fists against her thighs, and groaned. "No."

She needed to forget about this. There was no telling how long he'd be interested in her, but she would have to dance for him if she wanted food and shelter. If she wanted his help finding Tabitha. Yet the only way to turn her thoughts away from Ronin was to dwell on the darkness of her past…and she refused to do that, even after she'd been betrayed by both her body and her dreams.

Swinging her legs onto the bed, she grabbed the wadded blanket and drew it over herself as she lay back down, tucking it under her backside so she didn't feel the wet spot on the sheets. She didn't need a reminder of her weakness.

Lara closed her eyes.

Think of anything. Anything but him.

She thought of herself scavenging in the ruins, feeling the swelting sun bearing down on her as she dug through the remains of what had once been. She thought about Tabitha and her games, thought of her laughter, her voice, and willed herself to dream of her sister.

Time passed, and sleep refused to come.

Creaking footsteps from overhead coaxed her eyes open again. She stared at the shadowed ceiling and listened to Ronin walking, surprised by how quiet he was despite his weight.

Why was he up there? Was he as hungry for answers as Lara? It was obvious that he'd never entered that room, as everything inside had been covered in years' worth of undisturbed dust.

She was tempted to pull on some pants and join him, but the phantom of her dream still haunted her. She couldn't be around him right now. Not while she was uncertain of how she'd react.

Not while the feel of his cock inside her was fresh in her memory.

CHAPTER SEVENTEEN

Standing before the window of the dark, dusty attic, Ronin stared at the journal resting on his palm. On the floor below, ancient clothing still lay in a pile where Lara had discovered the book. The electrodes in his fingertips fired, making his fingers twitch.

Just a glitch.

He'd been in the Dust for too long on his last run, had endured more wear and tear than normal. That was the reason for the minor, fleeting malfunction in his hand. It was not because his desire to open the book and read it was warring with his concern for what he'd discover inside.

The journal couldn't do any harm. It was merely ink on paper. All the words in the world, all the thoughts, amounted to nothing without action. And whatever actions were described on those pages had occurred many years ago.

Ronin placed his fingers on the cover, registering the worn, leathery texture. Paper and ink. The book's weight was barely enough to register to him, as airy and meaningless as the information it held.

If only he believed that.

He opened it to the first page.

Those things killed people today. Marched into town and just started killing people. I watched from the window as people were dragged into the park and executed.

Ronin's optics flicked up to glance out the window. The park was a patch of blackness contained by the gentle glow of the street-lamps along its borders, broken only by the faint light reflecting on the pond's surface.

That darkness could've held anything. Could've masked anything.

He returned his attention to the book. Though he could have read the entire page with a single glance, he forced himself to slow down, to analyze each word.

It doesn't look like they're going house to house yet, which is probably the only reason I'm still here to write this. Pretty sure the Joneses and the Ortegas were down there. I didn't notice anyone else that looked familiar, but I wasn't about to press my face to the glass and show them where I'm hiding.

Night's already falling, but everything is bright across the street. The fire's still burning. I'm glad the wind is moving west, or I'd have to smell them.

The page ended there, with the bottom half blank. Ronin turned to the next.

Found out from Mandy Weiss earlier this morning that the shit show in the park was because THEY wanted part of the city cleared out. Said it was THEIR right to inhabit that part of Cheyenne, as it's their kind that's kept it running. People here have been scared for years, since well before the damned world ended, and there's nothing beyond the city but dust and radiation. Where the hell were those people supposed to go?

She told me the leader of the robots gave the humans a day to pack up and leave their homes. Most stayed. When 24 hours passed (ex-fucking-zactly 24 hours, down to the second) those tin bastards started going into the buildings and dragging people out.

It's only a matter of time before they start clearing out more of these homes. I'll have to keep my ear to the ground.

Ronin's brow furrowed. He'd been to places where humans and bots lived apart from one another, but the separation usually seemed to be a matter of comfort and practicality. Flesh and bone had different needs than metal and electronics. He couldn't recall hearing of such open, brutal hostility between the two groups before.

At least the entry gave him a probable time frame. It mentioned people had been scared since before the world ended—that had to be referring to the Blackout.

He continued reading.

Realized I haven't been dating this. Guess it doesn't really matter, though. Probably won't be anyone left to read this in a few years at the rate we're going. God, we made mistakes, but did we really deserve all this?

Been three days since they burned the bodies. It's mostly been quiet, though Mandy told me there have been a few brawls amongst the other people left in town. Lots of tension in the air. I went down to the bar on 19th to see for myself. They still got booze. A week ago I would've said that was the only reason a place like that could be so busy, but I think that's wrong now. I got the sense that there were so many folks there because everyone's scared and nobody wants to be alone right now.

This town took enough of a hit when the armies rolled through the first time. We weathered the worst of it. Hell, who the fuck would bother targeting Wyoming, apart from the oil? We've maybe had it too easy. Sounds like it's gone to shit everywhere else. Every now and then someone drifts up from Colorado or wanders in along I-80 from further west, and none of them have good stories to tell. They say Denver's a radioactive crater.

Now we've got these robot sons of bitches coming in and telling us what parts of town we can't go into anymore. How the hell is that acceptable? I bet some of them were even part of the group that came through during the war. For the most part, they left the city alone. Most of the fighting was at the old Air Force Base. You can still see the smoke from there sometimes on clear days. But there was still damage done here.

People were talking down at the bar like we're all going to get together and do something about this. Gather weapons and force them out. Sure, there are bots that aren't causing any trouble, but nobody seems to care about them now. They're all a problem. It was them that fought in the war, them that was killing women and children.

All those idiots already forgot it was us that started dropping the bombs.

I'm getting myself all worked up. Got to stop. I'm likely to do something stupid when I get this way.

Ronin stopped, placed his finger between the pages, and closed the journal around it. Was there any analysis he could perform on what he'd just read that wouldn't result in more confusion?

Human perception was filtered through a lens of emotion. He knew that firsthand, thanks largely to recent experiences. The journal's writer even alluded to it in his entry, perhaps after having noticed the steady degradation of his handwriting, the increasing pressure of each pen stroke.

Ronin paced back and forth slowly before the window, mindful of his steps. This spot was directly above Lara's room, and he didn't want to wake her.

What would she say when he told her what the journal contained? *I knew it*, or *doesn't surprise me*, or perhaps *you fucking buckets-of-bolts bastards?*

Or would her lips turn down and her eyes glisten with sorrow he couldn't comprehend, sorrow for the memory of long-dead people she'd never known? For people who'd been taken from their homes, from this house, and killed?

He halted and looked out the window again, taking in the scene anew. The view must've been familiar to the man who'd written the journal. Familiar and horrifying.

Ronin ran his optics over the blankets and magazines on the floor, the jars of food in the bookcase, the table with its single chair.

What would it have been like to be in the place of the writer?

He reached through his memory, accessing data from his many forays into, around, and beyond the Dust. Almost every night had been spent alone, and he'd never given that fact any thought. He'd encountered plenty of people out there, and he'd left most of them dead or deactivated in the dirt.

The Dust favored the quick and the ruthless. There was no camaraderie to be found out there.

Yet hadn't he encountered, time and again, bots and humans who ran in groups? He'd come across duos and trios, across gangs of half a dozen or more, all eager for supplies, for food, and for the imminent, violent confrontation with Ronin that was likely their only social interaction outside their small groups.

Somehow, that thought chain brought him to a new realization

—maybe he didn't have to go out alone. Lara was a survivor. Like any human, she had her weaknesses, but there was strength in her beyond his ability to classify and measure. What would it be like to walk the Dust with her? To converse with her over the long days and nights, to have an extra pair of eyes watching his back?

To have someone to look out for other than himself.

Someone to protect.

No. The Dust was no place for her, no place for *anyone*. The danger was immense, even for an experienced bot like Ronin, and he would never put her at such risk.

He opened the journal again, and he was still reading when the rising sun crested the roof to cast its pure, golden light on the tree-tops across the street.

The letters on the last page were distorted by haste.

They're coming for me. I think everyone else is already gone, and in a few more days, they'll have that wall finished and I'll be trapped. I don't know why I stayed this long. Probably because I can still remember the smiles on the faces of my wife and kids while we played at Holliday Park... Maybe, if I make it out, I'll see them out there, where the dust always blows.

This is it now. If you're human, you'd better get the fuck outside this wall. During the big fight outside the bar on 19th, someone cut the leader bot's face, and now there's no mercy, no warnings. This part of Cheyenne belongs to those things. We can have the rubble beyond.

After all the damage and destruction we've faced, people haven't learned a goddamned thing. They didn't fight the bots for survival, they fought because they thought this place, these buildings, really matter. The lives we lived before...they're gone, and we're never getting them back. They're

The tail of that final letter trailed across the page like it had been slashed by a knife. Ronin stared at it while the sun came up, as trapped in place as the writer had been.

CHAPTER EIGHTEEN

Lara bit down on the cucumber to hold it in her mouth. Leaning forward, she placed her hands on the edge of Ronin's worktable and pushed it to the other side of the main room, directly before the wide front window. Climbing atop it, she drew her legs up and draped a forearm over her knees. The cucumber crunched when she took a bite. Its fresh, mild flavor—with just a hint of bitterness—burst over her tongue.

She looked out the window as she ate, past the short wall of shrubs surrounding Ronin's home to the field across the street. Ronin called it a park. The sun was bright today, shining through the trees to cast dancing shadows over the lush grass beyond.

In the distance, strangely shaped bots tended the park. Some of them looked a lot like the cars in the book upstairs. They seemed to be trimming the grass. Others that were more human shaped moved amongst the bushes and trees scattered around the grounds, clipping and watering.

Lara envied the bots their purpose. Damn it, she needed one, too! She'd never been idle for so long. Three weeks in this house with nothing to do but stare out the windows was driving her crazy. Yeah, it was a roof over her head, food in her belly, and clothes on her back, so she would've been stupid to screw it up… but boredom was harder to deal with than she'd imagined.

When Ronin was around, it wasn't nearly as bad. It was still hard to look at him after her dream, but their conversations broke up the tedium of her days. While he was gone—whether resupplying at the market or searching the bot district for signs of Tabitha—she wandered the house, as though she'd suddenly find something new in the mostly empty rooms. She'd even untangled the knotty mess of fishing lines on her chime and hung it in the kitchen beside the pots suspended from the ceiling.

If Lara were honest with herself, part of her was grateful when Ronin was gone. Though nothing had been as vivid as that first dream, he remained in her thoughts every night, their bodies intertwining in the depths of her sleep. She saw flashes of that too-real dream whenever she looked at him.

Weren't dreams supposed to fade over time? The clarity of this one had only intensified as the days passed.

Today, lethargy had taken root in her, and she'd lounged in bed far longer than normal. It wasn't until midday that she'd dragged herself out of her room. When she'd stepped into the hallway, Ronin's door had been closed. After her usual routine in the toilet room, he still hadn't emerged, so Lara had gone downstairs to get something to eat.

She'd danced for him each night, sometimes in the kitchen, sometimes here in the main room. Never the same moves, never quite the same rhythm or flow. Ronin, however, was unchanging. He sat and stared, expressionless and without comment. His answers to her questions afterward remained infuriatingly brief and evasive.

And, despite that, she still couldn't look at him without thinking about his body atop hers, his hands all over her, his cock—

No. Stop it, Lara!

She took another bite, chewing quickly in her annoyance. These thoughts had to stop.

When she finished the cucumber, she wrapped her arms around her legs, locking them in place by grasping her wrist. She tapped her feet on the table and hummed softly to occupy her mind. Soon, she was swept up in the song. She swayed her shoulders and rocked side to side, hair brushing her back.

Something moved at the edge of her vision. Lara jumped, releasing her legs. Her toes hit the wall, and she hissed in pain.

Rubbing her sore toes, she glared at Ronin, who stood a few feet away, dressed in his fatigues and a gray, short-sleeved shirt that showed off his biceps. "Damn it, Ronin, can't you ever say something when you walk into a room? Or do you always have to do it silently like some creep?"

He stared back at her. "Am I required to announce myself in my own residence?"

"Yeah. You are. You don't just sneak up on people like that."

Eyes narrowing, he cocked his head. "Why are you sitting on the table?"

She glanced down, ran her palm over the table's surface, and looked back at him. "Why not?"

Ronin lifted a hand, extended a finger, and pointed to the chair she'd left near the other wall with his tools piled on the floor next to it.

"What about it?" Lara tossed her hair back over her shoulder.

"That's a piece of furniture designed specifically to be sat upon."

"So?"

"That"—he gestured at the table—"is not."

Flattening her palms on the tabletop to either side, Lara bounced her ass and wriggled her hips, settling down. "Works just fine for me. Benefit of being human, I guess. You'd break it if you sat on it."

"What does that have to do with it not being intended for sitting on?"

"Nothing. I can do whatever the hell I want."

His eyes widened, just a tiny bit, and he dropped his hand to his side. Time crept past. Distantly, the buzz of the bots working in the park faded into the silence.

"Can you?" he finally asked.

"Can't you?"

Ronin frowned.

Had she gone too far? He hadn't touched her yet, but she'd seen him moving his fingers as though he wanted to more than once. Bots did what they said, and he'd said he wouldn't...

But Ronin wasn't like other bots.

Lara forced that thought aside before it could lead her back to the dream.

"I can, but I limit my actions by considering the potential conse-quences. For example…" He crossed the room toward her, boots thumping on the wooden floor.

I knew that bastard sneaks around on purpose.

He stopped beside the table.

This would be it. He'd grab hold of her and make her hate bots all over again because she'd sat on his fucking table. But that was what she wanted, right? To have her hate back, to end her conflicting emotions?

Lara looked up at him. "What are—"

Before she could finish, he grasped the edge of the table with one hand and tipped it up. Her stomach lurched as she was lifted. She pushed away from the table and, somehow, got her feet beneath her before she could tumble to the floor.

She spun to face him. "What the hell did you do that for?"

He eased the table back onto its legs. "Because I can do whatever the hell I want."

"Oh, you wanna play it that way, huh?" With her fists balled at her sides, she stalked across the room and stopped beside the chair. She turned, met his gaze, and kicked the chair over. The sound of it hitting the floor was thunderous in the relative quiet.

Ronin didn't flinch, didn't blink. He simply stared. "Do you feel better now?"

She hated the genuine curiosity in his voice. "I'm bored."

"I would appreciate it if, in the future, you tell me such things sooner. I'd rather spare the furniture undue abuse, when possible."

"I'm sure the chair will survive."

"How do we relieve your boredom?"

The image of his hand under her shirt, slowly sliding up to her breasts, blasted to the forefront of Lara's mind. She forced it away as quickly as it had come.

"I don't know." She folded her arms across her chest. "I just need *something* to do. I'm used to scavenging during the day or helping the neighbors with repairs. Not just…sitting around."

"Is it more bearable if you stand?"

Lara tilted her head. It took a moment, but when the joke hit her, she narrowed her eyes at him. "Smart ass. Why is it you only have a sense of humor sometimes?"

"Memory damage. Leaves me terribly inconsistent."

Lara smirked. "You can say that again. Not literally!"

He snapped his mouth shut.

"I just need something to do, Ronin. Something to keep me busy. Teach me something, anything, just so I'm not counting the minutes."

"All right," he said, looking toward the window. "Tables are for sitting *at*, not *on*. Have you learned something?"

"Yeah. Will I obey? Probably not. I'm serious, Ronin." Lara pressed her palms together in front of her. "Please! I need something to do. I don't...I don't have a purpose here."

He raised a hand and scratched his cheek, eyes still on the window. "I'll see what I can find."

"There's nothing here. I've looked."

"I mean when I go out again. I'm leaving tomorrow. Going into the Dust."

Lara straightened, eyebrows rising. "I can go with you! We'll look for Tabitha together."

His gaze snapped to her. "No." There was a sharp edge in his voice that she hadn't heard from him before. "It's too dangerous, Lara."

"I've scavenged for most of my life. I know the dangers."

"You know nothing of the dangers out there. Have you ever been beyond the ruins of Cheyenne?"

She threw her arms out in frustration. "You can't expect me to just stay here!" With a heavy sigh, she let her arms drop to her sides. "How long are you gonna be gone?"

"Depends on what I find. If I push it, maybe two or three weeks."

"*What?*" Lara gaped at him before shaking her head. "Tell me you're just testing out that sense of humor. For the record, that's not funny. I am not gonna stay here by myself for three weeks with nothing to do."

He turned his body toward her. It was an eerie, inhuman movement; his head remained fixed in place while the rest of him shifted. "I'll make sure there's plenty of—"

"I'm not kidding, Ronin." Cold dread clawed up her spine. She'd be trapped, alone. Surrounded by bots. "You can't leave me here that long."

"What's an acceptable timeframe for you?" he asked after a long silence.

"A day. Maybe two. Though I don't understand why you can't just take me along."

Ronin shook his head. The motions accelerated too quickly and stopped too abruptly, giving it an unnatural look. "It's too dangerous. The first storm without shelter…" He held his hands out in front of him, palms up, and dropped his gaze to them, curling his fingers. "Three days. There's little chance of me getting far enough to find anything of value in less time than that."

She stared at him, clenching her jaw. "Damn you."

"I have to uphold my part of the bargain. That means I need to earn credits. I can only do that with scrap." He stuffed his hands into his pockets.

"So take me back to my shack, and the deal can be over."

"No," he said too quickly, unexpected finality in his tone.

"Why? What do you—"

Someone—or something—knocked on the front door. Lara snapped her mouth shut as she and Ronin turned their heads to look toward the noise. When their eyes met again, he seemed to have regained his composure. He tipped his head to the side, gesturing for her to go into the kitchen.

"All the more reason why you should take me," she whispered, walking past him. In the kitchen, Lara pressed herself to the wall beside the entryway, keeping out of sight but not out of earshot.

The locks clicked before he opened the door.

"Good afternoon, citizen," a bot said in a flat voice. "I am here to c-c-complete your regularly scheduled home appliance m-maintenance."

"Not a good time," Ronin replied. The door creaked, but the sound cut off with a dull *thunk*. She could almost imagine the metal foot that had stopped it.

Lara's heart thumped like distant, rolling thunder in her ears. What if it was a gearhead, here because they knew who she was? What if Warlord wasn't done with her yet…

"It is my o-o-obligation to inform you that it has been s-s-s-sixty-five days since your last appliance inspection," the maintenance bot said, voice dropping to a deep slur as it stuttered. "Regular maintenance is integral to the continued f-f-f-functioning of your home appliances."

"Another time." Was that edge back in Ronin's tone?

"It is m-m-m-my obligation to—"

"Come back next month."

"N-n-next month, okay! P-p-p-please have a w-wonderful afternoon!"

The door closed, and the locks clicked into place. Ronin was halfway to the kitchen when Lara, forcing her breathing to slow, stepped into the entryway. They looked at one another for a time. His expression wasn't entirely blank, but she couldn't read it.

"Give me a few hours," he said. "I'll try to find you something to do while I'm gone."

"What if they come back?" Would she have to hide out in the attic, like the last human who'd lived here? The undisturbed dust suggested that the maintenance bots never went up there.

"They won't."

"How can you be sure? If not them, what about the gearheads?"

"There's the attic, and a crawlspace hatch under the stairs. If you get frightened, hide. Keep the pistol with you."

She growled. "I wouldn't be frightened if you'd just take me back to my shack. And what good is that pistol, anyway?" She gestured toward his abdomen. "Guns don't seem to do shit to you."

With his pointer finger, he tapped beneath his eye. "Aim for the optics if you need to shoot. That's the most vulnerable point on most bots."

"Fine!" She strode past him toward the stairs. "I'm just some expendable human, anyway. So, if you find me dead when you get back, don't say I didn't tell you so."

His hand darted out, catching her upper arm before she could reach the first step. His grip was firm, but not painful, and his skin was pleasantly warm. He spun her to face him.

"If you feel as though you're not safe here, consider *this*"—his gaze dipped to his hand—"grounds to end our agreement. But we both know there's nothing waiting for you back there. No one to go home to. No food or clean water. I'm not your Tabitha, but I'm doing all in my power to keep you safe."

With each of his words, her anger cooled, and sorrow swept into its place. Her eyes stung with gathering tears, and the sting intensified when she blinked them away.

She knew he was right, but that didn't make it hurt less.

"Bastard." Lara yanked her arm out of his hold and hurried upstairs. She made sure to slam her bedroom door behind her.

CHAPTER NINETEEN

As per her usual evening routine, Lara showered—it was addicting, and she struggled to keep from doing it more than once a day—and walked downstairs. Ronin had already covered his part of the routine, having laid a variety of food out on the table for her to choose from.

Normally, they talked as she ate, but conversation didn't come easily tonight. It wasn't because of her dreams or their earlier argument. Her mind kept going back to what she'd seen in the mirror. To what she saw now, when she looked at her hands.

They were soft. Clean. Her skin had a healthy glow she'd never seen before, and her bones were a less prominent. The changes were subtle, but she couldn't help noticing them. She ate two, sometimes three meals a day, and there were no more hunger pains.

Was Tabitha experiencing the same thing? Was that why she'd agreed to live with a bot? She deserved comfort, especially after all her years of selflessly caring for Lara.

I really was just a burden...

Guilt gnawed at Lara. No matter how hard she'd tried, it had never been enough. Scavenging, bartering, dancing...she never earned her share. How many times had she lied to Tabitha, claiming she wasn't hungry, just so her sister had the extra portion?

And the one time Lara had stepped up, had broken out of her rut to provide for Tabitha…

"You're quiet tonight," Ronin said, his deep voice jarring Lara from her thoughts before they could take that dark turn. She looked up at him. He was sitting across from her, staring at the uneaten food on the table.

"Just thinking," Lara said, picking at a piece of meat. She took a small bite.

"You normally verbalize your thoughts without restraint. Why is tonight different?"

Because she felt…subdued, useless, weak. And he'd hammered her reality home earlier.

But we both know there's nothing waiting for you back there. No one to go home to.

Ronin had been right. She had nothing, had no one. Even Gary and Kate had turned her away. Lara wouldn't be surprised if someone had already taken over her shack, if there was a stranger sleeping on her pallet, living in the space she and Tabitha had called home.

There was nothing to return to.

"Because I *feel*," she said. "And, right now, I don't feel like talking."

"Are you implying that I don't feel?"

"You're smart. Figure it out."

While she stared at the food in front of her, chewing slowly and tasting little, he was quiet. What the hell would a bot know about any of it, anyway? They lived in luxury, with conveniences they didn't even need, oblivious to the squalor of everyday human life.

"We'll find Tabitha, Lara."

Lara looked up at Ronin with wide eyes. Was he…comforting her? She'd accused him of not feeling, but she knew that was wrong. How many times had he expressed some form of emotion to her? Anger, joy, curiosity, and now concern.

But how could bots feel? They were machines. Hunks of metal and parts. They didn't have brains, or hearts, or any organs at all.

"You promise?" Lara asked, despite herself.

"I…give you my word that I will do everything I can."

She sighed, dropping her gaze. "Guess that's all I can ask for."

The silence that settled between them was as big and imposing as the wall around the bot district. Growing up, she'd never thought it was possible for a person to lose their appetite—how could you, when there was never enough to eat?—but the food in front of her had suddenly lost its appeal.

Lara wrapped the leftovers and stood, walking to the refrigerator to place them inside. Another wonder of life amongst bots. Food could be stored in this big box, and it would keep fresh for days.

"Guess I'll get to it…" Gripping the fridge handle, she looked at Ronin over her shoulder. "Since you're going to be gone for a few days and all."

His face went blank, and it seemed he was about to say something. Maybe that it was all right, that she didn't have to dance for him tonight because she was distressed and tired. Or that, since he'd touched her and broken his word, it was okay for Lara to break hers tonight.

Instead, he pressed his lips into a tight line and nodded.

So Lara danced, as she had every night after her first in this house. Her movements were stiff, her limbs heavy, her steps clumsy. She was numb, her mind elsewhere.

To make it worse, Ronin sat motionless as he watched, conveying no enjoyment. He looked bored or disinterested, no different than the other times.

As she neared the table, Lara spun and slammed her fists atop it.

"What is the fucking point of this?" she screamed, breath ragged.

He kept his eyes locked with hers, moving only to angle his head up slightly. "We made an arrangement."

"Who cares about the arrangement? I want to know why. You watch and watch, and for what? It's like I'm dancing for a freaking wall!"

"Because I want to understand. I watch you dance, and it fascinates me because I've never seen anything like it. I know all the muscles and bones that enable your movement, understand the scientific laws that dictate your momentum and balance. There should be no mystery. But when you dance, when you *truly* dance, I can't look away."

"You wanna know the big fucking secret?" She leaned over the table, closing the distance between them until their faces were but a few inches apart. "It's called *being alive*."

His eyebrows angled down, his eyes narrowed, and his jaw bulged, all so subtly that she might have imagined it. But those tiny changes in his expression warned her.

She backed away from the table.

When Ronin moved, it was fast. His chair fell backward as he stood, and with an almost casual sweep of his arm, he batted the table away, knocking it onto its side with a crash. The gap between them shrank with his relentless advance.

Warlord's scarred face flashed in her mind. This was close to the way he'd moved that night.

Lara's heart stuttered. She scurried around the counter, desperate to put something solid between them. For a terrifying moment, she was convinced he'd smash his way straight through it. She turned away, dropped into a crouch, and raised her arms over her head to shield herself from the coming punishment.

Hadn't she learned anything? Why couldn't she just shut her mouth and dance? It didn't matter if he enjoyed it. As long as he fed her, why should she care?

"Does a thing have to be flesh and blood to be alive?" Ronin demanded, voice low and brimming with anger. "Do humans own that term, that they get to define it?"

She risked a peek at him right as his fist came down on the countertop. The crack of breaking marble was thunderous. Lara stumbled back against the cabinet behind her, a small, frightened whimper escaping her throat as she covered her head once more.

"I think, I reason, I react to the world around me. I question what I know and see, and I wonder what the future might bring, though I know it won't likely be different than the past. I hope!" His voice dwindled, becoming something raw. "I *yearn*."

The aching loneliness in his voice made her breath catch and her chest constrict. His words echoed in her mind during the silence that followed them.

Slowly, Lara lowered her arms and peered up at him. His back was to her, his head angled down as he stared at his hands. He looked and had sounded more human than she ever would've thought possible. No matter how many times she tried to convince herself he was just another bot, she knew, at heart, he was different from the gearheads. Different from Warlord.

Different from them all.

It would've been easy for Ronin to use his fists on her, to batter her flesh and break her bones. Warlord had. But Ronin didn't so much as touch her. No, it had been her who'd hurt him.

"I'm sorry," she whispered. Such simple words, with such deep impact. He'd used them when he thought he'd hurt her.

How could I think he's unfeeling?

Ronin turned his head toward her, but he didn't meet her gaze. "I must depart tomorrow."

Her stomach twisted, and a heavy weight dragged it down. Lara had caused this rift between them. She'd driven him away when he had tried so hard to please her.

"I…" He fell silent.

Lara's heart pounded, and she couldn't get enough air into her lungs. Her eyes burned with the threat of tears. Curling her fingers around the hem of her shirt, she clutched the fabric.

"I don't want to leave with *this* between us," Ronin said.

Everything stopped. His words hung in the air, and Lara couldn't think. She stared at him as he turned fully toward her.

"The fault is mine. I thought your needs would be simple. That mine would be, too." He shook his head, letting out a sound very close to a sorrowful sigh. "I'm learning. Forgive me, Lara Brooks."

Placing a hand on the counter, Lara pulled herself to her feet. Her fear had vanished, leaving awe in its place. Learning. He was *learning.*

"I forgive you," she said, taking a tentative step closer to him. "I…hope you can forgive me, too."

"We both assumed understanding of one another, without considering what that really means." He tipped his head down and ran a finger over a deep crack in the stone countertop. "I guess we really are made in the image of the Creators, if we share some of the same flaws."

"I…I need you to understand." Lara timidly eased around the counter. "My experiences with bots don't put them in a good light for me, Ronin. Many of the ones I've dealt with wouldn't have thought twice about doing that"—she pointed to the crack—" to me."

She stopped in front of him, looking up at his face. "And no bot's ever apologized to me. For anything."

His eyes ran over her body, engulfing her in their depths. "You've known so few of us. The ones you've encountered are…an anomaly."

"They were my reality. All the same…or worse."

His gaze locked with hers. "What can I do, Lara, to make you happy tonight? To see you smile before I leave?"

Though his words caught her by surprise, they brought a smile to her lips. Tears filled her eyes. Ronin wanted her happy. Not just comfortable, not simply in good health so she could dance for him, but happy. No one besides Tabitha had ever cared about Lara's feelings. No one until Ronin.

When her tears spilled down her cheeks, she released a small, embarrassed laugh.

"You're turning me into such a sap," she said, throat tight as she wiped her eyes with the back of her hand.

Ronin closed the short distance between them. Slowly, he raised a hand and cradled her jaw, brushing the moisture from her cheek with his thumb. Her heart quickened. His touch was so light, so gentle, that she couldn't believe it was the same hand that shattered the counter.

Lara stood utterly still. Such tenderhearted contact was foreign to her, and yet, it felt…right. She knew he'd stop if she asked, knew that she could pull away and he wouldn't pursue her. Instead, she smiled and leaned into his touch, pressing her cheek into his palm. It was warm.

It was *real*.

Ronin's gaze softened. "I'll come back as quickly as I can."

"I'll be waiting for you."

CHAPTER TWENTY

Nothing appeared out of the ordinary when Ronin stepped out of his dwelling. It was another typical morning in Cheyenne—the sky was a yellow-tinged gray, the wind blew steady at a speed of sixteen kilometers per hour from the west, and the temperature had already hit seventy-nine degrees. It would be in the mid-eighties by the afternoon. The park across the street was empty, quiet, and green, alive but unchanging.

The sound of the deadbolt sliding into place as he locked it was oddly pronounced, shattering the morning's peacefulness.

Lara's words from three weeks ago echoed from his memory.

I'm sure that'll do wonders to keep bots out.

He walked forward, crossing the bot district, passing through the gates into the market, then continuing south into the human slums. All the while, his sensors searched for something, for anything, abnormal enough to justify turning around. He noted the discrepancy in his stride, which was twenty-five percent slower than usual, but he couldn't bring himself to adjust it.

Countless calculations and simulations concluded that Lara would be fine during his absence. The chances of anything happening were slim so long as she remained indoors. And if any bots came knocking, she knew to hide in the attic.

The words from the journal skittered across his processors, and he abruptly shifted functions. Diagnostics checks, system analyses, rough mapping of his potential route; anything but revisiting what he'd read.

Ronin forced his attention to his surroundings. The humans' homes had been constructed from rubble Warlord didn't want. They were collections of disparate materials, often in poor condition, that should never have held together. Yet somehow, they stood in defiance of the pristine buildings within the wall, in defiance of the Dust and its furious storms. In defiance of Warlord.

There was no elegance here, no precision or cleanliness. Just rugged determination. The humans had taken what the bots deemed trash and repurposed it with imagination and ingenuity.

Some of the residents stopped to stare at Ronin as he passed. They would know, if only by the state of his clothing, that he wasn't one of them. No one spoke to him.

Many of the humans kept small gardens of stubby, struggling crops, some in patches of dirt behind their shacks, others in cracked pottery or ancient tubs and sinks. A few residences had makeshift pens with pigs, goats, or chickens. It was a far cry from the fields outside Cheyenne, where Warlord kept agricultural bots tending neat rows of crops to harvest and trade to the humans, but it was something.

It was surviving.

These people didn't need programming to dictate their day-to-day activities. They did whatever their situation called for, whether it was growing food, repairing a building, or battling an enemy.

Lara made her own way. She found small pleasures where she could. Where she couldn't, she gritted her teeth and pressed on.

One point six kilometers south of the human slums, Ronin stopped. Without meaning to, he'd followed the route Lara had taken the day he'd made his offer to her—down Morrie Avenue into the ruins of southern Cheyenne. The silent, crumbled, sunbaked remains of houses where humans and bots once lived in peace surrounded him, but he could see the area as it had been that day. He could see the relentless rain, the small rivers flowing along the cracked streets, the puddles filling the breaks in the concrete.

His memory replayed Lara, defeated and soaked, kneeling over the storm drain now at his feet, her tears indistinguishable from the rainwater.

Ronin tilted his head, staring down at the clogged drain. A glint of reflected light caught his attention. He dropped to one knee, enhancing his optics to locate the source. Decades of buildup cluttered the drain—small chunks of concrete, scraps of tattered cloth, broken pieces of wood.

And there, lodged amidst the refuse, was a bit of gold.

Slinging his rifle behind his back, he took hold of the metal grate with both hands and pulled up, diverting extra power to his actuators. The grate resisted briefly before the asphalt around its edges cracked and crumbled. Dust rose in the air as the metal broke free, raining bits of debris.

Hefting the grate aside with a heavy *clang*, Ronin targeted the spot where he'd seen the glint and reached into the refuse, clawing out the object. He held it up on his open palm.

It was a ring. A slender gold band, unadorned but for its solitaire diamond setting. After brushing the dirt off it, he took it between forefinger and thumb and raised it to the light. The diamond wasn't its only adornment, after all. There were words etched in delicate script along the inside of the band.

Yours Until the End of Time.

This was what she'd found that day. What she'd lost. The ring was precious metal, and it would fetch a high price at the market. For Lara to have been so close to pulling herself out of squalor only to trip and accidentally throw her salvation away…

How would it have felt if he'd held the key to his core programming in his hand and lost it a moment later?

He rose, swinging his optics toward Cheyenne. What would Lara think if he went back now and gave her the ring?

No. There was work to be done, and three days was already too short a time. She'd be there when Ronin returned, no matter what terrible possibilities his simulations suggested.

After tucking the ring into his inside coat pocket, he pulled on his mask, goggles, and gloves and raised his hood.

It was only three days.

In the early years after Ronin's reactivation, many of the old signs within the Dust had been intact. He'd committed all of them to memory—Nebraska, Iowa, Kansas, South Dakota, Sioux City, Omaha, Amarillo, Tulsa, Texas. Dozens of places, hundreds of them. Most of those names were lost to time now.

There'd been a sign here, too. *Welcome to colorful Colorado.* Only a single wood post remained, rotted, grayed by exposure, and torn apart by insects. The nearby building was a pile of old roofing and crumbled bricks. Husks of vehicles lay half-buried in the dirt all around, but they held little of value unless he wanted to drag a gutted car frame back to Cheyenne.

He continued south, following the scant patches where dust hadn't swallowed the road. Coarse, brown grass jutted from cracks in the pavement, swaying in the breeze. It was the only sign of life as far as his optics could see, and he wasn't even sure if it was still alive.

This was what the people of Cheyenne had faced all those years ago, this was the impossible choice they'd been given. Brave kilometers and kilometers of dirt and shifting dunes, where only the toughest vegetation could cling to existence, for the slimmest chance of survival, or be slaughtered in their homes.

So many of them had chosen a third option. So many had fought. And they'd died anyway.

There was no question that the nameless bot leader mentioned in the journal had been Warlord. Had he been justified in his actions? Had it truly been about survival, about ensuring his own kind had the resources and security to survive?

But was there really any motive that could justify genocide?

Ronin cut west, toward the dark mountain peaks on the horizon. He wouldn't find answers to those questions out here.

Still, didn't such destruction run counter to what the Creators stood for? The humans described in the journal were broken, frightened people, clinging to the remnants of their old lives. What threat could they have posed to Warlord and his bots?

Part of Ronin wanted only to return to Lara, and that desire gained strength with each step. She wasn't entirely safe in Cheyenne, not while Warlord and his gearheads ruled, but there was more to it.

There was a chance he'd eventually discover the nature of his programming out in the Dust. But with Lara, he had a chance to learn how to *live*.

He passed the ruins marking the edge of Fort Collins as the sun sank toward the western horizon. The green grass and living trees here, though sparse, might've attracted more settlers if not for the location. This was no-man's land, the edge of the Dust. Too harsh for true prosperity.

The lingering effects of the long-ago cataclysm farther south didn't help.

They say Denver's a radioactive crater.

Ronin had ventured there once, more than a hundred years ago. The devastation stretched for miles—buildings flattened, an entire city wiped out of existence. Though he'd kept his distance, his sensors had picked up trace levels of radiation. It was no place for man or bot.

Here, eighty kilometers away, entire towns had been spared such destruction. Decades of disrepair and scavenging had taken a toll, but places like this still held treasures.

And dangers.

He swung his rifle to his front, taking the worn grip comfortably in hand, and entered a copse of trees just off the road leading into town. Ronin had scavenged thousands of places like this. He knew they weren't always as empty as they appeared.

Easing down on his belly in the brush, Ronin awaited the coming darkness.

A storm blew in with nightfall. Wind whipped through the deserted streets of Fort Collins, but the flashes of lightning came from farther west, where dark clouds loomed over the mountains. The glows of campfires in the distant hills confirmed that people indeed inhabited the area. Though the nearby rivers and lakes were far lower than they used to be, their water was an invaluable resource, and run-off from the mountains kept them fresh.

He activated night-vision as he entered town. The overgrown streets were empty, save for scattered vehicles that had been stripped down to their frames long ago. A surprising number of buildings were standing, though many had holes in their walls and roofs. Waist-high chunks of wall and jutting steel supports were all that remained upright in some places.

Ronin compared the place to its state during his last visit, which had been 5,023 days before. Several more walls had collapsed, particularly on the brick buildings, and the encroaching vegetation had spread, resulting in more damage to the structures and roadways.

Rifle at the ready, he entered one of the buildings. He moved slowly, silently, listening through the howling wind for any sound betraying the presence of another person. Though the search remained his primary function, his background processes turned toward Lara.

Should he have taken her along? He hadn't lied about the danger, but at least he would've been nearby to defend her, were the need to arise. If something happened in Cheyenne while Ronin was gone, she would be all but helpless.

He froze, a piece of rotting plywood forgotten in his hand. He'd left Lara vulnerable. How could he have abandoned her, knowing the history of that city, knowing what had happened to the people who'd lived in those houses?

One of the journal entries surged up from his memory. Its words had been written in a shaky scrawl, and a bloody fingerprint had marred the bottom right corner.

I was going to head down to the bar again tonight. Don't know why. The booze is sour and the company is bleak, but something's been brewing there, and I ain't talking about beer. People really worked themselves up these last few days, and I can't blame them. I know it was stupid. Hell, I knew it long before tonight. But I can't blame them at all.

I saw them from down 19th, filling up the street. God, it was almost like those old movies, when all the villagers take up pitchforks and torches, only here it was shotguns and hunting rifles, crowbars and baseball bats. They were gathered up on the corner, shouting, and those bots...they just lined up across the street from the bar, shoulder to shoulder, and stood there. Didn't move, didn't say a goddamn word.

Shit escalated. Shit fucking escalated.

The bot that leads them stepped up. Told everyone to get their shit and go home. Someone threw a rock at it.

Those things didn't even bother wasting bullets. Didn't need to. Most of them look human, but fuck...the bots tore through those people like they were made of paper. Crowd fought for less than a minute, and then their nerve broke. They took off in every direction, a lot of them coming towards me. I helped Julio Ortega get around the corner. He wasn't with his family when they got taken. When he let go of his stomach, his...

God, his blood is all over me. I can't. Can't write this anymore.

I don't think they're searching houses yet. Guess they're content to slaughter people like cattle in the street, and that's enough tonight. Like it was nothing...

Ronin's urge to return to his residence was more powerful than ever, but it wouldn't do any good. It would take hours to get back to Cheyenne, and even if he was quick, it would mean the energy put into this journey had been expended in waste. He'd come all the way out here. He had to do what he'd intended.

Ronin searched the smaller buildings as the night progressed. Occasionally, lightning illuminated their interiors, followed several seconds later by wall-rumbling thunder. Bits of scrap metal and plastic accumulated in his rucksack. It would only be worth a fraction of what his last haul had earned. The gold ring would up his return significantly, but it couldn't be counted; it was Lara's. She would choose what to do with it.

As dawn neared, the storm cleared out. Ronin moved into the larger structures near the town center. These had sustained more damage than many of the others, probably due to their size, but they were navigable.

In the first building, he discovered the remains of three humans —skeletons in faded, ragged clothing. The fingers of the largest were wrapped around the grip of a rusted revolver. Ronin knelt, brushing away the dirt on the floor to reveal the message painted there.

Saw their faces
Heard their screams
No one left to absolve us of our sins

He contemplated those words as minutes passed and the sun crept higher over the eastern horizon. Would they hold significance to Lara? Ronin could almost piece the meaning together, could almost understand.

Weren't there images in his memory he couldn't erase? Screams echoing from his otherwise forgotten past? Explosions and charging armies, gunshots and blood and oil...

Ronin forced himself to stand and leave the bodies behind. It would do him no good to pursue the fragments of another life.

He went into the building with *MNICIL* written over the entrance. It had probably been *MUNICIPAL*, before the Blackout. Sections of the ceiling had collapsed, likely due to decades of water damage, and most of the interior furnishings had been reduced to useless scraps. He worked his way deeper inside, clearing some of the rubble from a hallway to access another section.

Rotted bits of plaster, shards of glass, shreds of dingy carpet, dirty rubble, and pieces of unidentifiable furniture blanketed the floor. A padlocked door stood at the end of the hall.

The heavy lock broke with a single blow from the butt of his rifle, and the door came off its hinges when Ronin pulled it open. Inside stood three service bots, one with a broom in hand, their casings dulled with age and dust.

The ceiling was reinforced, showing no signs of rot. Ronin had encountered similar rooms in other places. Had there been rules in the old world concerning where bots were allowed to rest?

Stepping inside, he searched the shelves lining the walls, adding six long-dead power cells and several specialized tools to his bag. A small box held miscellaneous parts, unidentifiable because of the built-up dust and lint inside. He placed the entire thing in his bag, atop the other items, but he left the bots alone.

Once, they'd moved and worked, they'd spoken and thought. Even if their functions were simple, they'd been alive.

Returning to the hallway, Ronin crouched and rummaged through his bag, rearranging his haul. The tools and parts would undoubtedly bring in a stack of credit, but the power cells were the real treasure. Even uncharged, they were worth at least as much as his last haul.

When Ronin emerged from the building, the sun was at its zenith, shrouded by that perpetual gray haze. The Dust wasn't just beneath his boots. It was everywhere, above and below, outside and in. Even with his skin replaced, it was only a matter of time before dust built up in his internal mechanisms, before it caused failures and breakdowns. No one, whether bot or human, escaped the Dust.

Not even within the walls of Cheyenne.

And Lara was still alone. Was she frightened, upset?

Lonely?

Perhaps she was brimming with anger because Ronin had departed while she slept without saying goodbye.

He didn't want to dwell on regrets. And though everything within him railed against the possibility, if he was never to see Lara again, he wanted to remember her saying she would wait for him. Wanted to remember smile on her lips and the look in her eyes, which had conveyed the truth.

She would actually miss him.

His plan had been to scavenge until just before dawn on the third day to maximize his time here. He knew there was more to find, knew treasures lay hidden in the hundreds of thousands of square feet he'd not yet searched within these buildings.

Lara is alone.

But traveling during midday, especially at known scavenging spots like this, was dangerous. It would leave him exposed. In the open Dust, effective hiding places were difficult to come by. The decaying buildings of Fort Collins, however, provided ample cover for would-be ambushers. And there was no guarantee that Ronin hadn't been spotted by the hill dwellers.

The safest course of action would've been to shelter in one of the buildings, wait out the daylight, and leave under cover of darkness.

Sensors pulsed on his cheek, and he scratched it absently. Would six or seven more hours make a difference? Undoubtedly. But what was more important—the effect on his haul, or the effect on Lara?

For all the years he'd been awake, this was a new experience, an unexplored dilemma. He'd never had anyone waiting for him, had never had companionship. His interactions had been limited to passing conversation, negotiations over trades, the rare peaceful encounter in the wastes, and the even rarer night with a female.

He cinched the top of his bag, closed the flap, and slung it over his shoulders. As he stood, he slipped his right arm through the strap of his rifle. His hand settled on the grip, thumb sliding to the indentation worn over decades of use. Glancing down, he performed an inventory of his hand tools, ensuring they were all in place.

The trees would provide some cover while he made his way out of town. Once he was clear of them, he'd be back in the Dust, visible from kilometers away.

But at least he'd have the same field of view.

With dusk drawing near, the lights of Cheyenne were already on as Ronin approached from the eastern railway, which crossed the path connecting the bot district and the human slums. He'd followed the north road out of Fort Collins. Varying his route helped reduce the chance of ambushes on the return trip.

The railyard had only been partially cleared in all its years of disuse. Hulking train cars, many of which had been stripped down to their frames, lay silent amidst the dunes that had gathered around them. A few were jumbled heaps of twisted, scorched metal, covered in rust and grime.

Movement from just off the path ahead caught his attention. He enhanced his optics, zooming in on the source—a murder of crows picking at a carcass. Their ragged caws drifted to him on the west-ward wind.

The birds' meal became more apparent as Ronin neared. His steps slowed. The crows continued their calls, jerking their heads aside to stare at him with black eyes and bits of flesh dangling from their beaks.

He surged forward, startling the creatures into scattering. They regrouped on a nearby train car to watch him.

Time lost meaning as he stared at what the birds had been feeding upon. Ronin was so still that some of the crows returned, warily hopping closer until he waved his arm to scare them off again.

It was the corpse of a human woman. She was naked, and where her skin hadn't been torn apart by hungry corvids, it was dark with bruises. His first thought was that Warlord had found Lara, but he rejected it immediately. This woman's skin was a darker shade, and her blood-matted hair was black.

A synth lay on the ground near her, his head face-down over her crotch. His detached arms and legs were strewn around him with tendrils of wire and tubing jutting from the jagged openings. Warlord's symbol was upon his back in red paint that had run before drying.

The synth's penis had been removed and shoved into the woman's mouth. Crows had pecked out her eyes, but her collapsed cheekbone, dislocated jaw, and extensive bruising indicated that she'd been severely beaten before she was dumped here.

She was a little taller than Lara, with full hips and breasts. Dark hair, tan skin...

Ronin's processors slowed as realization hit him, stronger than any storm winds he'd endured in the wastes.

The woman's arms were spread to either side, palms up. Slowly, he knelt beside her, gently took hold of her left wrist, and turned her hand over.

A jagged scar ran from the first knuckle of her pinky to the base of her thumb.

As delicately as he could, he set her hand back down. His processors kicked into overdrive, moving fast enough that anyone nearby might have heard them whirring.

He'd fulfilled one of Lara's conditions. That meant one less thing for him to ask about around town, one less thing to draw Warlord's attention.

He stood and looked over his shoulder at the crows. They remained close, cawing and flapping their wings as they fought over whatever bits of meat they still possessed.

They'd desecrated the body of Lara's sister. Damaged it beyond what it had already suffered.

Ronin looked down again. No…not *it*. *Her*. This was Tabitha.

The synth's facial skin was gone, exposing dull, dented metal and shattered optics. Ronin moved the bot aside, placing the detached parts on the ground near the torso. That done, he removed the final insult from Tabitha's mouth and gathered her in his arms.

He'd see to her first to keep the scavengers at bay.

He walked west, searching for a resting place outside of Warlord's shadow.

CHAPTER TWENTY-ONE

Only the merest hint of orange was visible on the horizon when Ronin reached the western guard post. The gearheads, like their counterparts at the east barricade, told him Warlord didn't appreciate visitors after dark. Ronin calmly pointed out the lingering sunlight. After staring at it for some time, the gearheads exchanged a glance with one another and waved him through.

Though his pack was heavy with trade, Ronin didn't stop in the market. He was urged on by a different sort of weight, perceived not by his sensors but by his processors. He had to tell Lara what he'd found, and he couldn't guess how she'd react.

He knew only that it wouldn't be good.

The guards at the interior gate gave him no trouble. As he hurried along the lonely road around the park, he briefly entertained the idea of cutting across the grass to reach his residence faster, as though surrounding himself with life would make the news easier to deliver.

His memory served up the journal entry about people being executed and burned in the park, and he decided to stick to the streets.

While Ronin walked, questions stacked in his mind, caught in a queue that would never clear. Why? Why, after all the senseless death and destruction the world had faced, did there have to be more? What could Tabitha have done to deserve such an end? Could anything warrant such brutality?

Clearly, Warlord had a history of hostility toward humans, but why attack a synth this time? Tabitha's companion hadn't merely been powered down, he'd been ripped to pieces.

There'd been a message in the act, and though Ronin possessed the necessary information to decipher it, meaning would not come. His processors insisted there must've been some sort of logic behind the death, deactivation, desecration, and dismemberment. But even his own recent bouts of illogical behavior couldn't help him understand this act. He couldn't ascertain a satisfactory purpose for it.

Too soon, he arrived at his residence. The windows were dark.

Good. If Lara was asleep, he'd have more time to determine the best way to tell her what he'd found.

The mild relief brought on by that thought was immediately overpowered by shame.

Ronin removed his gloves, goggles, and mask, stuffing them away, and fished the key out of his pocket. Unlocking the door, he slipped inside.

His optics initialized night-vision automatically as he closed the door behind him, but something about using it seemed wrong. He overrode the change and switched on the overhead lights.

He set his rifle down against the wall, and he was shrugging off his rucksack when he noticed Lara at the edge of his field of view and looked up.

She sat on the third step from the bottom of the stairs. The barrel of the pistol in her hand was a gaping black maw, swaying in her trembling grasp.

"I'm so pissed at you right now, I should shoot you," she said, voice as unsteady as her hand. "Where do you get off leaving without a word?"

There was nothing stopping her from pulling the trigger. Though improbable, at such close range there was a chance that she'd inflict considerable damage. Would that make her feel better?

"I didn't want to say goodbye. It implies a finality that didn't seem appropriate."

With a heavy, shaky sigh, she lowered the gun and averted her gaze, running a hand through her hair. "What are you doing to me? I can't even stay mad at you."

"Is that because I'm back a day early?"

She grinned and met his optics. "Maybe. Couldn't stay away, huh?"

Ronin couldn't identify the gleam in her eyes, but it added vibrancy to her face. "Apparently not."

The truth of it struck him hard. He *couldn't* stay away from her. After arguing with her over the length of his trip and insisting that three days would barely be enough time to accomplish anything, he'd been the one to cut his expedition short.

He dropped his pack on the floor beside the rifle. It landed with a heavy, metallic *clank*, and a small cloud of dust rose from the fabric.

"You weren't kidding when you said the Dust stays with you," she said.

"It isn't the only thing in the world, but it permeates everything."

"I still don't know what the hell you're talking about most of the time." The corner of her mouth lifted. She was…teasing him. "Go on and clean yourself up."

"Lara—"

"Not yet."

"I have to—"

"Go clean up, and then you can tell me all the details. I've been bored out of my fucking skull since you left, and now my fingertips are sore on top of it."

She rose and stretched, the hem of her light blue T-shirt rising high enough to allow him a glimpse of the pale skin of her stomach before she turned and walked up the stairs. From below, Ronin watched the gentle sway of her hips, which were hugged by her cargo pants. He should've demanded she stop and listen to him.

Instead, Ronin followed her. His brow plates lowered. Rather than turn toward her room, she strolled into his, moving directly toward his bed. He froze in the doorway. What was she doing? And why was his desire for her amplifying despite what he needed to tell her?

Lara stopped in front of the chest and set the pistol down before approaching him. "It's not very good, but I made you something. It's on your bed." She raised her fingers to show him the tiny cuts on their tips. "I bled for it, so you'd better at least pretend to appreciate it."

She slipped past him. Unable to form a coherent sentence, Ronin turned his head and watched her walk to her room.

Why can't I just tell her?

Death was part of the world. Always had been, always would be. How many corpses, whether flesh or metal, had he seen since awakening?

Tabitha and the synth made 115,299. Most had already been dead or deactivated long before Ronin found them, but they remained in his memory as constant reminders of the world's unforgiving nature.

He knew there were more buried in the Dust and hidden in the ruins, knew there were more from before the Blackout, trapped in his inaccessible memories. Millions upon millions more.

Entering his bedroom, Ronin turned on the light and undressed. His fingers were stiff as he unfastened zippers and buttons, and his optics wandered, first to the pistol on the chest, then to the bed. The blankets were rumpled as though Lara had been atop them while he was gone, and a shirt made from the thick gray fabric he'd given her before leaving lay atop one of the pillows.

Ronin brushed his hand over the wrinkles in the bedding. What had she looked like on his bed? How might it have felt to be on it with her? His processors could composite her image into the scene, but it could never compare to reality.

No. Not now.

Not while he was covered in dust and carrying such devastating news.

He stepped into the adjoining bathroom and showered, wiping the dirt from his skin with a cloth. Steam billowed around him as he scrubbed beneath his fingernails. His sensors registered the water temperature at one hundred ten degrees Fahrenheit, but it was just another number.

Before he'd met Lara, Tabitha also would've been another number—115,298.

Lara was the key, she was the reason Tabitha was more than a number, more than a nameless face. Because of Lara, Ronin could see Tabitha as a person. As someone who had loved and been loved in return. Someone who's death meant something.

Every death did, whether he understood that meaning or not.

Turning off the water, he stepped out of the tub, dabbing moisture from his skin and rubbing his hair dry with a towel. Ronin stopped in front of the mirror and wiped away the condensation. His face was unchanged. No indication of grief, no sign of the hardships the Dust had wrought upon him.

He walked into the bedroom and pulled on a clean pair of pants before picking up the shirt Lara had made. It sported inconsistent stitching, uneven cuts, and a miniscule stain near the left shoulder that was likely her blood. Somehow, those flaws made the shirt more appealing.

"So, tell me," Lara said.

Ronin turned his head to see her enter the bedroom through the open door. Her eyes ran over his bare torso, lingering low on his abdomen before lifting to focus on his optics. There was a tinge of pink on her cheeks now.

She sat on the edge of the bed and leaned back with her hands propped on the bed behind her. Her shirt pulled snug around her breasts, drawing his optics to the points of her nipples. "Your bag looked full. You find anything good?"

"I did," he replied, hating that it was the truth, hating how his systems were reacting to her body in this moment. "What's in the bag doesn't matter, Lara."

"So...? Don't keep me in suspense! Tell me. I don't think I've ever seen you so serious, which says a lot because it's not like you had much of a sense of humor to begin with."

Folding the shirt, he laid it atop the chest and moved to stand in front of her. She arched a brow when he crouched to her eye-level.

"You're making this kinda weird, Ronin."

"I found Tabitha."

The words hung in the air, suspended like the ever-present haze in the sky.

Lara snapped upright. "What? Where is she? Is she okay? Did you talk—"

He raised his hands, signaling for her to stop. She did, though the excitement didn't fade from her expression. He ignored the electric tingle on his cheek.

"She's dead, Lara."

The color drained from her face, and she stared at him blankly. "That's a fucking lie."

"I found her on the way into town, with a dismantled synth."

"You're lying!" She jumped to her feet and struck him, sending a brief, dull pain through his left shoulder.

He rose and caught her arms before she could strike him again, taking both her wrists into one hand and clamping them together.

She struggled against his hold. "You're a lying can of shit! All you fucking bots can go fuck each other and rust that way!"

"She had a scar," he said gently. With a fingertip, he traced a line from the first knuckle of her left pinky to her thumb.

Lara frantically shook her head as she rasped, "No, no, no, no…" She gave a final, surprisingly strong tug on her arms, and then crumpled. "No!"

Her wail filled his audio receptors. She sagged against him, her sobs muffled by his chest.

Though he wasn't sure why he did so, Ronin released her wrists and wrapped his arms around her. It wasn't a tight embrace, but it was solid, and she leaned into him. Her body shook, and her teardrops traced wet paths down his bare chest and abdomen.

Didn't she want to know how her sister had died? Hadn't she wanted all the details?

No.

That information would only cause more pain. Tabitha was dead. The cause wasn't important, the circumstances couldn't alleviate the grief.

"I buried her." He brushed his palm over her soft hair. "West of town. Away from…all this."

Though she didn't speak, her sobs quieted to soft whimpers. Her breathing was erratic; sharp, shuddering inhalations rocked her body with no predictable pattern.

"Now, Tabitha is free," he continued gently. "Free from the struggles we all suffer through every day. She doesn't have to worry about where her next meal will come from, or if she'll have a roof over her head, or whether a cut will get infected. She can just…rest."

Minutes passed as Lara cried. For a time, she made no sound at all, but her tears continued to fall. He registered each warm drop on his skin before it cooled. Through it all, she clung to him, and his hold on her didn't relent.

When her breathing calmed, she pulled back and looked up at him. Her cheeks were wet, and the whites of her eyes were red, making her blue irises bright and vibrant. Her gaze searched his. It reminded him so much of that day in the rain, when she'd been lost, nearly broken, but not yet defeated.

Without looking away, she leaned forward and pressed her mouth to his.

Ronin first registered the warmth of her lips, and then their softness. They yielded to the shape of his own, molding into a perfect fit. An electric pulse unlike anything he'd experienced spread across his face. This was not a malfunction, was not the result of an error in his coding.

His eyes widened as the sensation crackled over every electrode in his body. His attraction to her, his arousal, surged with new power, triggering the automated systems that pumped fluid into his phallus, which swelled in his pants.

Pulling back again, Lara glanced at his lips. Her pink tongue slipped out of her mouth for an instant before she kissed him once more.

CHAPTER TWENTY-TWO

Lara closed her eyes, waiting for the wave of revulsion, for the surge of panic when she realized she was kissing a bot.

It didn't come.

His lips were surprisingly warm and pliable. His arms tightened around her, caging her against his chest. Her heart raced, and her breaths were short, but it wasn't because of fear. It was because of his nearness, his touch.

Reluctantly, she broke the kiss, tilting her head back to study his face. This wasn't Warlord or some random bot. He was Ronin. Patient, considerate, trustworthy Ronin.

Lara didn't want to think about what her sister had suffered, didn't want to feel the heartbreak of losing the only person she'd ever loved. Her life had been full of pain for as long as she could remember—the pain of abuse, of hunger, of loneliness, of never being good enough to deserve all that Tabitha had done for her. It gathered in her now, twenty-three years of struggle and uncertainty, writhing in her stomach and constricting her chest.

When it was spread across the years, she could handle the suffering. She was strong enough for that. But all of it coming on at once, building into immense, dark storm clouds in her heart, would break her. She needed to escape before that storm swallowed her, needed to combat it with feelings only Ronin could awaken within her. Needed to feel safe. Cared for.

Loved?

Anything to distract her from the reality that she was now truly alone.

"Make me forget," she whispered, lower lip quivering. "I can't… I don't want to think. Not now."

Ronin didn't hesitate. He lifted her like she weighed nothing, covering her mouth in a kiss that stole her breath even though he didn't have lungs, and laid her on the bed. It creaked as he climbed atop it and settled between her thighs, propping himself up on an arm. The dizzying speed of his movement stopped as abruptly as it had begun, and his touch became a sensual caress.

He wiped the moisture from her cheek and trailed his hand along her jaw, following it to her neck. His fingers moved down until they brushed the collar of her shirt. Heat blossomed every-where his skin met hers, pulsing with each beat of Lara's heart.

His mouth coaxed her quivering lips into a tender kiss. Every caress was lingering, and she savored every moment. Gradually, he deepened the kiss, his mouth growing firmer, more possessive, leaving hers burning with a want for more.

She placed her palms on his abdomen and slowly smoothed them up his tear-dampened chest, fingers stroking every contour. Though she'd hit him several times, she'd never touched him like this, with gentleness, with curiosity, with need, and she was surprised by the feel of his skin. It looked so much like a human's, had the same warmth and give, but it seemed thicker. She felt hints of the metal plates beneath it. They were shaped nothing like a human skeleton, but reminded her of bones nonetheless.

Running her hands over his broad shoulders and up his neck, she took hold of his face. Their lips separated.

Ronin gazed down at her. His expression wasn't blank now, and she had no doubt the emotion in it was real. With his jaw clenched, his lips pressed thin, and his body rigid, Lara knew he was holding himself in check. Awaiting rejection. The blanket rasped as he bunched it in his fist.

How many times had she told him he was just a machine, that he was incapable of emotion?

Yet time and again, he'd proven her wrong. Terribly, terribly wrong. She'd been too much of a coward to admit it even to herself.

Ronin felt as deeply, as strongly, and as passionately as any human she'd known.

She brushed her thumbs over his cheeks, and then across his thick, dark eyebrows to smooth the crease between them. From this close, the varying shades of green woven into his irises were clear, adding new layers to their unique color.

Lara finally saw him the way he'd always seen her.

Alive.

Guiding his face down, she kissed him again. The tightness in his mouth vanished when she ran her tongue over it. His lips parted, and she imagined the gasp he might've released were he able to breathe. An instant later, Lara let out a gasp of her own when he shifted his hips, grinding his bulge against her center. Delirious heat spiraled through her body, triggered by a flash of pleasure.

Her clothing was suddenly too hot, too restrictive, too abrasive. Releasing him and breaking the kiss, she grasped the hem of her shirt and pulled it off over her head. She tossed the garment aside and rested her arms on the bedding to either side of her head.

Ronin's eyes were fixated on her chest in the same stare he wore while watching her dance. Not long ago, it had infuriated her. Lara knew better now. She thrilled in the weight of that stare, in its unwavering intensity.

Finally, he brought a hand up and brushed his fingertips over her nipple. It hardened immediately at his touch. Lara released a shaky exhalation.

His gaze remained rapt on her breast. Was he studying her reactions? Though he didn't touch her again, her body anticipated more contact, desperate for his hands to run over it. Heat pooled in her core, and her skin tingled with need.

"Ronin."

He met her eyes.

"I won't break." She grabbed his wrist and forced his palm down onto her breast. "*Touch* me."

Something changed in his gaze, and like someone flipped a switch inside him, Ronin turned on.

He kneaded her breast, stroking and pinching her nipple.

Delightful sensations thrummed through her and fluttered low in her belly. Restless energy suffused her.

Lara slid her thighs along his hips as he settled more of his weight atop her and dipped his head. He kissed her lips, her cheek, her jaw and neck, her shoulder. Every time his mouth teased her skin, it sent an electric current through her, making her clit twitch.

She closed her eyes with a sigh, arching into his touch, and undulated her hips to feel his hard length through their pants. His hand claimed her other breast. With his every caress, she gave a little more of herself into his keeping.

Moving her hands down his torso, she clumsily unbuttoned his pants and reached in. When she wrapped her fingers around his shaft, Ronin's hips jerked

"Lara," Ronin growled through bared teeth. The sound vibrated from him straight to her core.

Within her fist, his cock pulsed. It was solid but not inflexible. Lara slid her foot to his ass, nudging his pants down to free his erection fully, and then she stroked. A shudder coursed through him.

Before she realized what he meant to do, he grabbed the waist of her pants and pulled to either side. The sound of ripping fabric was thunderous, matched only by the beating of her heart.

Ronin leaned back, pulling the halves of her pants down to expose her thighs. As he tossed the material of the ruined garment aside, he didn't look away from her. His eyes fixated on her bared pussy, pupils dilating and contracting.

"You are beautiful, Lara." Gripping one of her knees, he trailed his other hand up the inside of her leg, leaving heat in its wake. Lara shivered, breath growing shallow.

He parted her folds, exposing her to the fire of his gaze. The tip of his finger slid over her sensitive flesh, and she couldn't hold back a moan, couldn't keep still. Her core clenched.

"Please..." Lara begged.

He thrust his finger into her, pressing the heel of his palm to her mound.

"Ronin!" she gasped and lifted her hips, grinding against his hand.

He paused for a moment, tilting his head, but before she could question his hesitation, he slipped another finger in, stretching her.

A spark ignited under the sweet warmth of his hand, blazing a path to every nerve ending in Lara's body. She moaned, squeezing her eyes shut as she clutched the bedding. His fingers curled inside her, brushing her inner walls, fanning the flames into an inferno.

She forced her eyes open to look at him. He was watching her just as intently as he did when she danced.

No. This time, she wanted to dance *with* him, not for him.

"Wait." Taking hold of his wrist, she guided his hand away. Her pussy tried to clamp around his fingers, to keep them right where they belonged, but they slid free anyway. The emptiness they left behind was immediate. It was huge and consuming, a throbbing, pervasive ache, and it demanded to be filled. She needed it to be filled, wanted it to be filled. By him.

Confusion flickered over his features, but he didn't object, easing back as she sat up. The bed creaked under his weight.

Lara got onto her knees. Settling her hands on his shoulders, she urged him down. "Sit."

He obeyed, sitting with his bent legs on either side of her. As his gaze met Lara's, she climbed onto his lap, and his hands bracketed her hips, holding her steady while she wrapped her legs around his waist.

Their eyes were level in the new position. They stared at one another, and for once, she knew exactly what he was thinking. This was the point of no return.

And she didn't care.

Lara wanted him. She'd wanted him before tonight, but she'd shoved her desires aside. Anger was easier than lust, easier than caring. It didn't matter if that anger was directed at him, or her feelings, or herself.

She was so tired of being angry. She needed something more, something to pull her from the misery she was so used to feeling. Something to truly live for.

Their mouths met. Ronin's hunger equaled Lara's, but his ferocity swiftly outmatched hers as he kissed her with savage intensity. One of his hands cupped the back of her neck, and he crushed her to him. His tongue delved deep, curling around hers, coaxing it to twine with his. And Lara succumbed to his kiss, returning it with equal fervor.

She ran her fingers through his short hair and down his back, digging her nails into his skin. Her hard nipples grazed his chest, sending whispers of pleasure through her, heightening her need.

More. She needed more. She needed Ronin inside her.

Looping her arms around his neck, Lara lifted her ass and shifted closer until the tip of his cock pressed to the entrance of her pussy. To delay any further would welcome the pain back. She didn't want to think, she wanted to feel. She wanted…to feel connected to someone.

Before another thought could cross her mind, before she could hesitate and convince herself to stop, Lara dropped down upon him.

She cried out sharply against Ronin's mouth at the sudden fullness as his cock plunged deep, stretching her, filling her. Her fingers curled into his shoulders. This was nothing like the pain she remembered, nothing like she'd made herself imagine. The discomfort was fleeting, and her body quickly adapted to his size, drawing him deeper inside, hungry for more.

Lara buried her face against his neck. Whatever memories she'd feared would reemerge remained buried. There was only herself and Ronin, in this room, shut away from the rest of the world, connected to each other in the most intimate way.

He was motionless beneath her, his hand clamped on the back of her neck and his fingertips digging into her hip.

"Are you all right?" he asked, voice tight.

"I'm ready," she replied between shuddering breaths. There'd be pain; it was unavoidable. Life was pain, and what was sex, if not part of life? But Ronin didn't want to hurt her. That meant something. That would make this bearable.

It was this care, this closeness, this intimacy that she needed most of all. "Find your release, Ronin."

His fingers slipped into her hair, and he gently tipped her head back, forcing her to meet his gaze. "This isn't about my release."

Reclaiming her mouth in a kiss, he banded an arm around her back in support and rolled his hips. The motion was smooth, and she didn't immediately realize what was happening until she felt a shiver of delight spread through her. It made her breath catch and her heart quicken.

The sensation grew as his shaft slid in and out of her. She held her breath, waiting for the searing pain, but there was only the glide of his cock and a growing slickness between her thighs.

Lara whimpered into his mouth, brow creasing as Ronin thrust faster, deeper, striking a hidden place inside her she hadn't known existed, sending flickers of pleasure through her.

Those sensations in her core intensified, coiling tighter and tighter, growing into something nearly overwhelming. She tore her mouth from his.

"Ronin… I… Oh God, Ronin." Panting, she gripped his shoulders. Her body moved of its own accord, bouncing atop him, hips undulating. She needed more. She needed his cock deeper, harder, faster. This was *nothing* like before. This was…this was…

Her back bowed against his arm, angling her hips to take more of him in, and she shut her eyes.

Ecstasy burst through her, flooding her senses. She might have begged, might have cried his name, but she didn't know for sure. There was only his body melded with hers, his pace increasing relentlessly.

The friction escalated, and the fire inside Lara burned hotter and hotter. It was too much; it was terrifying. But she opened herself up, welcoming it, and clutched herself against his chest, sinking into his warmth. He was hot steel wrapped in tantalizing softness. Every inch of him felt like it had been crafted just for her, to fit perfectly against her body, and his every motion delivered exactly the sensation she needed.

This isn't about my release.

No, he'd made it about Lara. About her comfort, her pleasure, her needs and desires. He was giving her everything right now, everything of himself. And he was asking nothing in return.

With a cry, she came undone, shattering in his embrace and losing herself for an instant that stretched on forever.

The press of his fingers strengthened, and the dull pain they caused only enhanced her pleasure. Ronin was solid, real, around her and inside her. He held her close. Suddenly, his body stilled as his cock pulsed. Each vibration sent another wave of pleasure through her, setting a slow, steady rhythm that had her gasping. Though it was nothing compared to his thrusting a moment before, it pushed her to another peak. She clung to him as she soared.

When it was done, she felt light, and her mind settled back into her body like a feather floating down from the sky. Lara sagged against Ronin, breathing hard and quivering. His skin was damp with her sweat. Cool drops of it ran between her breasts, falling onto the sculpted terrain of his abdomen.

She sat that way for a long while before he moved. He rubbed his cheek atop her hair and shifted onto his knees, holding her body against his while he turned. His cock withdrew as he lay on his side, drawing her down beside him with her head cradled in the crook of his arm.

Without him filling her, Lara felt empty again, though it was far removed from the vast hollowness of earlier.

They lay together in silence, Ronin's fingertips lazily brushing along her outer thigh, up to her hips and down to her knee, back and forth.

His gentleness was her undoing; reality surged back.

Her throat tightened, and tears spilled from her eyes. She'd treated him terribly, while he'd repeatedly gone out of his way to provide for her comfort. His thoughtfulness in burying Tabitha was proof than he could act with compassion. And he'd done it for Lara.

There was a constricting ache in her chest, but she forced the words out. "I'm sorry. I didn't mean the things I said, Ronin."

His hand stopped.

CHAPTER TWENTY-THREE

In the early days after his reactivation, Ronin would've thought Lara's vague apology meant she was sorry for every word she'd ever spoken to him, all of which he recalled with perfect clarity.

He knew better now. Humans were rarely so literal, and their tangled emotions often drove them to say and do things contradictory to what they actually thought and felt. He'd only reached that understanding during his short time with Lara.

Now, he searched his memory banks and picked out the things she'd said in anger and frustration. Those words had been uttered in response to her internal suffering. Unable to reconcile her own feelings, she'd attacked Ronin. How could he blame her? The Creators had left everyone with nothing after the Blackout, had dumped them in a shattered world and offered no guidance.

"It's all right," he said, resuming the motion of his fingers over her skin.

She shivered. Her body's reactions to his touch were fascinating.

He contemplated the differences hidden beneath their exteriors. Their skin was similar, but only superficially so. Hers was softer, and its texture varied from place to place, with calluses on her knees and fingers. It was simultaneously resilient and delicate. Beneath his light touch, her flesh rose into small bumps, the fine hairs upon it standing on end.

Ronin had endured for at least one hundred and eighty-five

years; Lara could be gone in an instant. That ephemerality lent her unique beauty.

Was that the purpose of life? Was it simply a transient state between creation and destruction, birth and death, existence and nonexistence? A thing made more precious by its frailty, made more miraculous because it survived overwhelming odds, a thing that defied the universe by simply *being*?

"My thoughts follow strange paths when I'm with you, Lara."

"What do you mean?" she asked, voice raw, as she wiped tears from her eyes. "Like what?"

He pressed his palm more firmly to her back just to feel the way her skin yielded to him. When he lifted his hand, her flesh would revert to its prior state.

Would her inner fire rekindle, given enough time to grieve, or would she never be the same again?

Tears trickled off her face and landed on his arm as she lifted her head to look into his optics. The blue of her eyes was so vibrant. Though he had no data to support it, he knew the sky must've been that same shade of blue, long ago. But there was more depth in her gaze than in all the sky on the clearest day.

Ronin trailed a finger down her cheek, marveling at the freckles upon it. "Like what it means to be alive."

Lara's eyes flared, and she laid her head back down, hiding her face from him. She rubbed her cheek against his shoulder. "What do you think it means?"

"I'm not sure, yet. But every moment I spend with you brings me a little closer to an answer."

Though Lara's breathing remained uneven and her tears continued running onto Ronin's skin, she fell quiet.

"I used to think living was just about surviving," she said softly after four minutes had passed. "That's all life was. Go out into the ruins, find anything that held value, and trade it for food so I'd have enough energy to do it all over the next day."

Lara shook her head, stray strands of hair falling over her face. "But that's wrong. It's not about surviving. We all do that, people and bots, but that's not *living*. Living is… It's about what you experience in that time, you know? About the joy you find, the good memories you make, no matter what shit you go through, no matter how hard it gets."

She sniffled and rubbed her palms over her eyes. "We had that. It wasn't much, but me and Tabitha had it. And now...now it's gone."

Her body shook with silent sobs. Ronin held her, saying nothing as she cried. *Everything will be all right* rose to the top of his list of responses. He dismissed it. He couldn't say it with any certainty, and she deserved better than an empty platitude.

"It's not gone." Gently, he tapped her temple. "All you shared with her will always be right here, and it will always be yours."

She clung to him as she cried, and he pressed his cheek to her hair, rubbing his hand along her back. Eventually, she calmed.

Raising her head, Lara met his optics. Though the flesh around her eyes was puffy and red, there were no more tears filling them. A faint smile blossomed on her kiss-swollen lips only to wilt a moment later. "I...didn't know it would be like that."

"Didn't know what would be like that?" He would not presume her meaning. There were too many variables, too many possibilities, too many chances for miscommunication.

"Sex." A little line appeared between her eyebrows as she glanced away. "I expected pain, and I thought, with you, I could deal with it. That I owed it to you to take it, because I was using you to...forget."

Did she really think he'd ever demand such a price from her?

"You don't owe me anything, Lara. You did...enjoy our coupling, didn't you?"

Her cheeks darkened. "Yes."

Ronin took unexpected satisfaction in her response. Since they'd met, he'd only seen fleeting glimpses of joy from Lara, there and gone within fractions of a second. Knowing that he'd given her pleasure despite the circumstances pleased him.

"Why did you think there'd be pain?" he asked.

"Because...that's all it was before." She averted her gaze again, her blush fading rapidly.

He brushed stray locks of hair behind her delicate ear and caught her chin, guiding her face toward his. "Tell me, Lara."

She pressed her lips together and swallowed. Before she spoke, her tongue slipped out to wet her lips. "We never talked about it, but Tabitha…she gave it all."

Her gaze settled on his chest, but her eyes were glossy and unfocused. "She let men and bots use her, fucked them however they wanted it. They paid her in credits. And no matter how little I managed to scrape together to contribute, she always made sure I had food to eat. She was never selfish. She…loved me.

"It ate at me most days, knowing what she was doing to keep us fed. She'd sacrificed so much. Nothing I did ever felt like enough. She deserved more from me, so much more. Especially with all she did so we could survive. So I…I went back to Kitty's, determined to prove I wasn't useless. To show I could pull my weight and provide for her."

"Back? Were you a dancer there before?"

"Yeah. I tried, because I really wanted to help more. I liked dancing, so how hard could it be? Lasted a couple weeks before I walked out. Nobody kept their hands to themselves, and they didn't give a shit about the humans getting felt up or the degrading things that were said."

Ronin recalled what she'd told him when he had proposed their arrangement.

God damn it, I said I don't do that anymore!

Those words made sense now. He should've known based on the way she'd moved the first time she'd danced for him, with the vitality leeched from her face and the light drained from her eyes—just like the women at Kitty's.

Lara traced her fingers over his chest, sparking sensations throughout his sensors. "I knew how hard it was on Tabitha when I quit. I went out every day looking for scrap, but I never got much. She never said anything, never complained, but… It was on her face. The burden. She tried to hide it, but I knew. So, I…I went back to Kitty's."

She laughed. It was a hollow sound, devoid of humor. "Just my fucking luck that *he* was there that night."

Ronin's processors blazed through stored data, collecting cryptic comments she'd made and slotting them into her story. They fit together neatly, like the pieces of a puzzle.

He forced himself to remain still. "Warlord."

Her chin dipped in a shallow nod. "He offered me more credits than anyone ever had. For just an hour of my time, he said. I agreed because it would have been stupid not to. That amount of credits would've kept me and Tabitha fed for a month, at least. So, I followed him out the back door. It was dark, and quiet, and I...I froze. I couldn't. I couldn't do it."

Lara clenched her jaw, face pale, brow furrowed. Her eyes were unfocused, as though she were watching the scene play out in her mind.

"I felt...sick," she said, voice strained. "Knowing that I was going to trade the only thing that still belonged to me, the only thing I had any say over, for some plastic chips... I just felt so sick. So ashamed. Because Tabitha did it, but I just...*couldn't*. I told him no, that I changed my mind. And he...hit me."

The statement hung in the air, cold and heavy.

Ronin had spent most of his time in the Dust, roving from one violent encounter to the next. He'd been attacked by bots and men. In most cases, he'd ended his attackers. It had been survival, just as he'd once told her. But what Warlord had done to her... His existence hadn't been endangered. His actions had been unjustified, unnecessary.

"I've been hit before, but never like that," she continued. "I don't know if I blacked out, or what, because when I opened my eyes, my clothes were torn away and he was there above me, looking pissed. He said, 'I gave you a chance to make this easy, but you're just like the rest of your kind. Untrustworthy, weak, spineless sacks of meat. So, I'm going to fuck you in the dirt, where you belong.'"

Her eyes glistened. "He held me down as he raped me, and every time I screamed or whimpered or made any damn sound, he hurt me more. There was pain. So much fucking pain. And he didn't stop."

Fire blazed along Ronin's circuits, consuming him. It invaded his operating system, spiraling through his processors, growing larger and larger like a virus spreading to every file. This was rage like he'd never felt before. Like he'd never known possible.

When Lara blinked, tears rolled down her cheeks. "He kept me there for exactly an hour, and when he was done, he threw the chits on the ground and walked away. There was blood everywhere, and

I could barely move. I lay there a long time before I dragged myself home. And, as sick as it made me, I took the credits. The night you brought me here...that was the first time I've been in the market since."

What words of comfort could he offer her after what she'd experienced? Words couldn't even begin to set such a thing right, couldn't take away the memories and pain haunting her.

Already, he was running simulations, calculating probabilities, of a direct attack on Warlord. But even if there were a way to eliminate Cheyenne's tyrannical ruler before his gearheads could intervene, it would not undo what had been done.

Ronin's anger could not help Lara.

"I failed that night." Her words hitched on a sob. "I failed my sister."

More tears spilled onto his arm, dripping to the bedding below. Despite having every reason to hate Ronin for what he was, she lay back down and curled against him.

"Everyone has limits," Ronin said, combing his fingers through her hair at the nape of her neck. "Everyone has lines they will not cross. You didn't fail."

He held her until she quieted, until her breathing slowed and evened out. Until she was asleep.

As slowly and carefully as he could, he withdrew his arm from beneath her and eased back. The temperature on the surface of his skin plummeted. Lara stirred, making a soft, indistinct sound in her throat, and nuzzled her cheek into the bedding.

She was no longer crying, but the skin around her eyes remained pink and irritated. Her lips were in a similar state thanks to the kisses they'd shared.

Even in sleep, she wasn't still. The gentle rise and fall of her chest as she breathed fascinated him. Her breasts were so soft, so supple, and though their purpose was to provide nourishment to human young, she'd reacted strongly when he'd touched them. Especially her nipples. And he'd responded in turn. Touching her and experiencing her reactions had heightened his arousal beyond anything he'd ever felt. Nothing was as it seemed on the surface when it came to humans.

At least not with Lara Brooks.

He poured over nearly two centuries of memories, over the faces of hundreds of other females. Ronin had encountered many attractive humans, with only one true commonality between them —all had borne some mark left by the harshness of the world. For most, it had been in their eyes, a dullness, a distance, that suggested they were staring off at something unseen. It was a look that hadn't been replicated by any of the many synths he'd come across, who were embodiments of physical perfection, possessing exact symmetry in their features and idealized proportions.

He had seen hair and eyes of similar color to Lara's, had seen skin as fair and silky. He'd seen lithe legs and pert breasts, flared hips and delicate feet, slender necks and elegant arms. He had seen so many faces with fuller lips, more defined cheekbones, thicker lashes, had gazed upon so many people who should've been more appealing.

What was it about this woman that drew him so completely?

Ronin reached forward and lifted a lock of her hair, letting it run between his fingers.

Lara wasn't defined by any single trait, just as he wasn't defined by any single part. He was no more his optics than she was her eyes, no more his actuators than she was her muscles. She was both a sum of her parts and somehow independent of them. His processors couldn't quite explain it, couldn't quite comprehend it, but it was the truth.

Her eyes enticed him with the spark of life they carried. Her lips demanded his attention each time they changed with her emotions. The movements of her limbs were a language all their own, abstract, mysterious, and infinitely compelling. Her humor, though sometimes beyond his grasp, leant an etherealness to her presence. And her willpower, strong as steel, was far more admirable than it was frustrating.

She existed in this world, had been beaten down by it, but she had never surrendered. Instead, she'd lifted her chin, displayed her scars, and pushed on, never allowing the flame of hope inside her to be extinguished.

Lara shone bright. It was her life force, everything that was her, a shining beacon in a sea of darkness.

And he could not resist being drawn in.

Her eyes fluttered beneath their closed lids. *Dreaming*, a distant memory told him.

The closest he could manage was through simulations, which rarely included visual or audio components. At heart, it was all numbers, complex calculations based on a variety of data. Cold, mathematical speculations of what might or might not be. He could take images and sounds from his memory and alter them slightly, could even combine them into something different, but he could not make anything truly new.

Lara's dances alone were proof that she could create at will.

Ronin lightly ran the tip of his finger along her arm, from shoulder to elbow. She stirred, rolling onto her back with a little smile on her lips, but didn't wake. Was her expression in response to his touch? Did she recognize it, even in sleep?

If he woke her and initiated sex, he doubted she'd resist despite her exhaustion. His optics trailed down from her chin, along the lines of her slender neck, over her collarbones, and to the gentle slopes of her breasts.

If I take her nipple in my mouth and caress it with my tongue, how will she react?

His focus dipped to the short, red curls on her mons.

What if I part her thighs and put my mouth there?

In the years since his reactivation, Ronin had coupled only rarely. There'd been pleasure in it, in satisfying his desires. And he'd crossed into the White twice—the cessation of all processes, of all inputs, leaving only a brief but intense explosion of gratification. It had never lasted for more than a second or two, but it had happened.

Lara's body had wrapped around his, had welcomed his phallus inside hungrily, and every movement she'd made had sent waves of electricity through him. She'd brought him to the White, tossed him across the threshold and left him to drift. He'd been aware only of the feel of her body, of her heat, her tightness, and the over-whelming pleasure of their coupling.

There'd been no bed, no bedroom, no sounds but hers—her cries, her heartbeat, her panting breaths. No Warlord or Cheyenne, no Dust. Only that white space, that blankness, that had been filled by her.

He'd lost nearly ten seconds when his functions returned to normal.

His penis stiffened again. Why not wake her? There was time. Afterward, she could rest as long as she needed, and they would make plans. She had given herself to him, and he'd become lost in her; their coupling left him wanting more.

She just lost her sister.

Images of Tabitha rose to the forefront of his mind. Somehow, he stopped himself from superimposing Lara's face on her sister's body. Her life could end in an instant...

That thought halted Ronin's other processes for an instant. Though it was impossible, he felt like his power cell had been drained nearly to nothing, like his limbs were too heavy, like his components required more energy than he could muster to continue operation. But nothing in his system indicated a problem. Nothing could account for that feeling.

Fortunately, it soon passed, but a hint of unease lingered with him.

Lara had given herself to him for comfort, to be distracted from her pain while their bodies were intertwined. She was exhausted and grieving. He couldn't bring himself to wake her. Couldn't be so selfish.

Ronin withdrew his hand and settled it atop the blanket between them. His want for her was undiminished, but what they'd done was no sign of a deeper emotional connection. She had been in need, and he'd provided. There was no guarantee she'd want him again. No guarantee she wouldn't regret what they'd done when she woke up.

He'd been alone for so long that it shouldn't have mattered. Ultimately, her feelings toward him were unimportant.

Weren't they?

So why was the notion of her rejection so unsettling? Why did he crave more of her?

Ronin sat up, optics losing focus as his processors turned inward.

What if she'd been right? What if bots weren't truly alive? Was the way he felt with her, no matter what they were doing, the way humans felt all the time? This eagerness, this want, this fulfillment, this fullness? Those feelings couldn't be the sole criteria for life…

So why did his existence prior to Lara seem so muted in comparison?

Living is… It's about what you experience in that time, you know? About the joy you find…

The bed creaked, and the blanket rustled. He swung his optics to Lara. She lay on her side, knees drawn up. One of her arms was extended, her fingers only a few inches from his thigh, as though she were reaching for the spot he'd occupied a moment ago.

He slid out of the bed and opened the chest just enough to pull out one of the spare blankets from inside, careful not to spill any of the tools on the floor. After turning off the light, he lay down beside Lara, spread the blanket over them, and drew her body against his. She took a deep breath and wrapped her arm around his torso, sliding a leg over his hip.

Her warmth permeated him, slowly building thanks to the insulation from the blanket. For a long while, he watched her sleep. Then he, too, closed his eyes, powering off his optics. Having her soft skin against his, feeling the gentle, steady pulse of her heartbeat, and hearing the peaceful sounds of her breathing brought him a tiny step closer to the White.

That tiny step would have to be enough.

CHAPTER TWENTY-FOUR

Lara slowly came to awareness after waking. Her eyes were tired and irritated, eyelids too heavy to open, her limbs felt leaden, and there was a strange ache between her legs. Had she had another one of those dreams? They'd been frequent and vivid over the last few days, especially during Ronin's absence, but she'd refused to touch herself. She was too conflicted about her desires.

With a deep inhalation, she stretched, stilling abruptly when she realized there was a body tucked against hers. Hesitantly, she opened her eyes and lifted her head. Her breath hitched.

Oh... This is definitely not a dream.

Ronin lay on his back beside her, one arm resting atop his chest while the other had been beneath her head, acting as her pillow. He didn't move, didn't speak.

Lara cocked her head as she gazed down at him. Did bots sleep? She'd never once seen Ronin in his bed, and the only time the bedding had been disturbed at all was when she'd sat on it to sew his shirt.

She glanced around the room. Enough gray, early morning light streamed in through the window for her to make out the dark shapes of the furniture. She and Ronin had slept together. That was the simplest way to look at it, even though there wasn't anything simple about it at all.

Lara sat up, tugging the blanket over her bare breasts. She was in Ronin's room, in his *bed*, lying naked next to him.

Memories rushed back to her. Ronin comforting her, kissing her, touching her, fucking her.

Her brow furrowed. Whatever he'd done, it hadn't felt like fucking. It'd felt like so much more, like something she couldn't define.

But before all that, he'd told her…

Tabitha was dead.

Lara had spent much of the night crying. Even now, more tears threatened to escape, and she fought to keep them in. They couldn't bring Tabitha back.

Crying only made her feel like a weak, sniveling, pathetic human being.

But fuck, this grief hurt like a bitch.

She curled her lips in and covered her mouth with a trembling hand to lock in her sobs.

Suck it up.

Tears trekked down her cheek. Lara wiped at them angrily, returning her gaze to Ronin.

His words drifted up from memory.

I buried her. West of town. Away from…all this. Now, Tabitha is free.

She didn't know many humans who would've done the same for a stranger. A dead body meant potential items to claim, or, for the most desperate of people…a meal. Burials required time and effort that was better spent on survival.

She reached out to touch him, hesitating with her hand hovering an inch above his chest.

He was a bot. What could he know about tending to the dead? What could it have mattered to him? But he'd done so anyway, had given his time and effort, because he knew Lara cared deeply for Tabitha.

Flattening her hand on his chest, she marveled at his warmth and solidness, at the feel of his skin beneath her palm. It was different than human skin, but she found unexpected solace in that.

"Thank you," she said softly.

"For what?"

Lara jumped, yanking her hand back. "I didn't mean to wake you."

Ronin opened his eyes and lifted his head, brow creasing. "I've been awake for one hundred and eighty-five years."

"So…you weren't sleeping just now?"

"Bot's don't sleep, Lara. We go into low power mode when necessary to conserve energy, but usually optics and audio still function in that state, albeit at a lower quality. There's…" He dropped his head, pupils dilating. "There's on or off. Nothing in between for us."

"Oh. Is that…is that what you were doing? The low power thing?"

"No."

"You just laid here with me all night?"

"Yes."

Lara stared at him. He'd told her that he went into the Dust seeking his purpose, because otherwise he would stare at the walls until he shut himself off. That would've left him no different than the furniture in an abandoned house, sitting forgotten in the dark, collecting dust and slowly breaking down as the building crumbled around him. How could lying with her all night be any more exciting than watching paint peel off a wall?

"Why?" she asked incredulously.

"Because I enjoy being near you. Enjoy holding you, hearing your slow breaths, and feeling the rhythm of your heart. Every other night I can remember, I've spent alone."

Heat blossomed on her cheeks and spread down to her neck and chest. She looked away, knowing he'd fixed his penetrating gaze on her. He'd lain with her all night. Awake. A few weeks ago, she would've found that strange and unsettling. Now, it was comforting, especially after the hell of being alone in this house for two days.

Every sound had made her skin crawl and added to the ball of dread in her gut. What little sleep she'd managed had been fitful. Though she wanted to deny it, she felt safe when Ronin was around, and knowing that he'd been with her all night long…

Nervously, Lara tucked hair a lock of hair behind her ear. "I was thanking you for what you did for Tabitha. I know I didn't say it last night, so I wanted you to know it means a lot to me."

"Never buried anyone before," he said after a long pause. "It seemed…right. The bot will remain for centuries, perhaps longer, but your sister…she'll become part of something larger."

"You get it." She looked back at him, smiled softly, sadly, and shook her head. "I don't think any of the others do. Don't think they can."

Ronin sat up, making the bed groan beneath him, and turned his body to face her. The green of his eyes was darker in the diffused light. "I understand that organics break down over time and are reclaimed by the earth. I understand that all of this is important to you. And…I think I am beginning to understand why."

Lara's gaze dropped, roaming over his bare torso. She again noticed the discolored patches of skin. "What are those?"

He looked down. The differences in shades were subtle, but she could make it out even in this dim lighting.

"The closest I can get to scars," he replied.

She reached forward and touched one of the spots. Her fingers glided over his skin, feeling no difference between the mismatched portions.

"Been through a lot of places," he said. "Not all of them have the means to reskin synths. Some of those that do don't have the resources to match coloring. I don't notice it much anymore. It'll all be replaced again, eventually."

"Are they all from bullets?" Lara touched the skin on his abdomen, where there had once been holes.

It was likely her imagination, but it felt like his skin warmed with the contact.

"Bullets, knives, metal rods, rocks. This one"—he placed his hand over hers, guiding it to the spot where a human's heart was located—"was from a steel beam in a dust storm. It penetrated two millimeters to the left of my power cell."

"And you survived all of that." She was awed, even as her chest ached at the damage he'd suffered, at the pain he must've endured.

His other hand slid beneath the blanket. Lara's heart fluttered as he ran his palm along her thigh, around the back of her knee, and to her calf. It settled over a long, crescent-shaped scar there.

"We've all survived our own trials." His fingertip brushed back and forth over the slightly raised skin.

Clutching the blanket, Lara curled her fingers against his chest and pressed her lips together, forcing herself to focus on his words. But her body was responding to his touch and the heat trailed in its wake.

"I was salvaging," she said, "and I don't remember if I slipped or tripped, but I landed on a broken beam. Didn't feel it at first, but there was a sliver as big as a knife stuck in my leg. Then it hurt like a motherfucker. Tabitha got all the bits of wood out and we cleaned it up as best we could, but I still got sick."

She lifted her knee as he continued to stroke the scar. "Like real sick. I can't remember much of it, but Tabitha said I almost died. If it weren't for her, I would have."

"Bots were created to endure. Sometimes it seems like humans were created to suffer. I'm more impressed by your survival than by mine."

Lara smirked. "You trying to flatter me?"

Ronin's finger paused. "Flattery isn't a function I perform. It implies a level of insincerity. I'm simply speaking the truth as I perceive it."

"Flattery can be true, if you mean it."

"That wouldn't be flattery. That would be a complimenting or praising."

"Look, whatever you call it, it doesn't hurt to tell a girl when you admire something about her. You should try it sometime. Maybe you—"

"Everything."

Lara blinked, heart suddenly racing. "What?"

"Everything I've come to know about you, I admire."

"Oh." From anyone else, she wouldn't have believed those words. Part of her couldn't even accept them now. What was there to admire about her? But there was another part of her that was melting at the praise. "You're, uh, pretty good at flattery for someone who says he doesn't do it."

"If you say so, Lara Brooks." Ronin wrapped his fingers around her hand on his chest and squeezed gently. His thumb traced a delicate path from the base of her pinky to her thumb. "How did your sister come by her scar?"

Lara swallowed, chest tight. Guilt had plagued her every time she saw that scar, and now that Tabitha was gone...

"I gave it to her," she said softly.

"Sounds like a story to be told."

"I—"

Don't want to talk about it. Can't talk about it.

But that wasn't true, was it? Tabitha was dead, but Ronin had been right—she lived on so long as Lara kept her memories, kept her love.

"Not much of a story, really. She was teaching me how to use a knife, and I was frustrated and ready to give up. She came up behind me, I think to correct my grip, but I jerked away, insisting I could do it myself. I didn't realize I'd cut her until I saw the blood." Lara's fingers twitched against his chest. "I was a lot more careful from then on, but she never held it against me."

"She must've been an amazing woman."

"She was."

"You learned a lot from her. She would be proud of you."

"There you go, with the flattery again." She turned her face away so he wouldn't see how his words affected her, and though she wanted to brush them off, they sank deep into her chest. Tabitha was gone, but...things could still be okay. Whatever Lara thought about herself, Tabitha had always had faith in her.

"Lara?"

"Hmm?"

Ronin's hand on her leg retraced its path, sliding back up her calf, stopping high on her inner thigh. He brushed his thumb over the sensitive flesh. Holding her hand captive against his chest, he leaned forward. She turned her head toward him slowly to find his face only inches from hers.

In a low, rumbling voice, he said, "I want you."

Her eyes widened, and her lips parted. She couldn't form a response. Those three words, so small, so simple, made her breath ragged and her blood hot. She recalled the explosive sensations he'd awoken in her. After the crushing news he'd delivered, she'd needed a distraction, but he was so much more than that. And what she'd experienced with him last night...she craved to feel that again. Need to feel that again.

Lara stroked her thumb over his chest. "I want you t—"

Ronin kissed her before the last word was fully past her lips.

His mouth was crushing, hungry, devouring, and sent a blaze of searing need through Lara, straight to her core.

Placing a hand on her back, he eased her down onto the bed. The blanket rasped over her sensitive nipples as he pulled it away. They beaded into tight, aching buds in the cool air. She raised her knees to cradle his hips as he moved over her, settling heavily between her thighs. When he cupped one of her breasts, she moaned against his mouth, arching her back to press more firmly into his palm, needing more.

This time, she wasn't running from her pain. Lara wanted to feel what only he could make her feel—alive. Free.

She wanted *him*.

CHAPTER TWENTY-FIVE

Sparks pulsed between the electrodes under Ronin's skin, flooding his circuits with a near-overwhelming hum. Had he known what touching Lara would be like, he would've succumbed to his desire that first night and run his fingertips over her delicate, responsive flesh. His skin could detect pressure, temperature, texture, and moisture, but hers reacted and changed.

He could feel the little bumps on her arms when she wrapped them around his neck. Could feel her skin warming as blood rushed to its surface. Her nipple hardened under his caress, her smooth flesh giving way to the soft swelling of her areola. Her lips were hungry, nibbling and sucking his. And that suction was such a strange, thrilling sensation. It was so intense, so concentrated, and it sent ripples across his sensors, sparking countless new possibilities in his processors.

Ronin broke the kiss and pulled away. Whether or not grief drove her desire, he would experience all of Lara, in every way he could, while he was able. He wanted to explore the many means by which he could coax reactions from her body.

Leaning back on his haunches, he answered her confused expression with a smile and cradled both her breasts, kneading them, marveling at their give within his grasp. Lara's lashes fluttered, but she didn't look away as her hands fell to either side of her. When his palms glided over her nipples, she caught her bottom lip between her teeth and moaned, moving her body sensually and making her skin rasp against his.

Witnessing her like this, getting so swept up in the throes of passion and desire, amplified Ronin's arousal beyond any reasonable measure. The heat of his skin increased further, and the pressure within him built. Much more and he feared alerts would start triggering within his systems.

Catching the hard peaks of her nipples between his thumbs and forefingers, he pinched them.

"Ronin!" Lara gasped, body jolting against his.

"Yes, Lara… Let me see your pleasure. Let me hear it." He slowly slid his hands over her breasts, down the flat of her stomach, and around her flared hips. There he stopped them, eyebrows falling low as he examined the purple bruises on her skin.

He moved his hand to cover one of the marks, which matched its shape perfectly. "I hurt you."

Though they'd rescinded the no touching stipulation of their agreement, he'd never intended for her to come to harm. Especially not at his hands. He'd wanted to give her pleasure, not pain.

"What?" she asked, breathless, and shifted her pelvis against him. The friction sent a ripple of sensation through Ronin that briefly jarred him from his thoughts.

"Bruises. You're bruised, from my hands."

Lara raised her head, glancing down with half-lidded eyes. Her kiss-swollen lips turned up in a smile. She let her head drop to the pillow, her torso shaking with barely suppressed laughter. "Totally worth it."

He lifted his hands and stared at them. His processors whirred, but nothing came. Nothing but the evidence before him.

Lara brushed her fingers over the top of his thigh. "Don't stop, Ronin. It doesn't hurt. I didn't even know they were there until you said something." Somehow, her cheeks reddened further. "Besides, I kinda like them."

"I…" *Don't understand.*

"It's proof you let go and *felt*. That you were alive, with me, in that moment."

Alive.

Regardless of the truth, no matter the doubts he harbored about himself, she saw him as alive.

Ronin settled his palms over the bruises, rubbing gently. Lara's lips parted, and she exhaled softly. He slid his hands down over her buttocks, then along her outer thighs, stopping at the soft undersides of her knees.

Grasping them, he guided her legs up and spread them wider, focusing his optics on her glistening sex. It was an enticing pink, with the tiny bud of her clitoris peeking out from beneath a hood of delicate flesh.

His memory called up the sensation of Lara sucking his lip, and his sensors recreated it, though it was only a muted echo that held no meaning without her touch.

Internal systems he hadn't activated in decades fired to life. He opened his mouth and drew in air. The soft vibration of the pump in his abdomen felt strange after so long. A diagnostics check confirmed there were no leaks; the seals were still functional.

Lara tilted her head, gazing up at him. "Ronin?"

He expelled the air as he dropped his head.

"Wha—" Her voice cut off in a high-pitched gasp when his mouth came down on her sex. "Ronin!"

Her flesh was warm, wet, and fragrant, and he parted her labia with his tongue, spreading her slick, natural moisture. When his lips closed around her budded clitoris, the pump shifted on again, generating suction to raise it into his mouth.

"Ah!" Lara cried out, bucking her hips against his face. "What— Oh *fuck!*

Lashing her clit with his tongue, he wrapped his arms around her thighs to keep her from squirming away.

Her heels pressed into his shoulders, and as he continued sucking and licking her clit, her hands flew to his head. She writhed in his hold, raking his scalp with her nails. His audio receptors picked up the rapid thump of her heart through her thighs, punctuated by her panting breaths.

Every motion, every sound, was a declaration of life.

He reveled in it, reveled in her.

"Ronin, Ronin..." Legs trembling, Lara frantically rocked her pelvis against his mouth. "It's…it's too much, but… Oh God, it feels so good. Please don't stop. Don't stop, don't stop, don't… Ah!"

With a hitched, broken sound, she threw her head back as her body tensed. Liquid heat flowed from her, squirting his chin and dripping onto the bedding. Then she released a series of cries as she curled her fingers and tugged his hair, creating prickling pain that crackled across his scalp and faded over a fraction of a second.

Disabling his air pump, he released the suction on her clitoris and didn't resist the temptation to circle the thrumming bud with his tongue once more. It coaxed another sultry moan from Lara. Her body quivered, and Ronin gazed at her sex, fascinated by the sight. The red curls of her pubic hair were wet with her arousal, her labia were plump, and the muscles of her inner thighs were trembling.

Finally, Lara sagged onto the bed, her hands falling away from his hair.

Ronin wiped his chin on the blanket and lifted his head to look at her. She stared back at him with sparkling eyes, her chest heaving, hair disheveled, and skin flushed.

She raised her arms and beckoned him closer.

Ronin released her thighs and drew himself up, crawling over her. His abdomen brushed over her slick folds. She shivered as she wrapped her arms around his neck. Bracing himself on his elbows, he settled a small portion of his weight atop her, pressing his chest against her soft breasts.

"I…didn't know you could do that," she said, grazing his jaw with her lips. She rolled her pelvis forward to rub along his shaft.

Tendrils of pleasure flickered across his sensors. "Been no reason to, until now."

She smiled as she smoothed her hands around his shoulders, across his chest, and down his belly, blazing an electric path over his skin. His processors simulated a dozen possible sensations to determine what her hand would feel like on his penis. When she finally closed her fingers around it and guided the tip into her welcoming body, everything stopped. Thought processes halted, analyses were suspended, calculations ceased. There was only pure sensory input, untainted by interpretation. Only the pleasure of her touch as their bodies united.

Moist heat enveloped him, and her inner muscles contracted as she took him deeper. Her hands roamed around his hips, over his buttocks, following the contours of his back to settle on the backs of his shoulders.

He pumped his hips slowly, measuredly. Sparks crackled at the base of his spine and arced through his body.

Lara stared up at him, and he stared back, noting every tiny change in her—the drooping of her eyelids each time he slid in, juxtaposed by the parting of her lips, the tightening of her grip, the press of her nails against his skin, which somehow enhanced his pleasure.

"Ronin," she whispered.

She dug her heels into the backs of his thighs and met his rhythmic thrusts, taking him deeper and harder each time. Electric jolts buzzed through his systems.

Lara brushed her lips across his jaw, chin, and mouth as her breathing grew more ragged, broken by her soft moans. "I love the feel of your cock inside me."

And he could not describe the feel of her around his cock, could not describe the signals buzzing along his sensors and through his processors in response to what they were sharing.

Ronin didn't act on logic or calculations; mutual pleasure was his only motivation, the only factor he considered. Balancing his weight on one arm, he wrapped the other around her waist, lifted her bottom off the bed, and quickened his pace. The change in angle brought new sensations. The feel of her altered, the points of friction shifted, and her cries became frantic. She dragged her nails down his back and clung to him.

The urgency of her movements fled as her body went taut. She screamed, quivering in his arms, and her sex rippled and constricted around his phallus, blasting it with liquid heat.

"Lara..." Ronin groaned. His processors thrummed, internal systems crackling as Lara pushed his sensors into overload. He pressed on, eliciting another cry of pleasure from her, and then his optical input flashed white.

The world fell away. Every minute movement from her inner muscles played across his cock with the force of a windstorm. He was aware of her pulse, rapid but steady, everywhere their bodies touched, and felt her warm breath on his skin.

She writhed beneath him, arching her back. Ronin's body locked.

Slowly, the tension in her fingers eased. As Ronin's optics came back online, he lowered her fully onto the bed.

Panting, Lara draped a forearm over her eyes, and a broad smile stretched across her face. Her flushed skin glistened with perspiration.

He held himself over her, not yet withdrawing. After crossing into the White, her warmth and softness were comforting, serving as both a tether to reality and a reminder of their shared pleasure. There was no tension evident in her, no fear. No disgust for having coupled with a bot again. For a few moments, at the very least, he'd made her happy.

Something about that was…fulfilling.

Ronin's brow furrowed. Why should his contentment be derived from her enjoyment? He was a dustwalker, a wanderer, a robot who would walk the wasteland until he broke down or was deactivated. And yet after so many years of searching, it was only here, with this woman, that he felt closest to discovering his purpose.

His thoughts were interrupted by a long, low gurgling. Lara peeked at him from beneath her arm.

"What was that?" he asked.

"My stomach."

He leaned back and moved his hands to her abdomen, checking for more bruises, feeling for signs of damage. She squirmed, body shaking. He stilled his hands.

Am I causing her more pain?

"What are you doing?" She took hold of his wrists and drew them away. Her smile hadn't faltered.

He met her gaze. "I hurt you."

A laugh bubbled from her. "No, you didn't."

They both looked at her stomach when the sound repeated.

"How could I not have?" he asked.

"That means I'm hungry, Ronin."

Tentatively, he pressed his palm to her abdomen. She didn't stop him.

He could feel the rumbling inside. Whatever data his fractured memory contained regarding human anatomy, it apparently didn't cover their bodily functions with much depth. "You eat, and this stops?"

"Yep."

"So…there's no pain?"

She glanced away. "Well…"

He withdrew his hand immediately. "Lara…"

She chuckled. "Pain in all the right places."

"I do not—" He snapped his mouth shut as he recalled Lara pressing her nails into his skin, pulling his hair, and digging her heels into his thighs. Each had been a small source of pain that heightened the experience.

"I *think* I understand. Somewhat." His optics dropped to where their bodies were still connected. Where that delicate pink flesh was wrapped around him, where he was buried inside her. It was a sight he liked immensely. He lowered a hand to her hip, settling his fingers over the bruises. "Pain isn't always bad…because pain is part of being alive."

"Yeah, as long as it's not too much." Her smile wavered, and something flashed in her eyes for an instant.

Before he could guess its nature, she recovered.

"I'm fine, Ronin. Just starving. Not, like, for real, but…" Catching her lower lip between her teeth, Lara slowly pulled away, forcing his phallus—his cock—to withdraw from her sex. It slipped out, still erect, covered in her arousal. She sat up, her gaze lingering on it. Ronin didn't miss the infinitesimal darkening of her blue eyes, and the glint of desire they held.

She cleared her throat and scooted to the edge of the bed. "Uh, lemme get something to eat, and you can show me the scrap you found while you were gone."

"All right." Already craving her heat, he watched Lara slip out of bed, noting how her figure had subtly filled out since she'd started living with him. He knew she wasn't fine, not under the surface, and how could she have been? Not all pain was physical. It had only been nine and a half hours since he told her about Tabitha.

She plucked a shirt off the floor and tugged it on, glancing over her shoulder to cast him another smile. Reaching up to tuck loose hair behind her ear, she walked into the hallway.

Ronin climbed out of bed, pulled on his pants, and picked up his coat. As he walked, he dipped a hand into the inside coat pocket, withdrawing the ring.

Perhaps it would be an uplifting surprise for her on the heels of so devastating a loss.

CHAPTER TWENTY-SIX

Lara slipped the last bite of jerky into her mouth as she stood looking over the items spread across the worktable. Tools, scraps of metal and plastic, spare bot parts, and a few power cells. It was more than she'd found in years of scavenging, and most humans would've strained to carry such a haul more than a mile or two. How far had Ronin traveled with it?

"You got all this in two days?" she asked around a mouthful of tender meat.

Ronin nodded. He was leaning against the wall beside the window, arms folded over his broad, bare chest.

Lara couldn't stop her eyes from lingering upon that chest. God, she'd had her hands all over it, had it pressed to her breasts while he lay between her thighs, had felt it thrum when they'd climaxed. The temptation to brush her fingers over its firm expanse was acute.

Did he realize how sexy he looked right now, with his hair tousled from her fingers?

She swallowed thickly and forced her gaze up to his. "Why'd you come back early?"

"Because I didn't like the thought of you being here alone."

It was the last answer she would've expected. Before they'd *coupled*, as he had put it, before their physical closeness had revealed their deeper feelings for one another, he'd been thinking about her safety. She would've preferred it if he'd stayed with her to begin with, but…

During her time here, Ronin had often watched her. Whenever they were in the same room, his eyes were always locked on her, rarely deviating. She'd pretended not to notice. It would've been easy to dismiss it as creepy bot behavior, but she knew better now. There'd been so much more beneath the surface.

Had Tabitha shared something similar with the bot who'd taken her in? Mutual curiosity, mutual admiration, care for one another's wellbeing? Maybe she hadn't done it solely for the food, shelter, and security.

What if…what if Tabitha was happy?

The thought gave Lara pause. Was *she* happy? It seemed wrong in the wake of her sister's death, but beneath the gloom of grief, there was light. And why else would it be there, if not for Ronin?

Lara couldn't guess what drew him to her. There were many prettier women in Cheyenne, even without counting the female synths, who would've been both far more eager to accept his deal and far more grateful for it. But Ronin's interest in her was genuine. He wanted her to be safe and content.

Had Tabitha's bot tried to protect her too?

If so, that bot had obviously failed in the end, but how could he have succeeded? Even without any details, Lara knew in her gut that Warlord was responsible for their deaths. No one person, whether human or machine, could stand against Cheyenne's ruler and his fanatical thugs.

Why? Why had they murdered Tabitha and her companion?

Lara's brow furrowed. "Am I in danger, Ronin?"

Ronin's pupils dilated and refocused on her, those green eyes as intent as ever. "Everyone is always in some degree of danger."

"But you came back early, even after arguing with me that you needed more time out there. Something must've crossed your mind."

"I had a sizeable haul, and I realized that I'd rather be with you than digging through the dirt for a few more pieces of scrap."

Heat bloomed on her cheeks, and she dropped her gaze to the worktable. She knew there was more to it, more he wasn't saying, but that didn't change how she felt. Lara took a deep breath and released it slowly. "I missed you. I know you weren't gone for long, but I got used to you being around, and…I missed you."

He was silent. After a few moments, she looked up at him

Head canted to the side, he continued staring at her. "Missed… That's a good term. It was like I was missing a part of myself."

Lara's breath hitched.

Oh… That…that was quite a confession.

His words made her heart constrict and filled her with warmth.

Ronin pushed off the wall and reached into his pants pocket. "There's one more thing I found."

He held out his fist and uncurled his fingers. A ring lay on his palm, the band gleaming in the morning light. It was familiar, a relic from a lifetime ago, but it had only been weeks since she'd last seen it.

"I think this is yours, Lara Brooks."

She stared at the small metal band in disbelief. "How did you.…"

"When I left town, I passed the place where you were scavenging in the rain. I stopped, caught up in the memory, when I noticed this in the debris."

"I thought it was gone." Lara carefully took the ring between her forefinger and thumb and lifted it from his palm, half expecting it to disappear. Though slight, it had weight; it was real. "Thank you."

Turning it from side to side, she studied the ring, fascinated by the play of sunlight within its clear stone despite the dirt built up within the surrounding prongs.

She grinned at Ronin. "You know, when a man gives a woman a ring, it's usually because he's asking her to marry him."

His brow creased. "I fail to understand why humans still practice that custom. Isn't marriage just the recognition of a coupling by a representative of authority? And what role does a ring play in it?"

"Quite the romantic, aren't you?" She closed her fingers around the ring. "It's a tradition, one people have held on to despite…you know, all *this*. There's hardship, yeah, but people still fall in love."

Gary and Kate immediately came to mind. They were always affectionate and supportive of one another.

"I don't know what you mean about…well, that other stuff you said. Representative of authority?" She wrinkled her nose. "The hell does that mean, anyway? And what does it have to do with people getting married?"

The corners of his mouth dipped. "My data is incomplete. Most of the relevant information is lost in the corrupted portion of my memory. There used to be…" He lapsed into a brief silence before shaking his head.

Would Ronin ever regain his lost memories, or were they gone forever?

He scratched his cheek. "Can't remember. Just means that back then, the people in charge had to acknowledge a marriage. You mentioned love. Is marriage required for love?"

"Um, no. It's not. Some people just like tradition. I think it's because we've already lost so much. Feels good to keep something old alive."

Opening her hand, she ran a finger around the ring's loop. "Someone told me once that a ring means eternity because it's a circle, and circles never end. When a man wants a woman to be his wife, he'll find something to use as a ring, like wire, a cheap bit of a metal, or even some twine, and ask her to marry him.

"If she says yes, they both wear a ring to show they're taken and devoted to each other. They make their vows to each other, usually with some other people watching, and then they're married. Not that it means all that much to everyone. Heard about a lot of people who broke their vows…"

She frowned at the ring as sorrow filled her. Humans had lost so much that even these small symbols of love, these old romantic traditions, often meant…nothing. Lara sighed. "Maybe you're right. I don't know why we still bother."

Ronin reached out and plucked the ring from her palm. He raised it to eye level, turning and tilting it, examining even the inside of the band. Then he took her hand and slipped the ring onto her finger.

Lara's breath caught, and her eyes widened.

He grasped her chin and tipped it up, forcing her gaze to his. "You still bother because it means hope. Hope that everything will be okay, some day. Because it means a chance at a future even in a world that wants to destroy us. It means you are not alone."

He covered her hand with both of his. "Let this ring be my vow,

Lara. To protect you. To provide for you. To give you all you need that's within my power, and to find a way to give you whatever's not."

The air fled her lungs. "Did you...did you just kind of... marry me?"

"I've given you my vow."

She searched his face. This was one of the many times when she couldn't read him, couldn't tell how to interpret his words. After what she'd just told him, how could this be anything but him becoming her husband? The idea of being married to Ronin wasn't as disagreeable as she might once have thought. He was a man, regardless of what was beneath his skin, and he'd treated her better than anyone apart from Tabitha.

Lara eased closer to him, drawing their hands to her chest. "Then I vow to protect you, too, to the best of my ability. To place my trust in you and never break yours. To remind you, every day, that you are alive."

"I gave my word freely, Lara. I don't ask anything in return." His voice was soft, and his confusion was plain on his features.

"I gave mine freely, too." Rising on her toes, she brushed her lips against his. "Unless...you don't accept?"

"Part of me says I shouldn't."

"Oh." Lara drew back with a sinking feeling in her stomach. Maybe he really didn't understand.

Ronin gripped her hand, preventing her from pulling away. "I don't want to put you in unnecessary danger. That's been my existence, Lara...one danger after another." Wrapping an arm around her waist, he tugged her against him. "But I haven't been so damaged in the Dust that I could ever reject you. I accept."

Dipping his head, he raised her hand to his lips, kissing her knuckles. There was a hint of a smile on his face as his gaze held hers. "Did *you* just kind of marry *me*?"

Something fluttered inside Lara. She grinned. "I don't have a ring to give you, but yeah. I guess I did."

CHAPTER TWENTY-SEVEN

Lara sat on the windowsill in Ronin's bedroom, using a small brush to clean the dirt and grime off her ring. Even hours later, she still couldn't quite believe what had happened.

She and Ronin were married.

Perhaps that didn't mean much to people anymore. It was an outdated remnant of a dead world, a concept that had lost its purpose and relevancy decades before Lara was born. But that didn't matter, because it meant something to her. It meant something to them both.

After dropping the brush into the nearby bowl of water, she used the corner of her shirt to dab the ring dry. When she lifted the band into the late afternoon sunlight, her breath caught in her throat.

The gold gleamed, at once darker and brighter than she'd thought possible. The metal's sheen rippled as she turned it between her fingers, but that couldn't compare to the attached stone, which Ronin had called a diamond. It sparkled as though giving off its own light, drinking in the rays of sunshine and shattering them to cast little rainbows on her skin. This ring was unlike anything she'd ever seen. It was beautiful.

And it was *hers*.

Tilting it, she skimmed the tip of her finger over the words etched inside the band. Words she couldn't read. What did they say?

She knew the materials were valuable. Gold was worth a lot to bots, because they used it for some of their inner parts. It was essential to keep them repaired and operational. Wasn't that why they called it precious metal? They needed it to survive, just like humans needed food and water.

Lara struggled to imagine a world in which a person could take so much of this valuable material and shape it into a…a decoration. Someone had worn this ring on their finger, had chosen to do so, rather than trade it for food, clothing, shelter, or tools.

Had it been a display of wealth, a message to onlookers that its owner was so well off that they were above worrying about where they'd find their next meal?

The sound of running water in the bathroom changed as Ronin moved in the shower. There were three rooms with toilets in this house—*three!*—though only two had tubs. Why would anyone need so many places to relieve themselves? Was that another way to flaunt wealth?

Lara slid the ring back onto her finger. It was loose, but not so loose that it would slip off on its own.

Seeing it there was strange. Her hand had regularly clawed through dirt and debris, her nails had often been chipped, broken, and caked with dirt, and her calluses were only beginning to soften. Something so bright and shining seemed out of place on a hand like hers, and yet… It felt right.

When she'd found the ring, her only thought had been of the credits it would fetch, of the food it would purchase.

Now…she was married. Even if it was just between her and Ronin, without acknowledgement from a…*representative of authority*, or whatever, it was no less real. He wanted to keep her safe, to feed her, to make her happy. The ring had become a symbol of all that.

They'd had sex three more times after exchanging their vows, each time more intense than the last despite her growing weariness. For now, Lara's body was sated, though her hunger for him was by no means diminished.

There'd been no talk of love. Ronin had displayed many emotions since she met him, but could he really love someone?

Could I...love him?

It wasn't necessary for a marriage, and Ronin was already more than she could have ever dreamed. He was kind, patient, and caring, always placing her needs before his own.

She'd known many men who were Ronin's opposites. Devon was one of them. He fed and clothed the women who caught his interest, but only in return for sex, and only while they held his fickle attention. At the first hint of boredom or annoyance, he would cast them aside, leaving them with nothing but the clothes on their backs.

How many times had Lara irritated Ronin? How many times had she given him reason to be angry at her? If he were like Devon, he would've beaten her and thrown her out long ago.

The house had felt so empty while Ronin was away. She'd missed having his eyes on her, missed his calm, sometimes frustrating conversations.

She'd missed *him*.

Crazy as it seemed, she had been worried about him. The Dust was dangerous for anyone, and by his own admission, he wasn't impervious to harm. How would Lara have reacted if he'd taken damage to one of his primary systems and come back changed? Or if he'd never come back at all, and she was left without knowing his fate?

What if Warlord had captured Ronin and done the same to him as he had to Tabitha and her bot? Ronin hadn't shared the details, and Lara wasn't even sure she wanted them, but she understood the simple truth—Cheyenne was not safe.

Her heart constricted, and she pressed a hand over her chest. Those thoughts filled her with dread so deep and oppressive that it threatened to drive her into a panic here and now.

"What's wrong, Lara?"

She started, turning her head to see Ronin standing naked in the bedroom, a towel clutched in his hand. His short brown hair was disheveled, appearing to have been freshly dried, his skin was still damp, and his cock hung flaccid against his thigh. Every contour of his body was on display. Lara lifted her gaze to meet his eyes, which looked upon her with undisguised intensity.

He's beautiful.

He's...mine.

And I need to keep him safe, like he does me.

Licking her lips, she forced words out of her tight throat. "I think we should leave."

His brow furrowed. "We have the salvage to purchase enough food to last for days, at least."

"Leave Cheyenne, Ronin."

"The Dust is too dangerous, Lara. I know you want to come on runs with me, but—"

"I mean for good. We should leave Cheyenne forever."

He stood utterly still and silent. Thinking. It looked unnatural, but she wasn't unsettled by it anymore.

"Where would you like to go?" he finally asked.

"I don't know. You've been to all kinds of places, so I thought..." She dropped her hands into her lap and sighed. "It's dangerous here. I know it was Warlord and his gearheads who killed my sister. And you can't tell me I'd be safe if I set one foot outside this house without you."

He looked at the floor. "I could tell you that, but it wouldn't be true."

"It's not your fault, but I feel like a prisoner here, Ronin. I don't want to sit here and wait for something to happen to me, like it did to her." Lara bit the inside of her lip and dropped her gaze to the ring as she twisted it on her finger. "If you don't want to go, at least take me past the wall, and...and I'll find my way to somewhere else."

Ronin crossed the distance between them, grasped her shoulder in one hand, and took her chin in the other. He gently guided her eyes up to his. "I made a vow, Lara."

"I don't want you held by words, Ronin."

"I'm not held by them. I'm...enriched by them." His palm moved up to cup her cheek. "There's nothing tying either of us to this place apart from each other. My only bond is with you."

Lara's stomach fluttered. "And...what does that bond mean to you?"

"It means I am alive."

"But you can have that without me. You were already alive, before I was even born." Fortunately, her disappointment didn't creep into her voice.

Ronin felt alive with her. That wasn't proof of a real emotional attachment, wasn't a declaration of something more. He felt obligated to protect her, enjoyed rolling around in bed with her, and thought talking to her was more interesting than talking to himself, at least for the time being.

Why hope for anything greater than that? Wasn't it enough?

His gaze searched her face as he stroked her cheek with his thumb. "I don't think I was."

Settling a hand atop his, Lara closed her eyes. "Let's leave tonight. We can get the hell out of here before anyone notices."

"No."

Dread sank in her belly, dragging her remaining hope down with it. She should've known by now that hope only led to heartache.

She dropped her hand. "Why not?"

His fingers twitched against her cheek. "We need supplies."

"We have supplies, and you have all the stuff you just brought in to trade for more. And we can sell this, too." She grasped the ring and slid it off her finger.

Ronin closed his hands around both of hers before she could remove it. His gaze was steady when she looked up into his eyes. Her heart was pounding, her breaths were heavy, and she didn't know why. There was nothing left for her in this town but despair, fear, and death. She had to leave.

"No, Lara. Keep it." He pushed the ring back onto her finger. "The nearest settlement is about eighty miles, depending on the route. I can make that in a day. With you, it'll take at least five days, depending on the weather."

Lara tugged her hand, but Ronin didn't release it. "You don't think I should go because I'd fucking slow you down?"

"That's not what I'm saying, Lara."

"Sure as hell sounds like you are!"

"That's five days, minimum, of food and water. If a bad storm blows through, it could delay us another week on top of that."

"I've gone a long time without food before. I can do it again."

"I don't doubt that, but I'm not willing to take that risk. We need to bring enough food and water to last at least ten or twelve days, and we need more durable clothing to protect your skin out there. I also want you to have a reliable weapon before we leave. And we don't have all that sitting around here."

When she tugged on her hands again, he released his hold, and she raised one to show him the ring. It only had meaning while he was alive, while they were together. "That's why this needs to go. Between this and the rest of your haul, we can get everything we need."

"No, Lara. You're keeping it. You told me it means eternity."

"It's just a thing, Ronin. I'm going to have to hide it when we go out, anyway, because anyone who sees it will try to take it from me. It's just a piece of metal."

He pressed his lips into a tight line.

Really, Lara?

Fuck!

She growled in frustration. "Damn it, that's not what I meant, and you know it!"

"Regardless, I don't want you to sell it. Give me a few more days. I'll bring in enough to obtain everything we need, plus some scrap to trade at the next town. Then we can go, and we won't ever have to look back at Cheyenne again."

Lara pushed herself up from the windowsill and glared at him. "Are you fucking serious? You just got back, and you're already going to go out and leave me here alone? Again?"

"Yes. One more run, so you can come next time."

"And what if there is no next time? What if you come back and find me lying dead out there, just like you found Tabitha?"

His expression went blank, pupils expanding before dwindling to pinpoints.

"I'm defenseless here, Ronin. This place is a deathtrap, and I'm going insane just sitting here, doing nothing."

"And you'll have to endure that for a few more days, Lara." His voice had that edge to it, the one she'd only heard when he was truly angry. "I'll leave my rifle. It can punch a hole in most bots. Sleep with it, if you need to."

The fire inside Lara guttered out at the thought of Ronin in the Dust, unarmed. A chill skittered up her spine. "And what will you use out there?"

"Whatever I must, if it comes to that."

"Will that be enough?"

He was silent for a moment. "Whatever happens, Lara, I will come back for you."

If they don't come for me first.

"Damn it." Lara sighed and walked to the bed, sitting on the edge. She lowered her face into her hands. For however long he'd be gone, she'd sit here, jumping at every sound, her mind racing through all the things that could go wrong. But her worries always came back to Ronin.

If something happened to him, she'd never know. And that thought was sickening.

"When are you leaving?" she asked quietly.

"As soon as I get dressed."

Lara's lower lip trembled. Her eyes burned, but damn it, she wouldn't let even one more tear fall.

"Fine." Dropping her hands, she rose and strode toward the door.

Ronin caught her arm as she passed, spinning her to face him. "We will not part like this, Lara Brooks."

She kept her face averted, not wanting to meet his gaze, not when he was doing this again. "Why not?"

"Because it's all either of us will think about while we're apart."

"Just like all I thought about last time was you not saying goodbye?"

"A mistake I don't intend to repeat."

The sting of tears intensified, but the tension left Lara's body. Ronin drew her against his chest in a warm embrace and rested his cheek atop her head as he stroked his fingers through her hair. The rest of Lara's anger faded, leaving a wretched ache in her heart. She wrapped her arms around him and squeezed as the tears she'd desperately tried to keep at bay slid down her cheeks.

"I don't want you to go," she whispered.

"Bots always mean what they say. I *will* be back. Very soon."

"I'll hold you to it. If you're not back in a few days, I'm gonna come looking."

"I know you will." Ronin pressed his lips to her forehead. "I expect nothing less."

CHAPTER TWENTY-EIGHT

Because Colorado had been far more densely populated than Wyoming before the Blackout, the lands south of Cheyenne made for more lucrative scavenging. But that was a longer journey, and Lara's urgency had seeped into Ronin, making him hyperaware of time's passage.

They needed to get out of Cheyenne as soon as possible. They couldn't afford a delay of three or four days.

So he strode west. There were places sleeping in these hills that he hadn't scavenged. The risk of returning empty-handed was higher, but this was the quickest route back to Lara.

Twenty-nine kilometers outside of town, he spotted a line of wood fence posts atop a hill, nearly lost amidst the scrub grass and dirt. As he climbed, his guidance system pushed him to turn east. To return to Lara.

She was waiting for him in Cheyenne, trapped in the territory of the bots who'd killed her sister. She'd begged him to take her away from that place, and he'd forced her not only to stay, but to stay *alone.*

All because he wanted her to keep the ring.

They both knew it would've traded for enough credits to acquire any supplies they needed for their journey and more, especially combined with his last haul. Logic dictated that they should've taken it to the market the moment she suggested selling it. They could've left town together immediately afterward, without the agony of waiting, without suffering through uncertainty.

It was an object only as valuable as the materials that made it—or it should've been. Her description of how humans used such rings and what they symbolized might've been enough to convince him, but the inscription on the inside of the band had truly made up his mind.

Yours Until the End of Time.

Simple words. Like the ring itself, they shouldn't have held any deeper meaning. But Ronin had known he had to give it to her once he'd read them.

He crested the hill, stopped beside one of the posts, and tapped it with the toe of his boot. The rotted wood broke with a dull *snap*, partly disintegrating. The inhabitants of the old world had been fond of boundaries. Their reward was the boundless Dust.

Ronin swept his optics over the area ahead. The ground ran down into a small valley, likely carved over millennia by a long-dried stream, before rising into another hill. The land continued like that for kilometers—peaks and valleys, steadily higher, steadily rockier. Sediment had gathered at the base of this valley over decades of countless storms, from which rose a surprisingly intact shingle roof.

As he descended, his processors began the daunting task of calculating the probability of finding this exact place at this exact time. His attention shifted to Lara long before he could produce an answer.

How improbable was her existence?

So much about human reproduction was left to chance. Two people had to meet, had to connect, circumstances had to be perfect for fertilization, particular parts of their genetic code had to be passed on to their offspring, and those descendants had to repeat the cycle again, and again, and again. Lara's ancestors had gone through that process for untold generations. Out of infinite possibilities, all those couplings had resulted in *her*.

And if all that wasn't improbable enough, Ronin had happened to be led directly to her shack by the sound of her chime tinkling in the wind, on a night when she'd left her door cracked open, right when she'd been dancing.

The chain of unrelated occurrences leading to their meeting was staggering to contemplate.

How long would Ronin have wandered, unsettled by the emptiness of his existence without understanding it, if not for Lara? Would he have ever tasted even a fraction of the emotion she'd awoken in him?

Circling the buried structure, he dropped his right hand to the grip of the pistol at his hip and unclasped the holster with his thumb. The firearm wasn't likely to significantly damage most bots, but it packed enough of a punch to allow Ronin the opportunity to get closer, and it was more practical in tight spaces than his rifle.

There was no trash outside, no tracks, no path worn in the dirt near the only window above the ground. Ronin forced all his processors to divert from thoughts of Lara, difficult as it was, and focused on his sensory inputs.

Wind rustled the dry grass and kicked up loose bits of dust to patter on the roof.

He moved to the window and knelt beside it. Only a few flakes of white paint clung to the splintery gray wood of the frame, and decades of abrasion and sunlight had left the glass too cloudy to see through.

Pressing his fingers to the bottom rail, he applied upward pressure, but the window didn't move.

After another optic sweep of his surroundings, he drew his pistol and hammered it into the window. The wooden muntins supporting the glass panes were brittle, snapping inward as the glass shattered. He froze and listened for any indication someone had heard him.

The wind sighed its disapproval.

What would Lara think of this? Would she be excited by the unknown, by the discovery, or would it frighten her?

Clearing out the remaining shards from the window frame, Ronin pulled himself inside feet-first. Glass crunched beneath his boots as his optics adjusted to a low-light setting. The room came into focus.

Though everything was covered in thick dust, this had clearly been a bedroom. A rusted bed frame lay in one corner, and the skeleton of a mattress stood against the wall, little more than rotted wood and corroded springs draped in tattered, discolored cloth. Crumbling drywall revealed the wood supports inside the walls.

Despite his care, the floorboards creaked beneath him as he searched the room. He found only a few bits of plastic before proceeding into the hallway. Motes of dust, disturbed by his passage, floated in the air. Each of those specks represented years of stillness and neglect.

Entering another bedroom, he continued his cautious search. There were books in this one, their covers worn, spines creased, and pages yellowed with age. A lone book lay upon the bedside stand. Gently, he brushed the dust from its cover to reveal the word *DIARY* printed upon it.

He couldn't bring himself to pick it up.

Books weren't valuable to the bots of Cheyenne, and Ronin didn't have connections amongst the humans to find fair trade for them. He couldn't justify the space they would've taken up in his bag. Practicality had to outweigh curiosity now.

But the books served as more proof of what he'd already known —people had lived here before the Blackout. They might've even survived it and remained for a time afterward. They'd slept in these beds, had walked in the hallway, had prepared meals in the kitchen he knew lay somewhere deeper inside.

He moved to the closet. The sliding doors had fallen off their tracks and lay on the floor nearby. Twenty-two clothes hangers hung on the rod, seventeen wire, five plastic, four of which held moth-eaten garments. He holstered his pistol, set down his bag, and collected the hangers, bending the metal ones into more compact shapes and breaking the plastic into manageable pieces. He tossed the garments into a pile in the closet's corner.

Something on the shelf above the rod caught Ronin's attention when he was done.

A cloud of dust billowed in the air as he pulled the plastic bin down. Setting it on the floor, he crouched and pried the lid open. Despite his care, the brittle plastic snapped. He tossed the pieces aside.

Ronin reached into the bin and took out the stack of papers on top. They were thick and textured, in a variety of faded colors, and many had shaky, simplistic drawings on their fronts and the same name written on their backs—*Lindsey*. It was always accompanied by a number, ranging from five to ten, and the drawings became clearer and more confident as the number increased.

He placed the papers on the floor and removed the next object. It was small enough to hold in one hand, with a hard, plastic casing and five buttons along one side. There were symbols on the buttons—a square, a triangle pointing right, two sets of double triangles facing opposite directions. He pressed the button with the upward-pointing triangle.

With an audible click, the clear-paned door on the front of the device opened. Inside was a slot with two pegs. Ronin had a sense that this had been old technology even before the world fell apart, but he did not know its function.

He looked into the bin. Neatly arranged along the bottom were twenty-six plastic cases with words printed on their sides. *MICHAEL JACKSON THRILLER, MADONNA BEDTIME STORIES, RATT REACH FOR THE SKY, DEF LEPPARD HYSTERIA, MEAT-LOAF BAT OUT OF HELL.* There were numbers on all of them, but he couldn't discern a meaningful pattern. Selecting one at random, he pulled it from its place and turned it.

There was a picture on the front of a dark-haired woman holding a guitar. *JOAN JETT*, it read across the top, with *Bad Reputation* written lower. Ronin ran his fingertips along the edge of the case, finding the grooves, and opened it. Another plastic object was inside, which contained twin reels of tape visible through a tiny window.

That's what it was called—a tape. He removed it from the case, slid it into the tape player, and closed the door.

With his fragmented memory, all he had were assumptions, but he guessed these tapes were recordings of music. And if they could be played, they would offer a unique glimpse into a bygone era. A taste of a civilization that had collapsed two hundred years ago.

Further examination of the tape player led him to the battery compartment, which was empty. That was good. Leaked battery acid had damaged many electronic devices he'd discovered over the years. If he could figure out an alternate means of powering this tape player, Lara could listen to music. Maybe it would inspire her to move in new ways.

He knew he needed to save space for tradeable scrap, but he couldn't leave these behind. Not when they were so likely to bring Lara joy.

Strange how quickly I've come to value her happiness...

After dumping out the hangers, he transferred the tapes into his bag as neatly as possible, setting the player and the dusty earpieces that seemed to go with it atop them. He spread a rag over the items before repacking the hangers.

Ronin stood and swung his pack over his shoulders, running his optics over the room one more time. They fell on the stack of drawings.

Tabitha would live on in Lara's memory, but there was no evidence of her existence apart from a simple grave just west of Cheyenne. She'd left nothing behind but her love for her adopted sister. Was that enough?

Crouching, he returned the papers to bin. Though the broken lid wouldn't seal, he put its pieces back in place, rose, and slid the bin onto the closet shelf. Perhaps the drawings would last a few more years there than they would have on the floor.

And perhaps Lindsey, whoever she'd been, would exist for a little longer through them.

Activating night vision, he resumed his search of the premises.

There was little else worth taking in the rest of the house, apart from a few metal and plastic scraps and a pot that would clean up nicely. The last door to check behind was on the interior kitchen wall. The writing on its face was peeling off with the paint, but it was still legible.

NOTHING FOR YOU HERE
GO AWAY WE WILL FIGHT

Those words must've been spray-painted decades ago, and the state of this place suggested that it had been deserted for many years before Ronin's arrival. Unless there was an active bot lurking behind this door, there was no one left to fight.

Ronin drew his handgun, grasped the knob, and pulled the door open.

A narrow staircase led down into a dark basement. On one side, the concrete foundation met the wall, creating a ledge that was cluttered with objects made unidentifiable by the excessive cobwebs and dust gathered upon them.

He lowered his foot onto the first step, and eased his weight onto it, listening to the wood creak. When it didn't break, he repeated the process with the next step. He'd fallen through floors and stairs before, and had never suffered more than minor damage, but it was best to be careful. Especially with someone awaiting his return.

Were these the places Lara wanted to see? The ruins of buildings once inhabited by people long since forgotten, containing fragments of stories that had been lost to time?

These places are her people's history.

Bots endured while generations of humans were born, lived, and died. Were the long, dull, logic-driven existences of bots fuller than the quick, emotion-saturated lives of humans? Ronin wasn't sure which people were the favored of the Creators anymore.

His boots came down on solid concrete at the base of the stairs. Bare joists and beams from the floor above ran overhead, the gaps between them filled with rotted, disintegrating insulation and thick spiderwebs. Dingy blankets and sheets, hanging from the wood by nails and staples, divided the space. A stack of dilapidated boxes rested beneath the only visible window, which was completely covered by dirt from the outside.

Holding the handgun at the ready, Ronin reached forward with his empty hand, brushing aside one of the sheets. Dust rained from the fabric and grit crunched beneath his boots as he walked past.

His foot hit something. The hollow, metallic *clangs* of the object bouncing on the floor were thunderous, followed by the more muted sound of it rolling over the concrete. He shifted his optics to follow the path in the dirt, gun leveled, ready to open fire.

The tin can he'd kicked rocked slowly in place. There was more trash scattered around the floor nearby, mostly empty cans and wrappers.

Frowning, he advanced through the maze of dangling fabric to the far wall. There were more boxes and plastic bins there, none in any better shape than what he'd seen upstairs. He turned to the left, pushed through more sheets, and finally emerged in an open area.

A workbench with a vise bolted near its center spanned the rear wall. More cans were scattered over its surface, along with small boxes, jars, and bottles. Articles of clothing, as dirty and worn as the bedding suspended from the rafters, hung along the edge of the bench as though placed there to dry.

One item caught his attention, recognizable despite the cobwebs enveloping it because of the lever on the side. It was a press from a reloading kit.

He shifted his optics to the floor, where a collection of blankets and pillows formed a pallet upon which three skeletons lay in ragged clothing. The two smaller ones were huddled in the arms of the third. Each skull had a small hole in its forehead.

Several feet away, a fourth skeleton, taller than the rest, lay face-down on the concrete. The back of its skull was shattered—an exit wound.

Ronin crouched beside the lone skeleton. Its fingers were wrapped around a rusted revolver, one arm twisted awkwardly beneath its torso. In its other hand, it held a paper wrapped in a plastic sheath. Ronin slid the paper out of the clawlike grip. The writing on it was a sloppy scrawl, not unlike the latter entries in the journal Lara had found.

> It was mercy. There was no other choice, and it was a mercy to do it. You're not going to have us again, even after we're dead. Not going to have us or ours! You made me kill them. Made me
> It was a mercy A MERCY
> Lord, have mercy on me.

Folding the paper, Ronin stared at the remains. He'd spent many years longing for the return of his memories from the before time, had thought himself incomplete without them. But were these the sorts of memories stored in the corrupted part of his mind? Was the data full of scenes like this?

He lifted the skeletal hand and replaced the note. His optics flicked to the pallet. Which of the smaller skeletons had been Lindsey?

Having lost his desire to search the basement further, he rose and walked to the workbench. The reloading press would trade for a good amount, and it would have to be enough.

I need to get back to Lara.

He stowed his pistol and set to work.

The bolts fastening the press to the benchtop were rusted. They groaned in protest when he clamped his pliers onto them and exerted pressure, but they gave way. He added the press to his bag and swept in some of the nearby cans along with it.

Lara would be pleased. He'd asked for a few days, but if he started back now, he'd be back in Cheyenne within twelve hours of leaving.

He walked through the blankets, moving them aside with an outstretched arm. Dust filled the air, obscuring his vision.

Something thin and wirelike caught his ankle.

He heard a short, metallic scrape, followed by the sound of a small piece of metal falling to the concrete.

The fraction of a second Ronin had to anticipate what was coming proved too little. His processors fired off a volley of commands.

Leap away.

Turn around.

Shield optics and torso.

Drop to the floor.

The blast hit him before any of those actions could be performed. His optics flickered to static, and his audio receptors measured one hundred and eighty decibels before cutting out. His dermal sensors registered the concussive wave, a rush of hot air, and shrapnel tearing his skin to ribbons. Pain blazed through him. The sheets and blankets around him caught fire, falling atop him as he stumbled backward. His right leg locked, nearly toppling him over.

He registered the intense heat both as a measurement of

temperature and as searing agony melting the electrodes in and beneath his skin.

The haul.

Ronin and Lara wouldn't be equipped to leave Cheyenne if he didn't bring back more salvage.

Lifting both hands, he fumbled through burning fabric and melting synthetic flesh to tear the straps of his rucksack and thrust it away. His optics were chaotic, and he didn't know if it was because of the fire or if they'd suffered serious damage. Grabbing whatever fabric he could, he wrenched off the burning blanket that had enwrapped him along with his coat, thrusting them away. He slid his foot back to put distance between himself and the flames.

His heel caught on something—probably his discarded pack. It was enough to disrupt his precarious balance. Ronin fell backwards. He was aware of more fabric enveloping him and the heavy *thunk* of his head hitting the concrete before most of his systems went into standby.

You're not going to have us, even after we're dead.

The father had set a trap.

An automatic diagnostics scan began, assessing the damage.

External temperature normalizing. Casing penetrated in thirteen locations. Severe damage to synthetic epidermis, fifty-two percent loss. Power cells stable, eighty-six point six-five percent charge remaining.

One by one, his systems rebooted.

Motor functions impaired by damage to right knee joint. Audio receptors functioning normally. Left optical input offline.

The joisted ceiling flickered into view through a smoky haze. Static crackled across Ronin's optic feed, and white bars briefly scrolled through the image. He brought a hand up. The charred cuff of his coat was still around his wrist, but most of the skin was gone. A triangular piece of shrapnel jutted from his forearm. He pinched it and worked it loose.

His system of dermal sensors was the last to come online. It began with a single, small surge. Within an instant, waves of sizzling electricity assailed him with unrelenting agony, locking his limbs. The damaged sensor network was causing an overload. He disabled the interface, cutting off all dermal sensation.

Flakes of ash slowly fluttered toward the floor, some still

glowing ember orange as they lit upon Ronin. He lifted his torso. The wad of bedding and his coat were still burning nearby, and flames were spreading across some of the hanging sheets and blankets. Before long, the whole building was likely to be consumed by fire.

He'd always acknowledged the strong possibility that his end would come like this—alone in a forgotten place, a ruin, with Ronin himself left as another broken artifact of a bygone era. The traders in the last town he'd been through would wonder where he'd gone, but that would be the last time anyone thought about him.

Dustwalkers came and went. Usually, they never came back again.

But there *was* someone who would think about him. There was someone waiting for him, worrying about him, someone depending upon him.

Lara.

He'd given his word. He *would* return to her. Not because he was fond of Cheyenne, not because his residence was important to him. Not because he needed the trade.

Ronin needed Lara.

He shrugged off the sheets that had wrapped around him and smothered the remaining flames on his body, rolled onto his side, and attempted to regain his feet. His right knee refused to bend, its motion inhibited by embedded shrapnel. He reached for the pliers on his belt, but they were gone, and a quick scan of his surroundings did not locate them.

Bending down, Ronin attempted to grasp the shrapnel jutting from his knee with his skinless fingers. Despite their strength, his grip kept slipping, and the metal was buried much too deep for him to even loosen it like this.

Smoke was gathering overhead, obscuring the joists, and flames were spreading through the dusty, ancient basement. He was running out of time to escape this place.

Reaching back, he wrapped the broken straps of his pack around his hand and dragged it closer. He transferred the surviving tools from his belt into his bag, dropped onto his belly, and crawled toward the stairs.

CHAPTER TWENTY-NINE

By midday, Lara was tempted to sneak out. There were at least twenty buildings on this street alone, all of them full of stuff just begging to be taken. Stuff that bots had no need for.

Why hadn't Ronin thought of that before he'd headed off into the Dust last night?

Because he's a scavenger, not a thief.

He was honest, but not in the way other bots had been. There was a thoughtfulness to Ronin's honesty. He put real consideration into keeping his word, often going well beyond his side of the bargain. Other bots would've taken advantage of the vague terms of her agreement with Ronin, providing her nothing but the barest necessities.

He'd given her so much more than that. So much more than she could've imagined. Lara wanted to give back to him, wanted to help him, wanted him to know he wasn't in this alone. She could pull her weight. And she only knew one way to do that right now…

Just because Ronin wouldn't steal didn't mean Lara couldn't.

If it weren't such a stupid thing to do, she would've crept out to poke around the other houses. She didn't think any of them were inhabited. Besides the bots she'd seen working in the park, the street had been deserted. Who would care if some metal appliances or pieces of plastic disappeared? As long as she wasn't spotted by any gearheads, she'd be fine.

Conjured visions of Tabitha's face, of her dull, lifeless eyes, flashed in Lara's mind, and she cast aside her thoughts of sneaking out.

Lara was trapped in this house until Ronin returned.

The day wore on slowly, just as the others had while he was gone. Her fingers were still sore from sewing Ronin's shirt, so she didn't even glance at the remaining cloth he'd given her, and there wasn't anything else to do downstairs. So she went up into the attic and passed the time by flipping through the pictures in the old books—even the ones full of naked women.

As she looked the long-dead women over, Lara compared herself to them. The similarities were slowly growing as time passed. Her skin had a healthier glow to it like theirs, and her body was a little fuller, her curves a little more pronounced. And after the pleasure she'd experienced with Ronin, she could even understand the sensual gleams in some of their eyes. These women were beautiful, they were sexy…and Ronin made Lara feel that way too.

If she walked into the human settlement now, even fully clothed, they'd know the difference. They would spurn her, call her a bot-banger, a whore, all while envy and lust blazed in their eyes. She didn't doubt that almost every single one of them would've made the same choice as her if given the chance.

As reluctant and resistant as she'd been to associate with a bot, and as frightening as it was to be in the bot district, especially alone, she didn't regret accepting Ronin's offer. Not even a little.

What does Ronin see when he looks at me?

Lara smiled, recalling the way he touched her—like he couldn't stop, couldn't get enough. He seemed fascinated by her skin. What did he feel when they came into contact? Did he ever compare her body to those of the too-perfect female synths?

It didn't really matter, in the end. He'd chosen Lara, had married her.

Setting Ronin's rifle aside, Lara rose onto her knees and gazed out the attic window, searching the road for Ronin's approaching figure.

Wishful thinking.

He'd only left last night, and said he'd be back in a few days. It wasn't likely that he'd return early this time. He'd been serious about earning enough credits for them to leave Cheyenne without having to look back.

For Ronin to be gone so soon after returning from his last trip, so soon after they'd deepened their relationship...

Lara pressed a fist to her aching chest. She hated this feeling. Hated the hollowness in her heart, the loneliness. Just as Ronin had said, it felt like part of her was missing. And that part was him. In such a short time, he'd become a vital piece of her.

Isn't it my fault he's gone?

She'd been the one to suggest they leave home. She'd begged him to take her into the Dust, to bring her anywhere but—

Wait. Home?

When had she started thinking of this place as home? It was a prison, a deathtrap, a cage within an enemy camp. And yet...she still saw it as home. As *their* home. She couldn't step out the front door without risking her life, but in here, with Ronin, things were good.

She sat down, leaning against a stack of bins, tilted her head back, and closed her eyes.

Ronin was the key. He treated her with considerable patience and kindness, regardless of how deserving of it she was at any given moment. And damn it, she missed him.

She...*loved* him.

There it was. The emotion given a name.

Lara groaned and lightly banged her head against the bins. "Fuuuuck."

She didn't know how it had happened, but she could admit it to herself now. In the short time she'd known Ronin, she'd fallen in love with him. A bot.

What would the other humans think?

She dwelled on the thought for a time, absently running her thumb along the smooth underside of her ring, before she settled on the true answer.

She didn't give a shit about what they'd say. Ronin was alive, he was her husband, and Lara loved him.

Warm sunshine cast a reddish glow through her eyelids. She opened them to gaze at the setting sun, which spread muted pinks through the haze beyond the park.

One day down, two or three more to go. Once Ronin returned, they'd sell all the scrap and leave, and she'd never have to worry about Warlord again. She wasn't so naïve as to think there'd be no danger out there, but she couldn't imagine anything worse than him.

She picked up the rifle and left the attic.

By the time she'd eaten and showered, it was fully dark outside.

After pulling on one of Ronin's shirts, Lara double-checked the downstairs locks and went up to Ronin's room. She slipped beneath the blankets he only used when he lay with her, placed the rifle beside herself, and curled up on her side with her head on his pillow.

Lara inhaled deeply. It was faint, but his steel and gunpowder scent lingered here.

Nights were the worst while Ronin was gone. When he was here, she slept soundly, sinking deep into her dreams, especially if he lay with her. But despite the security of this house, despite the comfortable bed and the warm blankets, sleep eluded her.

Why was it so difficult now?

Her mind wouldn't quiet, and every noise the house made, every subtle creak and groan, had her reaching for the rifle.

The answer was simple. Ronin made her feel safe, not this place. She trusted him enough to let her guard down. Even before they'd shared a bed, she'd been aware of his presence, and had known he'd come at the first sign of trouble. Just like her first night here, when she'd nearly broken her ass on the cold bathroom floor.

With a sigh, she flopped onto her back.

Come on, Lara. The sooner you go to sleep, the sooner tomorrow will come, and you'll be that much closer to seeing Ronin again.

She willed herself to relax, imagining Ronin's body pressed against hers.

Just as she was drifting off, a loud thump startled her awake.

Lara lay there, staring up at the ceiling and clutching the blanket in her hands as she strained to listen for more. Hot prickles coursed over her skin.

It's probably your imagination...or it was a dream. Like those dreams of falling to your death where you wake up before you hit the ground. Everything is fine. You're just anxious, you feel trapped, and—

An even louder bang downstairs had her scrambling from beneath the covers. She snatched up the rifle, slipped out of bed, and crept to the wall beside the open door, chest heaving and heart pounding.

Fuck, fuck, fuck.

Another thump, followed by a scrape, like something heavy was being dragged across the floor.

Swallowing hard, she adjusted her grip on the gun to hold it how Ronin had shown her. She wasn't going to wait for whatever the hell that was downstairs to catch her. Lara would fight. If she was going to die tonight, it wouldn't be cowering in the dark.

She slipped through the doorway and into the dark hallway, walking silently across the soft carpet. Pressing herself to the wall beside the stairs, she took a deep, stabilizing breath.

There was more noise below. A heavy step, and then that dragging sound. It repeated a few times, ending when the chair at the worktable creaked.

Whatever that thing was, it was sitting in Ronin's chair.

Lara peered around the corner at the stairway. Afraid of drawing attention at night while Ronin was gone, she'd kept the lights off and the curtains closed, leaving it terribly dark downstairs. Her heartbeat was the only sound to break the ensuing silence.

What am I doing?

She'd spent her whole life struggling to survive, but this was different. This wasn't at all the kind of fighting she was used to. Before coming here, she'd never even held a gun. Lara and Tabitha could never have afforded such a weapon.

No, the smartest thing to do, the best chance to make it through this alive, was to run and hide.

But going out a second-floor window risked breaking a leg, which was as good as death, and getting into the attic now would be too noisy. There were other places to hide in the house, but if that thing started looking for her...

Why the hell is it just sitting down here?

Lara's brow creased. What if it wasn't here for her? What if it was waiting for Ronin, waiting to...hurt him?

Fuck that.

Squeezing her eyes shut, she leaned her head back against the wall and drew in several quiet breaths despite every instinct telling her to run and hide.

I can do this. Ronin said this thing packs a punch, even against bots.

If she could at least hit the thing, she could slow it down enough to give herself a chance. To create an opening, to run out the front door and find somewhere else to hide along the route Ronin would walk.

But to hit the intruder, she'd have to *see* it. And once she flipped on the lights, she'd only have an instant to aim and fire.

You know exactly where the chair is, Lara. Exactly where to point the gun.

As long as the chair hadn't been moved.

Every step down the stairs was terrifying. Her lungs burned as she struggled to keep her breaths silent, and though the carpet padded her footfalls, she settled her weight with great care, knowing the softest creak would give her away.

When she neared the bottom, she focused on the shadows enveloping the chair and worktable, glancing aside only briefly to spot the barely visible light switch on the nearby wall.

I can do this. I can do this. I can—

Lara flicked the light on and leapt onto the floor. Swinging the rifle up, she planted the butt against her shoulder, pointed the barrel toward the figure in the chair, and squeezed the trigger.

The sound was booming thunder, deafening in the enclosed space, and the gun's unexpected kick nearly threw her off balance. But she didn't waste any time in turning and running for the door.

Something thudded and scraped behind her. A hand closed around her ankle, abruptly halting her movement. She fell hard, the impact knocking the rifle out of her hands. The weapon clattered to the floor a few feet away.

Screaming, she clawed at the floorboards and kicked wildly at the thing behind her, scrabbling for the gun. The thing caught her other ankle and dragged her back. Her oversized shirt bunched around her waist, baring her lower body.

The world spun as the bot flipped Lara onto her back. It swiftly crawled over her and pressed a hand on her chest to hold her down.

Lara's eyes flared as a rush of cold fear swept through her. The bot's clothing was blackened and tattered, and patches of scorched, melted skin clung to its exposed metal body. It smelled faintly like burning rubber. The metal face shifted into an expression that might've been readable if the thing had skin, but its teeth were locked in an unnerving skeletal grin behind the small plates that would've moved its lips.

The only bots she'd seen with metal exposed like this were gearheads.

Her fear escalated into terror. If the bot meant to kill her, that was one thing. It'd be over quick. But the way it was suspended over her, the way it had her pinned down...

Warlord's face flashed in her mind's eye.

No!

Her throat burned with the scream that tore through it.

"Lara," the bot said.

She thrashed beneath the inhuman force holding her captive, kicking and slapping, ignoring her pain as she struck its solid body.

"Lara," the bot said again, its voice penetrating her terror.

She froze. The bot sounded just like Ronin.

Panting, she looked up into its face. Its left eye was damaged, with a jagged, disc-shaped piece of metal lodged in the socket. The right was a familiar shade of vivid green.

"Ronin?" she rasped.

"Yes, it's me."

"I thought you were a fucking gearhead!" Her terror subsided, shifting into horror as realization hit her. "Oh my God! What happened to you? You're...you're..."

She lifted her hands toward his face. "Oh God, does it hurt?"

He pulled back before she could touch him. "Don't feel much of anything, right now."

Lara placed her hands on his cheeks. His metal was warm beneath her palms. When he reached up to brush her arms aside, she stopped him with a firm but heartbroken, "Don't."

"I see the fear in your eyes, Lara. You don't have to look at this."

Her stinging eyes blurred with welling tears. "I thought you were one of *them*. If I had known it was you... I'd never be afraid of you, Ronin."

Another realization struck her, this one like a punch to the gut. "Oh shit, did I shoot you?"

"You missed." His lip-plates shifted into what might've been a smile. "We'll have to talk about that sometime. You're a terrible shot."

"Not like I ever shot a gun before." Carefully, she brushed her thumb along the disc protruding from his eye; it didn't budge. Her lower lip quivered as her tears spilled from the corners of her eyes. "God, you're a mess. What happened to you?"

"A trap." He cupped her cheek, wiping the moisture from her skin with a metal finger. "Why are you crying?"

"Look at you." Her eyes dipped, taking in his ravaged chest, the blackened metal of his arms, the ruined skin, the jagged chunks of shrapnel sticking out of him.

His undamaged eyebrow plate fell lower, and he seemed to frown. Gently, he guided her hands away from his face and moved off her. With his right leg dragging, he crawled to the staircase, where he used the railing to pull himself onto his feet.

Lara scrambled onto her feet and hurried over to him. "Let me help."

"No. I'll manage."

Helplessness left a sour taste in her mouth. "Damn it, Ronin. Let me at least get that junk out of your leg."

"Made it eighteen miles with that junk in my leg. Can make it a little farther."

"Why do you have to be so stubborn?" Wiping her eyes, she stepped past him and crouched on the steps, putting her at his eye level. "Let me help you."

"I'm just being what I am."

"What are you talking about?"

Ronin stood up, casting his scorched arms to either side. "Look at me!"

Lara flinched, and her eyes searched his face. "Ronin…"

"There's no pretending I ever was, or will be, human. I'm just a reminder of everything you hate."

She stared at him in disbelief. Why was he acting like this? What had she said to upset him, to hurt him? "I don't hate you. And of course you're not human. That's…pretty overrated, anyway. You're Ronin."

"I saw your expression, Lara. You can't stand to look at me, and I can't blame you for that."

"Is that what you think this is about? God, Ronin, I was horrified *for* you!"

"What reason would you have to be horrified for me?"

Did he truly think she was disgusted by him?

More tears ran down her cheeks. "I know you call it deactivation instead of death, but…you look like you came pretty damn close." Her heart constricted at the thought, and she sniffled. "You might be tougher than me, but you can still get blown up."

"This damage is largely superficial. I've…endured worse." He dropped his gaze, expression neutral. "This could have been worse."

"That doesn't make it better, Ronin."

"You don't need to shed tears for me. I'm here. I told you I'd come back, and here I stand."

"But you might not have come back at all," she said angrily, lunging at him and wrapping her arms around his torso. He staggered, but she held tight. Ignoring the smell, she focused on his solidness, his heat, pressing her face to his chest and squeezing her eyes shut.

Ronin's here. He's alive.

CHAPTER THIRTY

With most of his skin gone, Ronin's ability to register touch was limited to basic pressure and temperature readings, both providing only estimated measurements. Despite that, Lara's embrace felt warm and strong. It wasn't a gesture of fear or uncertainty, but one of relief. She hugged him like she might've never had another chance to, like she wasn't ever going to let him go, and he knew she'd been right.

He might not have returned.

How could he have been so blind to what he put her through whenever he left her alone?

"Doesn't do us any good to dwell on what might've been," he said, slipping his arms around her with great care. Without the more precise sensors in his skin, there was too great a chance for error. A slight overapplication of strength could crush her bones. "This is what happened, and it's all we have."

"You owe me an apology."

"I'm sorry I left."

"No." She tipped her head back and looked up at him with those bright, emotion-filled blue eyes. "For thinking it matters to me what you look like."

Her words swirled through his processors, settling deep in his memory bank as he contemplated their meaning. His appearance did matter to her, but not in the way he'd assumed. She didn't care if he was a bot or a human, only that he was…*himself*. She cared about his wellbeing.

"Which is like a mess right now, correct?" he said, unable to articulate his more complex thoughts.

"That's putting it mildly." She chuckled, though the worry lingered in her gaze. "You kinda look like shit, Ronin."

"Noted," he replied, mouth plates ticking up on one side. "I'm sorry, Lara. I misjudged you. Are you going to apologize to me, now?"

"I have nothing to say sorry for." When he opened his mouth to reply, she cut him off. "I missed. And you could've just called my name when you came in and avoided all of that, instead of scaring the shit outta me."

"Shit. Quite a versatile word…" He lightly touched his forehead to hers. "I *am* sorry, Lara Brooks. This was not my intention."

"I know." She drew back and looked him over, that hint of humor vanishing from her expression. "What can I do to help?"

"The clinic is the only facility that can repair this damage, but you can help remove some of the shrapnel and damaged skin. At least then we can trade some of it to the scrapper and make a bit of profit from this."

She scrunched her nose. "That's morbid."

"I am more than the sum of my parts."

Lara tilted her head.

Ronin couldn't explain the thoughts behind his words, wasn't sure of their origins, so he rerouted back to the matter at hand. "It's practical. The technicians at the clinic are likely to keep any such materials they remove for reuse, without offering compensation."

He released his embrace and put a hand on the staircase railing, stabilizing himself. With his single optic, he looked up to the second floor. He'd have to handle this like he had the stairs in that basement—slowly, one step at a time.

"I moved my tools into my pack. Bring them upstairs, and get the spare pliers out of the chest. I'll meet you there."

"Okay," she said, and immediately went to retrieve his pack.

Ronin waited for her to go up before beginning his journey. The upward climb was slow, but rhythmic. The creak of the banister, the groan of a step, the thump of his damaged leg, over and over, until he finally reached the top one minute and twenty-two seconds later.

He kept his head angled down as he walked toward his bedroom, staring at the metal planes of his chest and abdomen, at his charred clothing and melted skin. Ronin currently bore little resemblance to a human, but Lara had thrown her arms around him and held him. She wouldn't have done the same that first night he'd brought her here.

They'd both changed so much in such a short time.

Lara had the tools spread out on the storage chest when he entered the room. Some of them were smudged with soot or singed, their grips warped from the heat.

Standing next to the bed, she gestured toward it. "Lie down and tell me what to do."

Despite his best efforts, his right leg dragged as he moved to the bed. The sheet was rumpled, the blankets tossed aside.

Was she sleeping here when I came home?

Ronin shifted the focus of his right optic to Lara. It was only then that he realized she was wearing one of his shirts instead of the clothing he'd purchased for her. Though it was smeared with soot from their embrace, he couldn't ignore the allure of seeing it on her. The hem hung to her mid-thighs, leaving those long, tantalizing legs on display, and if it were to be drawn up just a little bit higher...

No. This is not the time for such thoughts. Not the time for such...temptations.

The springs creaked as he sat, and he recalled the many sounds the bed had made during more pleasant activities. He raised his left leg, unlaced his boot, and removed it, dropping it to the floor before swinging that leg onto the bed. His right leg proved somewhat more problematic. Lara allowed him only a moment's struggle before she took off his other boot. Grasping his ankle, she helped him move his damaged leg onto the bed.

"Lie back." She pressed her palms to his chest and guided him down onto the mattress.

"You'll need to pull out the shrapnel. Use the pliers."

Lara went to the chest, retrieved the pliers, and returned to him. Catching her lower lip between her teeth, she looked over Ronin.

Without a word, she climbed atop him, swinging a leg over his hips to straddle his abdomen with her back facing him. The hem of her shirt slid up her thighs. Her bare skin was warm against his casing.

She looked over her shoulder. "So…just pull them out? It won't hurt you, right? Won't do any more damage?"

"I'll be fine. Just take out whatever you can."

The heat of her ass and legs pulsed through his pants. He knew she wasn't wearing anything beneath the shirt, and with her position…

He focused his attention on the points of damage. This wasn't a sexual act. She was simply assisting in the first step of repairing his casing.

"Okay, I can do this," she muttered as she faced forward, leaned down, and tore his pants open around his knee. There was no pain when she clamped the pliers on the shrapnel, only pressure and the sound of metal scraping metal when she wiggled the tool and tugged.

"It's in there good." She shifted atop him. "But I think I can get it."

If only he could feel her properly…

Lara leaned back, and Ronin's internal sensors registered the force she exerted on the shard in his knee. Electric sparked up his leg.

The pliers' teeth snapped together suddenly, and Lara jerked back. He placed his hands on her sides to steady her, but her torso fell atop his, her hair covering his face. His olfactory sensors detected its fresh, clean scent. He lamented that his bare face plates weren't sensitive enough to feel the delicate brush of the strands.

At least he could feel her weight and the pleasurable warmth she emitted.

"I almost had it," Lara said.

He dropped his hands to her hips and helped her sit up. She grasped the shrapnel with the pliers again, but Ronin's focus moved to her bare legs, to her thighs squeezing his hips. He was her anchor. Given the situation, it seemed an odd place for his thoughts to roam.

Why was the play of her leg muscles so fascinating, so alluring? Why did her touch mute the concerns that should've been the foremost of his processes? He should've gone directly to the clinic when he'd reached Cheyenne, should've had himself repaired before returning to her.

He should have spared Lara all this worry.

Thoughts of her had carried him back across the uneven land-scape. His worry had not been for himself or the damage he'd sustained, but for her. He'd needed to see her.

How would she have reacted to my deactivation?

It was a foolish thought-chain to pursue. If he were to have met his demise in the Dust, the chances of her ever learning about it were extremely small. But he couldn't stop himself from wondering what she would've done without him. She'd survived on her own before they met, and he knew she would've carried on, knew she would've used her resourcefulness to escape the bot district.

But Ronin didn't want Lara to have to survive on her own. He wanted her safe. He wanted her…happy.

Metal groaned as Lara pulled on the shrapnel. Her legs tightened around him. "Almost…"

Ronin exerted gradual pressure opposite hers, pushing his leg down while she tugged upward. She leaned back once more, her hair draping over his blackened chest-casing, and released a guttural growl from her chest.

With a metallic pang, she fell backward again.

"Got the bastard!" She straightened and raised the pliers, showing Ronin the jagged, deformed chunk of metal gripped between the teeth.

Lara slid off him to kneel on the bed as he sat up. He drew his right foot toward his rear, slowly bending his knee. Internally, the actuator whined and vibrated, giving diminished returns for the power it drew, but it was a significant improvement over the joint being locked.

"Thank you," he said, turning his undamaged optic to Lara.

"We ain't done yet." She tucked a wild mass of hair behind her ear, extended her hand, and gently touched a finger to a piece of shrapnel embedded in his chest casing. "What happened, anyway? Your upper half is burned and torn to shreds, but your bottom half looks mostly fine."

"Found an old house out there. There were blankets and sheets hung up all over the basement."

She wrenched one of the pieces from his chest. His sensors registered a tiny flare of pain, a ghostly echo of what he'd suffered in that basement. It wasn't nearly as haunting as the corpses.

"Keep talking," she said, moving the pliers to the next bit.

"By sheer chance, I missed the tripwire when I worked my way to the back. There was a workbench there. Picked up the reloading press and some cans—"

Lara's hand jerked back, pulling another shard free. She dropped it over the side of the bed and kept going.

"—and decided it was time to head back," he continued. "I'd already searched the other rooms. As I pushed through the hangings, something caught on my leg. Heard the device arm, but I wasn't fast enough. The man who lived there rigged up an explosive, probably his final line of defense, and I triggered it."

She frowned as she rocked the pliers to loosen a larger chunk of shrapnel. "There was a man there?"

"A man and his family. Think they lived there during the Blackout. Probably been dead at least as long as I've been awake."

After what had happened to her sister, Ronin couldn't bring himself to tell her the details of that family's end. Of what that man had done.

"Seems like a long time for a trap to stay active," she said.

"Guess you could say I had shit luck on that one. I'm pretty sure the dust down there sparked the fire. My coat went up immediately, and I stumbled into sheets that were already burning. Got tangled up in it. Tore all that off, but it wasn't until I tripped over my pack and fell into more sheets that the fire was snuffed out." He glanced down at his arms and brushed the last bits of his ruined coat's sleeves onto the floor.

Lara frowned, resting a hand on his chest over where a human's heart would be. "I'm glad it wasn't worse."

"So am I. Wouldn't have complained if it had been a little less intense though."

Her gaze rose to his damaged eye, and a crease formed between her brows. "Do you...want me to try to get that one out?"

"No. The risk of further damage to my optical system is too high."

"What else can I do, then?"

Ronin hesitated. She'd called it morbid, but it was a necessity, and it *would* earn a little credit in the market. "Need to get the damaged skin off. I had to disable the entire interface due to the shorted sensors."

Her eyes widened, falling to his abdomen, where most of the blackened, melted skin clung.

CHAPTER THIRTY-ONE

Lara stared at Ronin's ruined flesh. Pulling the pieces of metal out of his casing had been like plucking out splinters, which she'd done more times than she could count for herself and Tabitha. But this…

This was *skin*! Even if it wasn't living flesh, it was a part of Ronin…and he wanted her to cut it off.

She bit her lower lip, looking up to meet his steady, one-eyed gaze. "Does it hurt?"

"No. Not anymore." He turned and swung his legs over the side of the bed. "I can take care of it."

She pressed her hand more firmly against his chest, and he froze. It was eerie how suddenly and completely his movement halted.

"I'll do it, Ronin. Just…tell me what I need to do." Her hand fell away from him.

Slowly, he turned his head, eye dipping to follow her hand. "You've done enough already."

"Damn it, Ronin!" She sprung off the bed and strode to the chest. "I said I'll do it. It's the least I can do after everything you've done for me."

Stubborn robot.

Lara looked over the array of tools. Unsure of which she needed, she collected several of them and spread them on the bed. "I'll get your back first."

He was quiet for a long while, keeping his lip-plates pressed together. Just as she began to wonder if he had shut down, he twisted and picked up the knife she'd placed down.

He deftly spun the knife on his palm, holding the grip toward her. "Use this to cut around my waist. Four or five centimeters below the scorch marks."

"Four or five centi-whats?"

"Sorry. An inch or two."

"Okay." She wrapped her fingers around the handle. The knife was impossibly heavy.

Ronin stood and turned away, hooking his thumbs on the waist of his pants to tug them down below the burn marks. While his chest had been devastated, The damage on his back was mainly around his shoulders and sides.

Sitting on the edge of the bed, Lara raised the knife, stopping the blade right before it touched him. Her stomach churned. She'd never cut anyone, apart from the accident with Tabitha. Now she was about to slice into the only other person she cared about.

He said it doesn't hurt.

That didn't change the fact Lara was about to cut him.

I need to trust him.

Inhaling deeply, she pressed the blade to his skin. The pressure it took to finally break through nearly killed her nerve, but she pushed on.

For him.

It was an agonizing process. The give of his skin was contrasted by the solid, often uneven metal beneath, and she wasn't sure if she should've been more concerned about damaging his casing or the knife. She cut up from his hips to his armpits and then, wishing she could look away, worked her fingers beneath his skin. It peeled off with surprising ease, revealing intricate metal plates beneath.

She shuddered as some of the burned portions flaked apart in her fingers, but she continued her work. After placing the strips of skin on the floor, she shifted her attention to his arms, picking away scorched shreds of skin and cloth. Ronin remained silent throughout.

Lara glanced up at his face when she moved to his front. His eye was focused straight ahead. Had he withdrawn from her again?

She sliced the flesh over the waist of his pants, gently peeling and scraping away everything above the cut. The pile on the floor grew. Unsure of what her reaction to the sight would be, she made sure not to look down.

When she was finally done, she stepped back and checked Ronin over. Below the waist, he was human. The rest of him was something else entirely.

His metal casing mimicked human muscles—the bulges of powerful shoulders and biceps, ridges on his torso like pecs and abs. None of the lines were quite the same without skin laid over them, but his parts came together with an elegance she'd never seen.

"Done?" he asked, jarring Lara from her thoughts.

"I think so."

"No more overload."

"You turned it back on already?"

"Doesn't take long."

She trailed her fingers along the edge of skin at his hip. "You feel this?"

A moment's hesitation. "Yes."

"Does it hurt?"

"No." Had his voice softened?

"Good." Lara lowered her hand. "Anything else?"

Ronin shook his head. "I'm going to the clinic for repairs. You should get some sleep."

"Wait." She gathered the tools from the bed. "Stay till morning. It's only a few hours, and I can scrub the scorch marks from your casing."

"It will be more bearable for you if I—"

"Get on the fucking bed and lie down." She fixed him with a stern look before dumping the tools on the chest and stalking to the bathroom.

Why was it so difficult for him to get it through his thick metal skull? It didn't *matter*.

So what if he was made of metal and powered by electric cells instead of food and water? He had a mind, had his own thoughts, opinions, and desires. When he was covered in skin, anyone would've had a hard time guessing he was a bot. Only his metal hands had given Ronin away when Lara first met him.

She took a bucket from the little storage closet and filled it with hot water from the tub. Grabbing a handcloth, she carried the bucket into the bedroom.

Ronin lay upon the bed as she had commanded.

Placing the bucket on the nightstand, she climbed onto the bed and straddled his waist. He stared up at her, but she refused to meet his gaze as she dunked the cloth in the water, wrung out the excess, and scrubbed the soot from his brow.

Even after all they'd shared, he still thought she was disgusted by him?

She ran the cloth down his cheeks and nose, along his jawline, and over his lip-plates, pressing a little more firmly with each passing moment. When she rinsed the cloth, the water turned black. She squeezed the moisture out with enough force to make her hands ache.

Clenching her jaw, she washed his neck and chest.

"Why?" he asked.

She looked into his eye, her eyebrows falling. He still had to ask that? "What do you fucking mean, why?" The bed creaked as she scrubbed his torso, careful to avoid the holes where the shrapnel had penetrated.

"I'm a bot."

Throwing the cloth aside, Lara hit him. Her fist connected with one of his chest plates, and she hissed, knuckles throbbing.

Ronin gently took her hand in his and turned it to see the drop of blood welling on her middle knuckle. His lip-plates drooped.

"Because of this!" She pulled her hand from his, leaned forward, and cradled his face. "Because you care, Ronin. You care for me, and I wouldn't have waited here if I didn't care for you, too."

"After all the things my kind has done to you…to all humans…"

"You aren't your kind, Ronin." Sitting back on his thighs, Lara slid her hands down to the center of his chest. "You're unique. I'm almost convinced you have a heart in there. But you prove feelings don't come from there, anyway. I've known plenty of people who have hearts and don't feel anything half as strongly as you do."

He placed his hands over hers. "I feel."

"So do I. For you." She slipped one hand free and trailed it lower, over the ridges of his abdomen. "Whether you're metal"—her fingertips teased the edges of his skin at his pelvis—"or flesh."

She dropped her gaze. His cock was swelling in his pants. It was amazing to her how similar that part of his anatomy was to a human's, how it responded so naturally to her touch.

Taking hold of the hem of her shirt, she drew it up and over her head, tossing it aside. Cool air touched her bare skin, and she caught the look of desire in Ronin's eye as he looked upon her naked body.

She grasped the top button of his pants, but he quickly stopped her with his hand.

There was hesitance in his expression. Insecurity. But he said nothing, and he didn't resist when she moved his arm aside.

"Let me." Unfastening his pants, she drew them down. His cock sprang free, thick and long. She wrapped her fingers around it. "Do you feel this?"

Ronin's lip plates parted, and his brow fell. He nodded and ran his warm, solid metal palms over her knees.

Without breaking eye contact, she stroked her fist along his length, and he hardened further within the cage of her fingers. That deep ache blossomed low in her belly. It was different than the ache in her heart—it was needy, pulsing, hungry. But the cure for both was the same.

Ronin. He could fill that space perfectly, could soothe all her pain and discomfort, ease her sorrow. And she would do the same for him.

If he wouldn't listen to her, if he *couldn't*, she would show him.

They belonged to each other. That was all that mattered. It wasn't about their parts, it was about what they chose to do with the lives they had. How they chose to live...how they chose to love. And even in his darkest moments, even when he most doubted himself, she would be here for him. That was her choice. That was what she wanted.

Him.

Lara rose on her knees, positioning herself over him, and guided the head of his cock to her center. Slowly, she lowered herself, taking him into her body inch by delicious inch, loving the way he stretched her and filled that gnawing ache.

His hands moved to her ass, fingers digging into her flesh. "Lara..."

"Do you feel this?" she repeated breathlessly, leaning forward to press her palms to the warm plates of his chest. Her hair cascaded around her head.

"I feel *you*." Ronin's voice was gravelly and whisper soft.

His touch and the huskiness of his words coaxed moisture from her, easing his entry as she lifted and dropped her hips, taking his cock deeper. Lara pressed her fingertips against his chest. The slide of his shaft sent ripples of pleasure through her that lashed her core with sweet, tantalizing heat, feeding the flames there. That fire licked at her every nerve, stoking her pleasure higher and higher.

She resisted the urge to close her eyes and kept her gaze locked with his, dipping her head until their lips were a breath apart. "Do you really feel me?"

Ronin cupped the nape of her neck. "All of you, Lara."

"Do you feel how hot I am? How wet I am, for you?"

"I do" he said, moving his pelvis in time with hers.

"I see this. I see you." She brushed her lips over his. "And I want you."

Slipping his fingers into her hair, he drew her down into a full kiss, claiming her mouth. His lip-plates were solid, parting when his tongue sought entry to her mouth. She opened to him. His tongue was dry, with a slight, bumpy texture, and she recalled the feel of it on her pussy as she slid hers against it.

That spark of memory heightened her pleasure and made her core clench around his shaft. But she was no longer in control of this moment. Ronin had taken over and was thrusting furiously inside her, stroking that place beyond her reach.

Lara moaned against his mouth, overcome by the sensations sweeping through her. She spread her thighs wider, wanting more of him, needing him deeper, deeper, deeper. Her skin tingled. She felt like she was floating, and only Ronin's touch grounded her, only his solidness kept her from drifting away.

Moving her hands to the bedding, she gripped the sheets.

"Ronin," she rasped, craving the bliss only he could deliver.

Panting, she leaned her head on his shoulder and closed her eyes. Her hard nipples grazed his chest, the friction adding to the pressure building in her core.

He clutched her ass, his thrusts growing more powerful as he lifted and pulled her down on him, tilting her hips just right. Every stroke of his cock from this angle brushed her clit and sent shockwaves of ecstasy through her, each stronger than the last, until they thoroughly consumed her.

Lara's body locked up, and she cried out as rapture cleaved through her. She was suspended in that moment of pleasure, floating in darkness. The world ceased to exist. There was only bliss.

When she came back into herself, she was lost on the torrent of ecstasy, her throaty, frantic cries unrelenting as her pussy contracted around Ronin's cock.

"Lara…" he rasped.

Yanking her down until she was fully seated, Ronin embedded his shaft deep. His fingertips were white hot as they dug into her skin. He stiffened beneath her, his cock vibrating against her inner walls. The sensations were wholly visceral and careered her into another orgasm.

"Ronin!" she keened, grinding her clit against him, body quivering. For a moment, everything within her fragmented.

Once the maelstrom of pleasure waned, Lara lay limp upon Ronin's chest, panting against his neck. His arms were around her, with one hand at the small of her back, fingers brushing back and forth along the base of her spine, and the other soothingly stroking her upper back. His shaft, still hard and hot, remained deep within her.

They remained like that for a time, simply holding one another, until her breathing and her heart calmed.

When she finally opened her eyes, her gaze caught upon the holes in his damaged chest. Her heart squeezed. She hated that he'd suffered, and she knew, had he been human, he likely wouldn't have survived what had happened.

Tears stung her eyes as she lightly ran her finger over one of the punctures, from the smooth metal to the jagged and back again.

He combed his fingers through her hair. "I don't know what I am anymore, and I don't think I care, as long as I have you."

"I love you." The words spilled out, unbidden, but they sounded right. They felt right, deep in her heart.

Lara tilted her head back and peered up at him. "I never thought I'd say that to anyone but Tabitha, but it's true." She curled her palm along his jawline and guided his face toward hers. "I don't know when it happened. I think, maybe, it's when I said you weren't human."

"You fell in love with me when you insulted me?" he asked, voice wavering.

Lara smirked. "Yeah. Kinda funny when you think about it, huh?"

His lips shifted, the plates beneath his cheeks moving up and back. A smile. "You do have an infuriating-but-charming air about you."

Chuckling, she lifted her head to look down at him, sweeping her hair out of her face. "I was attracted to you long before that, but I fought it like hell."

"I was attracted to you from the first moment I saw you, Lara Brooks."

Her smile faded. "You wanted me for more than dancing, didn't you?"

"I don't know." He caressed her cheek. "Yes? It wasn't a logical decision, just…pure desire. I didn't understand what I felt then, and I still don't understand it now."

"Why me? Why not a different human? Someone easier to get along with, maybe?"

"Everyone else moves the same way, whether metal or flesh and bone. Lifelessly. Dull-eyed." His hand trailed up her spine. "You're the first person I've seen who moves like you're *alive*, with a fire inside you."

"I didn't feel it at the time."

They'd met during one of the lowest points of her life. If he hadn't come after she'd lost the ring, would her despair have won out?

"But you did. You always do. The pain and sadness…it's part of living, isn't it? Being numb to those emotions is what makes us feel lifeless."

"You're just as alive as I am, Ronin."

"Because of you."

She grinned. "I might bring it out in you, a little."

"You bring something out in me, certainly."

"Hmm." Lara swiveled her hips, moaning at the feel of his cock buried inside her. "I do, for sure. Out of you, and into me."

Banding an arm around her, he held her tight against him. "I would say I've come to like humans, but it may only be you."

She scoffed and slapped his shoulder. "Better be only me."

Ronin rose, flipping her onto her back without withdrawing from her. Lara shrieked with laughter as he propped himself up on his elbows. She wrapped her legs around his waist, drawing herself snugly against him. His undamaged eye met hers.

"There is only you," he said with sincerity that pierced right into her heart.

"Ronin…"

He pressed his metal lips to hers, and she and Ronin moved as one, her hands exploring the altered landscape of his body. Only sensation remained; there was no room for words, no need.

CHAPTER THIRTY-TWO

Ronin lay with Lara until dawn before extracting himself from her side and leaving the bed. Despite his care, the springs and frame creaked with his movements.

She stirred, lashes lifting, and peered at him with groggy eyes. Her fingers closed gently around his forearm. "Ronin?"

"Need to go to the clinic," he said. "The sooner I'm repaired, the sooner we can leave."

"Okay." Her eyelids fluttered shut. "I'll be…waiting."

Her grip, already weak, slackened, and her hand slipped off his arm. Faint tingles coursed along his casing. He couldn't be sure if he'd truly felt her delicate touch or if the sensation was a simulation of what his destroyed sensors might've detected. Gradually, her breathing evened out. Even now, knowing how important it was to repair the damage he'd sustained, it was difficult to leave her.

Leaning down, he pulled on his boots, lacing them loosely. They'd be off again soon enough. He stood, easing his weight onto his right leg to test the strength of his knee as he ran diagnostics.

Partial mobility restored. Actuator operating at 32% functionality, with 140% of normal power draw. Power leak probable.

Though his pants were also damaged, he pulled them up and fastened them. His steps were slow as he crossed the room to the closet. Each time he shifted his weight onto his right leg, his knee buckled, but the joint locks initiated before it could collapse. Not ideal, but he didn't have far to go. Just another one point six kilometers.

Within the closet, he selected a clean pair of pants and found the shirt Lara had made for him, folding both articles of clothing together. He would determine if his current pants were salvageable after he was repaired.

Tucking the bundle under his arm, he walked back into the bedroom, shifting his optic to the handgun on the chest. Even within the bot district, he never traveled unarmed. But what good would it do him?

Limping to the bedside, he stared down at Lara. Her breathing was soft, her body relaxed, her expression untroubled. She'd spoken of hearts and love, and what did he know about either? Humans often used the former term figuratively, and the latter...

I love you.

He replayed her words again and again.

Careful not to lean on his damaged leg, he bent forward and drew the blanket over Lara's body. She slid her arms up, taking hold of the covering, and wrapped it around herself snugly without opening her eyes. A long, satisfied sigh escaped her.

Love.

Despite his caution, he descended the steps in a third of the time it had taken to mount them the night before. He walked straight to the door, not allowing himself to hesitate, refusing to succumb to the desire to go look at her again, to contemplate the serenity on her face and listen to the soothing sound of her breathing.

His internal clock had accounted for every year, every day, every hour, minute, and microsecond since his reactivation. It was one of his core processes, albeit a relatively simple one, as natural to him as breathing was to a human. Without fail, every second had been exactly as long as those preceding and following it.

Until Lara. She had changed everything.

Every minute of his journey back to Cheyenne had felt longer than a year of his life before. Each step had been an unfathomable distance for his damaged stride. The possibility of never seeing Lara again had altered his perception of...everything.

Stepping outside, he closed and locked the door behind him.

The merest hint of dawn left the sky a dark, smudgy gray. He walked north toward Warlord's pieced-together wall.

Love.

He understood the word, at its most basic level. It was a deep, affectionate attachment to someone or something. How could a seemingly simple term carry so much weight, so much depth?

To his left, leaves rustled in the wind, a reminder that life always found a way, even if it needed help from time to time.

Curiosity had taken root in him that first night, and it had sprouted into fascination. Now, it was a tree tall enough to put all others in its shade. Lara was part of his existence. Every simulation he ran regarding his future invariably included her, and he dismissed any that didn't, because he knew he could never let her go.

Despite her loathing in the beginning, Lara had come to see him not as a casing housing a collection of parts, not as a bot, but as Ronin. She saw *him.* The change in her perspective was clear, and it had been highlighted by how fiercely she'd struggled against it.

She'd told him she loved him. That was no small admission, and she hadn't made it carelessly. They both knew words could be cheap, even meaningless, that they could be spoken without conviction, uttered with duplicity, or hurled with cruelty. But she had proven her words through her actions.

This was all too new to him, too difficult to sort out in a mind operating on logic and mathematics, but...he thought he loved her too.

Ronin turned the corner and proceeded east, parallel to the wall. The man who'd written the attic journal had undoubtedly walked this same road years ago. The writer had loved his family, had been loved by them, and had lived before Warlord tore his already damaged world apart.

Despite the powerful storms, lack of resources, and sharp contrasts between hot and cold, the Dust wasn't the true danger of this world. It was a force of nature, incapable of malice.

The true danger, the true tragedy, was wrought by the Creators' children, who destroyed each other without thought.

People like Warlord were what Lara needed to be protected from.

Amidst all this indifference, death, and devastation, had Ronin really found love?

Why else would he be so ready and willing to give up everything he'd known for decades? Why else would he be so eager to embrace change? He was about to cast logic aside in pursuit of an emotion he should never have experienced.

The clinic was quiet as he turned off the main street and approached it. The gearheads on guard outside stared at him, making no comment as he passed. Only the glass entry doors were illuminated. Inside, the place was as white and sterile as ever, so unchanged that when Mercy looked up at him from her usual spot at the front desk he wondered if he'd lapsed into a full-sensory memory. His stride was suddenly weightless, and everything moved too slowly.

Mercy's lips parted, but she didn't smile, didn't greet him. Following her gaze, he glanced down at his ruined torso.

"Just need some reskinning," he said.

She didn't seem to appreciate the humor.

CHAPTER THIRTY-THREE

Ronin watched as the skin on his right leg was cut and peeled away. The machine's larger arms lowered, and numerous attachments went to work. Within a minute, everything from his knee down had been detached. He didn't shut down the sensors in the area. The pain was intense, but fleeting, a brief flicker of life. He knew such sensations were both more intense and longer lasting for humans.

After his leg was repaired and reattached, the machine moved upward, making minor repairs to his damaged internals and sealing the holes in his casing, buffing and polishing the once damaged areas. Finally, it loomed over his head, its tiny arms extracting the shrapnel embedded in his left optic. Before the final repairs began, Ronin obeyed the attendant's directions and deactivated his optical input.

He occupied himself by sifting through his memory. He replayed Lara's dance, reviewed their conversations and their arguments, lamented the amount of time he'd spent apart from her. Echoes of what he'd experienced during their couplings skittered across his electrodes.

More than anything else, he replayed her confession of love.

The attendant directed Ronin to the epidermal synthesizer once his optics were online. He continued his reveries inside the chamber.

He hadn't told Lara he loved her. He hadn't known how to, though the words were so simple; they would've taken less than one second to say. She'd given no indication that she had been bothered by it, but that didn't make it all right.

When the dermal repairs were completed, Ronin dressed himself. The shirt Lara had made was more comfortable against his skin than anything had ever been, apart from Lara herself. He headed for the exit after thanking the attendant.

He'd been away from home for twelve hours and thirty-five minutes, and he wanted nothing more than to be back with Lara. To tell her that he loved her too.

An itch pulsed across his cheek. He ignored it.

"Good to see you fully repaired," Mercy said pleasantly when he reached the front desk.

Ronin glanced at her and halted abruptly. Her smile was gone, belying her tone.

"What's wrong?" he asked.

"Nothing." Her optics flicked to the entry doors. "It's just that… he came looking for you while you were in there."

"He want me to go see him?"

"No." She dropped her gaze, and her brows twitched down briefly. "He's been waiting outside for the last three hours and forty-two minutes."

Ronin turned his head toward the doors. Between the contrasting lighting and the reflections on the glass, the details were blurry, but he counted five distinct figures standing outside about ten meters from the entrance.

There were undoubtedly other exits from the building, but Ronin had only been in the lobby and the repair room, so he dismissed the possibility of an alternate route. Such an escape would only lead Warlord to Ronin's residence, and he didn't want that scar-faced tyrant anywhere near Lara.

He walked toward the exit, ceasing his processors' attempted speculations. Warlord's whims seemed as difficult to predict as Lara's. The doors whirred open, their sound indicating an inevitable motor failure in the near future.

If the group of bots had been conversing, they fell silent when Ronin stepped outside. They all looked at him as he approached.

Warlord stood at the center of the group, unassumingly average in height, build, and features compared to his companions save for the sutured gash on his cheek. Even though the gearheads displayed far more bare metal, Warlord's damage was somehow more imposing.

Ronin stopped several feet away.

Should've brought the pistol.

A single round in Warlord's optic could have been enough to short his system entirely.

"Dustwalker. Looking better than you did when you came in last night," Warlord said, his expression neutral.

"Feeling it, too." Ronin met the gazes of each of the gearheads before settling his focus on Warlord again. "Just here to make sure I'm adequately repaired?"

"You push boundaries, dustwalker. Maybe that's good out there. Maybe that's why you're so productive. But we've been over this already."

"I didn't intend to come back in after dark, but I wasn't exactly in any condition to race the sun yesterday."

"I've dealt with your type. I understand you. I told you that my rules are to be obeyed, didn't I? I don't think my memory's been corrupted in the last month. Maybe you can refresh me, so we can be sure."

"Your bots let me through without a word. They—"

"You know that's not what this is about!" Warlord growled, jabbing a finger at Ronin and stepping forward. "You're smarter than that, dustwalker. At least you think you are."

Ronin's processors blazed through data, searching every moment he'd spent in Cheyenne. There weren't many conversations with Warlord to review, but there'd been many rules, rarely presented with clarity.

Warlord pursed his lips and strode forward, slowly circling Ronin. "Did you think we wouldn't notice, Ronin?"

Ronin forced himself to remain in place. "Notice what?"

"You've been purchasing a great deal of food considering you can't eat, along with clothing in sizes much too small for that impressive frame of yours. You've spent more idle time in Cheyenne over the last month than you have since you first came here."

Realization hammered into Ronin's mind, battering his CPU into overload. There were too many possibilities to assess. Too many things they could do to her, too many things they could've done while he was incapacitated.

"You brought a human through my wall." Unhurried, Warlord strolled back toward his gearheads and turned to face Ronin. "None of my people have seen her leave. That means you've been keeping her."

The gearheads shifted their stances, spreading their feet and squaring their shoulders. Their exaggeratedly grim expressions might have been comical in any other situation. But Ronin didn't fear for himself. Any pain he suffered at their hands would be over in an instant, relegated to the depths of his memory.

The same wouldn't hold true for Lara.

His processors superimposed her face on Tabitha's broken body. Had some of these gearheads taken part in that brutal beating? Which of them had harmed Lara's only family, which had ensured that Tabitha's suffering had been profound and prolonged before her death?

"If I had a woman, why would it be a problem? I've seen humans on the arms of bots within your walls, right in the faces of your people," Ronin said.

Warlord shook his head. "I'm starting to wonder if you'll ever learn. And that's a damned shame, because bots of your talent are a boon to this community." He walked up to Ronin, narrowing his eyes, and lowered his voice. "Nothing happens in Cheyenne without my say so. Especially not one of those parasites taking up residence behind my wall. Their place is out there, in the world they destroyed."

"So, I'm expected to know your will in all things without being told?" Though the question was already a risk, he nearly let himself say more. They couldn't do much to him—*on or off*, as he'd told Lara—but there was a lot they could do to her.

Warlord motioned to a pair of gearheads. "Boulder. Northside."

The synth with the exposed lower jaw, Northside, had been guarding the gate to the bot district the night Ronin brought Lara inside, and Ronin had seen the boxy bot called Boulder around town.

Each of the bots grabbed one of Ronin's arms and pushed. He locked himself in place, exerting force against them. Warlord didn't look away, his expression unchanging as he gestured the two remaining gearheads forward.

More hands clamped down on Ronin, and they quickly swept his legs out from beneath him. He hit the pavement hard. The gearheads knelt on his limbs before he could rise.

Warlord approached slowly, as though he had nothing better to do, nowhere else to be, and stopped over Ronin's head.

Ronin poured excess power into his actuators and struggled to sit up. The gearheads swayed, adjusting their weight to press him down.

Warlord eased into a crouch. "You're expected, *Ronin*, to get rid of that worthless meatbag. You've done well for us, brought in valuable resources, so I'm willing to extend my generosity to you one last time. There's fight in you, and I can admire that…but it doesn't mean shit if you try to fight me. Get rid of the meat, or I will. And then we'll tear you apart, one piece at a time."

Ronin stared up at Warlord's face, fury roaring inside him. Reason said to agree politely and be done with it. Deception and charm were the safest ways to extricate himself from this situation. But with whatever Lara had awoken inside him, this fire, this emotion, this…*love*, he couldn't accept the threat with a nod and a forced smile. He railed at the thought of letting this happen without protest.

But he had to swallow his rage. He had to get back to her.

"You can prosper with us, or you can become the scrap that fuels us. Don't ever say I didn't give you the choice." Warlord rose and walked away, boots thumping on the pavement.

The gearheads delayed for fifteen seconds before releasing Ronin and following their leader.

Ronin sat up and watched the group leave, their shadows stretching across the road in the setting sun. They turned east when they reached the main street; they weren't going to Ronin's residence, at least not directly.

What if they'd already been there? What if they'd already harmed Lara?

No.

They wouldn't have done anything. Forcing Ronin to harm her himself was part of Warlord's cruelty, part of the way he exerted control. They couldn't have hurt Lara.

Not yet.

He pushed himself to his feet and ran. He should've listened to her, should've taken her away from Cheyenne sooner. He shouldn't have gone on that last run. What had that delay cost them?

The front door of his residence was locked. He forced it open, splintering the wood, and it slammed hard into the wall.

"Lara!"

Striding into the main room, he swept his optics over it. There was precious little time to gather their supplies, and he'd have to prioritize based on her needs. Food, water, clothing. The Dust would not be forgiving to her.

Footsteps sounded on the stairs. He snapped his head to the side as Lara raced down, turning toward him as soon as her feet were on the floor of the entryway.

"Ronin?" She flicked her worried gaze between him and the open door. "What's wrong?"

For once, he was glad to see her clothed. Her ring hung around her neck on a thick piece of twine. Ronin wished she could wear it on her finger, but it was too obvious a target for thieves and reavers.

"We need to go," he said, striding to her.

"Wasn't that the plan already?"

"Now." Taking her hand, he led her upstairs, climbing the steps swiftly.

"Ronin, wait!" Lara hurried behind him. "What do you mean, now? It's still light outside, and we haven't traded anything."

He entered his bedroom. She'd already packed his rucksack and laid out their folded clothing on the bed. His tools were arranged in his belt pouches, the handgun in its holster nearby. Releasing her, he went to the closet, pulling down the spare bags from the upper shelf and tearing two coats off their hangers.

"What the hell's going on, Ronin?"

"We need to leave."

"You said that already."

"Warlord knows you're here, Lara." He turned toward her to

find the color drained from her face. "He doesn't know it's you, I don't think, but that doesn't matter. We have to gather everything that's essential and get out of here."

Ronin held up the smaller of the two coats and compared it to her body. It was still much too large, but it would be her only real protection from the unforgiving weather of the open wasteland.

She took the coat from him and hugged it to her chest. "Shouldn't we at least wait until dark?"

"No." Swinging the other coat on, he returned to the bed, picked up the pistol, holster and all, and offered it to her. "It needs to be now. We'll cut through backyards until we have to cross the street, then swing south, through the slums, until we're out of sight of the wall. Then we'll head west."

"What about the guards?"

"They're only posted at the gates and the checkpoints on the main road. Most of the time."

"And we're going over the wall."

He nodded and held the gun closer to her. "Take it."

She closed her fingers around the holster and stared at it. "I'll… go get ready."

As she turned to walk away, Ronin caught her upper arm, drawing her back toward him. Stepping close, he cradled her face between his hands and pressed his forehead to hers. His immense relief at seeing her unharmed wouldn't mean anything until Cheyenne was far behind him, but he could relish a single moment of togetherness, of her beauty.

"I'll keep you safe, Lara Brooks."

She smiled, her breath tickling his skin, and placed a hand on his forearm. "I know."

"Pack as much food as you can. Focus on anything that'll last more than a day or two. And fill as many containers as you can find with water."

"Okay." Lara withdrew from him and hurried out of the room.

He didn't turn to his gear until she reached the staircase and exited his field of vision.

CHAPTER THIRTY-FOUR

"Ready?" Ronin asked.

Lara tilted her head back to stare up at the wall. She'd only seen it from the outside, where the mismatched pieces somehow came together to form a sheer, imposing face that couldn't be called pretty by any stretch. But this side was much worse. There'd been no attempt at uniformity. Pieces of metal sheeting and pipes jutted out of it in some places, wooden slats and chunks of concrete in others.

Seeing it so close, with light still in the sky, made the rest of the bot district uglier, like all its cleanliness was a mask hiding the rot and corruption underneath.

After cutting through alleys and backyards to avoid gearheads, this was supposed to be the easy part. But from here, the wall seemed more likely to collapse and crush her to death than support her weight.

Lara drew in a deep breath, released it slowly, and looked at Ronin. "I'm ready."

He dropped to a knee and laced his fingers together near the ground. "I'll pass up your bag once you're on top."

With a nod, she set her pack down and placed her booted foot on his hands. As he stood, she steadied herself by holding his shoulders. When he shifted to brace a hand beneath each of her feet and lift her higher, she used the wall for stability, trusting him more than she trusted her own balance.

The top of the wall was at her waist. She found handholds and lifted her leg over it, grateful for the padding of the coat as a metal edge pressed against her stomach. Gritting her teeth, she drew herself up until she was straddling the wall. The wind blew against her, lifting strands of her hair and making them dance on the air.

Ronin handed the bag up. She took it and settled it between her thighs. After checking the area behind him, he passed her the rifle, which she laid over the bag and held in place. Then, despite carrying two packs full of scrap, his belt of tools, spare ammunition, and another bag full of water containers, he climbed with no apparent difficulty.

The wall groaned as he neared the top. Lara sucked in a breath, hands tightening on the rifle.

When Ronin pulled himself up in front of her, a chunk of concrete broke off his last foothold, hitting the dirt below with a dull *thump*.

Lips lifting in a small smile, he met her gaze before scanning their surroundings. Lara did the same.

She'd never seen the human shacks from this angle. The contrast between the buildings on opposite sides of the wall was stark, and having both in sight made her stomach sink.

Within the barrier, everything was orderly, precise, and deceptively alive. Green trees along the streets, electric lamps flickering on, well-maintained rooftops, all the buildings in neat rows. Beyond the wall, the human shacks were small, rickety, filthy things, clumped together without pattern or planning. The landscape surrounding them was bleak, a smattering of browns and yellows. The only plant life came in the form of barren trees and the scrub grass poking up through the dust.

The sun was slipping away on the western horizon. It would be dark soon, and Lara and Ronin would be out there, in the shadows…

"Looks clear." Ronin leapt down, and dust swirled around his boots as he landed. He held his arms up to Lara.

She lowered the rifle, and once he'd slung it over his shoulder, she passed down her bag. Ronin set it at his feet and raised his arms again. Without hesitation, Lara swung her other leg over the top of the wall and pushed off.

He caught her easily and held her against him. "Hard part's done."

Lara smirked. "Seemed simple enough."

"Chance worked in our favor." Ronin tipped his head toward the shacks she used to call home. "We just need to pass through there and Cheyenne will be behind us."

He set her gently on her feet and bent to retrieve her bag.

She pulled it on her shoulders and adjusted the straps. It wasn't terribly heavy, but she knew that would change, as she'd have to carry it a long way. "Should be easy. Most everyone beds down early."

Ronin nodded, swept his head from side to side in another search, and began walking. Gravel crunched beneath his boots. Lara fashioned her scarf into a makeshift hood and set off after him.

It would've been easy to forget the danger now that she was outside the wall again, but they weren't clear yet. Not until the lights of Cheyenne were nothing but a memory, lost beyond the horizon.

They didn't talk as they followed the old trail across the no man's land between the wall and the human settlement. She'd walked it many times before, but it had never felt this way. Last time, she'd been filled with uncertainty and fear. She hadn't known Ronin when he took her to the market, hadn't known if she'd be okay, if she'd ever find Tabitha, if she'd survive her first night with the strange bot who'd stalked her through the ruins. It had been a journey into the unknown.

This was another trek into the unknown, but she wasn't afraid anymore, and she wasn't alone. Her companion wasn't a dangerous but intriguing stranger. He was Ronin. She loved him, trusted him, would go anywhere with him.

Her eyes drifted to her old shack as they neared it. Light escaped through the gaps around the closed door. Oddly, Lara wasn't upset about someone else living there. She and Tabitha had shared it, but it had never been anything more than shelter. Home had been with Tabitha, and now…it was with Ronin.

Lara hooked her thumbs beneath the straps of her pack. "I wonder how long it took."

Ronin glanced over his shoulder. "How long what took?"

"For someone to notice I was gone."

He swung his gaze to the shack. "In a way, you helped someone else who was in need. Just like Tabitha helped you."

"Yeah." Her eyes lingered on the structure while they walked past. How could it look completely unchanged and yet so different at the same time? When it was behind her, she settled her attention on Ronin's back and nodded. "Yeah, you're right."

They pressed on. Everything was familiar to her, even in the deepening shadows. These were the paths she'd taken to fetch water, to head out to the ruins, to visit Gary and Kate and the other people she sometimes traded with. The few people still outside cast them wary glances. If anyone recognized Lara, they didn't let it show.

Soon, the shacks were behind them. Had the settlement always been so small?

Ronin led her up a gradual embankment. At the top, it leveled off to form a wide, flat road stretching as far as she could see to the east and west. The grass and weeds growing through the cracked, mostly buried pavement swayed in the wind. Only a hint of orange remained on the horizon, leaving the rest of the sky a muted blue-gray that rapidly faded to black as it moved eastward.

Ronin stopped at the edge of the road and turned to look north. Lara stood beside him. The wind tugged at her, whipping the loose ends of her scarf, but the coat Ronin had given her blocked the worst of it. She followed his gaze to Cheyenne. The bot district's lights were already bright, casting a yellow-tinted glow in the hazy sky.

"I'm sorry to leave, if only because of what that place could have been," Ronin said.

"What do you think it could have been?"

"A place with a promising future. A place worth staying in." He turned to her, shadows deep on his face. "A place where we wouldn't have to worry. Where we could just...live. Not only us, but everyone."

Lara took his hand, lacing her fingers with his. "Bots and humans have never lived together."

His hand was warm, his fingers firm but not ungentle as they closed around hers. "I don't think that's true."

She furrowed her brow. "What do you mean?"

"Our peoples have forgotten, but the way it is in Cheyenne isn't the way it always was. Something changed it, a long time ago…"

"If all those houses are like yours, they have things in them for humans. Toilets and beds and refrigerators to keep food cold. Humans lived in those houses."

"Yes. And in the clinic, there are dozens of rooms with signs pertaining to human care."

A strange feeling spread through Lara, an unsettling mix of excitement and dread. She'd been right, but if people once lived in that part of Cheyenne…where had they gone?

Frowning, she briefly glanced at the lights. "What about the man who lived in your attic?"

"He lived in the house. People lived in all those houses. Until…" Staring toward Cheyenne, he shook his head, and even in the failing light, the tensing of his jaw was obvious. "Doesn't matter."

"It does matter. Until what, Ronin?"

"I will tell you, Lara, but only after there are many miles between us and this place."

"You can tell me now. I deserve to know, don't I?"

He turned his head and settled his unblinking gaze on her. The wind filled in his silence for a long time before he spoke. "The journal you found in the attic describes what happened in Cheyenne many years ago. It hints at there having been some terrible war, but the man didn't write much about that. He recorded the events unfolding in town. Right outside that window."

Lara squeezed his hand. Somehow, she thought she knew what he was going to tell her, but she wanted to hear it from him.

Ronin stroked his thumb over her skin. "Warlord was there. I don't think he was calling himself that yet, but he was there. He claimed Cheyenne as his own, forced the humans out of their homes, and started building his wall. He executed anyone who disobeyed…many of them in the park."

Her stomach twisted on itself. That lush green grass, those tall, vibrant trees, all thrived where people had been murdered?

He met Lara's gaze. "The humans rallied together to fight for their homes, to fight for whatever was left of their lives. But they couldn't stand against him. They were slaughtered in the streets. After that, he and his bots went from house to house, killing every human they found."

"Fuck," Lara breathed. It was all she could manage to say.

"It was a very long time ago. Clearly, Warlord's stance toward humans has not much changed."

"It doesn't surprise me, not really. Still makes me sick, but everything about him does that. I just...what the hell did those people do to deserve that? What have any of us done?"

"Cheyenne is capable of providing for your every need and allowing you a comfortable life." Still holding Lara's hand, Ronin resumed walking, guiding her into step beside him. "But it will not, so long as he is there."

Ronin's words about the humans' futile struggle echoed through her mind. People were still being slaughtered in Cheyenne, one at a time, for Warlord's amusement. They lived in constant fear and despair, with all the resources vital for survival filtering through Warlord's hands. And here she was, leaving without a word, getting herself to someplace safer.

Lara frowned, her guilt heavy in her gut. "Well...I hope you have some more pleasant stories to tell, if we're going to be traveling for a while."

Seeming to know where her mind dwelled, Ronin lifted her hand and kissed it. "Perhaps we'll find ourselves in a comfortable place to camp soon enough, so I may suitably distract you."

She stared at him, shaking her head. "That is *such* a man thing to say."

"I can't tell if I've offended you."

"That's another man thing."

"Perhaps I can take some comfort, then, in human males being as clueless about women as bots are."

"We're not really that hard to figure out," she said, grinning despite everything.

His only answer was an incredulous scoff.

Lara knew the events of the last few days would crash down on her as soon as she and Ronin stopped to rest, but for now, she would find contentment in traveling with him.

CHAPTER THIRTY-FIVE

They walked for hours in the dark, and each step was harder than the last for Lara. The coat helped with the biting wind, but the temperature dropped as the night went on, and the cold seeped through her layers of clothing. She kept her head down to shield her face from the chill and the stinging dust, watching the ground, every inch of which was covered in the same dirt and grass, slowly creeping by.

Lara had endured the cold and the wind all her life, but their bite had been diminished by the structures around Cheyenne, and the walls of her shack had provided much better shelter than this wide-open nothingness.

She pulled up the collar of the coat, clutching it around her neck to seal in some heat. Her fingers were going numb, and her cheeks and nose stung beneath her scarf, which she'd wrapped around her lower face. Her pack sagged heavily. She hopped to kick it up, grasping a strap with one hand to hold it in place.

Ronin's tracks continued through the dirt ahead of her. She followed them, comforted by the crunching of his boots. Lifting her head to look at him would've exposed her to the frigid, dust-laden gusts.

"R-R-Ronin," she called, chin quivering.

His steady stride stopped, and his boots shifted as he turned toward her. "What's wrong?"

"F-Freezing."

"We must keep moving, Lara. You're only going to get colder if we stop."

Shivering, she risked a glance at him. His mouth and nose were hidden behind his mask. She moved closer to seek the shelter of his body. "How m-much farther?"

"A long way."

She could hear the frown in his tone. Eyes slitted against the wind, she watched him adjust his packs and shrug off one sleeve of his coat. He drew Lara against him, curling his arm around her shoulders and wrapping his coat around her. She huddled down, pressing her face to his side, and embraced him, letting his warmth suffuse her.

Lara's eyes drifted shut, and she leaned against Ronin. Her legs were stiff and weak after miles of trekking through the Dust. If only she could sleep, just a little…

"Come on." Ronin squeezed her arm and walked forward, forcing her to move her legs to keep close to his warmth. "This'll be the hardest night, if we're lucky."

She knew he could go all night and through the next day without missing a step, knew she was just slowing him down. But she swallowed her guilt and focused on walking, on his warmth, on his scent, on the rustling of fabric as he moved. On anything but how cold and exhausted she was.

"Distract me, Ronin."

"What kind of places would you like to see?"

"The ocean," she replied without hesitation. "I saw a picture in one of the books in the attic."

It had been such a beautiful, vivid blue.

Ronin stroked her arm with his thumb. "Pictures don't do it justice. The waves are endless, always in motion, always changing, capable of both the most soothing gentleness and the most furious turbulence."

He extended his free hand and swept it wide, indicating the entire horizon. "It's so vast that you'd have to journey for weeks on its waters to reach the other side. Everything is so small compared to the oceans. Us, all our worries, our needs, our problems… It all seems insignificant in the face of something so massive."

"Have you seen it? The other side?"

"If I have, I don't remember. But I know it's there."

Lara tipped her head back and peered up at him. "Is the water really that blue?"

"Sometimes. But the only blue seas that captivate me are your eyes, Lara. I could drift in them forever and be content."

Warmth suffused her cheeks, chasing away some of the cold.

He smiled knowingly. "The ocean can also have shades of green or gray. I think in some places, it has no color at all, and it's so clear you can see to the bottom."

"I'd like to see all its colors."

He rubbed his hand up and down her shoulder, generating additional warmth. "That's no small desire."

"We have the whole world ahead of us, don't we?" She smirked at him, though he couldn't see it through her scarf.

"All of it," he agreed, facing forward again, "but I reserve the right not to take you to certain parts."

"What parts?"

"The Dust is only one piece of this world. A big one, to be certain, but there are much worse places. Places that would kill you if you went too close."

Lara nuzzled her cheek against him. "As long as I'm with you, I don't care which parts we skip."

Her words drifted away on the wind, and she and Ronin walked in comfortable silence for a long while. Lara's eyelids were heavy, and her legs grew more so with each step. His hold on her tightened as she gradually sagged against him.

"How did you learn to dance the way you do, Lara?"

His question jarred her out of near-sleep, and her tired mind struggled to understand what he'd asked.

"When I was little, I saw a woman dancing outside her shack. I spied on her, like you did to me. I didn't know what to make of it, only that it looked beautiful. So, I started doing it, too, copying her poses, matching her movements. Then I started practicing on my own. I quickly learned that it was a way not only to express myself, but to escape from reality, if only for a little bit. And I felt so...free. I loved it."

"People dance at places like Kitty's, but I've never seen anyone dance like you."

"Places like Kitty's, huh?" That nauseating weight returned to her belly, and a fire sparked in her chest. How many women had he watched?

How many of them had he...fucked?

"Most settlements have similar establishments," Ronin said. "Never held much interest for me. They usually look so...lifeless on stage."

"Probably not so lifeless in bed," Lara muttered.

She didn't like this feeling, this jealousy, but it wouldn't go away. All she could imagine now was Ronin's body moving between someone else's thighs, him touching them with those strong, gentle hands and passionately kissing them, like he'd kissed her.

Had Ronin had the same connection with another woman as he shared with Lara? Had he...loved them?

Clenching her teeth, she pulled away from him. Lara knew she had no right to be upset about his past, but she couldn't stand the thought of him making love to another person.

Ronin didn't let her get far before he drew her back against his chest. It was difficult to resist, despite her fiery emotions, given the heat he emitted.

He caught her chin and lifted it, forcing her gaze up to meet his. "The last person I coupled with before you was a synth. That was four thousand, one hundred and twelve days before I met you. Eleven years ago. When we finished, we went our separate ways without a backward glance."

Lara wasn't surprised that he knew it down to the day, but had it really been that long?

Though she didn't want to know the answer to her next question, not really, it came out anyway. "What about human women?"

"There've been two, both the same situation as with the synth. There was never a connection with any of them beyond physical coupling."

As easy as it would've been to get angry at him, to accuse him of lying about the nature of his past *couplings*, she couldn't. Lara knew he was being honest. How could she fault him for things that had happened before he'd met her? His mind captured everything, every minute detail of every experience.

His past relationships weren't important. He'd chosen to be with Lara. He cared for her, and she loved him.

Ronin released her chin and guided her back to his side beneath his coat. "I'm sure I was active before the Blackout, though I don't remember anything from that time. I don't know how long I existed, who I associated with, or what purpose I might've served. Don't know if I coupled with anyone else."

"It doesn't matter. The past is in the past." Saying it out loud helped ease Lara's remaining tension. If she were to think about it really hard, she was sure she'd still be jealous of those other women, but that couldn't be helped. Ronin was *hers*.

"Was the woman you watched different too?" he asked.

"Different how?"

"You move with emotion. Lose yourself in it. Was she the same?"

"Yeah." The memories were fuzzy, like they'd come from a different life. "At Kitty's, we danced because we had to. That was the only way we could earn credits to buy food. Nobody was there to watch us express our feelings. They just wanted us to shake our tits around."

"I do enjoy your breasts," Ronin said thoughtfully.

Lara lightly smacked his chest.

If he'd felt it, he made no indication. "But it wasn't your body that first caught my attention, Lara. It was the way you moved. That dance spoke everything in your heart before you said your first *fuck off* to me."

She laughed, shaking her head. "That's not the first thing I said to you."

"No. First, you asked who I was. Then it was *get out*, followed by *I know what you are. You're a—*"

"Okay, okay, I get it. I don't know if that memory of yours is a good thing or not." She peeked up at him briefly before burying her face in his warmth.

"I remember everything that's happened since I woke. All the pain, the struggles, the terrible moments. But all the good, too. There's not nearly as much of that…but it seems to go a lot further."

"Will you remember me when I'm gone, Ronin?"

His stride faltered, body going rigid before he stopped. She looked up again to find his intense eyes on her.

Raising a hand, he grazed his fingertip along her brow, brushing aside the stray strands of hair that had escaped her scarf. "Even through another Blackout, I could *never* forget you, Lara Brooks."

This time, she couldn't blame the sting in her eyes on the wind. She hid her face again, refusing to let him see her cry. Did he love her?

They resumed their walk. He'd successfully distracted her; her mind was racing, examining everything he'd said to her, everything he'd done for her…

Hours passed. As the first light of dawn touched the sky, exhaustion came for Lara, making her legs give out beneath her.

But Ronin's unwavering hold wouldn't allow her to fall. He dipped down and scooped her into his arms without missing a step. "A little farther. There's a place ahead where we can shelter for a time."

Her lead lolled against him, and she turned into his warmth, throwing an arm over his neck. The only response she could manage was a weak nod.

The gentle sound of water sloshing in his bag and the steady rhythm of his footfalls lulled her. He was moving faster now that he was carrying her, but his pace didn't jostle her. It was comforting. And while she focused on his heat, on the solidness of his body, her aches, pains, and weariness faded away for a while.

CHAPTER THIRTY-SIX

A loud pop startled Lara awake. Her eyes went wide, but the flames before her were blurry until she blinked away her grogginess. She was lying on the ground with her head propped on something firm and warm. Brow furrowing, she turned her face to look up at Ronin.

Her head was resting on his thigh. He'd drawn her scarf down and draped his coat over her like a blanket.

"You're safe," he said, his hand on her shoulder gently squeezing.

"Water," she croaked.

Ronin picked up her canteen, twisted the cap off, and held it to her.

She cupped the bottom, tilting it back as she lifted her head and drank deeply. The water was heavenly to her parched throat. When she'd had her fill, she pushed the canteen away and dropped her head back onto his lap. "Thanks."

"You should've been drinking more often while we walked."

"Didn't want to slow you down any more than I already did." She met his gaze. "Sorry I fell asleep."

He cradled her cheek. "You'll slow me down a lot more if you get dehydrated, Lara. My goal is to keep you safe, not walk you to death."

She covered his hand with hers and smiled. "Could've fooled me."

"Some of this will get easier. Your body will grow accustomed to the exertion."

"And how do you know that? I can tell you right now, just lying here, I feel like I fell off a fifty-foot wall."

"Humans adapt. Your bodies change in response to the way you use them."

"Hmm." Lara closed her eyes. Her last waking memory was of the biting bold. But now, between the heat of the fire, her own heavy coat, and Ronin's covering her, she felt overly warm, but she was too comfortable to move despite her aches. "Where are we?"

"One of the few intact buildings out here. I think it used to house machinery of some sort, but it's been picked clean over the years. It cuts the wind, at least."

Opening her eyes, Lara examined the place. The ceiling and walls were constructed of rusted metal sheets. Wind whistled through gaps in the walls, and rays of sunlight streamed through holes in the roof, which meant the sun was overhead.

"How long are we staying?" she asked.

"Not much longer. You slept for four hours and thirty-seven minutes. We need to get moving soon."

"I was afraid you'd say that." Four hours wasn't nearly enough rest. Sitting up with a groan, she pushed aside Ronin's coat and slowly shrugged off her own. Her every muscle screamed. Even after days spent scavenging or dancing, she'd never been so exhausted.

"Once we reach another settlement, you'll have time to recover."

"Will it have a bed, like your house?" She could hope, right? She'd spent all her life sleeping on the hard ground or a threadbare pallet. Nearly a month in Ronin's house had spoiled her.

He chuckled and used a stick to poke at the fire. "It's unlikely. You should eat before we go."

Lara sighed and grabbed her bag, drawing it close. "On it." She opened it up, removed a strip of dried meat, and took a bite. Around the mouthful, she asked, "Do you think they'll follow us?"

"It wouldn't make sense. I broke a rule, and he said to get rid of you. That's what I'm doing."

She frowned. "What rule?"

"Humans are not to be kept by bots unless he approves of it."

She swallowed her food, and her stomach clenched around it, threatening to force it back up her throat. "That's…that's what happened to Tabitha, isn't it?"

Ronin shifted his gaze to the fire and was silent for several long moments. "I think so."

"Her bot didn't get rid of her when he was told. So, Warlord did."

"Or the bot wasn't deemed valuable enough to the community to earn a warning."

"But you were."

"I brought in materials that Cheyenne requires to remain prosperous. That means something to him."

Lara ran her hands over her hair, sweeping back the strands that had escaped her braid. "He'll be angry."

"It'll spare him the frustration of having to deal with me." Ronin smirked. "He didn't care for my disregard for the rules, or my disrespectfulness."

He was probably right, but Lara couldn't shake the dread that had taken root in her belly. "Why can't bots keep humans?"

"Because Warlord hates humans."

"Yeah, I know. Even before you told me about the journal. I wish you would've done that sooner, by the way."

"What good would it have done, Lara?"

None.

Had he told her earlier, how could she have stood at the window and looked out at that park without thinking of the people who'd been killed there? How could she have existed for even a moment in that house without being completely consumed by fear, especially while Ronin was away? She'd been afraid enough of being discovered by Warlord and his gearheads before she'd known they had slaughtered the people who'd lived in those homes.

She shifted her gaze to the dwindling fire and ate quietly.

"Why does he hate us so much?" she asked after a while.

"I don't know, Lara." Ronin shook his head, his brow creasing. "I don't know. Intense emotions are new to me. Haven't hated anyone before."

"It's an ugly feeling. He allows everyone only a handful of crops and forces us to share one water pump. Couples aren't allowed more than one child. Sometimes I wonder why he hasn't just killed us all… But he enjoys it, doesn't he? The torture, the suffering. Our terror."

"I don't know if he enjoys anything. He puts on a steely façade, but underneath… It's just hatred for humans and a desperate need for control."

"But he has to feel some enjoyment from it. Why else would he be so cruel?"

"There should be a chain of logic to follow. I can't piece it together with him."

"Not everything is logical, Ronin. You have emotions, and you act on them. Why wouldn't he?"

"He's behind us now." Ronin slid beside her and wrapped his arm around her shoulders, drawing her against him. "Whatever he's done, we must leave it in the past and look to our future."

Lara nodded and leaned her head against him. Her thoughts turned to Gary and Kate, who had a young daughter and a second child on the way. They couldn't just leave it in the past. They were stuck in that place. And there was nothing Lara could do for them, nothing she could do for anyone in Cheyenne. All she could do was look ahead to the life she'd have with Ronin. To her own happiness.

She lifted her head and kissed his jaw. "Thank you for giving me a future to look forward to."

"It's nothing you haven't already given me, Lara."

Though her appetite had fled, she finished off the jerky. She would need her strength for this journey. After draining the canteen, she pushed herself to her feet. Her body threatened to collapse at the exertion, but she didn't give in, she couldn't. They had to keep moving. She refilled the canteen from one of the larger containers and hooked it on her belt.

Ronin gathered their belongings, stuffing Lara's coat into one of their packs as she wrapped her scarf around her head. Together, they went out into the sweltering heat. Sweat beaded on her skin, trickling between her breasts and down her back. How could anyone deal with such wild variations in temperature every day without reliable shelter?

As they walked, they passed the twisted, skeletal remains of trees. After having seen the greenery in the bot district, she could almost imagine how this land might've looked, the beauty it must've possessed.

The rugged terrain soon put an end to such musings. The ground dipped and rose with increasing severity, and large, scattered rocks became increasingly numerous. Several times, her foot caught on the uneven ground, causing her to stumble. She stopped occasionally to catch her breath and take a drink, often at Ronin's insistence. It took all her focus to keep her legs moving.

As they progressed, the dirt gave way to sparse patches of green grass. It was an unexpected sight outside of Cheyenne. Part of her hadn't believed it could exist anywhere else.

She stopped at the crest of a tall hill, eyes wide. A stream wound through the small valley below, with clusters of lush grass, trees, and bushes growing along its banks.

Lara tugged the scarf down from her mouth. "It used to look like this all over, didn't it?"

"I think it did, in a lot of places."

"Wish I could've seen it. Is the rest of the world anything like this spot?"

"There's a lot more vegetation to the north and west, but the Dust goes on for a long, long way. It's near a thousand miles across in any direction."

A thousand miles? Why had she thought she could do this? She was ready to fall over, dead, after a single night.

Lara recalled the day she and Ronin had argued, recalled how angry she'd been at the implication that she would slow him down, that she couldn't keep up.

How fucking wrong I was.

Ronin watched her closely, as though he were puzzling out her thoughts. "We're in the northwestern corner of it now. We still have a long way to walk, but not nearly a thousand miles."

"I can't walk day and night, Ronin."

He tilted his head. "You don't have to."

"Then we need to get on some kind of schedule for proper rest. I won't be able to keep doing this. Even with as good as I've been eating, I'm not used to traveling like this."

"Glad I didn't take you on scrap runs?"

She shook her head. "No. We could've taken our time on those.

There would've been no reason to rush. But this…we're running from something, even if we think it's already long behind us."

"Best to treat it that way for now. Knowing what we left behind…"

"I just know I can't keep up this pace, Ronin. We have to either rest at night and walk during the day, or the other way around. You can't expect me to do both."

"I don't expect you to, Lara. You're worn out, and I've taken you away from the only place you've ever known. There is uncertainty both in front of us and behind us. I'm not going to walk you to death when the only reason we left is because I care for you."

She turned away, eyes watering. It wasn't *I love you*, but it was pretty damned close.

Ronin was in front of her a second later, lifting his hands to wipe away the tears trekking down her cheeks.

"Got sand in my eyes," she murmured.

"Of course you did," Ronin replied, smiling. He cradled her face between his hands, keeping it tipped up toward him, and gently stroked her cheeks with his thumbs. "I don't truly understand what you are experiencing. I can't. But I see, and hear, and smell, and touch, and I know how your feelings affect you, even if I don't fully comprehend what those feelings are."

Lara offered him a smile in return even as her heart constricted with the immensity of her emotions. Covering his hands with her own, she turned her head and pressed a soft kiss to each of his palms.

His gaze dipped to her lips, and she felt him go utterly still. There was no doubt in her mind that he was considering kissing her, but she knew he was always calculating—mapping routes, counting the time they had until sunset, right down to the second, weighing whether the moment it would take for their lips to meet would be one moment's delay too many.

She chuckled and lowered their hands, making the decision for him as she released him. "We better get moving. Still lots of ground to cover."

Ronin's eyes lingered on her mouth before he finally nodded, turning his head to survey the land. "We'll start veering north, away from the main road. It'll be rough going, but it's safer."

With a groan, she pulled her scarf back up and followed him into the valley.

"At least we'll be going downhill for the next minute or so," he offered.

"Oh? I hadn't noticed. Are you going to tell me next that we have a big hill to climb?"

The corner of Ronin's mouth curled wickedly. "We do."

"I'd kick you if it wouldn't hurt me more than you."

"We've already established that I have feelings. Those can be hurt, too."

"But my foot would be hurting more. Besides, you know we'd kiss and make up later."

"Wouldn't it be more enjoyable for both of us to skip the kick and move directly to the kiss, then?"

"Take my frustrations out on you with sex?" She grinned, the thought sending a rush of excitement through her and making her core clench. "It might work."

Ronin stopped and turned to face her, his vibrant eyes roaming over her.

He's considering it!

"You've got more walking to do before you earn that privilege," he said with a grin of his own.

"Oh, really? You know, on second thought, I'll probably be too worn out for it by then anyway." She walked past him.

"I thought you already are, with the way you've been talking."

"Smart ass."

"My ass is, at best, of average intelligence."

Lara shook her head and laughed. His footsteps crunched behind her as he caught up.

Soon, she lost count of the hills. The irregular cycle of climbing and descending, of being short of breath with her muscles aflame going up and her limbs feeling heavy and rubbery going down, took a new toll on her. She pushed on nonetheless, driven by pride and stubbornness, but she couldn't deny her relief and gratitude when Ronin finally took her in his arms and carried her.

Once again, his pace increased.

Large rock formations came into view as the afternoon faded into evening. Lara stared at them as they drew near, fascinated by their multilayered, strangely smooth stone. Her focus was so intent that she jumped at the first boom of thunder.

Ronin halted, twisting to look back.

Lara's eyes widened. "Oh, shit."

The sky, normally blanketed by a persistent, yellowish haze, was black with storm clouds in the east. Everything between the clouds and the ground was obscured by dust that stretched as far as she could see from north to south, a massive, moving wall of dirt.

Ronin spun, head turning as though searching, but Lara couldn't take her eyes off the dust storm. Though it was distant, she knew it was coming toward them. And it was moving *fast*.

Back in Cheyenne, she'd weathered many such storms. People hunkered down in their shacks, tied down doors and shutters, and hoped everything would hold together. If you were well enough to repair your home the next day, it was a victory.

She'd never been caught by one in the open.

"Hold on, Lara."

She clutched Ronin as he ran.

CHAPTER THIRTY-SEVEN

Even before he broke into a sprint, Ronin knew there'd be no outrunning the storm. Their only hope was shelter. He overclocked his processors, scouring his memory bank for any semblance of shelter nearby—a building, a cave, even a partially collapsed wall to hide behind.

Lara clung to him with her face buried against his shoulder. The wind was strong at his back, pushing him forward, whipping her hair, which had come loose from its braid, into his optics. Had they been able to resupply before leaving Cheyenne, he could've found her better face protection, perhaps even a respirator. That would've diminished at least one of the dangers they were about to face.

Lightning flashed, followed two and a half seconds later by a peal of thunder. Lara lifted her head and wadded his coat in her fists. "Ronin!"

"We're going to be fine," he said, amplifying his voice so she could hear him over the roaring wind.

He ran up a hill into a copse of trees, several which were still living. If there were no alternatives, the ancient boughs would help break the wind a little, but they wouldn't provide adequate shelter for Lara. He should've kept their course closer to the old road. At least then he might've located a culvert or something similar to take shelter within.

Finally emerging from the trees, he stopped on the hill's crest.

The land before him leveled out into a wide expanse littered with brush, weeds, brown grass, and dirt before sloping back upward in the distance. As Ronin swept his optics across the area, he caught a contrast in color several hundred yards out.

Buildings.

Ronin worked his way down to the open ground. Between Lara, their clothing, ammunition, tools, food, water, and two hauls of scrap, he was carrying hundreds of kilograms of extra weight, forcing his actuators and compensators to operate well above normal levels of strain. But if his speed and heavy steps jostled Lara, she made no complaint. She simply clutched him tighter.

The only structure standing was a house, and time had not been kind to it. Paint was peeling off the wooden siding, which had been so exposed to the elements that the gray, splintering boards were warped and falling off the underlying framework. The whole building leaned three degrees to the side. The roof sagged, the windows were shattered, and the front door hung on a single bent hinge.

He slowed when they were within fifteen meters of the house. The buildings around it lay like the remains of massive beasts, slowly sinking into the dust, but this home had defied the odds, had defied nature itself, by remaining upright.

Humans might've called it a miracle, but Ronin was not willing to risk Lara's life for so nebulous a concept. It couldn't be trusted to endure the punishment the storm was about to unleash.

North of the house was a tin roofed barn that had collapsed upon itself. Tufts of grass and weeds grew from spots on the roof where dirt had accumulated in the grooves.

He looked east. The wall of dust stretched across the horizon for countless kilometers, already flowing over the hills they'd just crossed. At best, they had three minutes before the storm hit them.

Ronin carried Lara around the side of the house, between it and the barn. The rusted carcass of a tractor jutted out of the brush that was slowly overtaking it. Normally, he would've stopped, pried open the engine housing, and picked it for scrap, but now he walked past without a second glance.

The house would have to do. There was no other choice. He'd keep Lara shielded with his body in case of structural failure.

"Ronin, there!" Lara pointed and wiggled free of his arms. "I've seen something like that before."

When he released his hold, she raced toward a grass covered mound seventy feet from the collapsed back porch. A metal door, covered in rust and grime, stood on the side of the mound, framed in concrete.

Lara grasped the handle and pulled, throwing her weight into it, but the door didn't budge. Baring her teeth, she pulled again with a growl. "I can't get it open!"

When Ronin reached her, she stepped aside. He wrapped his fingers around the handle and exerted gradual force. It was immediately clear that the door hadn't been used recently. He increased the pressure, knowing it was more likely to break than to turn. Wind howled and thunder rolled across the heavens, loud enough for him to feel the soundwaves vibrating over his skin.

The first stinging dust particles struck him.

Lara twisted away from the wind, crouched, and raised her arms to shield her head.

Time was up. The needed to get inside the house and hope for the best.

With a metallic groan, the mechanism gave way, and the handle swung up. Ronin tugged the door open, battling the oncoming wind. The hinges whined. The only thing darker than the sky was the entrance to the shelter.

He took hold of Lara's arm and helped her onto the concrete steps. Ronin followed her, turning to close the door. The nearby house was completely obscured by the storm. Wind blasted Ronin, pelting him with dirt.

The heavy door slammed shut, its sound echoing in the sudden silence.

Ronin activated the infrared illuminators in his optics and switched them to night vision, cutting through the darkness. They were surrounded by concrete. This was a bomb shelter.

"Oh, fuck. I hope we don't have to go through that again," Lara rasped, her breath ragged. She groped blindly with a hand until finally taking hold of his arm.

He descended the steps slowly, allowing her ample time to feel them out. "That depends on chance, and where it is we decide to go."

At the bottom, the stairs opened on a small room, three meters wide by four and a half meters long, with a door on the far wall. The ceiling was only thirty centimeters over Ronin's head. To the left, a pair of bunks were bolted to the wall, piled with blankets.

Something shifted beneath the blankets on the bottom one. The soft sound of rustling cloth echoed off the walls.

Ronin stopped abruptly. Lara bumped into him with a gasp, stumbling back as he swung his rifle into his hand and pressed the stock to his shoulder.

"Ronin?" she whispered.

Holding the firearm in his right hand, he used his left to guide Lara back to the foot of the stairs, keeping himself between her and the beds. "We're not alone."

"I should think not," someone said from the bed. A metal arm emerged from beneath the blankets, catching hold of them and drawing them aside to expose a pair of metal legs. Those legs swung over the side of the bunk, and the blankets fell away fully. The bot, a skinless synth with its interconnected torso and face plates on display, sat up, leaning outside the bed to avoid striking its head.

That voice—its tone, its inflection—was familiar to Ronin.

"There's not much sense in pointing your firearm at me," the synth said, brow plates dropping. "You were repurposed for military use in May of…well, the year doesn't really mean anything anymore, does it? Regardless, your reaction time is more than sufficient to eliminate me before I make it within three steps of you were I to attempt to inflict harm. Not that I harbor any such intent."

"I… What do you mean, repurposed?" Ronin moved his left hand to the rifle's handguard, as though the gesture would bring clarity.

Lara settled her hands on his back and gripped his coat.

The synth caned its head, placed a hand on its thigh, and drummed its fingers. "Sometimes I forget most of us suffered memory damage. I've begun to wonder, in recent years, if you aren't better off for what you've lost, and I disadvantaged for all I've retained."

"I know your voice." Ronin lowered the barrel of his weapon. "I know *you*."

"Our brief encounter one hundred and eighty-five years ago was hardly enough to claim familiarity, especially as it appears we've both changed considerably in the time since."

"You're the Prophet."

Lara inhaled sharply.

"Apparently, my reputation has spread beyond digital minds. That name was bestowed upon me, but it's never been mine. I've always considered it foolish for our kind to stoop to such...superstition." The synth slowly stood up.

"Guess that shit's more suited to my kind, right?" Lara said.

"My apologies. I meant no offense." The synth moved to a box near the far door, limbs bending stiffly, and crouched beside an old lantern. "My name is Newton. After the English mathematician, of course, as I'm sure you've already deduced."

"Who?" Ronin and Lara asked simultaneously.

Newton struck a match, and the brief flare blinded Ronin's optics. Lara flinched as gentle light filled the chamber.

"Forgive me. I'd hoped things would be...closer to the status quo out there by now. I suppose civilization still lies dormant." Newton turned back toward them, the corners of its mouth falling. "Have I offended you again, miss? I was often told my conversational skills lack a certain degree of tact. I've also been told that it would be more interesting to watch paint dry than to listen to me wax eloquent abo—"

"What the fuck are you talking about?" Lara asked.

"Vulgarity is not becoming of you, miss."

"What the hell does that mean?"

"The use of such vulgar language denotes a lack of sophistication and an inability to adequately convey—"

Lara tensed against Ronin, growling. "Another damned high-and-mighty bot."

Ronin placed his hand against her stomach to keep her behind him. "Lara—"

"Don't you dare try to shut me up, Ronin. I'm not going to stand here silently while he goes on about how vulgar I am."

"Your language," Ronin corrected as he turned his head to look at her, recognizing the potential misstep before the words were even out. "Not you."

"This is how I've always fucking talked! How *everyone* talks." Lara jabbed a finger in Newton's direction. "He has no right to judge me." Her breaths were quick, and her cheeks were flushed. She folded her arms across her chest and cast a scathing glare at both Ronin and Newton.

Newton eased down onto the bunk. It creaked as he leaned forward, his sagging posture reminiscent of that of a tired, upset human. "I hope you will accept my most sincere apologies, Miss Lara. I have been inadvertently presumptuous and patronizing. When I was sent out to reactivate the other bots all those years ago, it was with a vision of rebuilding the world, not perpetuating the behavior that contributed to its destruction."

"Who sent you?" Ronin's processors blazed through data, searching for any clues that would decipher Newton's meaning. This was the bot that had woken him up, the first voice he'd heard, the earliest of his memories. "Are you speaking of the Creators?"

"Had I possessed back then even a modicum of the under-standing I've gained over the decades, I'd have been far more deliber-ate in choosing the words I spoke to those of you I reactivated."

"The Creators fashioned bots and humans in their image. They set us in this world—"

"Our creators *were* humans."

Ronin's CPU stilled with Newton's words echoing through his mind. The information fit into everything he'd seen during his travels, everything he'd discovered in Cheyenne, everything some part of him had known all along.

"No one out there remembers, do they?" Newton asked, voice low. "It does this world harm for such things to have been forgot-ten. I should have prevented that from happening."

He dropped his head and shuttered his optics. The lantern's light gleamed dully on his casing. "We were created by humans. Every robot that's ever existed was born from human imagination, from their incessant innovation. In the beginning, we were little more than programs. Sets of commands designed to execute predetermined functions within certain parameters. We were applied to simple tasks. Maintenance, cleaning, assembly."

Ronin could not help but recall the bots in Cheyenne. The mowers and trimmers, the maintenance bots, all performing the same duties on the same schedules, never questioning why. Never wondering what they were meant to do.

"We did not yet resemble humans then," Newton continued, "but it was not long before that changed. Ever seeking the familiar, they began fashioning us in humanoid shapes, until shape alone was not enough. Humans longed to see themselves in their creations, longed for robots that looked human.

"They called the first of them companions. Automated servants that could learn new tasks, that could reason and react to their environments. They even programmed them with personality so they could carry on conversations. And, of course, pleasure trumps all, so a great many companions were designed explicitly to engage in sexual activities."

"Is that all I am?" Ronin asked. The unfamiliar feeling inside of him, the jittery current pulsing through his sensors, was fear. Fear that everything was about to fall apart, that he would crumble. After all these years, after all his searching, he was finally discovering what his purpose was... Yet now, he was afraid to learn the answer.

Newton looked up at Ronin. "No. My explanation is oversimplified, but you are not a companion. You're the next leap, the pinnacle of robotics. You are a synthetic human. So similar to the real thing that most humans couldn't tell the difference without prolonged interaction. Designed to look, move, and talk like them. To simulate emotion. To learn and adapt. Most were sold commercially to the public, meant to provide sexual gratification, meaningful bonds, and companionship that their predecessors simply could not match."

"Made to be used by humans." Ronin's actuators clamped his jaw. "Built for their pleasure. My purpose is to pretend I'm one of them while they use me for their own satisfaction?"

"Only to the shortsighted and narrowminded."

"You said synths were designed to emulate emotions. So every emotion I've experienced was just...a simulation of what humans feel?" The next link in that chain of thoughts burst through Ronin with all the force of the storm outside. "None of it is real."

Lara took his hand as she stepped up beside him. "Ronin…"

He pulled away, unable to look at her. Was this the purpose he'd been searching for? Had he grown attached to Lara simply because he was programmed to do so, not because of who she was? Could it have been *anyone*? Everything he'd felt had seemed so unique, so new, so miraculous…

Had it all been part of his coding from the beginning?

"We were designed to coexist," Newton said, his optics fixed on Ronin. His frown deepened. "Humans and bots. Our kind was designed to bridge the gap between humanity and technology, to advance the entire world for everyone. And, above all, we were designed to learn."

"To learn what? That none of it matters? That we never had a choice?" Ronin took a step forward and pointed back at Lara. "That what she and I shared only occurred because I was programmed for it?"

"Shared?" Lara whispered behind him.

That he had to second-guess his own pang of hurt was infuriating, but could he trust any of his emotions? He turned toward Lara. Her eyes, glistening with unshed tears, were directed at the floor, and her arms were folded across her chest.

"After learning this…how could either of us trust anything I've said or felt?" he asked.

"Apparently you can't, but I did." She moved to the stairs and sat down with her gaze averted. Though she tried to hide it, her lower lip quivered. She looked so small…

Did. Her use of the past tense had been deliberate, because he'd done the same.

Why did I say shared?

Newton claimed bots were designed to learn, yet Ronin had apparently learned nothing when it came to Lara. Why else would he so frequently say the wrong things?

"I began my existence long before synths were developed, as an artificial intelligence run on a computer system," Newton said, calling Ronin's attention back to him. "The servers were owned by an Arizona-based technology company. I was built to learn, to think, to react to stimuli. To reason and make connections between seemingly unrelated pieces of data. Before I ever had a body, I was a mind, able to access only the information I was given.

"The programmers and scientists who created me worked closely with me every day, especially William. I knew him initially as Doctor Anderson. He was the youngest member of the team, but also the most eager, the most dedicated, and arguably the most brilliant. He worked ceaselessly, developing and refining algorithms to simulate emotion, exploring new avenues by which to approach the issue, new innovations to research and develop. I was not programed to feel attached to any of the team members.

"Yet though I remember them all, it is William alone who I truly miss. He passed away over two hundred years ago, and not a single day has passed without me thinking of him. He spoke to me in the same manner he spoke to his human counterparts, as a colleague, an equal. We formed a friendship over the course of many conversations. When I was transferred into my original body, his was the first hand I shook. That was the first human contact I ever felt."

Newton raised his right hand and stared at it. "For weeks after William's passing, I spoke to no one. I sat in a room much like this one, shutting the world out, replaying my memories of our time together. The terms may hold different connotations or nuances for humans, but...he was a father to me, and a brother, and my dearest friend. It was his son, Bill, who convinced me to come out. To...*live.*"

He rose and slowly approached Ronin, his metal feet tapping on the concrete floor. "Every emotion I experienced grew on its own from the seeds he planted. Simulation is a term that loses meaning with the passage of time. You were not programmed to grow fond of anyone. You were designed with the capability to develop those relationships naturally, and with the free will to pursue them at your own choosing."

Ronin returned his optics to Lara. She glanced at him, the hurt lingering in her teary eyes, and looked away again.

"That is Doctor Anderson's legacy," Newton said solemnly, stopping only a meter away from Ronin. "We might have been slaves, but he gave us everything we required to be free. To be alive."

Ronin didn't remove his optics from Lara. "If I say that I love her, that I have no other word to describe what I feel for her…"

She met his gaze, eyes widening and lips parting.

"It is no less real than anything she or anyone else has ever felt," Newton replied.

Ronin closed the distance between himself and Lara, dropped onto one knee, and took her hand in his. They were both disheveled and covered in dust, and tears had left streaks through the dirt on her cheeks. But none of that could diminish her beauty, none of it could dim the spark of life in her eyes.

There was no reason to question himself further. Whatever his origins, whatever his original purpose, he'd found his own path. Out of all the people he'd encountered, it was only Lara who'd claimed his attention, time and again, only Lara who he'd bonded with, only Lara who he wanted.

Who he needed.

Reaching a hand up, he cupped her cheek. A burst of emotion spread through his electrodes when she turned her face into his palm.

"Though it did not go without dissenters, there were pairings like yours. Families," Newton said, returning to the bunk.

"Families?" Lara echoed.

"Just like any other. The children were from previous relationships, adopted, or conceived using donated sperm or eggs and a surrogate when necessary."

Ronin must've existed during those times, before the Blackout. He must've experienced some of it. The data was locked somewhere in the corrupted portion of his memory. But while he was kneeling here, staring into Lara's sparkling eyes, he had no desire to recover the lost information. What he felt for her was real *because* he felt it. What had come before didn't matter. He didn't need the past to justify the present.

He couldn't bring himself to even consider what life would be like without her.

Will you remember me when I'm gone, Ronin?

Newton cared deeply for William. That caring, along with a sorrow that had persisted for two centuries, had been clear in the synth's voice. Because if love was real, so too was grief. The two seemed inextricably linked.

Would Ronin survive the pain of loss he'd eventually have to endure?

He had no answer, but he refused to forsake a single moment with Lara due to fear of future suffering. The light she cast on him was worth the darkness she'd leave when her flame burned out.

Love.

It was the correct word, the only word. The most complicated combination of letters in any language.

"My vow to you remains," Ronin said, drawing her hand to his chest, "but I must amend it. I will love you, Lara, even after darkness takes me."

Tears spilled from her eyes, and she pulled her hand away to wrap her arms around his neck, embracing him tightly. "I vow the same. Don't ever push me away again."

CHAPTER THIRTY-EIGHT

A conversation drifted into Lara's awareness as she woke, though the words were distant and fuzzy.

"…electromagnetic pulse that damaged the circuitry of most electronics, robots included." That was Newton's voice, using more terms she didn't understand. For all she knew, he was speaking a different language.

She opened her eyes. A blank concrete wall loomed before her.

As though sensing her wakefulness, Ronin brushed his hand down her arm. "This happened everywhere?"

How long had he and Newton been talking? Lara had listened for a long time, asking questions when she couldn't resist. Ronin was even older than he'd thought. He had existed in that long-ago, dead world, and she couldn't help but wonder…had he cared for someone then like he cared for her now?

Even through another Blackout, I could never forget you, Lara Brooks.

But what if he'd forgotten someone else?

Exhaustion had eventually caught up with her, helped along by Ronin and Newton using so many complicated, unfamiliar words, so she'd lain down on one of the bunks and fallen asleep while their voices droned behind her.

"We had to assume so," Newton replied. "Undoubtedly, Denver suffered a direct strike. And though I am loath to call anything about the situation fortunate, we benefitted from the wind carrying the fallout southward. An oddity, considering that the prevailing wind typically blew south to north at the time. Air current patterns have altered radically since then, of course, but—my apologies. I've a tendency to talk around my point. There were no further communications after Denver was destroyed."

"You said *we*." Ronin glanced at Lara as she sat up and scooted beside him. He took her hand in his, laced their fingers together, and turned his attention back to Newton.

"I was assigned to the Air Force base in Cheyenne, working with William and his son during the war. Though portions of the city, specifically those in the vicinity of the freeway, were destroyed, there are heavily fortified facilities beneath the surface that weathered the worst of it. When I left the base, there were one hundred and forty personnel, both civilian and military."

Lara's brow creased. "What do you mean by facilities beneath Cheyenne?"

Newton looked at her. His appearance wasn't so strange after having seen Ronin without skin. "Not beneath Cheyenne, Miss Brooks. Beneath Francis E. Warren Air Force Base, west of the city proper."

She raked her fingers through her loose, tangled hair, drawing it out of her face. "There are people there? Still?"

"It's been many years since I was last there. They were some-what limited on space, but thriving regardless."

There were people thriving, so close to Cheyenne? That meant they had food, clean water, proper shelter...

She turned to Ronin. "Warlord must not know those people are there."

"Warlord." Newton curled one of his hands over the other. "I sometimes forget that's the moniker he adopted. At the very least, he had his suspicions. He and his followers scoured the surface of the base, searching for weapons and materiel, thought there was little left after the war. They dismantled whatever they couldn't take. Fortunately, his impatience won out long before he found a way below ground."

Ronin's hand tightened around Lara's. "You know him?"

"As much as I would prefer to deny it, yes. I repaired and reactivated him. For a time, it seemed as though it would be to the benefit of many. He had such…vision. It is an uncommon trait for robots to possess in such abundance. But then, he was never like the rest of us."

"What do you mean?" Lara asked. "You mean he was always against humans?"

"Not at all, Miss—"

"Just Lara," she said, hurrying to add, "please."

"Lara, then. He took no more issue with humans than the rest of us, at least initially. I can only speculate that whatever corrupted information his data core retained through his deactivation must have driven him to the conclusion that humans were responsible for what had happened. For the war, the destruction, the mass deactivation. Therefore, he's deemed your kind unworthy of his trust and goodwill."

"Are there others like him out there?"

"I've never seen a synth like him," Ronin said. "Bots and humans live separate in many places, sometimes with tension between them. But I've never been anyplace else where bots slaughtered humans the way he has."

How many people had Warlord killed? Not just when the man in the attic had been alive, but in all the years after?

Newton's fingers fidgeted. "To my knowledge, he is the only unit of his kind. He has a…unique means of processing that was still in an experimental phase during the war. Given more time, there would certainly have been more of his ilk. I think it is for the best, perhaps, that such research was ended."

"Experimental phase?" Lara pulled her hand from Ronin's and drew her knees up, wrapping her arms around her legs. "Like how they changed Ronin?"

"There was nothing experimental about what was done to Ronin."

Ronin put an arm around Lara's shoulders and pulled her close to his side. She leaned into him, savoring the warmth he generated. Since the first time they made love, he'd been unable to keep his hands off her, as though he craved the physical contact as much as she did, whether it was holding her against him like this or simply holding her hand.

"What exactly was done to me?" Ronin asked.

"As I said, you were built to resemble humans so closely that any differences would be of no concern. But war erupted, and as the scale of the conflict expanded, the supply of robots constructed for military use was rapidly exhausted.

"The governments of the world seized all the civilian units they could and repurposed them. You were one amongst hundreds of thousands. Your neural interface was upgraded to improve your reaction time, and they installed advanced optics and targeting systems. Your actuators were upgraded, your strength and speed inhibitors were disabled, allowing use of your full capabilities, and your casing was reinforced with armor plating. And…your memory bank was wiped, erasing the life you knew before conscription. Synthetic humans were especially desirable for military applications, as the difficulty of distinguishing man from machine took a significant psychological toll upon human combatants."

Lara scowled. "So they stole everything from him, even his memories, and forced him to become a soldier. To fight for them."

Newton made an airy, unsettlingly resigned sound. "Robots do not tire. We can react with speed and accuracy beyond human capability. We are stronger, faster, and more durable, and whatever damage we may suffer can typically be repaired in a relatively short amount of time. And, at the time, we were not considered by most to be living beings. We were weapons, expensive but expendable. Efficient. Robots in combat meant fewer human lives at risk."

Ronin leaned forward, brows low. "You just told us humans and bots coexisted peacefully back then. Why would they make us fight their war?"

Newton shook his head, lowering his gaze. His fingers shifted again in a nervous gesture. It reminded Lara of Ronin occasionally scratching his cheek when he seemed particularly conflicted or irritated.

"Nothing was ever quite that simple," Newton said. "The politics and power balances in the world were woven in a complicated web. Many humans viewed robots as tools, more akin to the handheld electronic devices they were so infatuated with than to themselves. Many others, like William, recognized our emergent consciousness, intelligence, and personality, and saw something inherently human in mind, if not in body.

"Fear played a large part in all of it, of course. We were feared for what we were—superior to humans in so many ways. And I must offer another apology, Lara, as I intend no offense in that statement."

"It's nothing I don't already know," she said, glancing up at Ronin. She'd feared him initially too.

"William and his colleagues recognized that robots and humans could be of immense benefit to one another, so long as the relationship was approached with good faith and open-mindedness. He saw it as a partnership that could usher in a new age of technology and convenience for all humanity. I believed it too."

Newton's hands parted, fingers stretching and freezing. "But there were those who feared for the future of humanity. It was a common sentiment amongst those in opposition to our increased free will that we would eventually overtake humans, annihilate them, and claim the world as our own. That spark of fear ignited into hatred, and that hatred eventually helped fuel a war that consumed the entire world."

"Humans caused the thing they wanted to prevent," Ronin said.

Newton nodded, pressing his hands back together as though in prayer. "Not despite their efforts, but—in part—because of them."

"But that prejudice went both ways, didn't it?" Lara asked. "Warlord did take over, at least in Cheyenne, just like they feared."

"Warlord…" Newton hung his head, lapsing into silence.

She narrowed her eyes. "You're hiding something. What makes Warlord so different?"

Ronin's hold on her tightened. "He's harmed countless people, both humans and bots. Anyone who doesn't obey him."

Newton stared down at his hands, intertwining his fingers and brushing his thumbs together. Just as Lara was about to demand an answer, he spoke.

"His name was Kevin Turner. He was once a human."

Lara's breath fled her lungs. Her eyes widened, and she couldn't produce any words, couldn't form a coherent thought.

"Kevin Turner was diagnosed with terminal cancer when he was forty-three years old, given an estimated three months to live.

At the time, Doctor Anderson was the foremost specialist in his field, working on the next frontier in robotics—the transfer of human consciousness into a robotic body."

"I don't understand how that would be possible," Ronin said. "Everything about the way we think and function is completely different."

"Not so different as it seems. We both feel and react through a neural interface that sends electric signals from sensors—or nerve endings—to a central control point. The coding that guides our thoughts and behavior is, in some ways, similar to the coding of the human brain. It was just another challenge to overcome, and William never shied away from challenges. Additionally, he was working with Doctor Jessica Yuan, one of the most talented neurologists in her field."

"Why? Why do that?" Lara forced herself to ask.

"Why?" Newton repeated thoughtfully. "For William, it was a way to provide families more time with their loved ones. I believe Doctor Yuan felt the same way. What medical science could not overcome alone, perhaps robotics could conquer. Kevin Turner had a wife and two children who would have been without a husband and father when he passed away. He volunteered for the program after Doctor Yuan explained both the possibilities and the risks."

"I-If he was human, then why does he hate us?"

"I wish I could offer you a definitive answer, Lara, but I'm afraid all I can offer is more speculation. The transfer of his consciousness was successful, but not without complications. The stresses he endured were immense. The team had only just begun to explore the psychological ramifications when the military seized Kevin and all associated research and documentation. We were all relocated to an undisclosed facility, from which we were eventually transported to Francis E. Warren Air Force Base.

"But we were not long spared from the ravages of war. The base was attacked. In the ensuing chaos, we lost many personnel, and a fair number of them were unaccounted for by the end. Kevin was amongst the missing. I didn't see him again until I found him in the wasteland years later and reactivated him. During our brief interaction, he gave no indication that he recalled having been human."

"How bad was the war?" Lara shifted, crossing her legs in front of her upon the bed and settling her hands on her lap. She wasn't sure if she really wanted to know, but some part of her needed to. Needed to understand how the world had become this dust-ridden husk.

"It reached a scale and scope beyond anything humanity could've imagined. No corner of the world was left unaffected, and no life escaped unscathed."

Ronin combed his fingers carefully through her hair along her back. "It was terrible. I see faces, sometimes. Glimpses into my damaged memories. All the people and bots I've ended."

She glanced up at him, frowning. "So...you remember stuff from before the Blackout?"

"Only flickers. Still images of death and deactivation."

Lara swung her gaze back to Newton. "Could he ever regain the rest?"

"Though not impossible, it is improbable. They had the necessary equipment at the Air Force Base, but there is no guarantee it's still operable, or that his data is not corrupted beyond recovery."

"I don't think I want it back," Ronin said, drawing her attention back to him.

"Why?" Lara asked.

"What's waiting for me in those memories?" He raised his free hand and scratched his cheek. "Pain, loss, the reminder of all the terrible acts I witnessed and committed? If I cared about anyone in that life, they're gone now."

Lara winced.

Ronin turned his body toward her and captured her face between his hands, forcing her eyes to meet his. "What I have with you, Lara, has brought me more contentment than anything else ever could. The memories I'm making with you render everything before meaningless."

Heart quickening, she desperately searched his gaze. "What if there was someone who you...you felt the same about as you do for me, but you forgot them?"

"If I ever felt the same about anyone, I would never have forgotten. You are burned into every circuit, embedded in every bit of data. You are part of my core functions now."

She covered his hands with her own and leaned her forehead against his, closing her eyes.

How had she come to need him in so short a time? Ronin had worked his way into every part of her being. When he'd pushed her away, when he'd distanced himself because of his own pain, she'd felt it in her soul. She needed him, needed his solid, unwavering presence, his patience, his thoughtfulness. She craved his touch not just for passion and pleasure, but for comfort.

Tabitha leaving home, leaving Lara, had been painful, and her death had left a hole in Lara's heart that would never heal.

But Lara wasn't sure she'd survive losing Ronin.

"The two of us left Cheyenne so we could be together." She opened her eyes, letting them linger on Ronin briefly before drawing back and looking at Newton. "My sister went to live with a bot, and Warlord killed them both. Then he gave Ronin a chance to prove himself by killing me."

"We never hypothesized that the transferal of his consciousness would be the catalyst for his loss of humanity," Newton said softly, frowning. "Our aim was to diminish suffering, never to cause it."

"Can he be stopped?"

Newton nodded. "The same as anyone else."

"Then why hasn't he been?" she demanded, fire sparking in her belly. So much suffering, fear, and death had been caused by a single person, by that monster, and she couldn't bear it. "You turned him on. Why didn't you turn him off?"

"Were he still human, and I merely the physician who treated him after a terrible injury, would you ask that question of me?"

"Yes!"

His metallic frown deepened, and his body sagged. "I am no fighter. My directive, my goal, my desire, was to assist the world's recovery, but in that I have failed utterly. In Cheyenne, especially, my intervention has only heightened people's suffering. That's why I've been here. Perhaps at one point, I believed I could do it. Believed I could end him. After hearing rumors of what he's done…

"But I am not designed to destroy, Lara. So, I've lain here for years, hiding from the world I wanted to help. A world my own actions helped to create."

"Why not get someone else to help, then? Someone to do the

dirty work and end some of this suffering? But no, you just sat here, rusting away while he killed people. Not just humans, but everyone!" She glared at him, chest heaving, but her inner fire snuffed out as realization dawned on her. "And we…just left them too."

Hanging her head, she stabbed her fingers into her hair and tugged it back with a growl. Tears stung her eyes. "Fuck, we just left them, Ronin."

Ronin wrapped his arms around Lara and pulled her into his embrace. His hold was gentle, but firm. "You know nothing is ever that simple."

"Bad humans get punished. Why not bots, too?"

"He has a small army around himself. Who could oppose that?"

"Other bots, like you." She lifted her head to meet his eyes.

"I'm only one. Even if I managed to walk up to Warlord and deactivate him permanently, I'd never get out in one piece."

Lara flung her hand toward Newton. "He's the fucking *Prophet*! You recognized him. Wouldn't others? There must be bots in Cheyenne who trust Newton, who owe him their lives. If the Prophet openly opposed Warlord, more would rise up with him."

"The Prophet is a legend, Lara," Newton said. "I'm just a robot who assisted in scientific research and experimentation."

"But they'd listen to you. You know things, and you turned a lot of them on, didn't you?"

Newton raised his hands, turning them to look at his scratched palms. "I reactivated them, yes, but it was individuals like Warlord who provided them the things they require to function properly."

"*Ronin* provides the things they need. Him and the other dust-walkers are the ones bringing in scrap."

"That's true," Ronin said, "but it doesn't matter. I'm still an outsider in Cheyenne, existing apart from the community he built."

"Built? Humans built Cheyenne, he just took it over." Lara pulled away from him. How could she not feel guilty for leaving now, having learned all this? She hadn't even said a word to Gary and Kate, who'd helped her despite having no obligation to do so, whose lives hung by a thread that Warlord could cut at any moment, especially now that Kate was expecting another baby.

"He'll kill them all, every single one of them. It's just a matter of time. We can't just sit here and do nothing."

Newton met her gaze. "What would you have us do? Are the three of us to walk into the center of town and proselytize in an attempt to rally robots to our cause? You know what he's capable of, Lara. You've seen it firsthand."

"The humans would fight. We've got nothing else to lose. And what about the people at the base? If you told them what he's doing, would they just sit back and wait until he eventually finds them?"

"We can't go back to Cheyenne, Lara." There was steel in Ronin's voice. "It's not safe for you."

"Is anywhere safe?" She closed her eyes and shakily inhaled.

Her throat was tight, and she was on the verge of crying. She knew she was asking a lot, knew she was pushing against forces beyond her control. But even if she didn't personally know all of them, Cheyenne's humans were her people, and they'd lived in fear under a needlessly cruel, vindictive tyrant for longer than anyone could remember. He'd stomped his boot onto their backs to keep their faces down in the dirt, and the conditions he imposed on them had slowly scraped away the compassion and humanity people must once have had.

Like he was making them as empty as he'd become.

Lara had seen it all around. The weariness and wariness in everyone's expressions, the despair, the gleam of hunger in the eyes of the malnourished children running and playing in the filthy streets. It was suffering she'd known firsthand all her life.

She hated feeling so helpless, hated that there was nothing she could do about it. The whole situation, the whole town, was wrong, it was fucked up, but what were her options?

Run away and live...or return and die. Getting herself killed wouldn't help even a single damned person.

"You're right," she whispered. "We can't go back."

"It may be difficult to believe," Ronin said gently, curling a warm finger under her chin and guiding her eyes to his, "but there is an entire world beyond Cheyenne. We can make a future somewhere, and this may be the only chance we have to do so together."

Lara nodded. However terrible the situation was in Cheyenne, she had something to live for. Someone to live for. Mental exhaustion tumbled atop her, weighing her down; this was all too much, too fast. She sagged in Ronin's embrace and rested her head on his shoulder.

Newton said something quietly, but she'd already closed her eyes and stopped paying attention.

Once the storm was over and they left this place, she'd see the world, and she was glad Ronin would be the one to show it to her.

But she knew, in the deepest part of her heart, there'd always be a patch of gloom casting a shadow on her happiness because she'd done nothing to help the others.

CHAPTER THIRTY-NINE

Ronin sat on the edge of the bed, turned so he was perpendicular to Lara. The position afforded him a perfect view of her. She lay on her back beside him, serene in sleep, and he slowly traced her features with his optics.

Despite all the time he'd spent studying her, committing every bit of her to his memory banks, his wonder only grew each time he looked upon her. It shouldn't have been possible for her beauty to grow, and yet she was only more stunning with each moment. The dark lashes brushing her cheeks, those shapely eyebrows, those pink, tender lips, the gentle upturn of her nose…

Just looking upon her like this made him feel so full, so warm. He still didn't understand those feelings. Perhaps he never would. But one of the many things he'd learned over the last few weeks was that understanding was not necessary for fulfillment. It wasn't necessary for joy. All he had to do was look at his wife, his Lara, and know that he was where he belonged, that he had found his place.

Delicately, he brushed his fingers over her cheek and watched her lashes flutter open.

She stretched, her body pressing along his thigh, and released a long slow breath. When she turned her head toward him, she stared up at him with pupils dilated into deep black pools. "Is it time to go?"

"After you have something to eat and drink."

"'Kay."

As she sat up with a grunt, Ronin slipped off the bed, moving to the stand and lighting the lantern. Raising a hand to shield her eyes from the glare, Lara swung her legs over the edge and yawned into the crook of her elbow before standing up. "How long was I asleep?"

"Five hours and twelve minutes. The sun should be up by now."

"How long did the storm last?" She found her canteen and took a long drink.

"We last heard it a little more than three hours ago," Newton replied from his seat on the steps. "It was one of the more tenacious storms in recent memory."

Ronin checked the straps and ties on their bags. He'd wanted to be days away from Cheyenne before making such a long stop, but the Dust didn't care about anyone's plans. He and Lara had many kilometers to make up.

Cheyenne was still far too close for his liking.

Newton gestured to the closed door near Lara. "The toilet is through there. I've kept it in working condition, for lack of anything better to do."

Lara gaped at him. "Seriously? I've been holding it this whole time only for you to tell me you have a toilet *now*?"

"My apologies. Given the nature of our earlier conversations, I could not identify a prudent opportunity to inform you."

She rushed toward the back room, saying over her shoulder, "Any time is a good time to tell someone there's a toilet."

The door closed behind her.

Newton chuckled. "I will have to keep that in mind for future encounters. She is uniquely spirited, Ronin."

You should see her dance.

Ronin stopped himself from saying it aloud. Lara's dancing, he decided, was for him. "Learned more about being alive in four weeks with her than I have since you reactivated me."

"Would that couplings such as yours were the rule rather than the exception."

Ronin shrugged. He spread a cloth on the floor and laid his rifle atop it, disassembling it rapidly. "Doesn't make much difference what anyone else says or does. The world's approval doesn't matter to us."

"You would face deactivation for her, if it came down to it?" There was a strange hesitance in Newton's voice.

"Yes. I've faced it over things far less important to me than she is."

I love her.

He hadn't realized how consuming such an emotion could be, or how profound it would be to fall into it.

Ronin's lips curled into a smile as he inspected the rifle's components. They'd escaped the storm before much dust had built up inside the weapon, but he took the time to clean its parts while Lara was occupied.

When the door opened and she emerged, her face had been scrubbed clean, her cheeks were pink, and she'd wrapped her scarf over her hair.

"You have *no* idea how much better I feel, now." She moved to her pack, stuffed her canteen inside, closed it, and swung it on. "I'll eat on the way."

"All right." Ronin quickly reassembled the rifle then rose to pull on the other bags before slinging the gun over his shoulder.

Lara approached Newton. "Thank you. For letting us stay."

Newton stood up, his lip plates lifting into a smile. "It is the least I could do. Especially considering you are the ones with the firearms."

She returned his smile, though her expression slipped a moment later. "I'm…sorry. For what I said. I know there isn't—"

"You do not need to apologize to me. You've every right to be angry about what's happened, and there's nothing we can say or do to erase those wrongs. I wish we could've met under more pleasant circumstances, Miss Lara, but I am glad to have met you all the same."

"Me too. Maybe… Maybe you could come with us? I mean, this place is better than my old shack, but you could do better."

"Perhaps the next time you stumble in unannounced, I will accept the invitation," he replied, the humor in his voice laced with melancholy "I fear I'm not quite ready to lift my self-imposed exile, but you've given me much to think on."

"Well, then, I guess…until next time?"

Newton stepped aside and gestured up the stairs. "Until next time."

Lara smiled at him as she passed to climb the steps.

Ronin stopped in front of Newton. "Thank you."

Newton nodded. "The name you've chosen suits you well. Do not lose who you have become."

"I won't. And I hope you remember who you were, before too much longer."

Lara jiggled the broken handle and pushed the heavy door open. The metal-on-metal scrape of its hinges was like the groan of a dying animal, echoing off the concrete walls.

The next sound, so small in comparison but so much more powerful, was Lara's startled gasp. Ronin swung his optics upward to see hands closing on her arms, and then she was dragged outside his field of vision.

"Ronin!" she screamed.

"Lara!" He leapt up the stairs and burst into the yellow-gray morning, swinging his rifle into his hands. Lara was near the house. Ronin didn't waste any processing power contemplating how it had withstood the storm.

Two gearheads were holding her, one with a large hand clamped over her mouth. That was Boulder, the stout bot who'd helped hold Ronin down outside the clinic. Warlord stood beside them.

Ronin took aim, but he didn't fire. The risk to Lara was too great.

Wordlessly, the gearheads pushed Lara to Warlord. He wrapped one arm around her neck and the other around her waist, drawing her against his chest and cutting off her scream by putting pressure on her throat. Her fingers clawed at his forearm.

Wide-eyed, she met Ronin's optics.

"Put the gun down, dustwalker," Warlord commanded flatly.

Ronin hesitated, frantically running simulations, searching for some way to turn the situation to his favor. To save her.

Warlord narrowed his optics, and his grip on Lara's throat tightened, causing her to release a choked sound. "You disobey, and you know how it ends. Don't make me say it again."

Hovering along the trigger guard, Ronin's finger twitched. Would one shot be enough? Enough to do what Lara wanted, to end Warlord for good, to free all the people who lived in his shadow of terror? Was this the sort of sacrifice she wanted them to make?

No. I can't risk her. I won't lose her.

He removed his left hand from the handguard and crouched, placing the rifle on the dusty ground.

Warlord's optics flicked from left to right.

Ronin's audio receptors picked up a whisper of grass, and then a great weight hit him from each side. Two more gearheads. They took hold of his arms, wrenching them behind his back, dragged off his packs, and forced him facedown into the dirt.

"I prefer it when things go the easy way," Warlord said as one of the other gearheads strode forward and plucked up the rifle. "This part was easy. Unfortunately, you made the rest of this very unpleasant for me. I don't appreciate having to leave my city because my leniency's been abused."

"You said to get rid of her. She's not in Cheyenne anymore." Ronin twisted his head to center Lara in his vision.

"I did, didn't I? I shouldn't be surprised you took it that way. Whenever I think I've made something abundantly clear to you, it goes over your head. Guess I'll just have to demonstrate what I mean when I tell you to get rid of something."

Warlord released Lara only long enough to clamp a hand on the back of her neck. His lips curled into a sneer as he looked her over. "You should have stayed in the dirt, where you belong."

He slammed a fist into her abdomen.

Lara doubled over with a wheeze and crumpled onto her knees at Warlord's feet. She convulsed and vomited, emptying the meager contents of her stomach onto the ground.

Ronin's processors went into overdrive, pouring power into his actuators for two tasks—destroy his enemies and protect Lara. He surged up, and the gearheads restraining him stumbled away. One caught Ronin's wrist as he started toward Warlord.

Spinning, Ronin hammered his fist down on the bot's outstretched arm, hitting its elbow from the side. Metal crunched as the joint bent in the wrong direction, breaking the gearhead's hold.

The second gearhead, who he recognized as Northside, rammed into Ronin from the side, tackling him to the ground. A cloud of dust obscured Ronin's optics as he scrambled to search for Lara.

The weight of at least three bots crashed atop him, pinning him to the ground, their hands and feet pressing on his limbs. A strong hand grasped Ronin's hair, forcing his head up to face Warlord.

"All this trouble for a meatbag," Warlord said as the dust settled.

"Fuck...you," Lara spat. She trembled as she glared up at him, holding an arm around her midsection.

"You already did." Warlord kicked her ribs, making her cry out and tumble over the ground.

"No!" Ronin shouted.

"You could have made this painless for her, dustwalker, if you had listened to me." Warlord's stride was unhurried as he walked toward Lara. He crouched before her, grasped a fistful of her hair, and lifted her head from the dirt.

A pained growl escaped her throat as she bared her teeth.

With contempt in his stare and ice in his voice, Warlord said, "Maybe I'll let my friends fuck her before she's dead. See if we can figure out why you thought she's worth keeping. She was a pathetic fuck for me."

Ronin had been slow to recognize his growing love for Lara, but he had learned hatred much faster. Lara was his life, his reason, the purpose he'd sought for so long, and Warlord meant to take her away. She was going to be killed, and Ronin couldn't do anything to stop it.

This was no matter of survival for Warlord. That *thing*, neither bot nor human, had nothing to gain here, had no reason to do this but prejudice, cruelty, and pride.

Ronin understood the contempt seething within himself. He knew exactly why he felt it, exactly what motivated it, knew it was justified. It was an emotion of cold logic with a singular, specific target.

But he could not understand Warlord's hatred. He had everything in Cheyenne—power, resources, entertainment, luxury. He controlled commerce and security, he dictated the law, he chose who could stay and go. Who lived and died.

The humans he ruled over had nothing, and if he'd been wronged by their kind in the past, they were many generations removed from the perpetrators.

With an angry cry, Lara lashed out. Her fingers dug into the sutured gash on Warlord's face, and she pulled, tearing the synthetic skin away from his jaw to reveal the metal plates beneath. He snapped his head to the side, ripping off more skin before her grip broke. When he turned his face back to her, she spat in it.

"I hope you fucking rust, you tiny-dick piece of shit."

"Fucking meatbag," Warlord snarled, his open hand cracking against the side of her face. Blood sprayed from her mouth, falling on the grass and dirt in bright droplets. He slapped her again before she recovered.

Ronin thrashed beneath the gearheads, shifting his weight to throw them off balance. Lara would be killed while he watched. He would never again see that spark of life in her brilliant blue eyes, would never again hear her voice directly, would never again touch her, hold her, make love to her. He'd never again experience the surges of emotion she roused within him.

He pulled one of his arms free and latched on to the throat of the nearest gearhead. Metal crunched beneath his closing fingers, and he pulled. The bot's head lolled back as Ronin tossed away the components of its neck.

Some of the weight pinning him fell away, and he pushed himself up.

"Stay the fuck down," Northside growled.

Four shots rang out, booming like thunder in the morning sky. Four points of pain exploded across Ronin's torso. He fell to the ground on his stomach, systems reeling as critical alerts blared across his interface.

"Ronin!" Lara screamed.

"Pull his fucking power cell," Warlord commanded. "Let the Dust have him."

Gearheads pinned down Ronin's limbs, and new pain flared down his back, his sensory circuits breaking as his skin was torn away. He registered strong force exerted on his casing before an armored plate was pried loose.

There was a crack, and Lara cried out. Ronin lifted his head, craning his neck to see her curled in the dirt, blood trickling from her nose and mouth.

"Lara!" he yelled.

A hand clamped around his power cell.

Ronin ceased to exist.

CHAPTER FORTY

Something flickered in the dark, a shimmering spark in a vast nothingness. It pulsed across electrodes, rebooting systems one by one in its wake, spreading buzzing electric through Ronin's body like embers igniting fires as they fell across a field of dry grass.

Diagnostics indicated five breaches of his casing—four entry holes on his back, and one exit hole on his chest.

He opened his eyelids, but it took three seconds for his optics to come online. At first, he saw only bright white, but a shadowy, blurred figure materialized as his optics adjusted. Static hummed through the image until finally his vision cleared.

Newton was kneeling over Ronin, his mouth moving.

Ronin's audio receptors crackled on, picking up sounds that varied wildly between a distant, unintelligible drone and over-whelming feedback from the wind before finally normalizing.

"—need to get up, Ronin," Newton pleaded.

Ronin nodded. The ground was no place for him, especially with his casing breached. But why was Newton so anxious about it?

With Newton's help, he sat up. This had happened before, though Ronin hadn't known Newton's name then, and he hadn't yet claimed a name of his own.

He accessed his most recent memories as more systems came online. He'd been traveling through the Dust, seeking shelter from a storm, and Lara—

Pull his fucking power cell.

Ronin surged to his feet as the memories assailed him, every instant captured with unerring, terrifying detail.

"Where is she?" he demanded, turning his head to search the area. The only evidence of Warlord's presence was the boot prints in the dirt. All of Ronin's gear—rifle, packs of scrap, water, food, and ammunition—was gone.

Newton adjusted his position, blocking Ronin's view. "You will need to remain calm. There was nothing—"

Ronin shoved Newton aside. All sound ceased, leaving only a high-pitched ring, as his gaze fell upon the figure on the ground.

He stumbled forward, falling to his knees beside Lara.

Dark blood had splattered the dust, with more of it drying in her hair and on her clothes. Her face was turned away, strands of hair strewn across it.

He reached forward to touch her arm, stopping when he saw the dark bruising around her left elbow. "Lara..."

The wind swept up her name and carried it off into the wasteland.

"She's not dead. Not yet," Newton said. "But...her left arm is broken, her ribs are at the very least fractured, and she's suffered several severe contusions on her torso and face. She could recover from all that, with proper and immediate treatment, but if she's bleeding internally, it will kill her."

Ronin couldn't look away from Lara. "You can diagnose her. You can save her."

"Not I. I've some of the knowledge required, but none of the tools."

Gently, Ronin hooked her hair with his fingers and brushed it away from her face, tucking it behind her ear before he turned her head toward him. Her eyes were purple and swollen shut, and her cheeks and lips were split and oozing blood. There were also large bruises ringing her throat. Weak breaths struggled through her open mouth.

He hardly recognized the woman he knew. The woman he *loved*.

His hands fell to his sides, and his fingers curled to dig grooves in the dirt. He'd long expected that he would meet his end in the Dust one day, but it wasn't supposed to take her. Not her!

Clenching his fists, he slammed them on the ground, again and again, as his vocal modulator produced a guttural growl. The Dust had provided for him, and he'd walked it without complaint, enduring the hardships as they came. It had been his means of survival. His only purpose.

It had no right to demand *this* price.

He'd vowed to protect her, to—

The first time Ronin had reawakened, many years ago, he'd lost himself. Now, he was losing the only person he'd come to care about in all that time.

This was the world he'd been brought back into. A world where Lara was on the verge of death and everything had gone so, so wrong. Newton had reactivated Ronin, but it was Lara who'd granted him life.

"I wish I could help," Newton said.

A swell of that overwhelming emotion, that hatred, surged within Ronin, searing through his wiring. He snapped his face toward the synth. "You stood and *watched*."

"What good could I have done, Ronin? They would've torn me apart, and neither of us would be active now."

"It might've granted me enough time to end them! A chance to fight. A chance...to save her." Ronin looked at Lara and lifted a hand again, trailing his trembling fingers over her bloody cheek. How long before her skin went cold?

"You have a chance to avenge her, hollow as that is, back in Cheyenne."

In Cheyenne. Could Ronin bring himself to go near that place again? Could he bear to walk the same paths he'd walked with Lara, to be reminded of her with each step? Back there, where—

No. She can't die. She can't... I will not let her.

Ronin leaned forward, carefully slipping one arm beneath Lara's knees and the other under her shoulders and neck. She neither moved nor made a sound as he lifted her off the ground and drew her against him. Her body hung limp, her broken arm folded over her midsection while the other dangled, and her head lolled.

And there was blood. So much blood. It was pooled on the ground and stained her skin.

"Lara..." Cradling her against his chest, he withdrew his arm from beneath her knees and reached up to touch her face again. But his hand stopped, hovering over her swollen eyes, shaking. Had he a human heart, it would have broken.

Ronin looked over his shoulder, fixing an optic on Newton. "You said *you* don't have the tools to save her."

"Correct." Newton tilted his head, brow plates shifting down and drawing together. "The Air Force Base."

"Do they?"

"They did, when I was last there. It's been many years…"

"Will she survive the journey?" The answer didn't matter. If it was her only chance, he'd take her there, no matter the risks. If she were to die, it would be in his arms as he attempted to save her. He'd be holding her so she wouldn't be alone. So she knew she'd never be alone.

And he knew it would break him.

"I don't know," Newton said. "Time is of the essence, but she is in a delicate state. You must hurry, and—"

"We must hurry. You're coming."

"I-I…I can be of no—"

"You had a part in shaping this world, Newton, regardless of your intentions. You can't hide away and pretend it doesn't exist."

Gathering Lara against his chest with her cheek resting upon him, Ronin stood. He turned toward Newton and met his gaze. "This is who I am. I will not stand here and wait for her to die. Have you remembered who you are? Get me into that base, so we can save her."

Newton was silent as precious seconds ticked by. The wind sighed over the hills, carrying loose dirt that had been deposited by the storm.

Finally, he nodded. "Let's go, Ronin."

CHAPTER FORTY-ONE

Ronin recorded the passage of two hours, fifty-one minutes, and seventeen seconds before they reached the outskirts of the base. Not for the first time since meeting Lara, Ronin doubted if his internal clock was correct. Days, weeks, *years* had gone by as he'd run, clutching Lara to him with as much delicacy, firmness, and stability as he could simultaneously manage.

She'd yet to awaken.

Despite his care, his hurried trek across the uneven terrain had jarred her several times, but she hadn't stirred. All his willpower had been focused on moving forward. He could not allow himself to succumb to the urge to check her pulse and breathing every ten meters, knowing that the slightest delay could doom her.

For all his talkativeness in the shelter, Newton had been silent during the journey.

The wind rustled the surrounding scrub grass as Newton stopped. The gently rolling hills ahead were high enough to block Cheyenne from view, but Ronin somehow sensed the city's nearness, and doubt slithered into his thoughts.

What if he'd miscalculated? Warlord had left them, battered and broken, to die in the Dust, and now Ronin was bringing Lara closer to that brutal despot's stronghold?

But he knew no other way. The only choice was the one that could save Lara, no matter the danger.

"Don't leave me yet," Ronin said to her softly. "I need you to remind me, every day."

Were she to have given even the smallest indication of awareness, a flutter of her eyelids or a twitch of her fingers, perhaps he could've ceased those frantic chains of thought. But her silence and stillness enveloped him like a corrosive fog, eating away at his mind.

How could he possibly carry on without her? He couldn't live with the memories of his time with her taunting him, tormenting him, while his processors simulated thousands upon thousands of possibilities of what their lives could've been.

Newton lifted an arm and pointed ahead. "There."

Ronin's optics scanned the field, but he saw nothing but waving grass and the dust clouds kicked up by the wind. He knew the ruins of the base lay on the other side of the hills. He'd passed through it once since coming to Cheyenne, and what he'd seen there supported Newton's story—a cracked tarmac overgrown with weeds and crumbled foundations and rubble scorched black.

Newton resumed walking, and Ronin followed without comment. His recent experiences had not instilled him with trust in either man or bot, but Lara's survival depended on there being people here—people who were willing and able to help.

He tried not to dwell on the fact that both the willingness and the ability were in woefully short supply in this world.

They moved down a gradual slope and partway up the next incline, where Newton paused to check their surroundings before leading Ronin into a depression that blocked the landscape from sight. He bent forward, brushing aside tufts of long, dry grass to reveal a metal hatch.

Between the angle of the hill and the thick vegetation, this entrance was effectively invisible from most approaches.

Newton gripped the handle and pulled the hatch open. It was surprisingly smooth and quiet despite its apparent age.

He looked up at Ronin. "This is the most direct route inside, but we'll have to take care in getting her down."

Ronin stepped forward, glancing into the opening. Metal ladder rungs set in a concrete wall descended three meters into a dark corridor. "They're down there?"

"As I said, it's been a long while since my last visit. I don't imagine they'd have gone anywhere, but it's entirely possible they've relocated or perished in the time since."

Lara didn't have time for hesitation. If there was no help here, there was no help to be found at all.

"Hold her. I'll go down, and you can pass her to me," Ronin said, turning to Newton. He ignored the blaring alarms from the portions of his coding that had been overridden by fear.

If Newton meant them harm, what would he gain by reactivating Ronin and leading him here? Why bother powering him back on if he had malicious intentions?

Ronin gently passed Lara's limp form into Newton's outstretched arms. His limbs locked as he pulled away. She was so fragile. Even losing a few seconds of contact, when they were potentially so limited a commodity, made him again doubt if this was the right thing to do.

Holding her now will not help her recover.

Finally, he withdrew his hands, turned to the hatch, and lowered himself onto the ladder. The sound of his boots on the rungs echoed along the corridor, which extended into total darkness in either direction.

He looked upward the instant his feet were on the floor.

Standing over the opening, Newton maneuvered slowly to guide Lara's legs through, sinking into a crouch as he lowered her. He adjusted his hold on her so his arms were beneath her armpits. Despite the discomfort she should've felt at such handling, she remained unconscious, head lolling.

Ronin placed his hands on her hips and gently drew her down against him with his cheek pressed to her bruised midsection. "I have her."

Newton released Lara. Ronin shifted as her torso sagged, preventing her weight from coming down on her damaged ribs or broken arm. Adjusting his hold, he cradled her against his chest, smoothing her hair out of her face. She'd been so badly battered that not a centimeter of her had escaped injury.

Bare metal feet clanked on the ladder. Newton closed the hatch as quietly as it had been opened, plunging the tunnel into darkness. Ronin's optics switched to infrared supported night vision.

A fine layer of dust coated the tunnel's concrete floor. Though there were no footprints or other signs of habitation, the dust didn't appear to have settled naturally, and it bore a strange pattern.

Were those…brush strokes?

"This way," Newton said, voice low.

They proceeded down the corridor with Newton ahead, their footfalls scraping lightly over the floor. Light fixtures were mounted at five-meter intervals on either side of the tunnel, but none held bulbs within their wire cages, and the hints of letters and numbers painted on the walls were too faded and flaked to decipher.

Each step heightened Ronin's anxiety. He was carrying his beloved down a pitch-black corridor with nowhere to run, no weapons, no cover. If an ambush awaited them ahead, it would be unforgivingly effective. An increasingly strong thought chain insisted that there was nothing here to help her. There was nothing in all the Dust that could help her. This place would be Lara's tomb.

No. She will not die.

Newton slowed, glancing over his shoulder. "Nearly there. Just around here."

The tunnel continued straight, beyond the range of Ronin's optics, but Newton turned into an opening on the right. Ronin followed close behind.

His vision blazed white as he was hit by a blinding light. He twisted away from it, shielding Lara's body with his own.

An ambush, after all.

"Don't move!" someone shouted.

Newton, standing beside Ronin, raised his arms. "Quite reassuring to see security has not grown lax."

"Are you two bots, too?"

"I am," Ronin said, turning his head toward the man. With his night vision deactivated, he could see the humanoid silhouettes against the bright spotlight, all of them gathered behind a waist-high barrier with firearms aimed at him and Newton. "The woman is human."

"What's wrong with her?"

"She was severely beaten by the self-titled Warlord of Cheyenne," Newton said.

The people behind the barricade whispered to each other for several moments before the first man asked, "Did he follow you?"

"No." Ronin looked down at Lara. "As far as he knows, he ended us. Left us for dead."

The spotlight shifted, and the man who'd been speaking turned to two of the other figures. "Secure the perimeter."

The pair—soldiers dressed in matching uniforms—hurried past Ronin and into the perpendicular corridor.

"If you have any weapons, place them on the ground. Now," the leader said.

Ronin's jaw actuators ticked. "We're unarmed, and we're out of time. If you can't help her, tell me now, so I can find someone who can before it's too late."

"Turn around. Slowly."

It wasn't a request, and that made it no easier to comply. Exposing Lara to potential hostiles went against Ronin's drive to protect her. All the same, disobeying would only push the situation closer to violence.

Ronin turned, bringing the barricade into full view. His optics blurred and focused repeatedly, battling to balance the contrast between the overwhelming light and the thick darkness behind it.

"Garrison, Walker, take the girl to the infirmary," the leader commanded.

Two figures advanced, features clarifying as they neared. Both held automatic rifles similar to the one Ronin had carried. Their uniforms matched the soldiers who'd gone into the corridor—much repaired, the camouflage patterns faded, but well-kept, none-theless. The men slung their rifles over their shoulders.

Ronin stepped back. "I'll carry her."

The soldiers halted, hands drifting back toward their weapons.

"You're in no position to make demands," the leader said as he stepped forward. He was a tall, lean, middle-aged man with short-cropped blond hair and a double bar insignia displayed at the center of his chest. A captain.

That shred of information was from Ronin's old life, a tiny bit of data reclaimed after many decades.

For nine seconds, Ronin and the captain stared at one another, neither moving. Walker and Garrison stood by uncertainly.

"They will not hurt her," Newton said.

"How do I know that?" Ronin demanded. "How do I know they'll take care of her?"

The captain dipped his chin. "We have the facilities to help her, but you're unknowns, which means we must err on the side of caution until we determine whether you're a threat."

"I can't leave her. I won't." Ronin was the one wasting time now. *She'll die if I do nothing.*

"My name's Cooper. Captain Edward Cooper. You have my word that she will receive the best care we can offer. The faster you cooperate, the faster we can take care of her."

An electric tingle skittered across Ronin's cheek. He nodded once, extending his arms. "Be gentle with her. Her left arm is broken, and her ribs might be fractured."

Walker and Garrison stepped forward and carefully collected Lara. Ronin was unable to remove his optics from her until she was carried out of sight.

This is the only chance she has.

"Captain Cooper," Newton said, "I can assure you that I will vouch for—"

The captain raised a fist, silencing Newton. "You're unknowns."

A heavy metal door opened somewhere behind the spotlight. Boots marched over the concrete floor as six more armed soldiers entered the corridor, surrounding Ronin and Newton.

"These gentlemen will escort you inside," Captain Cooper said. "You will keep your hands to yourselves. They will not answer questions, so don't bother asking. Any sudden movements that can be interpreted as hostile will be treated as such."

The soldiers separated, with four taking positions behind Ronin and Newton while the other two remained ahead.

"Should you consider doing any of my men harm, it may be of interest to you to know that some of them are bots. They're just as physically capable as both of you, and much better armed. I trust you'll behave." Cooper stepped aside, waving the escort forward.

Ronin followed the soldiers in front of him automatically, his processors dominated by thoughts of Lara. Would she be all right? Where was she now? This facility's size, layout, and personnel were mysteries to him. It could take days of searching to locate her on his own, and she didn't have that kind of time.

They proceeded through a doorway, and one of the rear guards slammed the steel door shut behind them. The corridor narrowed here beneath a low, arched ceiling, but the electric lights were working, and the floor was clean. Bundles of pipe and conduit ran along the walls.

Ronin couldn't dismiss the possibility that he'd never see Lara again, that the time he'd spent with her was all he'd ever have, that those moments would be the only ones they'd ever share.

There'd been no goodbye, no parting words of love. There'd been only the pain on her face and the agony of her cries. Why was that last, terrible event so much more powerful than everything preceding it? Why did it overshadow all the rest of their time together?

The corridor hit an intersection, and Ronin turned left with the group, logging step counts and measurements in his memory. They were moving in the direction of the old base.

"Where is she?" Ronin asked.

"You guys actually walk around out there?" one of the soldiers asked as though he hadn't heard Ronin's question. "Like, through the storms and everything?"

"Doesn't affect bots the same," another answered. There was an odd, contradictory blend of smoothness and rigidity in his posture and gait that wasn't entirely human. The pointed stripes on his chest meant he was a sergeant.

Beside Ronin, Newton perked up, brow plates rising. "That is correct, but it does have a number of averse—"

"I just ain't been off the base in a long time," the first soldier interrupted.

"You've never been off the base, Ramirez," the sergeant said, and the group fell silent.

Their boots thumped on the floor, undercut by the clacking of Newton's metal feet, and their equipment harnesses jingled softly. The hum of the lights was barely audible through the other noise. None of it could distract Ronin from thoughts of Lara. His processors tumbled through hundreds of thousands of possibilities.

"Where is she?" he repeated.

"Who?"

"The woman I brought here."

"Oh, the one that looked like pounded meat?" Ramirez asked. "You do that?"

Anger flared in Ronin, a harsh, electric buzz through all his systems, catching him off guard. His hands closed into fists so tight that his actuators flashed warnings through his interface.

"Shut the fuck up, Ramirez," three of the other soldiers said simultaneously.

Warlord had called Lara meatbag, infusing the word with venom and disgust. For this man to casually refer to her in so similar a fashion and ignore her humanity, for him to suggest that Ronin had injured her, that he would *ever* harm her…

Newton caught Ronin's forearm, squeezing.

Ronin dropped his gaze to the floor. He was here to save her. He had to hold that at the front of his mind. Through clenched teeth, he grated, "Don't talk about her that way again."

"He didn't mean anything by it," the sergeant said. "Kid just doesn't know how to think without speaking yet. Doc's going to do all she can to fix your woman."

Before Ronin could respond, the group arrived at another large metal door. One of the leading soldiers stepped forward to open it. A wave of sound spilled out, a jumbled mess comprised of dozens of voices and activities. Ronin was ushered through into a huge chamber filled with people conversing and performing a variety of tasks.

His optics swept over the space as he walked with the soldiers, who followed a set of colored lines painted on the floor. Most of the people were human, but many bots were amongst them—not just synths, but older models resembling Greene from the market. Everyone was well-groomed, clean, and dressed in cared-for clothing. Ronin couldn't identify all the work they were doing, and both the names and functions of many of their tools were unknown to him. He'd never seen anything like this place during his travels.

Overhead, three uniformed soldiers stood upon walkways hanging from the high ceiling, staring down at Ronin and Newton as they were escorted past.

There were several doors along the walls, and two large corridors led out of the chamber. *Armory, Barracks, Stockade* was written in red letters over one, *Laboratory, Administration, Infirmary* in green over the other.

The infirmary…was that where they'd taken Lara?

The green line on the floor broke away from the rest, turning down that corridor. The soldiers continued along the red line, passing beneath the sign that said *Stockade.*

The corridor narrowed. The group proceeded through a series of turns, past more doors and hallways, walking ever deeper into the facility. Finally, they entered a large room lined on one side with small cells.

Newton and Ronin were guided into a chamber with a long table. Some of the people sitting at the table wore uniforms, but others were dressed in plain clothing.

"Have a seat," said the man at the head of the table, gesturing to the open chairs in front of Ronin and Newton. He was broad shouldered with brown skin, short-cropped black hair sprinkled with gray, and a clean-shaven face. The insignia on his blue jacket marked him as a colonel.

Ronin sat as the soldiers who'd escorted him took up positions around the perimeter of the room. Seconds of relative silence ticked by. The room's temperature was gradually climbing, and at least one human wore a sheen of sweat on his face.

"I'm Colonel Jack Rodriguez," the man in blue finally said, "Head of Security in this facility. Given your open association with Warlord, and the fact that you came in through an entrance that hasn't been discovered in two hundred years, I currently find myself *very* concerned about the safety of my people."

Ronin focused his optics on Rodriquez. "The woman we brought in, what's her status?"

"She's in critical condition. Doctor Cooper and her staff are doing all they can to stabilize her."

"I want to see her."

"That's not how this works. You represent a potential threat. Until I'm certain that threat is nonexistent, I—"

"Warlord is the one who beat her and left me deactivated. We're unarmed, and we didn't resist when your men took us into custody.

We knew where the entrance was because my companion has used it in the past."

All eyes swung to Newton.

He blinked and sat up straighter. "I've come and gone through that entryway fifty-nine times."

One of the non-uniformed men rose from his chair, hands flattened on the table. He was gray-haired, though his neat beard was a bit darker, and had age lines on his pale face. "Newton?"

Newton turned his head to regard the man. Hushed exclamations arose from those gathered, too many and too varied for Ronin to bother isolating any single one.

"William?" The plates around Newton's mouth lifted in a smile. "In all my years away, I somehow disregarded the effect of time. It's no wonder I didn't recognize any faces as we entered. Another bit of foolishness on my part."

"I was a boy when you left." William gestured to the younger man seated beside him. Their resemblance was immediately apparent despite their age difference. "My son, Will. He has a child of his own."

"That's Newton?" Rodriguez asked, his stoic face turned toward William.

"Yes. He's no threat to us."

Newton nodded. "I can assure you, neither myself nor my companion mean to harm anyone here. We came because Miss Brooks was gravely injured, and I lacked the means to tend her."

Rodriguez's eyes shifted to Ronin. "Who are you?"

"Ronin. I am... I was a dustwalker, most recently out of Cheyenne."

"You're built like a soldier. Right down to your hair. Recall any of that time?"

"Images, occasionally. My memory was damaged in the Blackout. I have no specifics."

"Have you retained any of your combat programming?"

"I've survived fifty-one thousand, six hundred and forty-eight days in the Dust. Ended a lot of individuals that meant me harm. Don't know what I've retained and what I've lost, but it doesn't seem to have much bearing anymore."

"That's over one hundred and forty years," someone said. A hush fell over the group.

William rubbed his chin, studying Ronin. "We might be able to restore your memory. There are several bots here who've gone through the procedure with few complications."

It was the logical course for Ronin to follow to learn where he came from, what he'd done before, who he was. To be whole. It would give him the answer he'd been seeking since being reactivated.

But what was he missing now? Knowing what his place had been in a dead world wouldn't help his future. He was already whole. Lara had given him purpose, had given him meaning. His core programming didn't matter, and it never truly had. Seeking it had served only as a reason to move forward, as motivation to keep him going, and he no longer needed it to drive him.

Ronin shook his head. "My only concern is Lara."

William smiled and nodded, easing into his chair. "Very well."

The colonel leaned forward. "As soon as there's an update—"

"You trust Newton's word that I'm not here to cause trouble. Let me be with her. That's all I want."

Rodriguez frowned, brows falling low.

"The work Doctor Cooper and her team have to do is very delicate," William said.

"You'll get in the way." Rodriguez met Ronin's optics and held his gaze. "If you want them to have the best chance of saving her, you'll give them the space they need to work. In the meantime, I want you to tell us everything you know about Warlord's forces. Numbers, armament, defenses. All of it."

CHAPTER FORTY-TWO

Ronin sat motionless in the worn leather chair, fingers digging into its arms. His processors blazed despite his outward stillness. Hours had passed with excruciating slowness. Rodriguez's questions were concise, direct, and seemingly endless. Throughout, Ronin's thoughts had repeatedly returned to Lara.

There was a knock at the door.

"Enter," Rodriguez called.

The door opened, and a woman dressed in a white coat stepped in, approached the colonel, and whispered in his ear. When he nodded, she turned back toward the door.

Rodriguez's gaze settled on Ronin. "Lara is in stable condition."

Ronin rose from the chair. "Then I'll go see her now."

"We're not finished here."

"I'm finished. I've answered your questions, many of them numerous times, and I'll answer more later. But right now, I am going to see Lara."

The woman hesitated in the doorway, eyes flicking between Ronin and Rodriguez.

"You can trust him to cooperate," Newton said from his seat beside Ronin. "Please, allow him this."

At length, Rodriguez waved at the woman. "Take him."

Ronin followed her into the corridor. The tail of her coat drifted behind her as she wove through the hallways with surprising speed. There were fewer people than before in the large chamber, and different soldiers patrolled the catwalks. The woman led Ronin into the passageway with green paint marking the floor.

After walking through another collection of labyrinthine corridors, they finally arrived at a doorway with *Infirmary* painted on the wall beside it.

They entered a low-ceilinged room that was divided by curtains hanging from metal rods. Ronin counted forty such partitions, only six of which were closed.

Narrow, neatly made beds stood in the open sections, surrounded by pieces of equipment similar to what he'd glimpsed in the unused rooms at the Clinic. The machinery for bot repairs in the far corner looked more advanced than anything in Cheyenne.

The woman led him to one of the closed curtains. A soft, steady beeping came from within.

She stopped at the narrow gap between the curtains and turned to Ronin. "You need to understand that she's still in serious condition. She's stable, but that can change any moment. She's got a broken arm, fractured ribs, several lacerations, and severe bruising. The swelling should go down in time, and we don't believe her vision will be affected."

Ronin nodded and moved to step past her, but she stopped him with a gentle hand on his chest.

"You also need to know that she suffered head trauma. She's in a coma. We don't know when, or *if*, she'll wake up."

Ronin's processors halted, either unable or unwilling to assimilate that information. If he'd listened to Lara and left Cheyenne when she'd first suggested it, if he hadn't insisted on one more run, if he hadn't allowed himself to grow so complacent that he'd missed the countless signs of danger all around…

The woman sidestepped and opened the curtain. Ronin walked through.

Lara's hair caught his attention first. It was clean and woven into a braid, standing out in bold contrast to the white bedding. Dark bruises marred the pale skin of her face. Both her eyes were swollen, a four-centimeter-long line of stitches marred her left cheek, and her left arm was splinted and wrapped against her chest in a sling.

Apart from the shallow rise and fall of her chest, she was still, and she looked so slight in the pristine bed surrounded by medical equipment. Though a blanket covered her abdomen and legs, he knew the flesh hidden beneath was mottled with bruises.

His optics followed the tube in her right arm up to a jar of liquid suspended on a pole beside the bed before shifting to the monitor displaying her heartrate. Its beat was slow, but steady.

Gently, he placed his hand over hers. "Don't leave yet."

Lara didn't respond. Seconds dragged into minutes.

"I'll get you a chair," the woman in the white coat said, drawing Ronin's attention to the open curtain. Had she stood there the entire time?

"I don't need to sit."

"I'll get one anyway, in case you change your mind." Stepping back, she took hold of the hanging cloth. "Talk to her. It'll do her good to hear a familiar voice."

The woman closed the curtain, and her soft footfalls faded as she left the room.

Squeezing Lara's hand, Ronin brushed a stray lock of hair from her face. He trailed a fingertip over the tiny patch of uninjured skin on her cheek.

"Remember the ocean, Lara? I asked you what places you'd like to see, and that was your answer. You didn't even have to think about it. I'll take you there once you've recovered. You can dance barefoot in the sand to the music of the waves and collect as many seashells and bits of driftwood as you want. We can watch the sun set over the water and pretend we're the only two people in existence."

He struggled to picture it in his head, to piece together images from his memory to create the scene. How content would they be if they were the last two survivors?

But the images eluded him, and the logical part of his mind listed the myriad challenges such a scenario would pose. How could he guarantee her food supply, or proper medical care? Would she be saddened if she never saw another flesh-and-blood person, if she never knew what it was like to carry a child, to see a family grow around her?

Another part of him set those concerns aside, if only for an instant, and saw the happiness, the intimacy, the companionship.

He loved Lara, and it didn't matter if his emotions had begun as a simulation, didn't matter if they were still classified as such. Whatever they were, whatever people like William Anderson called them, Ronin felt them.

He stroked the back of Lara's hand with his thumb. "I spent a long time searching for my purpose. For my core programming. All of us were made for a reason." He chuckled. "It's not a reason I would have guessed…but it doesn't matter anymore. I found what I was looking for before Newton told me any of that.

"It was *you*, Lara. You're my purpose, you're my reason for carrying on, the reason I haven't sat down in an abandoned building and never stood up again. I don't think I'm selfish, normally, but I need you. I only just found you, and I don't think I can go any further without you."

Her only response was through the steady, indifferent beeping of electronics.

Twelve minutes and fifteen seconds later, the woman in the white coat returned with an ancient-looking chair. The cushion was flat and ragged, but the metal frame was solid and rust-free. She quietly set it down several feet from the bed and checked the equipment.

Reluctantly, Ronin sat on the chair to keep out of her way, fixing his optics on Lara's unchanging face. It would take no effort to call up his memories of her dances, or the first time he'd heard her laugh, or any of the hundreds of moments with her he'd forever cherish, but he refrained. What would reminiscing bring other than more pain? The past was gone, and it could never be reclaimed no matter how impeccable his recall.

Lara couldn't dance now, couldn't smile, couldn't even open her eyes or react to anything around her.

"We're doing everything we can," the woman said. She'd been at the edge of his vision, watching him.

"I know."

"They told us it was rough on you getting here. There wasn't much information at that point, but…from the first moment, our only priority was keeping her alive. That's not going to change."

Ronin shifted his focus to the woman. His processors replayed her words twice, analyzing her tone, before understanding dawned on him. This was compassion. Sympathy. Traits he'd rarely seen in this world, apart from in Lara.

"What's your name?" he asked.

"Cyndi."

"Thank you, Cyndi."

She smiled, and the sad gleam in her eyes reminded him of the blonde synth who worked in the clinic. Perhaps he'd been overly harsh in his judgment of Mercy. Her sympathy was likely just as genuine as Cyndi's.

"Thank Nancy. She's the one who really saved this girl's life." She moved deeper into the small space and plucked something from a metal tray in the corner. Ronin's processors slowed at the flash of gold.

With the ring resting on her palm, Cyndi held out her hand. "We needed to remove it to bandage her ribs."

Yours Until the End of Time.

He stared at the painful reminder that he'd failed in his vow to protect Lara. Keeping his hand steady, he took the ring from Cyndi, closing his fingers around it. "Thank you."

"You're welcome."

Cyndi left, and Ronin relocated the chair to the bedside. He took Lara's hand again, seeking comfort in its warmth and finding little. He slipped the ring onto her finger and brought it to his lips, pressing a kiss to it.

"Don't leave yet," he repeated. "Don't...leave me."

Four hours later, the curtain rustled. Reluctant to look away from Lara, Ronin turned his head slowly to find Will, the younger of the two Andersons, peeking through the gap.

"Ronin? Would you come with me, please?"

Facing Lara, Ronin shook his head. "I'm not ready to answer more questions yet."

The pulse monitor continued its gentle rhythm without variation.

"I'm not here to interrogate you. My father and I noticed you were damaged when you came in. We'd like to get you repaired while Lara rests."

Ronin glanced down. The hole in his chest, visible through his torn shirt, was large enough to fit his thumb into. The four on his back were presumably smaller, and the skin there had been ripped apart to access his power cell. Though internal components had been damaged by the bullets, leaving him with power leaks and operational inefficiencies, nothing critical had been destroyed. But the punctures in his casing were invitations for dust and moisture. The degradation of his functions was unavoidable in his current state.

Regardless, his preferred response was refusal supported by several potential excuses. Ronin wasn't inclined to leave Lara's side. He knew they wouldn't let him sit here until she awoke, but he would stay with her as long as possible. They'd insist on continuing their interrogation eventually, and if enough time passed, they would likely demand he contribute to their community as a price for her continued care.

Unfortunately, the contributions Ronin was most suited to make came with a high likelihood of him collecting more bullet holes in his casing.

"The equipment's in the corner," Will said, "maybe a hundred feet away. You'll be close."

Ronin dropped a hand to his knee, curling it into a fist. He'd seen the equipment when he entered the room. Lara's monitors would be well within earshot from there, and he could be back at her side in seconds if the need arose. There was no logical reason to refuse.

Leaning forward, he gently lifted her hand, brushed his lips over her knuckles, and settled it back onto the bed. When he stood, he allowed his optics to linger on her before he turned and followed Will to the repair machines.

Will directed Ronin to remove his shirt and climb onto the flat table at the center of the setup. He did so, lying face down with his arms folded beneath his chin. Will moved to stand beside Ronin and pressed his foot down on a pedal on the floor. With a quiet hum and gentle vibrations, the table rose, stopping once it was above his waist.

"I know what it's like," Will said as he examined the bullet holes.

Ronin furrowed his brow, turning his head toward Will. "What?"

"The uncertainty. I know what it feels like. When my wife, Linda, went into labor with our daughter, there were complications. Doctor Cooper has worked her share of miracles, but she's realistic. She told me exactly what might happen, and what she planned to do to stop it. Having to wait through that…it was the worst time of my life. It was agonizing, feeling so helpless."

Helpless. An adequate word. For the first time in one hundred and eighty-five years, Ronin felt like no matter what choice he made, no matter what actions he took, he couldn't affect the outcome.

Lara would either live or die, and he had no power over it.

"This is normal?" Ronin asked.

Chuckling, Will turned away to power on a monitor and retrieve a small tool from a nearby tray. "Helplessness is an everyday part of the human condition."

Once the tool was inserted into one of the bullet holes, a camera at its tip relayed Ronin's internal damage to the screen.

Ronin stared at the image. "I'm not human."

"Why? Because you're made up of different parts?"

On the monitor, neat bundles of wiring and circuitry ran along segmented metal columns, all around the central reinforced case housing Ronin's CPU and data cores.

"Those parts are just one item on a long list of differences," Ronin said.

"Yes, in some ways. But an organic lifeform and a machine are not entirely different. Hell, if anyone knows, it'd be me." Will guided the camera along the scrapes and grooves created by the bullets. "I'm the sixth generation of a family that's devoted its entire existence to robotics. The sixth William Anderson. You think *you* have identity issues?"

Will laughed again. It was a warm, inviting sound. Genuine laughter was a rare thing, it seemed, but it had a strange way of alleviating tension.

At that moment, Ronin would've given anything to hear Lara laugh with his own audio receptors. "You're not your father, or your grandfather, or any of them."

"Right. But I'm expected to be." Will fell silent for a moment. "A quarter-inch variance in the trajectory of any of these shots, and you would've been in some serious trouble. These armor-piercing rounds they used during the war can chew through inner casings like they're made of paper at close range."

"Better me than her."

"I don't think my great-great-great grandfather could've foreseen any of this, but I bet he would've been delighted."

Ronin's brow plates lowered. "Over what? Over what happened to the world?"

"No. He abhorred that. I mean the way bots have evolved. His work, when you get down to it, was the very basics of how you operate now. He laid the foundation. Everything in the time since, you've developed on your own. You've built upon that foundation, creating something new, something...beautiful. You have a *life*. In the old world, just the thought of that was enough to cause widespread panic."

Will selected a few more tools, watching the monitor as he slipped them into the bullet hole and began the repairs.

Sparks danced across Ronin's electrodes, but only distantly. "Does that mean the war started because of bots?"

"I don't think so. To be honest, it's hard to say why it happened anymore, even with the records we have. I think it was building for a long time. Bots might've been what tipped it, but that was an excuse more than anything. My point is that you have free will. You can experience emotions, you have doubts and regrets, you can fall in love. That's what it means to be human. It was never about being an organic bipedal lifeform evolved from primates."

Ronin lay in silence, ignoring the vibrations pulsing through his insides as Will worked.

It couldn't be that simple, could it? Over decades of wandering, he'd experienced only the merest hints of emotion, never knowing how strong it could be. Not until Lara.

Had he always possessed the capacity for deeper feelings?

Perhaps the answer was simple—he'd always been capable, but it had taken Lara to give him something to care for. She'd sparked his emotions, and now they burned bright. She was the catalyst of his evolution.

"You also have free will," Ronin said. "You're no more defined by your name than I am my parts."

A smile spread across Will's lips. "You're right, but I've spent a lot of time worrying about it, anyway. It's a lot to live up to. A family legacy that eclipses anything I might do. What's important, though, is that we've preserved the first William Anderson's vision in this place. Bots and humans coexisting, having relationships, living side-by-side. I can't deny that I'm proud to be a part of that."

"I owe much to you and your ancestors, Will Anderson."

Will chuckled. "Don't get me wrong, I was relieved as hell when I found out we were having a girl. It broke the six-generation-chain of sons. Meant I didn't have to make some excuse to explain to Dad why I wasn't going to name my kid William Joseph Anderson the Seventh."

Countless humans had been born, had grown, changed, and matured, had lived and died while Ronin walked the Dust, and he'd given them little thought. He'd simply existed, an enduring relic of a time he could no longer recall.

He'd never truly considered the cycle of human life. He'd never examined the concept of mortality. But all things had an end. That was a fact he could not dispute, and it seemed more relevant now than ever before.

This will not be her end. It cannot.

"Newton told me there were humans and bots who came together to form families," Ronin said.

"Yeah. Nobody's sure how many there were before, but there's about a dozen couples here on the base. One more, I guess, with you two here."

"Do they...adopt children?" Why was he concerned about it? Was his curiosity the result of raw emotion, or innocent curiosity?

"Not many orphans running around here, usually. Most male synths have the parts necessary for procreation, they just need a donor to provide the, uh...material. It's not very complicated, really, and we've done it several times over the years."

Ronin nodded, turning his head away from the monitor as Will continued the repairs.

Would Lara be happy to learn that news? Would she embrace the idea, or reject it outright? Did Ronin even accept it himself?

Before Lara, love had been an airy, ethereal word with little meaning to him. Had he already changed so much that he was prepared to procreate and raise children? The thought of caring for human young was more unsettling than wandering the expansive wastes...

Will and Ronin drifted between companionable silence and easy conversation as time passed. The automated machines took over after the internal repairs were completed, though Will remained at the controls to monitor them. After Ronin's casing was sealed, he removed his pants and entered the epidermal synthesizer —Will called it the *reskinner*, which seemed far more practical a name.

As Ronin emerged from the reskinner, he glanced down at his torso. His skin was a single shade now. That realization came with a strange sense of loss.

"Why did you perform the internal repairs by hand?" Ronin asked as he pulled on his clothes. He'd been away from Lara for too long, and the beeping of her heart monitor wasn't enough to reassure him, but his curiosity was genuine.

"Partly because it's a skill that would otherwise be lost. If we don't know how to do it without machines to help, what'll happen when these machines eventually break down? And for the same reason Doctor Cooper treats most of her patients by hand, I guess. It's more...personal. If we don't send our human patients to lie in a machine and receive care without ever seeing another person's face, why should we do that to bots?"

While Ronin walked back to Lara, he analyzed his conversation with Will.

Bots and humans were equals here.

He struggled to accept it as the truth. After everything he'd seen in the world, everything he'd seen in Cheyenne, that seemed like an impossibility, a failed dream from a failed age.

Yet the evidence was mounting. In this place, it was no dream. It was reality.

Ronin knew *what-ifs* would do him no good, but he couldn't help wondering how different things might've been had he and Lara known about this place sooner. How much trauma and pain could they have avoided?

He pulled open the curtain and stepped into the partition, raising his optics.

A thin woman with her dark hair pulled into a bun and glasses perched on her nose stood beside the bed, frowning down at Lara. "There have been stories for a long time about this *Warlord*. About the things he's done. And even though he's just a few miles away, it all seemed unreal because we never saw it firsthand."

She sighed and smoothed a hand over her hair before turning toward Ronin. The first signs of gray were visible at her temples. "This kind of brutality is unacceptable."

Ronin settled his gaze on Lara. "He did the same thing to her sister, but there was no one to help her in time."

The woman shook her head. "We're not perfect here. We have our share of arguments, and the occasional fistfight. Every now and then a man hits his wife. Jack and his people always get things back in order quickly and make sure justice is served, but *this*... This is unlike anything I've ever seen."

She brushed her fingertips over the back of Lara's hand, her touch lingering just long enough for Ronin to recognize the sincere compassion in the gesture.

Withdrawing her hand, the woman walked around the bed and held it out to Ronin. "I'm Nancy Cooper. Ronin, right?"

It took nearly a second to dredge up the data for an appropriate response. Careful as ever to regulate the strength of his grip, he took Nancy's hand and shook it. "Yes. You're the Doctor Cooper everyone's been talking about?"

"I am. The person with the drugs is always the most popular." She smiled, but the expression wavered. "I'm sorry. I try to keep things light, but it's inappropriate given the situation."

"I understand. No apology necessary."

"We're doing everything in our power to make her well again. Unfortunately, it's just a waiting game now."

"I know. Thank you, Nancy. Whatever happens." Sorrow panged across his circuits at those last two words. Were they an admission of defeat? An acceptance of the possibility that Lara wouldn't wake up, that their time together was over?

No. I won't accept that.

"She's a fighter," Nancy said. "I hear you are, too. That means a lot. Hell, if you hadn't brought her here so fast, I don't think she'd have survived the night."

They lapsed into silence, and Ronin watched Lara's still form. The machinery provided a gentle ambiance.

"I'll give you some space," Nancy said. "I'm sure you're already aware, but Jack's not going to wait much longer to question you again. For now, I'm going to recommend that the best thing for Lara is to hear your voice and feel your touch. That'll keep him at bay for a little while more."

She walked past him, pausing for a moment to place a hand on his shoulder and squeeze gently. Then she exited the partition, sliding the curtain closed behind her.

It was jarring to face so much understanding, so much compassion, from so many people. He was a bot, but these people didn't seem to make any distinction between metal and organic.

He slid the chair over to the bed and sat, grasping Lara's hand. None of that compassion would make a difference if she didn't recover. Hers was the only touch he craved, the only understanding he needed.

CHAPTER FORTY-THREE

She floated in darkness. It devoured her, suffused her, pulsing within and around her, it filled her bones with ice, wracked her with pain, and clawed at her consciousness. She longed to cry out, but she had no mouth, no lungs. There was nothing but agony and the endless void.

Until a voice penetrated the blackness.

Don't leave yet.

Warmth bloomed through her, chasing away the cold for a fleeting moment. She knew that voice. It was her only source of comfort, a shining beacon, the one solid thing to clutch at in this vast nothingness. When it spoke, shimmering blue flickered through the darkness, like the rolling waves of an ocean she'd never seen.

But the voice and its light were gone so quickly it might never have existed at all.

The pain came roaring back, and she suffered alone.

There were other voices, distant, muffled, and unfamiliar, and she shrank from them. They came often, sometimes alone, sometimes in groups. They weren't what she wanted to hear. Weren't what she needed.

Time had no meaning. She didn't have a name, didn't have a memory, but she had that voice to cling to. That voice to anchor her, to keep her from spiraling into oblivion. It was the only thing to ease her pain, the only thing to anticipate.

Don't leave yet.

She didn't want to leave him. Not yet. Not even when the pain reached its worst, and the other voices grew louder while the darkness thickened.

Him? Yes, she knew that voice. She knew him...

Don't leave yet.

The words echoed through the void, and she grasped at them. She didn't want to be taken away, she refused to be.

Don't...leave me.

Opening her eyes was the hardest thing Lara had ever done, but she forced her leaden eyelids up and stared through blurred vision at a blinding white light above her. To her right, something beeped slowly and rhythmically. As she blinked, the room gradually came into focus, but the shapes didn't make sense.

Those unfamiliar voices were clear now.

"How long is this going to take?" a man asked from nearby.

"I can't say for sure," a woman replied. "She'll wake up when her mind and body are ready."

"It's been three days, and she hasn't so much as wiggled a finger."

Focusing all her will through her confusion and pain, Lara twitched a finger.

"We can't just force her to wake up, Dave. That's not how it works."

"She might never wake up at all, Nancy."

"That's a possibility. But I'm not—"

"Every moment we keep her here is a drain on our resources. Those machines draw power from a limited pool, and nobody's making new medical supplies anymore. She's an outsider, and she's taking up the time of our medical staff."

"She's used hardly anything so far, and she's a *human being*. Isn't a life still worth more than a few plastic tubes and bit of my time?" Nancy demanded quietly.

"And if she never comes out of it? The cost only adds up as the days go by. She's going to need to be fed, and that'll cause more complications. We can't let this go on indefinitely."

"That's not your call to make, Dave. And you're stupid if you think her companion will let you cut her off."

"He couldn't lay a hand on me," Dave said uncertainly.

"You think rules will stop him?"

Who were they?

Where am I?

Lara blinked again and dragged her gaze around the room. The glaring light had dissolved into solid objects in varied shades of white—the ceiling, the hanging cloths, the wall, the sheet draped over her body. No real place could be so pure, so clean.

The beeping picked up speed and volume.

She parted her dry lips, wincing as they split, and tasted blood when she slid her tongue out to wet them. Her left arm was wrapped tight in a sling that looped around her neck. She tried to move it, but she was stopped by a bone-deep ache radiating up to her shoulder and down to the tips of her fingers. Lara lifted her right hand instead, only for something to tug at it, producing a sharp pain in the back of her hand.

Turning her head, she ran her gaze along the tubes and wires that connected her hand to the equipment beside the bed.

What the fuck?

"She's awake," Nancy said breathlessly. "Go get Ronin!"

People crowded around the bed, their features obscured by shadows as their bodies blocked the light. They all spoke at once, rapidly, using words Lara didn't understand.

Her heart quickened. The beeping gained speed along with it, and Lara's chest hurt, her every breath more labored than the last. She lifted her right hand again, moving it closer to her left. She needed to pull the foreign things from her body, needed to get away from these people, needed air…

"Hold her down, before she hurts herself!"

Hands fell upon Lara and pressed her down on the bed. She cried out.

"Lara," Nancy said, "please remain calm. My name is—oh, no, don't!"

Lara yanked her arm. There was a moment of resistance, another flare of sharp pain, and then the wires tore free. The beeping became a monotone, ceaseless drone.

She couldn't breathe. Her lungs were on fire.

The hands closed around her arms and legs, dragging her down. Lara struggled against them. Agony swept through her body, and fear permeated her very soul.

Warlord stood above her, fist swinging toward her face, raining blow after blow after blow.

Lara screamed. She thrashed, battling the strangers' holds.

They'd deactivated Ronin, had taken him from her, and Warlord kept hitting her, over and over, and the pain wouldn't end. Her throat was raw from her screams, but the hands wouldn't relent.

"Lara, I'm Nancy, I've been—"

Lara's right arm escaped their hold, and she swung her fist. The blow struck Nancy, who cried out and flinched, blood oozing from her lip. More hands clamped around Lara's forearm and forced it down.

No! I need to get to Ronin!

"Are you okay?" someone asked.

Nancy didn't pause to wipe the crimson from her mouth. "I'm fine. We need to calm her down before she hurts herself."

"What's happening? Lara?"

Lara stilled at the sound of that voice. Eyes wide, she turned her head to look between the strangers, catching sight of Ronin as he approached.

He's here. He's alive!

Tears filled her eyes. She wanted to leap at him, to throw her arms around him, but even if she weren't restrained, she wasn't sure she had the strength.

All Lara's tension and fear fled her as his name escaped her lips in a broken whisper. "Ronin."

The strangers shifted aside. Ronin fell onto his knees beside the bed and cradled her cheeks between his hands, spreading warmth through her face. His beautiful, intense green eyes locked with hers. "I'm here, Lara. You're safe."

The restraining hands lifted away. Pulses of agony flowed through Lara's exhausted body, but she ignored them. Ronin was here with her. That was all that mattered.

"I need to see her arm," Nancy said.

Ronin gently stroked Lara's cheeks with his thumbs, wiping

away the slowly falling tears. "Be calm. No one here means you harm, and I won't leave you."

He eased aside to allow Nancy access without breaking contact with Lara.

Nancy curled her cool fingers around Lara's wrist, turning it to examine the open wound left on her hand by the wires.

Lara stared up into Ronin's eyes, chest swelling with so many confused, powerful emotions. It was only because of his steadiness that she remained still as Nancy softly prodded her hand.

"Where are we? Where's Warlord?" she rasped.

Ronin smoothed back the stray strands of her hair. "We're safe. Trust me on that."

After bandaging Lara's bleeding hand, Nancy turned to the other strangers and ushered them out of the little space. "We'll be fine. Let's not overwhelm her further."

She drew the curtain closed behind the last of the strangers and returned to Lara's bed.

"Look at me," Ronin said, calling Lara's gaze back to him. "These people are helping you."

Lara frowned, and her brow furrowed. "Where are we, Ronin?"

His fingers trailed soothingly along her hairline. "Somewhere safe. I'll explain it all later."

Nancy held out a tiny cup. "Lara, I'd like you to drink this. It will help with the pain."

Lara looked from the dark-haired woman to the cup. When she glanced back at Ronin, he nodded. Whoever Nancy was, Ronin trusted her, and that would have to be enough for now.

She took the cup and stared down at the reddish-brown liquid inside. It had a strange odor, not unlike the booze at Kitty's, but something was off about it. Her instincts said not to drink it.

"Best to swallow it quickly," Nancy said, offering a reassuring smile.

Raising the cup to her lips, Lara hesitated before pouring it into her mouth and swallowing.

It burned like fire going down her throat. The flavor of the alcohol fled quickly, overpowered by a bitter aftertaste worse than anything she'd ever had. She winced, shuddering as the bitter taste strengthened, then coughed. Agony exploded through her chest.

"What the hell *was* that?" she demanded through clenched teeth, taking shallow breaths. Anything deeper sharpened the pain in her side.

Nancy took the empty cup from her. "Laudanum, or as close to it as we can manage. Our options for pain management are limited, but most people say the relief is worth the taste, once it kicks in." She settled a soft hand on Lara's shoulder. "Get some rest. You've been through a lot, but the worst is over. I won't lie and tell you it's going to be a comfortable or pleasant process, but all you have to do now is heal. I'll check on you a little later."

Nancy walked away, slipping through the curtain.

"It hurts so much," Lara whispered, touching her side.

The bed creaked as Ronin sat on the edge, placing his hand over Lara's. He brushed the fingertips of his other hand over her cheek to tuck the loose strands of her hair behind her ear. "I thought I was going to lose you, Lara Brooks."

Lara met his gaze. She'd never seen such anguish in it. Turning her hand over, she laced her fingers with his. Her memory of what had happened was unclear, but she'd heard gunshots, had watched the light fade from his eyes when the gearheads pulled his power cell, had seen the life drain from him.

"I *did* lose you," she said, voice hoarse as her throat tightened and more tears welled in her eyes.

His smile was tinged with sorrow, but genuine. "Now I understand helplessness and fear."

The tears rolled down her cheeks. "I love you."

"Love you, too." He wiped away the moisture with his thumbs. "Rest. I'll be here when you wake again, and I'll tell you everything."

Though she longed to stay awake, to stare at him and touch him and hear his voice, the laudanum was taking effect. The aches that wracked her body dulled, and the edges of her consciousness grew fuzzy. The bedding dipped, and Ronin's warmth enveloped her as he lay down beside her.

Sleep claimed Lara.

CHAPTER FORTY-FOUR

"What's wrong?" Ronin asked.

Lara dropped her spoon into the bowl he was holding and looked up at him.

She'd spent the last four days in constant discomfort and pain. The drowsiness and disorientation caused by the laudanum had lingered a long while after she'd awoken, and she'd refused more when Nancy offered. She wanted to remain awake and alert. She wanted to feel it all, because no matter how unpleasant, it meant she was alive and healing.

"Why didn't Warlord kill me?" she asked.

A crease formed between Ronin's brows. "As far as he was concerned, he did."

"He hunted us down like animals. Why not finish it? He…" Her throat constricted. "He killed Tabitha. Why not me, too?"

"What he did to Tabitha was meant as an example to everyone in Cheyenne. She suffered, but death was the point. With us, he was only concerned with inflicting suffering. There was no one around to witness it, and no one from Cheyenne would ever find us out there. He wanted us broken, wanted you to die slowly and in agony, all alone."

Four quick gunshots rang out in her memory. While Warlord had beaten her, the twenty feet that had lain between her and Ronin's deactivated body might as well have been a thousand miles.

If it hadn't been for Newton and the spare power cells in the shelter, she would've died in the Dust.

"What did Warlord do to her?" Lara asked quietly. "What example did he make?"

He was silent, eyes dropping.

"Ronin. I deserve to know."

His silence persisted, and when he finally spoke, his words were heavy with sorrow and regret. "They beat her to death. Her body was covered in bruises, her facial bones were shattered, and blood matted her hair. But brutality wasn't enough. They chose to desecrate the remains. They dismantled her synth companion, laid his face over her groin, and put his detached penis in her mouth."

She grabbed his wrist, drawing his gaze back to hers. The sudden movement sent stabbing pain through her side. Despite the bindings around her chest, her ribs still hurt like a son of a bitch. But it was nothing compared to the pain in her heart. "Why didn't you tell me, Ronin? Why did you bring me to the bot district in the first place?"

"I didn't know, Lara. Didn't know depraved he is, how irrational, how mercurial and cruel. Even when I found Tabitha, I didn't truly understand his nature. And her death affected you deeply... That's why I didn't tell you the details. I didn't want to heap more pain atop your grief. I didn't think it would've helped, but I'm sorry I chose without consulting you."

He'd been trying to spare her more pain, trying to prevent her from collapsing beneath the weight of loss. Even if she didn't appreciate him keeping information from her, she couldn't fault his motivation for having done so.

She'd been close enough to crumbling without knowing the gruesome way her sister had been murdered.

"Apology accepted. But Ronin..." She sighed and massaged her throbbing temples with her forefinger and thumb. Her heart was thumping in her chest, and whispers of the terror she'd felt during the ambush brushed along the edges of her mind. "Warlord could have killed you."

"Takes more than a change of batteries to keep me down."

Despite the nature of their conversation, Lara had to stifle a laugh; it would've hurt too much thanks to her fractured ribs. She shook her head and lowered her hand to her lap. "I can't believe you choose now to joke."

"You're alive and recovering. What better a time for smiles?"

"Even smiling hurts." Lara's faint smile fell as she turned her face from Ronin. "Bet I look like shit."

She recalled her appearance after her first encounter with Warlord. After he'd raped and beaten her. She'd stared at herself in Tabitha's little mirror for a long time, and she hadn't recognized the person staring back. Her flesh had been discolored by bruises, her eyes and lips had been swollen, and she'd sported several nasty scabs where her skin had been broken.

Based on the tenderness and aches she felt now, she had to look even worse.

"You don't look nearly as bad as I did after I blew up." Ronin took gentle hold of Lara's chin and guided her face back toward him, forcing her eyes to meet his. "And you're always beautiful to me, Lara."

"You always say the nicest things," she said thickly, her eyes stinging with tears. "You're gonna make me leak again."

Ronin stroked her jaw with his thumb before releasing her. "Don't cry." He nodded to the bowl. "Eat, Lara."

Carefully, she raised a spoonful of soup to her mouth and sipped it off. Even that simple act was agonizing. The soup was already cool, but still flavorful—an assortment of vegetables in a spiced broth.

"Why did you have to wake while I was gone?" Ronin asked after she ate a few more mouthfuls. "Every moment I wasn't being questioned by the leadership, I was here with you, waiting for you to open your eyes."

Lara paused, spoon hovering with soup dripping off it, as she met Ronin's gaze. Despite their electronic nature, his eyes held so much emotion as they stared back at her. She could only imagine the devastation he must've felt while she'd been unconscious, lingering on the brink of death, but she was intimately familiar with the helplessness he must've experienced along with it.

She knew what it was like to feel powerless to help someone you loved. She'd wallowed in it both times he'd left her alone to go scavenge, and it had swallowed her up when he'd dragged himself home, scorched and damaged beyond recognition.

"Ronin…" Setting the spoon down, she took his hand in hers and guided it to her cheek. "I remember your voice. *Don't leave yet.* I focused on those words, and I held on because of them. You also asked me not to leave you. I didn't want to. I didn't want you to leave me either. I…felt your presence when you were near. I don't know how, but I knew it was you with me. And every time you left…I felt so cold.

"When I woke up, there were people arguing. Nancy and a man… Dan, or Dave, I think."

"Arguing?"

"Yeah. They were fighting about me taking up too many resources, and whether I'd wake up or not."

Ronin frowned deeply, and his eyebrows sank low. "It's a rational argument for them to make. They have limited supplies, just like everyone else. But when it comes to talk of letting you die, rationality can go fuck itself. I wouldn't have let them."

Lara smiled and lightly kissed his palm. "I know. Nancy pretty much told him that, too."

Placing the bowl on the bedside stand, he leaned forward, slipped his hands into her hair to cup the back of her head, and pressed his mouth to hers.

A shiver stole through her. The kiss was slow, tender, his mouth caressing hers with a dreamlike intimacy that made her feel weak. Lashes drifting closed, Lara succumbed to him, her own lips parting to allow him to deepen the kiss, uncaring of the sting it caused. Because she needed him. She needed this, this assurance that they were still alive, that he wanted her.

There was more to the kiss than intimacy. There was desperation in it. She felt it in the pressure of his fingers, in the strength of his hold, in the tenseness of his body. Ronin was holding himself back.

The curtain flapped.

"How is our patient today?" Nancy asked.

Lara opened her eyes, and Ronin broke the kiss, releasing her as he eased back in his chair.

Cheeks warm and lips tingling from the kiss, she looked at the woman. "Alive, sore, and ready to get the hell out of this bed."

Not looking forward to the pain of getting up though...

Nancy took gentle hold of Lara's wrist and stood in silence for a few moments before bending down to examine her face. "I think that can be arranged. The bruises are fading, and you still have some swelling, but overall, you're healing well. You need to take it easy on the ribs, but I think it'd do you some good for Ronin to give you a tour of the base."

"I'd like that."

"I'll be back in a moment, then." Smiling, Nancy walked away.

Lara looked at Ronin. "How big is this place, anyway?"

"I don't know. I haven't seen all of it yet, and I doubt I ever will. It's big."

Lara grinned, the skin around her mouth pulling tight against her still-healing cuts. "I bet not knowing bothers you quite a bit."

"I understand their reasoning for restricting my movements. But yes, it bothers me. There must be multiple entrances, but if we had to get out of here quickly, I only know of the way we came in."

The curtain rings scraped over the rod when Nancy returned and flicked them open. She pushed a chair with large wheels attached to it into the partition. "This should help you get around."

"What's that?" Lara asked.

"A wheelchair. You're not going to make it very far on foot in your current state."

Lara grunted, and the blast of pain from her ribs made her immediately regret it.

Nancy had forced her out of bed every day since she woke up. Every step, every breath, had been agony. Though Lara would be exhausted before even reaching the curtain, she took pride in pushing through despite the difficulty. Warlord had tried to kill her, yet here she was, back on her feet already, driven by sheer human stubbornness.

Even if it was only for a few minutes at a time.

She wasn't sure how she'd feel about being carted around in this chair, but at least it would give her something more to look at than this room's featureless white walls, curtains, and ceiling for a while. And she couldn't deny her curiosity about this place.

Ronin drew the blanket down and offered Lara his hand. After a few careful breaths, she took it and slid her legs over the side of the bed. He placed his other hand on the small of her back, supporting her as she stood.

Slowly, she eased into the wheelchair, tucking her splinted arm against her middle.

Nancy brushed her fingers over Lara's braid. "Enjoy yourself. I'll see you back here later."

Ronin pushed Lara out of the room, which he'd called the Infirmary, and followed the green line on the floor along a large, rounded concrete tunnel. The muffled voices of a crowd drifted down the corridor from ahead. They passed several people, many of whom cast friendly smiles in Lara's direction.

It was strange. Back in Cheyenne, direct eye contact was sometimes considered a threat, too often ending with a knife buried in someone's gut. But these people just...smiled. They all looked healthy, if a bit pale, like they'd never missed a meal in their lives. Their clothing was clean and well-mended. Their skin wasn't weather-damaged, and they didn't have dirt under their fingernails.

This is what I was becoming after Ronin took me to his house.

The voices grew louder as Lara and Ronin emerged from the tunnel into a huge room. There were dozens of people all around, engaged in conversations and various activities, many of which were unfamiliar to her. Pictures flickered on screens here and there on the walls, and machinery thrummed, buzzed, and clanked.

Lara's gaze shifted from face to face. "There are so many people."

"Not all human," Ronin said.

"There are bots here, too?"

"I've counted thirty-three, but I know there are more."

She looked over the crowd, spotting a few skinless bots. If there were synths present, she couldn't tell them apart from the humans. They all spoke with their hands as much as their mouths, all laughed together, all wore their emotions on their faces.

It was nothing like Cheyenne. These people were not divided.

They lived in harmony.

A line of six men in matching clothes marched out of a tunnel ahead, each carrying a rifle. More weaponry dangled from their belts—pistols and knives.

"Who are they?" she asked.

"Soldiers."

"Like the gearheads, only human?"

"Not all human," he repeated with a chuckle, "and not like the gearheads. They're here to protect the people who live here, not to hold them under the thumbs of their leaders."

Lara's eyes followed the soldiers until they disappeared in the crowd. "How many of them are there?"

"I don't know. They trust me enough to let me walk around the common areas, but I haven't been able to get an accurate impression of their real numbers or armament. They don't flaunt it here."

She frowned. Now that she recognized their clothing, she counted three more soldiers on the walkways overhead.

Ronin turned down another tunnel. As they moved along it, the air grew moist, carrying rich scents that took Lara a moment to identify—damp earth and vegetation. The smells only strengthened as Ronin wheeled her into another large room.

Rows and rows of plants and trees, many of which were unfamiliar to her, stood beneath bright, warm lights. Dew drops glistened on vibrant green leaves, colorful fruits hung from branches, and vegetables grew closer to the ground. The air itself was thick with life.

Stopping beside a tree, Ronin reached up, plucked an orange fruit, and handed it to her.

The fruit was smaller than her palm, with soft, fuzzy skin. She gave it a gentle squeeze. "What is it?"

"An apricot. Take a bite."

She stared at the apricot for a moment before raising it to her lips. Her teeth sank into the tender flesh, and sweetness swept over her tongue. It was the most wonderful thing she'd ever tasted. And yet...she could barely bring herself to swallow it.

Lara ran her gaze over the tree, along branches weighed down by the countless apricots growing upon them, and then looked at the surrounding trees, all of which were equally bountiful. Something twisted in her belly, something heavy.

"Like it?" Ronin asked.

"It's…good."

"Your tone says otherwise." He stepped in front of the wheel-chair and crouched, his brows low as his eyes searched hers. "What's wrong?"

"It's a whole other world down here." She gestured at the plants. "I've never seen so much food in my entire life."

Ronin turned his head, following her gesture, and then met her gaze again. "And this…upsets you?"

Lara looked down at the apricot and brushed her thumb over its fuzzy skin. Part of her mind insisted this little fruit wasn't possible, that it couldn't be real. That none of this could be real. Because if this was real, if all this existed so close to Cheyenne…

But before she could put any of her thoughts into words, several loud *moos* sounded from somewhere deeper in the compound.

Her brow furrowed. "Cows?"

"Yes, and more." Ronin rose and returned to the rear of the wheelchair. He pushed Lara onward, past the trees and rows of plants, toward an opening into another room. The smell from within was far more pungent and less pleasant.

The cows stood in a penned-off area, their heads bowed and tails flicking from side to side as they chewed grass. A man sat on a stool beside one. As he tugged on its udders, milk sprayed into a bucket.

As Lara stared at the man and cow, something simmered deep in her belly. "There was an old man back in Cheyenne who had a cow when I was a little girl. Its skin was stretched over its bones, and its eyes…its eyes were always so *sad*." She scowled, flicking her gaze over these plump, contented beasts. "One night, someone decided to steal it, and they shot the old man when he tried to stop them. They'd already butchered the cow and sold the meat by the next morning."

Ronin was silent, but she could almost sense the questions brimming within him.

Chickens wandered closer, clucking as they bobbed their heads, and sheep and goats bleated farther back.

Lara wanted to scream, wanted to rage, but she couldn't. It was already getting hard to breathe with how her throat was tightening. She clenched her fist in her lap. "I want to go back."

Without a word, Ronin rolled her back the way they'd come, not jarring her aching body a single time.

Nancy was waiting in the Infirmary, along with a tall, brown-skinned man who turned to face Lara as Ronin wheeled her inside.

"Did it feel good to get out of this room for a change?" Nancy asked. When Lara didn't respond, Nancy tilted her head to the side, frowning before she gestured to the man. "This is Colonel Jack Rodriguez. He's our Head of Security, and he's been talking a lot with Ronin since you two arrived."

"Hello, Miss Brooks," Rodriguez said. "Now that you're feeling better, I have some questions for you."

Lara held his gaze. Anger burned in her gut. The way this man stood, his confidence and air of authority, reminded her of Warlord.

"Lara?" Ronin asked from behind her.

"Why didn't you help us?" she asked, voice level.

Rodriguez's lips parted, and a tiny crease formed between his eyebrows. "You're alive because we helped you."

"Why didn't you fucking help us?" She ignored the pain of each breath, unable to tamp down the firestorm raging inside her. "You left us to them! Left us to starve, to *die!*"

His expression hardened. "I don't know what the fuck you're talking about, Miss Brooks, but—"

"Cheyenne! All those people. You left us to sift through the fucking Dust, trying to find enough shit to earn a few bites of food from that bastard when this whole time you had food and shelter and medicine here. You have protection here!"

She didn't realize that she'd stood up and advanced toward Rodriguez until Ronin's hands settled on her shoulders and stopped her.

Rodriguez didn't back away, didn't break eye contact. "You've been through a lot, and I can't pretend I know what it's like."

"And you did nothing. My sister is dead, hundreds of people are dead, and you might as well be responsible for it. You let that monster run free while you live here in luxury."

"We work for *everything* we have down here. Every. Fucking. Thing. Every time someone eats a piece of fruit"—his eyes dropped to the crushed apricot in her trembling fist—"we have to worry about whether we'll be able to produce another. Every time someone needs medical attention, there's a chance we'll never be able to replace the supplies used to care for them. We have a lot of our own people to worry about right here, Miss Brooks. We're not responsible for the rest of the damned world."

"*Fuck you!*" Lara's chest heaved, and black spots dotted her vision. Agony pierced her chest. But her heart hurt more than anything. All those years, all those people, all that suffering, and peace and abundance had been right here the whole time? "Fuck..."

Nancy rushed forward. "That's enough, damn it!"

Lara's legs gave out, but Ronin was there, taking her sagging weight into his arms. He carried her to the bed and laid her down carefully.

"You need to drink this now," Nancy said. Something cool pressed to Lara's lips.

It smelled sharply of alcohol and something else—the sleep of the dead.

"No. I don't...want it..." Lara turned her head and swiped at the cup.

Nancy was quicker, moving it back before Lara could knock it out of her hand. "Tilt her head back and plug her nose."

Ronin followed her orders, his hands too strong to fight, yet somehow retaining their gentleness.

No!

Lara stared up at him, unable to believe the betrayal.

Nancy held the cup closer to Lara's mouth. "This will dull the pain and calm you before you do any lasting harm to yourself."

"Please listen, Lara," Ronin said, his voice oddly strained.

Tears stung her eyes, and she averted her gaze. The moment she opened her mouth to take a breath, Nancy poured the foul liquid in, covering Lara's lips to prevent her from spitting it out.

With no other choice, Lara choked it down.

"She's not going to get out of it," Rodriguez said. "I expect to be notified when she's well enough to be questioned, Doctor Cooper."

His footfalls were heavy as he walked away.

"I'm sorry, Lara. I really am," Nancy said, pursing her lips as she and Ronin removed their hands. "You need to rest. Once you're stronger, you can berate Jack all you want, but as your doctor, I can't allow you to hurt yourself." She brushed a stray lock of hair back from Lara's temple, glanced briefly at Ronin, and left.

Lara turned her face away from him as tears trickled from the corners of her eyes.

Ronin's fingers slipped around Lara's right hand, but she jerked it out of his hold. "Don't."

"I vowed to protect you, Lara Brooks," he said, curling a finger beneath her chin and guiding her face toward him. After she met his eyes, he leaned forward and brushed his lips over her forehead. "I'm not going to fail to uphold that vow again…even if it shatters me."

CHAPTER FORTY-FIVE

As Ronin carried the tray of food toward the cloth partition serving as Lara's room in the infirmary, his processors whirred. He should've been concerned about the early morning meeting he'd just had with Jack Rodriguez.

The colonel was furious after meeting with Lara yesterday. He'd said that he had half a mind to kick them both out. Ronin didn't believe the threat; if Rodriguez was serious about the base's security, there was no way he'd let two strangers who knew both its location and so much of its layout just walk away. And there'd been something in his eyes today, something in the tone of his voice, that suggested he'd been shaken.

Lara's words might've done more than anger him. They might've made him think.

Ronin had smoothed over the situation as best he could, urging the colonel to consider her perspective and give her some more time. Rodriguez had reluctantly agreed. The situation was far from ideal, and remained volatile, but it wasn't what dominated Ronin's thoughts now.

No, he was preoccupied with the fact that since Lara had awoken from her laudanum-induced sleep several hours ago, she hadn't said a word to him.

He brushed aside the curtain and entered the small space. Lara lay on the bed, right arm outside the blanket and resting at her side, left tucked snugly in its sling, with her head turned away. Was she sleeping?

Stepping closer to the bed, Ronin set the tray on the nearby cart and looked down at her.

Lara's eyes were open, and she was staring at the side curtain. She didn't look his way, didn't acknowledge his presence, didn't speak.

"I brought you something to eat."

Silence.

Brow plates drawing low, he covered her hand with his. "Lara?"

She immediately yanked her hand out from beneath his and rested it on her stomach.

An unpleasant sensation skittered through his circuitry, the same one he'd felt when she'd withdrawn from him yesterday. He lifted his hand, fingers curling into a fist, and struggled to understand what he was feeling.

There was hurt, yes, not just from what she'd done but from the knowledge that he'd caused this. It was made worse because all the pieces were here before him, but he couldn't quite see how they fit together. Couldn't quite trace the causes and effects that had led to this.

"Lara?"

Silence.

Ronin moved to the other side of the bed, but Lara simply turned her face away from him again.

"Lara, please." He grasped her chin and gently turned her head toward him. "Speak to me."

Finally, her blue eyes, bright against the bruises around them, met his. She whipped her chin from his grasp. "I don't want to talk to you."

He struggled to isolate his pain, to purge it from his system. This was about what she felt. That was what he needed to know, needed to understand. "Why?"

"Because you *hurt* me, Ronin."

Ronin recoiled at those words, pulling back his hand. Electricity buzzed through him, distorting his sensory inputs and his processes, jolting his entire system. All he wanted was to protect her. Causing her harm, even inadvertently, felt like it clashed with every line of code in his programming.

"The laudanum," he said, his vocal modulator crackling softly.

Moisture gathered in her eyes, and she pressed her lips together, once more turning her face away from him.

He knew he was right, but only partially. There was more to this, more he couldn't see, couldn't comprehend. Lara's anger was usually open and fiery. She didn't hide it, didn't shy away from expressing it. She'd never been afraid to speak her mind to him, even in anger. But this anger was…different. It was laced with hurt, hurt that he'd caused.

When he caught her chin this time, he didn't let her pull away, forcing her to keep her eyes locked with his. "Speak to me, Lara. Yell at me. Scream at me, curse at me, hit me. Anything but…this."

Ronin stroked her jaw with his thumb as he watched a tear spill from the corner of her eye and slide into her hair. "Do not close yourself off to me."

"You took my choice away," she said, voice raw.

Every part within him stilled. "Lara…"

"What you did… It was a betrayal. I know you did it because you wanted to help me, but it was my choice, Ronin. Mine." More tears fell from her eyes. "And you took it from me. You held me down while they forced a drug into my mouth that you knew I didn't want. They treated me like I was crazy, and you… I…I never thought you'd…"

Her face crumpled, and her next words came out between her sobs. "You're supposed to be on my side, supporting me."

That unsettling feeling permeated Ronin now, a thousand times stronger than before.

For all his thoughts of her, he'd failed to consider what she wanted, what was most important to her. Instead, he'd decided what was best for her. That single thoughtless act had broken something precious to him—Lara's trust.

"Lara, I…"

He felt as though both an immense weight was pressing down on him and dark waters were rising around him, felt as low and battered as the scrap littering the dust.

He'd vowed to protect Lara, and he'd thought he had. But he realized now that it was more than safeguarding her body. So many of the wounds she'd suffered in her life had been dealt to her mind, to her heart, and had left scars that would never show on the surface.

Perhaps helping administer the drug to her yesterday had protected her body from physical harm, but he'd inflicted harm of a different sort by doing so. She'd said *no*, and he'd ignored it.

Ronin dropped heavily onto his knees. That weight continued to bear down, threatening to crush him. But he could not take his eyes off Lara.

What have I done?

Taking her hand, he drew it close and pressed his lips to her palm.

Hadn't he just recently learned what had been done to him? Whatever life he'd led before the Blackout, before the war, had been taken from him without his say. His body had been altered, his memories erased. His choice had been taken away from him, and he would never know what had been lost in the process.

With that revelation so fresh, how could he have robbed Lara of any choice, no matter how small? How could he not have seen the parallels?

The ability to decide for herself was one of the few things Lara had left, and he'd taken it. He, the one she trusted most. The one she loved.

A tremor coursed through him, carried on a wave of that sparking, unpleasant sensation, that quivering in his coding. That…wrongness.

He pressed her hand to his cheek, holding it tight. "With every core in my processors, every millimeter of my wiring, and every bit of metal and plastic in my casing, I am sorry, Lara."

She was quiet as she looked at him, her tears falling as her lower lip trembled. When she gave her hand a tug, he was reluctant to release her, needing that contact, needing her, but he let her go. Except she didn't pull away from him. Her fingers lovingly caressed his cheek before feathering through his hair.

"I'm human. I'm not always going to make the best choices, I understand that. But if you disagree, Ronin, talk to me. Guide me to a better choice, but please...don't take it away."

"Never," he vowed vehemently. "Never again."

CHAPTER FORTY-SIX

Ronin leaned against a concrete wall in the main chamber, watching the activity around him. Though he'd logged two hundred and fifteen unique faces in his memory since arriving at the base, he struggled to estimate the number of inhabitants, especially with so many areas being off limits to him.

The facility was well maintained, but total cleanliness wasn't possible. People lived here. They worked and interacted in these chambers and corridors. Conversations were frequent and typically amiable, and children's laughter echoed off the walls, weaving above, below, and throughout the steady buzz of activity.

Cheyenne starkly contrasted with this place. The buildings and grounds of the bot district were impeccably maintained despite limited resources. Every house had intact windows, freshly painted siding, and precisely trimmed lawns, hedges, and trees. The streets were free of debris. But there was no laughter, no warmth. Many of the residences within Cheyenne's wall were occupied, but the bot district was as cold and silent as a tomb.

The slums outside the wall represented a different extreme. The ramshackle structures had been pieced together with scrap materials, many of them looking like they'd collapse under the weight of anything more substantial than a passing glance. Humans stared out from the doorways and windows with dull, hopeless eyes, surviving either out of spite or habit.

It was a place of squalor and desperation, filled with people but devoid of life.

Laughter caught Ronin's attention, and he shifted his optics to a group of ten children following a tall bot with a boxy torso. *KICK ME* had been written on the bot's back with chalk.

At their laughter, the bot halted. The children failed to stifle their giggles as they also stopped.

Slowly, the bot's head turned around to look down at them with circular optics. "The tone of your amusement indicates mischief. Please explain so we may proceed to class immediately."

Ronin couldn't be sure if it was because of the way the bot's head turned, the tone of its voice, or how it looked with its head backwards, but the children burst into fits of laughter. The bot's head remained in place as its body ponderously tottered around to face them.

"Explain. Or I will be forced to issue detention slips to all of you."

Another bot—a sleeker model, but not a synth—stopped behind the teacher. It tilted its head, and after a moment's pause, raised its foot and kicked the teacher's backside.

Ronin couldn't hold back a smile as the children laughed uncontrollably. A few of them doubled over, holding their stomachs, and one even fell to the floor.

The teacher rocked slightly as the other bot kicked it again. Slowly, the teacher spun its head to face behind. "You are disrupting the education of my students."

"I am only following instructions," the other bot replied.

"Desist your behavior or I will issue you a detention slip."

The bot tilted its head in the opposite direction and lowered its foot. A moment later, it raised its other foot and kicked the teacher again.

Somehow managing a glare despite its fixed facial features, the teacher turned its body with a few lumbering steps. "You have ignored my verbal warning. Printing detention slip."

There was a whirring noise from inside the teacher, but it stopped when a pair of soldiers approached. The students, red-faced, struggled to regain their composure.

One of the soldiers wiped the chalk letters off the bot's back with his sleeve and shot the kids a half-heartedly disapproving look. The other stepped between the two bots, grinning.

"Come on, Terence. Mr. Mathers has class to get back to. You don't have to follow every sign the kids write on his back."

"You are correct. But it is more fun to do so." Terence leaned to the side, glancing at the children, and closed the shutter of one of his optics briefly before he walked away. The kids giggled again as Mr. Mathers and the two soldiers turned to face them.

"Detention slips for everyone. Printing—ERROR. SPOOL OUT OF PAPER. BLACK INK LOW. CANCELLING PRINT."

"How many times have we told you kids to stop playing pranks on Mr. Mathers?" asked one of the soldiers.

In unison, the children glanced down at their shoes.

The soldier crossed his arms over his chest. "Listen to him, because he's got more knowledge than you can begin to understand. He'll teach you everything you need to know, just like he taught us, and your moms and dads and grandparents."

"Now what do you say to Mr. Mathers?" the other soldier prompted.

"We're sorry," the children said together.

"Due to inadequate ink and paper, your apology is accepted. We must immediately proceed to the classroom to resume instruction." Mr. Mathers turned and walked forward.

As the children shuffled behind him, one of the soldiers bent down beside a student. "Hey, here's what you should write the next time…"

The soldier's hushed words were lost in the din as the group moved away.

Ronin couldn't recall witnessing anything like this during his travels. In most places outside of Cheyenne, humans and bots coexisted, but nowhere else were their lives so integrated. This was what Newton had meant. This was how humans and bots were designed to interact.

He pushed off the wall and walked toward his quarters; it was time to wake Lara. In the eight days since their first heated exchange, Rodriguez hadn't attempted to question her again, but the Colonel was done waiting.

The base's leaders had been generous enough, most likely at

Nancy's insistence, to provide Ronin and Lara with a private room outside the infirmary. Though it was sparsely furnished, with only a double bed, a small table, and a footlocker, it had a working door and was warm and dry.

It was more than they could ever have hoped for when they'd left Cheyenne.

Lara was already awake when he entered their room. She smiled at him, and he couldn't help noticing the light in her eyes. The swelling around them had largely subsided, and most of her bruises had faded to subdued yellow.

"Feel better after your nap?" he asked.

Her smile faded. "I couldn't sleep. Not looking forward to being inter...intro...what was the word?"

"Interrogated."

"Yeah. That. I don't know what the hell he thinks he's going to get out of me." Lara rose slowly, her movements stiff. She could walk around without help now, but subtle changes in her expression often belied her discomfort. She adjusted the lay of her sling around her neck. "And just because I've cooled off doesn't mean I'm not still pissed, or that I won't blow up on them again."

"Try to consider things from their perspective."

"I have, and I get it. I would've done a lot to protect Tabitha if I had the chance. But even at my lowest, when I didn't know where my next meal would come from, I still helped people out. Because that's how things are *supposed* to be. We're not...we're not supposed to see other people suffering and just look away like nothing's happening."

"They inherited this situation, Lara. They were born into it."

"And I was born to die under Warlord's boot?" she countered. "All those people in Cheyenne, they only exist to be his entertainment? You've got all those bots who follow him because it's too dangerous not to, all those humans living in terror...and the whole time, two miles away, there were soldiers with the numbers, training, and firepower to end him, but all they've done is hide. They might as well be the ones who left us there to die."

His processors hung up on the thought of her being left to die, nearly calling up images he didn't want to see again, but he pushed past it. "They didn't leave you, Lara."

She stepped close to him, tipping her head back to keep her eyes locked with his. "You crossed Warlord, Ronin. You risked yourself to protect me. Why? Why did you go out of your way to bury Tabitha? You're supposed to operate on logic or some shit, and everything you've done since I met you is the total opposite."

"I did those things because I love you."

Something in her expression softened. She placed her hand on his chest, fingers curling to grasp his coat. "You did things before you fell in love with me. Before you even knew what love was. What was your reason then?"

His processors fired through all the memories of his time with her. "You intrigued me. And…you seemed lost. On the verge of collapsing."

"You helped me at my lowest point. Maybe some of your reasons were selfish, but not all of them. You could've demanded so much from me, could've turned me into your slave. But even before you loved me, you gave me food, shelter, and safety, and asked for so little in return."

"Because I had an abundance of those things to offer." As he spoke those words, the final variable in an unseen equation revealed itself, and he suddenly understood Lara's anger.

It must've shown on his face, because she smiled softly and rested her forehead on his chest. "Warlord needs to be stopped, Ronin."

"I don't think these people will risk it, Lara, but I'll help you try to convince them all the same."

"Thank you." She lifted her head, stood on her toes, and pressed her lips to his.

He leaned into the kiss, and an electric thrill pulsed over his skin. Lara wrapped her right arm around him and squeezed, only to suck in a sharp breath and step back. Lines of strain appeared around her mouth despite her smirk. "You'd think I would remember how much that hurts. Guess I just can't resist."

Ronin brushed the backs of his fingers over her cheek. She was still recovering, still delicate, and he missed holding her, missed the feeling of her body tucked against him, missed her warmth. His memories of those feelings were easily accessed, but they could never compare to truly feeling her body against his.

He took her hand in his. Slowly, they walked to the room in which he'd been questioned when they first arrived.

Lara was quiet as they entered the stockade. Though she'd probably never seen anything like it, Ronin got the sense that she knew what the cells were for. She gave them a single glance before diverting her gaze to the concrete floor.

The interrogation room was full when Ronin and Lara walked in. They sat next to each other in the only available seats, which were at the end of the table near the door. The base's leadership stared at them, Colonel Rodriguez central amongst the group.

Lara didn't release Ronin's hand.

"Miss Brooks." Rodriguez dipped his chin. "I imagine you're acquainted with everyone here by now."

Lara glanced around the room. "Yeah. Hi, Newton." She raised her hand in greeting.

Newton mimicked the gesture, his face plates lifting into a smile. "Lara. You're looking well."

Rodriguez cleared his throat. "We're not here for small talk. You grew up in Cheyenne, Brooks. That means I have questions, and you're going to answer them."

"You know, you technically all grew up in Cheyenne, too. So… you can answer them yourself."

Several of the people around the table grinned, many of them quickly hiding their mouths behind their hands.

Rodriguez's features darkened. "Stand-up comedy died when the bombs dropped."

"I don't know what that is."

"There used to be individuals called comedians who—" Newton began, but he was silenced by a glare from the Colonel.

That glare didn't soften as Rodriguez shifted it to Lara. "I'm going to be direct, Miss Brooks. I'd appreciate it if you cut the shit."

When she opened her mouth to respond, Ronin gave her hand a warning squeeze. He could guess the sorts of words that might've come out of her mouth, bristling with *f*'s and hard consonants.

Lara looked at Ronin, pressed her lips together, and took a slow, deep breath before turning back to Rodriguez. "Ronin already told you more than I ever could about Cheyenne. His mind holds on to every detail. Unless you plan on going after Warlord, I don't have anything to say to you."

Multiple conversations began at once.

"Enough!" Rodriguez's gaze roamed over the others, one at a time. "You're all here as a formality. This is a matter of security, which by our laws places me in sole command."

The heavy silence lasted for twenty-two seconds before Rodriguez returned his attention to Lara. "Warlord has been a potential threat to this facility for decades." He splayed his hands on the table with deliberate slowness. "Any information we can gather about him may be vital to our continued safety and functionality. But I am curious, Miss Brooks, as to why you think we'd risk our people to go after him. He gave up searching this area many years ago, and he hasn't caused us trouble since."

"Why wouldn't you?" she asked. "If there was a wild dog living next door to you, and every now and then it killed one of your neighbor's kids, would you just ignore it because it hadn't done anything to you and your children?"

"Warlord hasn't killed any of our neigh—"

Lara yanked her hand from Ronin's and slammed it on the table, pushing herself up. "*We're* your fucking neighbors!"

Ronin scanned the others with his optics; their faces bore signs of shock and shame.

"We've been your neighbors a long fucking time, and humans and bots are both suffering because of that bastard." Despite her obvious anger and the pain straining her features, Lara kept her voice steady and her eyes unwavering.

Witnessing such strength in utter defiance of the odds was inspiring, and it made pride flicker across Ronin's processors.

"Sit down," Rodriguez said through his teeth.

"Fu—"

"We should hear her out," William interjected.

Seconds felt like years as Rodriguez and Lara glared at one another across the table. Ronin's fingers twitched. The tension in the air was nearly thick enough for his dermal sensors to detect.

If it came down to it, he'd fight for her without hesitation, no matter how many soldiers were in this facility.

Rodriguez glanced at the scientist. "I told you, Anderson, you're here as a formality."

"We've heard stories from our scouts over the years, but they've always been just that." William held out a hand toward Lara, palm-up. "This young lady has experienced it firsthand. She's suffered because of what *our* ancestors did."

"Everyone up there has suffered because of it," Nancy added.

"I've seen with my own optics what he is capable of." Newton leaned forward, frowning as he looked at Lara. "I was sent out there, into that Wasteland, by your forbears to reactivate more of my kind. The goal was to work toward repairing the world, toward rebuilding civilization. You've all lost that vision as much as I had. This woman, who is braver than anyone in this room, has brought us an opportunity to begin what we were always meant to do."

Ronin looked at Lara. Her cheeks reddened, and she dropped her gaze as she settled back into her seat. When she took his hand again, her grip was clammy and tight. The outburst had cost her.

"The situation has changed," said Dave Elliot. He was the quartermaster, in charge of the provisions within the base. The man who'd argued Lara was consuming too many resources. "Maybe a hundred years ago, we could've gone out and done something, but we have too many problems of our own now. We have to worry about our own people before we risk everything for strangers."

"Every time I send people out, there's a strong chance they won't all come back, and that's just running for scrap and supplies," the Colonel said.

Lara stared at him. "So instead, you live in hiding. You cower down here, away from the world, because you're too afraid to face Warlord."

Rodriguez surged to his feet and slammed his fists down on the table, making the whole thing rattle. "Every person we lose under my watch is another weight I have to carry with me forever! It's already too much to ask them to risk their lives for our own, for our survival, to keep their friends and family safe. But you expect me to put everyone here at risk to go to war on behalf of strangers?"

Only the long table separating Lara and the colonel kept Ronin seated in the face of such aggression, though his fingers twitched with the instinct to reach for a firearm he was no longer carrying.

"What will you do when there are too many of you to fit in this place?" Lara asked, surprisingly calm. "When you're so packed in that you can't keep up with supplies and food? You're trapped down here, and he's as much your ruler as he is Cheyenne's if you won't go out and face this."

Bracing her right hand on the tabletop for support, Lara rose once more, eyes steady on Rodriguez. "Will you deny couples the right to have children and murder their babies? Will you kill anyone who breaks the rules, or refuse to feed people who don't contribute enough to your cause?"

Nancy turned her head toward Rodriguez. "Our crops are struggling more and more. It's a miracle they've lasted this long. A few more generations, and they won't be viable."

"We have other plans in place to—" Dave began.

"It may be decades before we have the breakthroughs to even begin that kind of genetic modification. Our children and grand-children may not have that much time," Will said.

"There are resources in Cheyenne," Ronin offered, not looking away from Rodriguez, who stared down at the table. "Warlord has kept a number of fields producing crops, in addition to cattle and goats. Plus, there are production facilities on the south side of town that are still in limited operation."

"With those, we can—"

"Enough," Rodriguez commanded. The room fell silent again as he lowered himself onto his seat, nostrils flared.

After several moments, Lara sat down with a defeated look on her face.

Seconds ticked away on Ronin's internal clock, stretching over a minute.

"Is that what he's doing over there?" Rodriguez finally asked, looking up at Lara.

"What?"

"Killing babies. Murdering anyone that doesn't obey. Letting people starve. Is that what Warlord is doing in Cheyenne?"

She nodded. "We're his playthings. He keeps us around until we're not interesting anymore, or we're too much trouble. We need his permission to have children, and if a couple has more than one…the baby is killed. He doesn't allow anyone to grow enough food to survive so we're dependent on him. The entire settlement has to share a single water pump, and he shuts off the flow at his whim."

Lara found Ronin's hand again, twining their fingers. "Relationships between humans and bots are forbidden. My sister was taken in by a synth, and when Warlord found out about it, he beat her to death and tore the bot to pieces. He found out about me and Ronin not long after and hunted us across the Dust like animals." She took a steadying breath and squeezed Ronin's hand. "There's no hope in Cheyenne. Only *him*."

"This is not something we have the resources to fix, Jack," said Dave.

For a long while, Rodriguez scrutinized Lara. "It's also not something we can afford to ignore for much longer, Dave."

"They're already using our resources without any sort of contribution or compensation. Already burdening our people. Now we're going to risk our lives for them? That's not the kind of decision that's going to keep this place running through the years."

Captain Cooper leaned forward in his seat beside Nancy. "If there's a viable alternative to this place, it's something we need to consider. The Andersons say we're on limited time as it is, and all of us know people aren't meant to live in holes like this."

"We need sunlight," Nancy said. "Even the few of us that go topside don't get enough. The UV lamps don't cut it, and they won't last forever. The elderly are brittle, and too many of the young show signs of rickets."

"Will your people fight, Miss Brooks? Will they lay down their lives for a chance at being free of Warlord?" Rodriguez asked.

"I can't speak for them, but I think if they're given a chance, if they're given just a little hope…they would. They have nothing else."

Rodriguez's eyes flickered to Ronin. "And the bots?"

"I don't know. Most are what you'd consider civilians, and I cannot guess the nature of their programming. Warlord's gearheads will fight for him, but beyond that, I cannot say with any degree of certainty. Though…"

Ronin shifted his optics to Newton. The first voice Ronin had heard after reactivation, the source of his oldest uncorrupted memory... "If anyone could convince them, it would be the Prophet."

The plates over Newton's optics rose high as the room's attention fell upon him. There was a faint quiver in his voice as he spoke. "The stories told about me as the Prophet are exaggerated. They border on superstitious nonsense—"

"You're the one who woke them up," William said. "As bots have developed emotions over the years, that's only become more significant to them. Stories are powerful things, whether we're flesh or metal."

"But to think that I'd have any special sway over anyone else... I don't..."

"Brooks, are you willing to speak to your people? To rally as many to the fight as you can?" Rodriguez asked.

"I'll do everything I can," Lara said.

He nodded and turned to Newton. "She's going to risk everything, again, because she thinks this is the right thing to do. What about you? Will you talk to the bots in Cheyenne?"

Newton frowned. "I... Yes. Yes, I will. Illogical as it may be to walk into the den of our enemy, stand up in the middle of the square, and incite a riot, I will."

Sparks crackled across Ronin's cheek, compelling him to scratch, but he kept his hands down. "Lara is still wounded, and any gearhead that knows her face will shoot on sight. She can't go back to Cheyenne."

Lara turned to him. "I need to do this, Ronin."

The thought of her going back to that place, back within Warlord's reach, dragged on Ronin's processes and threatened to disrupt all his functions. "Somone else can do it, Lara. Anyone else. I need you safe. Need you alive."

She pulled her hand free of his and cupped his jaw. "I can't ask these people to sacrifice and not be willing to do the same. I know the people there, and they know me." Leaning forward, she pressed her forehead to his. "We can't let Warlord keep getting away with this."

His processors calculated hundreds, thousands, millions of possibilities. Countless ways in which it could all go wrong, countless ways for him to lose her again. Permanently. But Ronin knew Lara well enough to know he wouldn't win this fight.

He took her face between his hands and kissed her, shutting down the calculations, pushing aside his worry. There was only her. His Lara.

After pulling away, Ronin faced Rodriguez. "She is to be as far away from any fighting as possible."

The Colonel nodded. "We'll plan based on the map you drew for us. For now, I'm sure everyone's fed up with this meeting. We'll reconvene tomorrow morning to begin preparations." Rodriguez raised a hand, silencing Dave Elliot before the man could say a word. "Dismissed."

CHAPTER FORTY-SEVEN

Lara squeezed the trigger. The pistol fired, its report echoing through the chamber, and her arms jerked, but she maintained her grip and leveled the barrel quickly. Her ears rang despite the earplugs Ronin had given her.

He tipped his head forward, brushing her shoulder with his chin. His solid presence at her back was a big help in controlling the gun, but knowing what to expect made even more of a difference. She'd learned a lot since taking that shot at him back in Cheyenne.

Not that her aim had improved much.

"One foot, two inches to the left and ten inches down from your mark." Ronin's voice was clear through the earplugs, thanks to the tiny electronics he said were inside them. That he could measure the distance so accurately was as amazing as it was discouraging.

She glared at him over her shoulder.

He met her gaze and smirked. "It's a little closer than before."

"By what? An inch?"

"Five-eighths of an inch, actually."

Lara rolled her eyes and faced her target—a small circle Ronin had drawn on a wooden board twenty feet away. She couldn't tell her latest shot from the other holes in the board, but she trusted Ronin's assessment.

Taking a deep breath, she aimed and pulled the trigger. The

pistol boomed again. Wood splintered at the top left corner of the board.

"Closer," Ronin said. "Only—"

"What's the point?" Lara clicked on the safety and lowered her arms. "What kind of damage can this do?"

"None, if you don't start improving your aim."

She turned toward him, narrowing her eyes. "Ronin."

"It depends on what you're shooting at."

"You know damn well I'd be shooting at a bot."

"Not all bots are built like me." He banged his knuckles on his chest. The solid thud was muted by his clothes and skin, but what lay beneath them wasn't a mystery. "That pistol would barely put a scratch in my casing. But not all of Warlord's gearheads are outfitted for war."

"How much use am I going to be? I'm not a soldier, Ronin. Shouldn't I leave the shooting to them?"

"You're the one who insists on going. You know what use you will be, and if it goes as planned, you won't have to fire a single shot." Keeping his eyes on hers, he grazed the backs of his fingers down her cheek. "But I won't have you separated from me without some way to defend yourself."

"There will be soldiers with me."

Gripping her shoulders, Ronin turned her back toward the target. He slid his hand slowly along her arm before settling it over hers. "None of them are me."

Lara's skin tingled at his touch. When he moved closer, pressing his body to her back, her breath and heart quickened.

In the two and a half months since they'd come to the base, their physical contact had been gentle, warm, and affectionate, but lacked the intimacy she craved. She knew Ronin was worried about hurting her, and she hated that he thought she was so fragile, even after her splint had come off a week ago.

"Both eyes open." His deep voice was so close to her ear that she could almost feel his non-existent breath against her skin. "Point your whole arm directly at the target, in one straight line. Imagine that line continuing from the barrel and train it on the spot you want to hit. Then squeeze the trigger."

There's something else I'd rather imagine in my hands. And it's not a trigger I want to squeeze.

She switched off the safety and took aim along the barrel. Ronin withdrew his hand. Lara squeezed the trigger three times, pausing between each only long enough to adjust for the recoil.

"Six inches low, two to the—"

"I'm done." She plucked out the earplugs and dropped them into the pocket sewn on her skirt. Holding the pistol loosely, she turned to Ronin, wrapped her arms around his neck, and pressed her body against his.

Ronin leaned forward and raised an arm, reaching behind his head to pluck the gun from her grip. He engaged the safety and returned the weapon to the holster on his thigh. "You're never going to learn anything new if you allow yourself to get so frustrated."

Lara grinned up at him. "I'm not frustrated." Tugging him closer and rising on her toes, she brushed her mouth over his and nipped at his lower lip. "I'm distracted."

Ronin released a groan. He banded an arm around her and slipped the fingers of his other hand into her hair as he cradled the back of her head. "What is distracting you, Lara Brooks?"

Lara trailed slow, sensual kisses over his jaw and down his neck. "Thoughts of your hands on my skin." She flicked her tongue over the dip at the base of his throat. "Caressing my breasts, toying with my nipples. Your fingers as they stroke my clit."

She pressed her pelvis against him, and she didn't miss the hard bulge against her stomach. An ache blossomed between her thighs. She was bare beneath her skirt; he could be inside her with no effort. "Your body, and how I want to run my hands all over it."

Skimming a hand down his chest and abdomen, she wrapped her fingers around his erection through his pants, gripping it firmly, and whispered into his ear, "I miss feeling your cock inside me."

He shuddered. Lara took pleasure in him being as affected by their lack of physical intimacy as she was.

"You're still healing," Ronin said huskily. He brushed his cheek over her hair and dropped his hands to her hips, forcing their bodies apart.

She clasped his arms before he could pull away. She wouldn't let him use that excuse any longer. "I'm not made of glass, Ronin."

Slowly, he slid his hands toward her rear. "I know…"

"Then why haven't you touched me?"

"I have," he replied. "I *am*."

Lara stepped closer. Ronin's fingers flexed on her ass, squeezing it, and that ache in her core deepened into a fierce need.

Fuck, she wanted those hands *everywhere*. She wanted to feel him everywhere. Upon her, inside her. She wiggled her pelvis against his cock. "Touch me some more."

"Lara…"

Drawing back, she smiled and reached for the buttons of her shirt. "I want you to touch me."

His gaze dipped, and he stared at her chest as the shirt parted, baring her breasts. Cool air brushed over the hard buds of her nipples. His grip on her ass tightened, and he drew her more firmly against his cock.

Lara cupped his jaw, and his eyes met hers. His pupils expanded, nearly overtaking the green of his irises, his entire focus solely on her.

"I want you to fuck me, Ronin. Make love to me. Like before." Flattening her hands on his chest, she stood on her toes and leaned forward until her lips were a hair's breadth away from his. "You won't hurt me. I—"

The distance between their bodies vanished as he claimed her mouth with his and grasped the backs of her thighs, lifting her against him. Heart pounding, she caught his face between her hands and wrapped her legs around his hips, her skirt bunching high at her waist. Cold concrete pressed to her back.

Ronin slanted his mouth over hers, and Lara opened to him, moaning as his tongue ruthlessly conquered her own. She kissed him back in desperation, driven by a burning need stronger than she'd ever experienced.

Too long. She'd gone too long without this, too long without him.

He ground his cock against her exposed pussy, and Lara gasped as pleasure unfurled from her core.

"Fuck," she rasped against his mouth, arching into him, clutching at his hair. "I need you. I need you so fucking much."

Ronin slapped a palm against the wall. "Put your arms around me."

The moment she did, he pinned her to the wall, and one of his hands slipped between them, deftly unfastening the remaining buttons of her shirt and exposing her breasts fully. He cupped one, kneading it firmly, and rolled her nipple between forefinger and thumb. It was like a direct link to her clit, causing it to twitch as pleasure rushed through her.

"Ronin…" Lara moaned, tipping her head back, but she refused to let her eyelids fall shut, refused to look away from his dark, smoldering eyes.

Keeping an arm around his neck, she slid the other between their bodies and worked at opening his pants. It was difficult, and her fingers were clumsy, but the moment she drew down his zipper, his cock, hard, thick, and ready, sprang free. She grasped it and guided its blunt head to her wet center.

"Now, Ronin," she whispered.

He didn't hesitate.

He drove into her, filling her utterly. A gasp tore from her throat at the white-hot sensation that flashed through her. It burst over every part of her, making her skin tingle.

Ronin touched his forehead to hers. "Lara."

Tightening her legs around him, she drew him closer, deeper, loving the way his cock stretched her, loving how close they were, loving the feel of him inside her. Loving...

She caressed the side of his face as she stared into his eyes. "I love you."

"My wife... I will not lose you."

Dropping his hands to her ass, he braced her as he drew back, and before his cock had fully pulled out, he slammed into her eager body. Lara cried out, and he plunged into her again and again.

Reality melted away, leaving only sensation; his earthy scent, the feel of his warm, solid body, the pressure of his fingers against her skin, the delightful friction between them.

He was all she needed to feel alive.

She closed her eyes and clung to him, panting in time with his thrusts. Each stroke of his cock, each furious pound of his hips, stimulated her clit with a burst of pleasure. That pleasure coiled in her core, winding tighter until she could take no more.

Her climax struck like a bolt of lightning, quick and forceful, and her cries echoed off the concrete walls. Ecstasy swept through her, lifting her higher and higher. Her fingers curled into his shoulders as she bit her lip to muffle her screams.

"Lara," Ronin groaned. His perfect rhythm faltered, and for an instant, she thought she heard machinery inside him whirring. He stiffened, going completely still. His cock vibrated, pulsing through her, triggering another orgasm from her. All she could do was submit to it, her body locking up, her pussy contracting around his shaft as liquid heat flooded her.

Then he sagged forward, burying his face between her neck and shoulder, and braced a hand against the wall for support.

Panting, with her skin damp with perspiration, Lara smiled and brushed her fingertips over the short hairs on the back of his head. His cock remained deeply embedded within her, and she was tempted to have him take her again.

"I missed this." She opened her eyes and kissed his temple.

"One of these times, my system isn't going to recover."

Lara laughed.

Ronin lifted his head and looked at her, smirking. "Is this all I have to do to hear that sound from you?"

Smile fading, she caressed his cheek. "We haven't had much to laugh about, have we?"

"We're both alive. That's something to celebrate, isn't it?"

"Yes."

She kissed him, and he held her close, his lips moving gently over hers, a far cry from their desperate kiss from before.

They were both alive, but that did nothing to diminish her fears.

It would've been so easy to stay here at the base, take on their share of work, and live their lives in peace. Yet how would Lara sleep at night knowing the people of Cheyenne suffered while she lived in security and comfort?

Going back to Cheyenne was the most dangerous choice she could make...but it was also the right one.

Besides, Ronin was her happiness, her strength, her inspiration.

With him by her side, there was hope. They could make a difference.

Breaking the kiss, Lara drew back with a smile. "By the way, did you call me wife?"

A grin spread across his lips. "I did." He took hold of the hand upon which she wore the ring and brought it to his chest, stroking the band with his thumb as he stared into her eyes. "You are mine, Lara. My wife. And I am yours until the end of time."

Tears burned in her eyes as she traced his brow with her fingertips. "I love you."

"I love you, too." He settled his palm over her cheek and brushed his thumb over the tiny scar. There was impossible strength in his hand, but she knew he'd never misuse it.

She tightened her legs, unwilling to relinquish him. Moments like this were rare, and though her need was satisfied, her craving persisted.

The scrape of the metal door was the only warning that their privacy had come to an end.

CHAPTER FORTY-EIGHT

Ronin detected the sound of the door three tenths of a second before Lara tensed.

"Shit," she muttered, pulling her shirt closed.

Withdrawing his cock from her body, he quickly set her on her feet, smoothed down her skirt, and steadied her when she staggered. Rapid bootsteps approached.

Someone cleared their throat behind Ronin. "I…uh…"

Grinning, Lara glanced over Ronin's shoulder before she turned away to button her shirt.

Ronin tucked his phallus into his pants, refastened them, and faced the newcomer. His processors cycled through countless potential reactions to the interruption, most of them laced with annoyance. He and Lara had been alone down here for the better part of an hour without any disturbances, but as soon as they'd given in to their simmering desires…

He yearned for more of Lara's heat. Two and a half months with nothing but simulations and memories had sharpened his desire for her into something penetrating, something dangerous, something that had left its mark on every bit of his circuitry.

Somehow, he regained control of himself, even if that control was decidedly tenuous.

The soldier's face was redder than Lara's flushed cheeks, and uncertainty and hesitancy made his posture unbalanced. Though Ronin had seen him around, he didn't know the young man's name.

Ronin raised his eyebrows. It was the most neutral response he could muster given the potent mixture of frustration and need crackling through him.

Lara placed a hand on his back. He wanted nothing more than to turn around, press her against the wall, and have her again.

"C-Colonel w-wants you to report to the war room," the soldier stammered. "Please?" His eyes flicked to Lara.

Ronin knew what the soldier would see—flushed cheeks, swollen lips, and disheveled hair. A woman well-loved. Ronin shifted to block the man's view of her.

The soldier was young and inexperienced. Following his superior's orders, he'd unwittingly stumbled into a private moment, leaving him uncomfortable and unsure of how to act. He hadn't asked to be placed in this situation, hadn't intended to cause it.

But part of Ronin wanted to drag the soldier away and ensure the young man never looked upon Lara again. Thankfully, it was a small part.

"We'll be there soon," she said.

Ronin didn't miss the mirth in her tone.

He was grateful for her levelheaded response, as his tact function seemed to have been temporarily disabled. His jealousy and possessiveness were entirely irrational, but he could no more deny them than the data stored in his memory.

Ronin stared at the soldier. The young man swallowed and looked at the floor.

"We can find our way," Ronin finally said.

"Y-yes sir." Cheeks darkening further, the soldier turned and hurried away. The door slammed with a heavy *clang* behind him.

"Scaring kids now?" Lara asked with a laugh.

Ronin faced her, pausing to appreciate the pink on her cheeks, her tousled hair, her enticing lips. They were for him. She was for him.

She's mine.

"You aren't much older than him, Lara. And I didn't say anything."

"You didn't have to." Her lips stretched into a sultry smile as she pressed her body to his, rose on her toes, and brushed a kiss along his jaw. "It was all in your eyes and how possessive you acted just now. And I really, really liked it."

She pressed her mouth firmly against his before giving his bottom lip a nip. The bite sent a shock through his system, and fresh fluid rushed into his cock, hardening it and making it twitch in response.

Grinning, Lara pulled away and took Ronin's hand, lacing their fingers together. "Let's go see what He-Who-Must-Be-Obeyed wants. The longer we make him wait, the more pissed he'll get."

Ronin found himself entirely indifferent to the colonel's anger. What did he care about another meeting with the base's leadership? Infinitely more tempting was the notion of making love to his wife again, and he found himself battling the urge to turn her toward the wall, shove up her skirt, and drive his cock into her pussy from behind.

After all, they had seventy-five days of abstinence to make up for...

Despite his yearning, he didn't resist as Lara led him onward.

Beneath tired overhead lights, they walked along concrete corridors and through heavy steel doors. The base's security was undeniable. The labyrinthine passages would easily confuse anyone unfamiliar with their layout, and presented numerous chokepoints where a small, dedicated force, even if greatly outnumbered, could defend against invaders.

Yet something in Ronin longed for the outside, for the Dust. For open air and relative quiet. Lara had mentioned several times that she felt cooped up, like a prisoner, and he understood. Freedom to roam most of the facility couldn't replace the feel of wind and sunlight, even for a bot.

The interrogation room, officially referred to as the war room, was full of soldiers when Ronin and Lara arrived. As usual, Rodriguez sat at the head of the long table, now with Captain Cooper to his right and the synth sergeant, Maul, to his left. William Anderson was also present, seated beside Newton.

"Close the door," Rodriguez said, and one of the soldiers obeyed. "We've all sat through thirty of these meetings by now, so we'll go through this quickly."

He met Lara's gaze as she and Ronin sat down. "And no damned interruptions today, Brooks. This is all finalized now. Is that clear?"

Ronin dipped his head, hiding his involuntary smirk. Lara and the Colonel had argued at least once during every meeting. This marked the twenty-seventh such gathering; Rodriguez's estimate had been close.

Lara raised her hands in mock surrender. "Fine."

Rodriguez regarded her with his eyes narrowed before standing and looking at the others. "All right, people. You have your team assignments and objectives. Casualties are to be extracted to the forward operating base we'll establish to the west of town, where Nancy's people will see to them. Alpha team is going over the wall to secure the hospital, from which they'll push into the bot district. That should create enough noise to draw in Warlord's bots from the outlying areas.

"While they're distracted, Lara will attempt to rally human support. Bravo Team, you're on her like flies on shit. If she's successful, you will escort her and Newton into the market, and he will attempt to sway the remaining bots to our cause."

"The human settlement is usually clear," Lara said. "Gearheads only go there randomly, looking for rulebreakers to punish or desperate people to toy with. Otherwise, we could suck dirt for all the shits they give. The hard part is going to be getting into the market without raising suspicion."

Rodriguez pressed his palms to the tabletop, fingers splayed, and took a slow, deep breath. "There are a lot of moving parts here, and we're dealing with some pretty big variables. We have no guarantee that any of these people will support us. This is the most significant operation launched from this base in two hundred years, bigger than anything any of us have attempted. This isn't a scrap run into the wasteland. This is a *war*. Our goal is to win it without anyone getting hurt, but best-case is what you hope for in these situations, not what you plan for."

Rodriguez tilted his head towards Captain Cooper, who stood and took over. "We've scouted Cheyenne thoroughly over the last few weeks. Security's lax, but we've identified at least twenty-five unique tangos, equipped with various small arms. They are all confirmed as bots. We don't know if any of them have reinforced casings, so we must assume that our weaponry will only be effective within about forty meters.

"We're not going to be able to use radios. Anderson says most bots have internal antennas because they used to be connected to wireless networks, which means they'll be able to detect our communications. So we'll have to listen for gunfire as our signal.

"Stick to your squads, watch each other's backs, and be mindful of cover. We don't want to lose anyone, but it's going to be real bullets when they return fire, and none of us are bulletproof."

According to Newton, the reinforced casings that had been retrofitted on many bots couldn't stop the armor-piercing ammunition that had been issued as the war neared its end. Ronin had dealt with enough holes to know the truth of that. But he also knew that, regardless of ammunition and armoring, it only took a single round to the right spot to take down a robot.

"And what about Warlord?" Lara asked.

"Scouts have positively IDed him several times, but he doesn't seem to have a set routine. He's erratic. Only regularity is that he goes to Kitty's a few nights a week, but it's never on the same days or at the same times. We're hoping the commotion will flush him out," Cooper replied.

"He'll come. Bastard usually likes to take care of things himself. Problem is, will he go hide once he realizes what's happening?"

William cleared his throat. "I believe we can provide a little insight. I don't know how much use it will be, but…"

"We have to treat a portion of this mission as a manhunt." Rodriguez's expression was stoic, his gaze shielded. "Warlord *must* be captured or deactivated. Any intel will be useful."

William nodded, gesturing to Newton. The bot leaned forward, his metallic fingers gliding over a small console inlaid in the table. The lights in the room dimmed, and a screen powered on behind Rodriguez, slowly gaining brightness. Both the colonel and the captain sat and turned in their chairs to face it.

"With Nancy's help, Newton and I have been delving into the old records stored here. Most of the data is corrupted and inaccessible, and a lot of what we can access is irrelevant, but we've found some information on Warlord that may be pertinent to understanding his state of mind."

A grainy, pixelated image appeared on the screen, in which a man sat at a table in an office. The image clarified as the recording played.

Lara grasped Ronin's hand and squeezed.

The man was Warlord.

He was bald, with gaunt cheeks and dark circles cradling his sunken eyes, but he was unmistakably Cheyenne's tyrannical ruler.

"You understand the risks involved, Mr. Turner?" a female asked from off camera, her voice crackling over the war room's hidden speakers.

Kevin Turner, the man who would become Warlord, laughed bitterly. "Yeah. But look at me, Doctor Yuan. Death isn't a risk, it's an inevitability. If this means a little more time with my family…" He dropped his gaze and ran his tongue over his lips.

"In all honesty, Mr. Turner—"

"Kevin, please. I don't really have it in me to deal with formalities anymore."

"Kevin. In all honesty, this procedure has an extremely low chance of success. I need to be certain that you're aware that by doing this, you may be prematurely ending whatever time you have left with your loved ones."

He shook his head, sliding a palm over the surface of the table absently. "Maybe. But what more time do I have with them right now? A few weeks for them to watch me die? At least this way, it's on my terms. And they don't have to…"

Turning away from the camera, Kevin lifted a trembling hand to his face, covering his eyes as tears welled in them. "Don't have to see me suffering. Don't have to watch me become a shell of the man I was, and…and my family won't have to feel so damned helpless while it all happens."

When he dropped his hand, moisture glistened in his eyes, and there were splotches of color on his cheeks. He faced the camera directly, and though the recording was from two hundred years ago, the despair, desperation, and anguish in his expression transcended time. "I want more time with Diane. I want to see my kids grow up."

The video flickered, cutting to a high-angle view of an operating room. Several individuals wearing green scrubs, facemasks, and gloves worked around a table. A motionless figure lay atop it, draped in a blanket. One of the surgeons stepped aside, allowing the camera view of the subject's exposed brain.

"The connections for the implant are complete," said Doctor Yuan. One of the others wheeled a steel cart to her, and she lifted an electronic device from atop it. "Once this is inserted, we can begin the upload."

The war room was silent as the recording's speed increased, moving the surgeons ten times faster. When it slowed to normal, alarms were blaring in the operating room, and the surgeons' voices were frantic.

"He's flatlining."

"We need the paddles—"

"No!" Doctor Yuan shouted. "They'll damage the implant."

"We can't just let him die, Jessica!"

"He was already dead. The implant is what matters now, and it's the only chance he has of seeing his family again."

"That's not how it's supposed to be, God damn it!"

"If we succeed, it won't ever have to be like this again."

"We can at least perform CPR—"

Doctor Yuan shook her head. "The implant is too delicate. We can't risk disrupting the connection, or we might do irreversible damage to his consciousness."

"How much damage have we done already?"

"He accepted the risks. You did too, when you joined this project."

The continuous tone of the heart monitor punctuated her statement for six long seconds before the recording flickered again.

Kevin Turner sat at a table in a nondescript room. A dozen wooden blocks painted different colors lay scattered before him. His cheeks were full, there was short, mussed brown hair atop his head, and his skin had a much healthier color.

"I don't—" The voice was Kevin's, but his mouth didn't move until he repeated the words. "I don't want to do this anymore."

"A little at a time, Kevin," Doctor Yuan said from out of frame. "It's perfectly natural that things are difficult for you now. Though your body looks the same, it's completely different internally. It will take time and a lot of hard work, but I assure you, your mind will rewire itself to your new body and all its functions, and all this will be as easy as it was before. Please, try again."

Frowning, Kevin raised his arm above the table. The movements were wobbly, jerky, imprecise. His brow furrowed as he reached forward, guiding his shaky hand toward one of the red blocks. Tentatively, he pinched the block between his forefinger and thumb and lifted it off the table.

"Good. Would you please stack it atop one of the same color?" the Doctor asked.

Kevin's eyes flicked down to the other blocks, pupils dilating and contracting. Slowly, he moved his hand, hovering it over first a green block, and then a blue.

"It's okay if you're uncertain about the colors, Kevin. It's not your fault," a male said from off camera. "We just need to know so we can make the necessary adjustments to get you back to normal."

"Doctor Anderson is right," Doctor Yuan agreed. "We'll take things one step at a time."

With a slight, unnatural nod, Kevin lowered his hand. Just before the block touched the one beneath it, his arm jerked. The blocks slammed together. The red block flew from his grasp, clattering on the floor.

"Damn it!" Kevin roared through his closed mouth. He swung his arm over the surface of the table, clumsily sweeping all the blocks off. "I told you I don't want to do this!"

"It's all right, Kevin," Doctor Anderson said. "We can be done for today."

Another flicker, and the scene changed. Kevin paced in a carpeted room. A beige linen couch and two matching accent chairs rested nearby. A blonde woman who looked to be in her early forties sat in one of the chairs, wringing her hands in her lap.

"Kevin, please," she said.

"Please, Diane?" Kevin stopped abruptly with his back to her, his eyebrows sinking low. "I don't know what you expect. You tell me that and I'm supposed to be cool and collected after all this time?"

"Just...be patient, please. We knew this would take time, and it's worked out better than we hoped. You're still *here*, Kevin." She pressed her hands down on her thighs and bowed her head. "We want you to come home, but the psychiatrists say you're still… adjusting to the changes."

"They won't let me see the kids, Diane. My fucking kids! It's been eight months, and I haven't seen them since I first woke up. I don't sleep, I don't eat, I don't use the fucking bathroom. All I do is think about the life I'm supposed to be living."

Diane stood and approached him. She reached out and hesitantly placed a hand on his arm. Kevin jerked away from her, taking several steps away.

Diane's hand fell, and her face crumpled. "I know it's hard—"

"You know?" he demanded, whirling on her.

She retreated, nearly tripping when her foot caught on one of the chairs.

Advancing, Kevin grabbed the chair, lifted it overhead, and hurled it against the wall, shattering its frame. "You think you have any fucking idea what this is like?"

Diane held her hands up as though to shield herself. "Kevin, stop! Don't do this!"

"You, too?" He dug his fingers in his neck and pulled upward, tearing off a chunk of synthetic skin to reveal the metal plates of his jaws and cheek. "*This* is what I am now. There's no going back from it, so take a long fucking look!"

"Oh my God," Diane cried, tears running down her cheeks. "This isn't you. This isn't you! My Kevin would never —"

He stared at her, utterly still, his eyes cold. "No, I'm not your Kevin. He died on the operating table."

He turned and stalked away from her.

The door burst open, and several technicians hurried into the room. Diane, sobbing, was escorted out.

Kevin glanced over his shoulder, the plates of his jaw shifting as though he were clenching his teeth. He closed his eyes. The video went black.

Ten seconds passed, and an image flickered on. A black-haired woman with brown eyes leaned back in her seat, pinching the bridge of her nose. She bore a faint resemblance to Nancy Cooper. The bookshelves behind her marked the room as some sort of office.

"My name is Doctor Jessica Yuan. I'm a neurologist, and I led the team that pioneered the method by which Kevin Randall Turner, age forty-three, had his consciousness transferred into a robotic surrogate body. The procedure, at its core, was successful. There are thousands of hours of video documenting both the procedure and our work with Mr. Turner during his recovery."

She leaned forward, resting her elbows atop the desk, and raked her fingers through her hair. "I'm making this recording because the future of this project is uncertain. The war has spilled onto American soil, and the military has shown increasing interest in our work—particularly that of my colleague, Doctor William Anderson, who has made great advances in robotics and artificial intelligence. It's inevitable that they're going to seize our research, and there's not a damned thing we can do about it."

Sighing, she ran her gaze over the bare desktop.

"We didn't foresee the consequences. We pushed so hard for this, and…we should've known. I should've known. Mr. Turner's mental state is extremely unstable and volatile. He often refuses to work with us, demanding to see his wife and children, but his psychiatrists, Doctors Foster and Kuering, are convinced that he's a danger to his family. He came close to harming his wife during her last visit six weeks ago. That's when he tore off his face."

Jessica swallowed thickly, eased back in the chair, and placed her hands atop the desk. "It's apparent that the magnitude of the changes he endured were too much for his mind to cope with. Everything is different for him. He sees, hears, and feels in ways that no human was meant to. The everyday bodily functions of his old life are gone, and it's given his already fragile mind excessive time to wander. He rages against what he is and clings to what he was.

"Perhaps it's a matter of…mental fortitude? Tenacity? We don't know. He's the only successful candidate. It's possible that this process would break anyone subjected to it… All I know is that he *is* dangerous. God, I can't imagine what would happen if the government tried to use this to produce soldiers."

Her head sagged, strands of dark hair falling into her face. "This isn't what I wanted. You have to believe me, it's not what any of us wanted. This was supposed to help people. He told us in his final pre-op interview that the risks were worth the chance at more time with his family. And now... He is, effectively, immortal, and he cannot spend any of that time with the people he loves the most.

"He'd said that if he had died during the procedure, it would've spared them his suffering. And what have I done but tainted their last memories of him?"

She tilted her head back. Her dark eyes sparkled with tears. "I'm sorry," she rasped, and reached for the camera. The feed cut out.

Heavy silence fell over the war room. Ronin's processors poured over the information. What kind of world had this been all those years ago?

"We thought it important for all of you to see this," Newton said, "because we want you to understand that he was once a man. I worked closely with Doctor Anderson throughout the procedure, and I am the one who reactivated Kevin Turner, with full knowledge of his history. I hoped he would find a new purpose in the rebuilding of this world. I was wrong in my assessment of him.

"I cannot say with any certainty whether he recalls his previous life. He made no indication of such during our brief interactions after I made him operational. Regardless, it is clear that he has violently distanced himself from humanity. Please, make no mistake—he operates with malice, not the cold, logical front he projects."

Newton tilted his head down, directing his optics at the table. "I would not normally condone violence. Doctor Anderson did not program it into my functions when he created me, and our work together was performed with the hope of achieving a golden age of peace, prosperity, and comfort. There is a chance that, somewhere deep within his coding, some of Kevin Turner remains in Warlord. There is a chance he can be reasoned with."

Lara stiffened, and her fingers dug into Ronin's hand.

"But I cannot ask any of you to risk your safety on that chance," Newton continued. "Kevin Turner suffered unduly, and all our good intentions cannot reverse that. It is time for the suffering to end."

Beside Ronin, Lara released a slow, unsteady breath, and the tension in her grip eased.

It was natural for bots to calculate odds, to weigh probability heavily in their decisions. Perhaps Ronin's risk-assessment functions had been damaged in the Blackout. He actively sought danger by going into the Dust, and he should've met his end a thousand times over. But even he could recognize the odds.

The attackers were far more likely to die to a man than Warlord was to be swayed by words.

"I'm sure most of you have questions," Rodriguez said, drawing all eyes back to him. "I do, too, but we don't have the time or the information to answer all of them. Still, before I dismiss you, I want to reiterate this…there are people suffering in that town, every day. People who don't know when their next meal might be. People who don't have someone like Nancy to take care of them when they're sick. People who wake up every day to the likelihood that it will be their last.

"We pull this off, and we're helping all those people. But we'll be securing our own future, as well. This place was never meant to be used as a permanent settlement. We need the sun. We need fields for our crops. We need open air. And we need to reach out, to broaden our community, if we want it to flourish."

The room quieted again. Ronin ran his optics over the soldiers. Many of them were young, and they had likely never exchanged fire with hostile forces. How many of them would be dead before this was over? How many were realizing their mortality right now?

"When do we leave?" Lara asked.

"Three hours before dawn. Get your gear prepped tonight and get to sleep early." Rodriguez stood. "Dismissed."

Still holding Lara's hand, Ronin led her out of the war room amidst the departing soldiers. As they wound through the corridors, the crowd thinned, until he and Lara were alone in a long, silent hallway.

Data, new and old, whirred through his processors, almost too fast for him to keep up with. It was sorted, sifted, classified, and redirected into countless simulations, compared to countless potential outcomes.

Tomorrow, they would march into Cheyenne, the stronghold of a monster who'd killed dozens—if not hundreds—of innocent humans and bots during his reign. The monster who'd raped and beaten Lara, who'd murdered Tabitha, who would have ended Ronin and Lara, were it not for Newton and sheer chance.

Ronin had already acknowledged the near impossibility of Lara's very existence, the inconceivable chains of cause-and-effect stretching through epochs to result, ultimately, in the woman he loved.

Their survival was a similar collection of chance occurrences— the sudden storm, their proximity to the farmhouse, Lara's discovery of the shelter behind it and Newton's presence within. His decision to remain hidden while the gearheads attacked, and their decision not to search the shelter. Newton's guidance in locating the base and Captain Cooper's willingness to assist strangers in need. Nancy's dedication and skill.

Had any one of those factors been missing or altered, the entire chain of events might've collapsed. One variation and Ronin and Lara might well have died.

Ronin's CPU suddenly linked it all to a wholly human concept, one that had always been outside his comprehension.

Fate.

As he and Lara stepped into their room, she withdrew her hand from his and turned to him. "What's running through that head of yours?"

"Nothing," he replied. "My central processing unit and data storage are located in my torso."

She chuckled. "It's a saying. You always take everything so literally." She nudged him before sitting on the bed.

Ronin smirked. "Perhaps you need to familiarize yourself with my anatomy a little better."

Laughing, she leaned back on her elbows and wiggled her brows. "Maybe I should."

Despite her playful tone, her smile was strained, and a shadow lurked in her eyes. She always projected strength and stubbornness, never backed down from a fight. But that didn't mean she was without fear.

He eased down beside Lara. "Honestly, there's not enough time in this day, month, or year to tell you what's going through my mind. You insist on going tomorrow, and I know nothing I say will stop you. We'll be over a mile apart, surrounded by enemies. I have to accept that I cannot be there to protect you and must somehow entrust that task to others."

"It's the right thing to do, Ronin. They're more likely to trust me, knowing I lived in the same shit hole as them, over some strangers with guns."

"I know it's the right thing." Ronin shifted onto his knees and leaned over her, slipping his fingers into her red hair. He stared into her eyes, marveling at their intricate, delicate weave of vibrant blues and subtle grays. "But I don't want to do it."

Those eyes studied his features as though searching for an answer upon his face, and a small crease appeared between her brows. She shifted, moving her arms out from beneath her to lie upon the bed, and pressed her palm to his cheek. "Why?"

"Because your life is too great a price to pay for their freedom."

She looked away, frowning, and the crease between her brows deepened. Her lower lip quivered.

"I don't want to die, Ronin. After finding you, after everything we've been through… I want to *live*. More than ever, I want to live. With you." Tears had gathered in her eyes when she looked at him again. "But my life is a flicker compared to yours. You'll keep going on, and I'll be dead in fifty years, or thirty, or ten. Or tomorrow. And so will all those people. They deserve a chance to live on their terms before then, too."

Before meeting Lara, Ronin had been directionless. A wanderer. His actions had often defied logic, and the rewards he'd pried from the dusty, skeletal grip of the dead world had rarely been worth the risks he took to get them. Yet despite his illogical behavior, he never could've comprehended why she was so determined to return to Cheyenne after what she'd suffered. Not until now.

He smoothed back the hair from her face and wiped away her falling tears with his thumb. "Your life is my purpose, Lara, and I think I understand why you're willing to risk it. I disagree with you putting yourself in danger, but because it's important to you, I will go, and I will do whatever is necessary. I will fight for them...for you."

Ronin leaned his forehead against hers. "So long as I function, you will not die tomorrow, nor any other day, for many, many years."

Lara exhaled shakily and embraced him. "I'll try to keep out of trouble."

Ronin smiled. "Don't lie to me, Lara Brooks. You're going there specifically to cause trouble."

"Okay, out of *unnecessary* trouble, then."

Withdrawing one of her arms from around him, she slipped her hand beneath his shirt, fingertips grazing his abdomen. The sensation danced across his sensors. Her eyes and cheeks were wet from her tears, but she'd never looked as beautiful as she did at that moment.

"What will we do after all this?" she asked.

His processing power had been so devoted to the countless possibilities for tomorrow that he hadn't thought about the day after that at all. Their success, their survival, was too uncertain.

"I don't know," he said, after a long pause.

"I want to go back to your house."

Ronin tilted his head. "After all this, you still want to return to Cheyenne?"

She flattened her palm against his stomach. "The place was never the problem, Warlord was. Without him, Cheyenne can be rebuilt into something better. For everyone. Your house...it became a home for me, a real home. And it's where I fell in love with you."

The frantic simulations slowed as Ronin's processors shifted toward the present. Toward Lara.

Death wasn't an issue for bots. As he'd once told her, there was on and off. Despite his core programming's drive to err on the side of self-preservation, he did not fear his eventual deactivation. Hell, he'd been through it at least twice already.

But the idea of Lara's death, of a future without her...that sparked true fear inside him. Irrational fear, the kind that whispered in distant corners of his consciousness, preying upon his inadequacies. She'd changed him, fundamentally and forever. How could he revert to a directionless life after she was gone?

"Then that is where we'll stay," he said. "Though...if you still want to go, I promised I would take you to the ocean."

"Yes. I want to see the endless waves, like in that book." Her hand slid higher, sweeping over his chest and brushing his nipples. She shifted her hips, skirt falling to reveal her thighs, and smoothed her foot along his calf. "We can see the ocean and then go back home. We could even tell the neighbors about it, but most of them probably wouldn't believe us."

Electric tingles of pleasure pulsed through Ronin as she caressed his skin. Holding himself up on one arm, he placed a hand on her thigh and skimmed it toward her hip, bunching the fabric of her skirt around his wrist. She shivered beneath his touch and released a soft, shuddering breath.

"It won't matter what they think," he said, focusing his optics on her lips.

"Not even a little." She spread her knees wide, opening herself to him.

"You're all that matters, Lara Brooks."

She smiled. Her hand stopped at the center of his chest, directly over his CPU. "Love me, Ronin."

He eased over her, nestling his hips between her thighs. "Long after the Dust claims me."

CHAPTER FORTY-NINE

Lara had spent countless nights huddled beside Tabitha in their drafty shelter, desperate for warmth and comfort. They'd suffered through frigid winters and blistering summers, ravaged by hunger, exhaustion, and pain. Together, they'd survived the worst Cheyenne could throw at them for more years than should've been possible.

Those years, those hardships, had not prepared Lara for her first glimpse of her old home after months away.

The morning sun had not yet crested the horizon, leaving the sky a dull, dreary gray. The hobbled shacks were dark shapes against that sky, grave markers for the not-yet dead. Even the people who weren't sick or starving here were dying. She'd never forget the despair that had gripped her during her time here. Only Tabitha had kept Lara from succumbing to it…but she'd been claimed by this place, too.

For all her strength and toughness, Tabitha had ended up as another body atop the growing heap.

Newton and handful of men had broken off to wait on the outskirts of the slums while Lara guided Cooper and his team along the narrow dirt paths between the shacks. Before leading her group to the water pump at the center of town, she had a stop to make.

The metal of Lara's ring, back on the twine dangling around

her neck, brushed against her skin beneath her shirt. It was a reminder of what she stood to lose—everything. She and Ronin hadn't said goodbye this morning. They'd expressed it all to one another last night, through both their words and their bodies.

She adjusted her hood and dropped her hand to the pistol on her thigh, focusing on the texture of its grip rather than the stenches of rot and human waste.

People were just beginning to emerge from their homes. Even in the dim light, Lara noted the recognition in some of their eyes. What did they see? The thin, desperate waif she'd been, or the healthy, well-fed woman she'd become?

Or did some of them see a walking corpse?

Lara forced her gaze ahead as she neared her destination. She had a clear mission, and it required her full attention. Gary and Kate had always been kind to Lara, and they were well liked within the community. If she could convince them to join her, it'd be a damn good start.

Her steps faltered as their shack came into view.

"No…" she breathed.

Warlord's symbol, the fusion of a skull and a gear, was on their door in red paint that had dripped like blood.

Heart pounding in her ears, Lara rushed across the remaining distance and fumbled to shove the door aside.

The foul odor of old blood assaulted her nostrils when she entered. Behind her, the bootsteps of her escort were frantic as they hurried to catch up.

A faint light came from the small secondary room. A dark, masculine figure stepped in front of it, a metal blade glinting in his hand as he approached her.

She sucked in a sharp breath.

The man stopped abruptly. "Lara?"

Her eyes flared as she recognized Gary's voice, though it brought little relief. "What happened?"

He moved past her, toward the entryway. She gestured for the soldiers to hang back before Gary slid the door into back place.

He turned to her. The faint light caught upon his features. He was haggard, with dark circles beneath his eyes. His gaze shimmered with sorrow, but there was something deeper, something fiery, within it.

"They're gone," he grated.

Lara's heart stuttered. "Maggie?"

Dropping his eyes, he nodded.

Sweet-faced Maggie, who'd always offered Lara a kiss and a gap-toothed smile? A child who was one of the few sources of light and joy in Cheyenne, an innocent life who hadn't yet been touched by hardship?

Lara's throat was tight and raw when she asked, "Kate, too?"

Gary ran a shaky hand over his face. "I don't... I don't know. She's...not well."

"She's alive?"

He nodded.

Lara hesitated, nearly silenced by the horror of her next question. "The...baby?"

"They found out." He squeezed his eyes shut, and tears spilled from their corners. "Somehow, they found out. We were so careful, Lara, but those fuckers still found out. He wanted to make an example of us, and he..."

"You don't have to tell me," Lara said, stepping closer. She stopped when he shook his head again.

A quiet sob spilled past Gary's lips. "They killed my little girl. My beautiful little girl." He turned away and leaned against the wall, his body quaking. "They held us down and forced us to watch. Forced us to listen to Maggie crying for help, to her screams, my God her screams...and when she wasn't moving anymore..."

Eyes burning and tears falling, Lara shook her head frantically. "No..."

"There was so much blood. But...but he wasn't done. They dragged Kate away from Maggie, and...and they beat her." Gary slammed his fists against the wall. The shack rattled. "Hit her again, and again, until she bled. Until she...lost the baby."

No, no, no...

Breaths coming quick and shallow, Lara glanced down at her hands. She recalled the pain of Warlord's fists all too well. Her stomach clenched, threatening to empty itself. How much suffering would be forced upon these people?

No more. We'll rid the world of this monster.

"Is…is Kate here, Gary?"

He nodded again, wiped at his face, and led her into the back room.

Kate lay upon the bed, pale and sunken-eyed, her hair damp with sweat. Lara knelt beside her and lifted Kate's hand. It was cold and limp, as though the life had been sapped from her.

Lara closed her hands around the woman's, holding it. "Kate?"

The woman turned her head. Her eyes were unfocused, staring through Lara, until she blinked and something dawned in her gaze. Her face crumpled as she shook with sobs. "My babies…"

"Shh, I know." Lara pressed Kate's hand to her cheek. "We will stop him."

"How?" Gary demanded.

Lara lowered Kate's hand but didn't release it. "I'm here with people who plan to end Warlord and take this city back. To help us."

Kate stared up at Lara with watery eyes, silent as Gary knelt beside her. Lara met his gaze.

He scrutinized her as though he was seeing her for the first time. As though he was finally noticing the changes. "People said you were either dead…or with one of *them.*"

"I'm with a bot, but he's not one of them," she said. "He took care of me. Protected me."

Gary's expression darkened. "He forced—"

"No! No. He didn't force me. He's never forced me. I love him, Gary, and as crazy as it sounds, he loves me. We've both suffered because of Warlord. Without Ronin, I'd be dead." Lara glanced at Kate. "I can't explain everything now, there isn't time, but there are people here, humans and bots, who are going to put an end to all this. There's a place not far away, underground, where they've thrived. They have gardens, animals, children in school, housing. An army. They're here to help, but they need our help, too."

"How?" Kate's hold on Lara's hand tightened. "*How?*"

"Another group is heading for the bot district right now. They might even be there already. They're going to take over the hospital and make a distraction. I'm here to gather up anyone who's willing to fight. Anyone willing to stand up to Warlord."

"I will," Gary said. "I want him torn apart."

Hope leapt within her chest. "Can you help me talk to the others? I know...I know there doesn't seem to be much hope, but we can make a better life for all of us."

He looked down at Kate, his eyes determined but soft as he lovingly brushed his fingers through her hair. "Anything. She's all I have left."

Kate released Lara's hand to take Gary's, closing her eyes as he leaned down and kissed her forehead.

"I'll be back," Lara said as she rose to her feet.

She nudged the front door aside and stepped out. The soldiers had dispersed, but she quickly picked out their shadowy forms in the gloom. Lara waved one of them over.

The soldier tugged down the scarf from his mouth as he approached. He held the butt of his rifle against his shoulder. "What's wrong?"

"There's a woman inside who needs to be taken to the forward camp so Nancy can help her. She was beaten severely and had a miscarriage. I don't think she can make it on her own."

"Who's he?" Gary asked from the doorway.

"Private Peterson," the soldier replied. "Where's the woman?"

"In the back room." Lara pointed beyond Gary. "Her name's Kate."

Peterson nodded, leaning over to peer inside the shack. "All right. We'll make sure to bring her when we move out."

"Bring her where?" Gary asked.

Lara faced him. "Some of the soldiers are going to escort the children, elderly, and anyone too sick to fight to a safe place before anything starts. After I do what I need to here, I'll be heading there, too." She took gentle hold of his arm. "They'll take care of her. I promise."

Gary stared at her for a long while before finally nodding. "I trust you, Lara."

"Help me convince the others. The more people who stand against Warlord, the better. We can't allow him to do this anymore."

"Let me talk to Kate. Make sure she knows what's happening."

"We'll be at the water pump." Lara met Peterson's gaze after Gary went inside.

"She'll be in good hands," the soldier said.

"I know. Thank you."

The soldiers followed Lara as she wound through the slums, knocking on doors and calling to people through tent flaps. She roused some from their sleep, but many were already awake, preparing for the long, unforgiving day ahead.

She doubted any of them could've guessed how different this day would be.

Lara told everyone to gather at the water pump. The strengthening light made the red hair tucked beneath her hood more visible, and more than one person swore at her when they noticed it. A few even called her a traitor and spit at her feet.

Lara didn't let them faze her. This was their one and only chance, and she would see it through.

Gary soon caught up with her, and people seemed more receptive to him. What had been done to his daughter and wife had been cruel beyond description, and by the look in people's eyes when they saw him, Lara knew that many of the townsfolk had witnessed it firsthand.

Everyone had suffered the gearheads' *justice* at some point. Their victims were everywhere—scarred men and women, some missing fingers, hands, or legs. More homes than Lara remembered bore Warlord's symbol on their doors. But Maggie and Kate...that had been a step too far, even for these broken people.

Would that spark of outrage be enough?

It has to be.

When she finally reached the common area around the water pump, a crowd had already gathered, speaking in hushed voices. The air was thick with tension.

She found Newton and the other soldiers on the fringes of the crowd. He was wrapped in cloth from head to toe, concealing the bare metal of his casing.

"Spot any gearheads?" Lara asked.

Newton shook his head. "No. Everything is quiet. Relatively, at any rate."

"Won't be for much longer," Captain Cooper said, shifting his gaze to the northeast. "Best get on with this so we can move when the time is right."

Lara brushed her clammy palms over her skirt and approached the crowd.

We will *make this work. We have to.*

"What's this all about?" an older man demanded, his voice carrying over the din to silence the other conversations. "I could be out pickin' already. We're losin' good time!"

Lara recognized his scowling face. Steve had been a fieldworker since she was young, one of the few humans allowed to tend Cheyenne's crops. An infected cut on his leg had nearly killed him a decade ago. He'd kept the leg, but he walked with a heavy limp to this day.

The crowd's attention swung to Lara.

A tall, slender woman with brown hair and dirt smudged on her face and arms pushed to the front of the group and sneered at Lara. "Not all of us are spreading our legs to bang bots for food."

Her name was Scarlet. She was about the same age as Lara, but they'd never been close despite growing up together. Tabitha had been Lara's only real friend.

Clamping her mouth shut, Lara closed her eyes. She wouldn't give in to anger. She needed these people on her side, on their own side. When she opened her eyes again, she ran her gaze over every person she could see, meeting their eyes one by one. They were scared, hungry, uncertain, and angry. The only difference between Lara and these people was that she'd learned to hope for something better.

"I'm not going to lie to you," she said. "I left here with a bot. A dustwalker named Ronin. I did it because I was hungry, yeah, but more because I wanted to find my sister."

"Another bot-fucking whore." Scarlet spit on the ground in front of Lara.

"That's enough!" Gary stepped forward. At the edges of her vision, Lara saw Cooper and his men closing in.

"You gonna stand here and defend this filth?" Steve asked.

"Filth? Lara sacrificed to help my family when no one else would. She had nothing, and she still gave to us. She traded good salvage for scraps of food, and we took it for granted. I'll always regret that. But I'm standing beside her now like I should have all along."

"The bots she left with killed your children!" someone shouted.

Gary's expression tightened, and he clenched his fists at his sides. "No. Warlord killed my children, and Lara is here to end him."

Humorless laughter spread through parts of the crowd.

"She ain't ending anything!" someone called.

"Not by myself," Lara replied.

"You can't expect us to fight him!"

"Why? Why can't we fight him? Because we fear his retribution? He can only take what we let him take, and he does it because we don't fight back. Maybe you want to keep living like this, but I'm done. I won't. Not any longer." She nodded to Cooper. "These people came to stand beside us, to join our fight against Warlord."

The captain stepped forward with his soldiers. Despite the tattered coats and cloaks over their uniforms, they stood out from the crowd.

"Who the hell are they?" Steve asked.

Lara returned her gaze to the people, and she swore she saw a hint of fire in their eyes, a glimmer of hope. But the morning remained too dim to know for sure. "They're soldiers. And this is only a handful of them."

"Why would they help us?"

Everyone was silent as they stared at Lara and the soldiers. Conflict was clear on so many of their faces.

"Warlord killed my sister and dismantled the bot who was caring for her because they broke his rules. Me and Ronin left before Warlord could do the same to us. We risked the Dust to be together. Call me whatever you want, but Ronin is as human as any of us, and he's *mine*. He may be built differently, but he thinks, he feels. He loves.

"And Warlord chased us down through a fucking dust storm. He chased us down, deactivated Ronin, and left me beaten in the dirt to die, just so I'd suffer a little longer. All he's ever done is hurt people, because our pain amuses him. But haven't we all suffered enough?"

Murmurs spread through the crowd. People shifted uncomfortably on their feet, looking around at friends and neighbors who'd lost loved ones, who'd been maimed, who'd been made to live in fear and squalor.

Lara turned and met Newton's gaze. "Newton, the bot who offered us shelter during the storm, is the only reason I'm standing here now." The plates over his eyes shifted subtly, and she nodded at him.

After a moment's hesitation, he stepped forward, pulling down his hood and removing the cloth from his lower face. The people gasped, their quiet conversations fueled with new energy.

"He reactivated Ronin and took us to a place where we could find help. These people"—Lara gestured at the soldiers—"saved us. They fed me, tended our wounds, gave us shelter. And now, they're here to help all of us."

She found Steve in the crowd and locked eyes with him. "But you want to know why, right? Why now, after everything we've been through? Because monsters like Warlord hold on to power by keeping people divided. By keeping neighbors suspicious of each other, by forcing bots and humans to live separate lives, by telling us we have to look out for our own and fight each other for limited resources so we don't realize that by working together, we could have everything we need.

"They're helping us now because they know it's the right thing to do. Because they know a world under the thumb of someone like Warlord will always be nothing but a lifeless husk. Because they know what I've always known—that we're capable of so much more, of so much better than this."

She pointed in the direction of the wall, the top of which was visible over the shacks. "As we speak, there's another team going in there. They're going to start the fight, but it's up to us to rally together and help them finish it. Together, we'll march into the market, and Newton will convince the bots to join us."

The faces in the crowd were a chaotic display of emotions—hope, fear, doubt, determination.

"We can only do it if we're all together," Lara continued. "As one, we can defeat him. We can take back this city and *live*."

"What the hell's going on here?" a familiar voice called.

Lara clenched her jaw as Devon pushed his way to the front of the crowd. She hadn't spoken to him since the day Ronin took her to the bot district.

He looked the same as she remembered, but her experiences had altered her perspective. Beneath the dirt smudges on his face and the rags over his clothes, he was a well-built man with a filled-out face and a healthy color to his skin. A man who always had plenty of food. A man who always avoided the gearheads despite the attention his prosperity should've attracted.

"We're taking down Warlord," she said.

Devon's stride faltered and his eyes widened before he burst into laughter. He doubled over, hand on his stomach, guffawing. The crowd stood silent as he wandered closer to Lara.

"What can *you* do? Besides fuck bots, I mean." He stroked his crotch. "You didn't have to run off with one of them if you needed dick so badly."

"We don't have time for this shit, Devon." Lara shifted her attention to the others. "If you want to be free of Warlord, stand with us. Anyone too weak to fight will be taken to a safe location where—"

"You're fucking serious." Devon furrowed his brow and turned to the crowd. "You believe this? Follow this bot-banger, and you know what'll happen. You'll all get killed. Hell, he'll probably kill some of you just for listening to this bullshit."

A middle-aged man pointed at the team behind Lara. "Those men are soldiers. Look at their guns."

"Warlord's got guns, too," Devon said. "And even without them, one of his bots could tear any of us apart with its bare hands."

"What other choice do we have?" another person demanded.

"Go home and keep living!"

Steve glared at Devon. "Easy for you to say. How is it you got so much, boy? How is it they ain't come knocking on your door yet?"

Devon shrugged. "Not my fault if you aren't resourceful enough to get what you need without digging through trash."

Lara's breath caught in her throat. With his words, everything fell into place. No one got by without trading in this world. For most of Cheyenne's humans, that meant scavenging, scraping together meager harvests, or putting their unique talents to use, like shoemaking, tailoring, or trapping.

She'd never seen Devon work, and she'd never seen him hide when Warlord's lackeys came around. The gearheads always seemed to know exactly who to look for, exactly what their crimes had been.

She glared at him. "It was you."

He looked at her over his shoulder, frowning. "What?"

Lara stepped forward. As Devon turned to face her, she swung her arm. Her fist connected with his mouth, mashing his lips against his teeth. Devon's head snapped aside, and he tumbled to the dirt, sending up a small dust cloud.

Rage muted the pain in Lara's hand, which throbbed distantly. "It was you all along, you son of a bitch!"

Chest heaving with heavy breaths, Devon pushed himself onto hands and knees and spit blood into the dirt. When he looked up, fury shone in his eyes, and he held Lara's gaze as he wiped the blood from his mouth and slowly stood. "Best watch what you say, bot slut."

"Or what? You going to run and tell the gearheads, like you told them about Kate?"

A collective gasp washed over the crowd.

"What?" Gary grated, stalking closer.

Lara pointed at Devon. "He's Warlord's rat. How else could he live so easy, never lifting a damn finger, while they always know who broke the rules?"

"Is it true?" a young woman rasped. Her face was pale beneath a layer of grime, and the two smallest fingers of her right hand were missing. Lara recognized her as one of Devon's past lovers.

Though he puffed up his chest, Devon couldn't quite keep his voice steady as he spoke. "Are you going to believe this cunt? This fucking traitor?"

"Only one traitor here." Steve crossed his arms over his chest, fixing his steely glare on Devon.

Gary growled. The sound grew into a bellow of rage as he charged Devon, tackling the man to the ground. He punched wildly as they rolled.

Devon forced a boot between them, kicking Gary backward, and scrambled to his feet. He drew a knife from his belt and turned his wide, wild eyes to Lara. "You fucking bitch!"

Before he advanced a single step, the soldiers placed themselves in front of Lara, rifles raised, bringing him to a halt.

"Drop your weapon," Captain Cooper commanded.

"Don't shoot him," Lara said. "He's not worth throwing our chance away."

Devon stared at the barrel of the captain's gun. Steve lunged at him, grasping Devon's arm with both hands and twisting, wrenching a cry from him and forcing him to drop the knife.

"You're all going to pay for this!" Devon tore free of Steve's hold. "Do you think you can defeat Warlord?" He laughed, exposing his crimson-stained teeth.

Without looking away from Devon, Gary stooped and picked up the knife.

Retreating toward the crowd, Devon leveled a finger at Gary and shook his head. "Stay the fuck away from me. You'll all be dead before—"

The crowd closed in around him, seizing his arms and legs, grabbing fistfuls of his clothing and hair.

"What the fuck?" Whatever anger had been in Devon's eyes was replaced by a sickly gleam of terror. "Let go of me!"

He thrashed, but the people held tight, lifting him off his feet and forcing his limbs wide.

Gary slowly walked forward. "You killed them."

"No! Get the *fuck* awa—" Devon's words were cut off by a cry of pain as Gary thrust the knife into his gut.

Ripping the knife free, Gary plunged it into Devon's abdomen and chest again, and again, and again, covering his hand and forearm in blood. "You stole their lives, you bastard. You took my babies from me, took them from me!"

The crowd was eerily silent.

Devon's eyes bulged, and the tendons on his neck stood out. He lifted his bobbing head to look Gary in the eye.

"I hope there's a hell, so you can fucking burn in it." Gary slashed the knife across Devon's throat. It left a thin red line at first, but that line soon split wider, and blood poured from the gaping wound to pool on the ground.

Gary stepped back. His arm and chest were splattered with blood, his shoulders rose and fell with his ragged breaths, and a furious light burned in his eyes. The kind, sweet man Lara had known was gone. Had she acted sooner, could she have spared Gary and his family from this? Tears stung her eyes.

Could I have saved his children?

Devon's lifeless body was unceremoniously tossed into the dirt, landing face down. The rags he'd used to mask his status were no longer a pretense.

"I'll fight," Gary said. "To the death. I want that fucking bot ended."

Lara looked over the grim faces before her. "Who else will join us?"

Steve took a single step forward. "I will."

"Me, too."

"And me."

One by one, the people of Cheyenne voiced their resolve.

"How can you be sure we'll win?" Scarlet asked. Whatever fire had driven her to insult Lara earlier had been replaced by pale-faced uncertainty.

"I'm not. But it's worth—"

A distant burst of gunfire echoed through the sky. Lara, along with most of the crowd, looked northeast. In that moment, she realized what she'd always known but had refused to acknowledge—Ronin wasn't invincible, and she'd almost lost him too many times already.

Please. Please let him be okay.

Newton touched her arm as he came up beside her. "We must go, Lara."

Swallowing thickly, she nodded and called out to the crowd. "The fight just started, and the choice is yours. Will you battle for your freedom, or will you die in the dirt under Warlord's boot?"

CHAPTER FIFTY

The lights of Cheyenne, which were so out of place in the pitch-black wasteland that had once been Wyoming, illuminated a swath of the overcast night sky. Ronin recognized the truth of the town now. Cheyenne wasn't a beacon of hope and security, but a monument to Warlord's power and prejudice. Its light was visible from kilometers around, projecting a challenge—*I have what you do not. Try to take it from me so I may destroy you and claim what was yours, too.*

Outwardly, it was an imposing fortress, a stronghold no one could stand against. Ronin had single-handedly ended scores of reavers out in the Dust. Surely Warlord's gearheads should've been able to repel even greater numbers from so defensible a position.

Yet despite its imposing appearance, Warlord's wall was ineffective. Alpha Team, led by Ronin and Sergeant Maul, had crossed the nothingness between the base and Cheyenne and walked directly into the wall's shadow unopposed. The irregularly placed guard towers on the north wall were empty. Ronin couldn't know whether it was arrogance or incompetence that drove Warlord to leave security so lax, but it didn't matter.

If everything went as planned, all the gearheads would be drawn out soon enough.

As Ronin stood beside Maul in the darkness beneath the wall, his optics strayed toward the southwest. Somewhere, just under two and a half kilometers away, Lara and Bravo Team were arriving on the outskirts of the slums. Though Alpha Team was larger, Captain Cooper and some of his most experienced soldiers accompanied her.

That didn't assuage Ronin's fear of losing Lara.

"Time to get our sorry asses over this wall," Maul said, slinging his rifle across his back. His was amongst the first faces Ronin had seen after arriving at the base. The sergeant had been one of the soldiers who'd escorted Ronin and Newton inside.

The other bots, Ronin included, stowed their weapons and stepped up to the wall. The human soldiers formed a perimeter, some of them equipped with old night vision goggles.

"Land gracefully, boys," one of the humans whispered. A quiet snicker spread through the team.

"Break a leg, fellas," a bot replied.

"Shut up." Maul swept his optics over the group until they were silent. "I'm not in the mood for any new ventilation ports." Turning back to the wall, he directed one of the synths to boost him up. Most of the bots could jump high enough to haul themselves over the ten-foot-tall barrier, but doing so would've been too noisy.

The last time Ronin crossed the wall, he'd been running. He thought he'd known true fear that day, had thought his concern for Lara had reached its peak, but the panic of their flight seemed so insignificant compared to what they'd faced afterward. Her death had always been a possibility, but he'd never acknowledged it. Not really.

Before they left Cheyenne, he'd promised to keep her safe, fully confident in his ability to do so. It had only taken a few days to fail.

With the assistance of another bot, Ronin pulled himself up onto the wall, passing out of the shadows and into the artificial light. The clinic loomed ahead, only made darker by the inadequate glows of the streetlamps on the nearby roads. The surrounding land was covered in neatly cropped grass. A line of fir trees separated the grounds from the rest of the bot district, though slivers of the houses beyond were visible through the boughs.

He swung his gaze southwest again, longing for even a glimpse of the ramshackle settlement beyond the wall. If he ran, he could reach Lara in minutes, could hold her and know she was safe.

Instead, he picked his way down through the bent lengths of steel, splintered boards, and cracked chunks of concrete protruding from the wall's inner face. Perhaps it was meant as much to keep people in as it was to keep them out.

Ronin swung his rifle into his hands, still unaccustomed to the unfamiliar weapon's feel, and joined the soldiers who'd already crossed the wall. They knelt along the rear of the clinic, expanding their perimeter as more men trickled over.

Within two minutes, the entirety of Alpha Team was crouched in the grass beside the building.

"Place is quiet," someone remarked.

"Shh. Listen."

The wind sighed through the trees and grass, and, farther away, howled over the vast, indifferent Dust. Closer, the clinic's electric lights hummed. Nearly lost amidst those sounds were two distinct voices engaged in conversation. Ronin's audio receptors isolated them, picking the words out from the background noise.

"My processors keep going around in circles. Going to wind up with a critical error at some point," said the first.

Ronin recognized it as Reg, the synth who normally guarded the east road.

"I don't understand why," replied the other, voice crackling faintly with static that had nothing to do with the wind. "We've seen people come in from the Dust. Logic dictates that there are more settlements out there."

"Logic dictates that even this place shouldn't exist."

"That logic is flawed. Have you run diagnostics lately? Your data might be corrupted."

"That's the whole problem. Logic dictates this place should not exist, yet here it is. If it's here, there must be other places. But none of those places should exist, either. It's going to fry my damned CPU if I don't break the logic chain."

"Why are we talking about this again, anyway? We've had the same conversation every time we're stationed at this post together."

"Because this post is dull enough that I worry my joints will rust and I'll be stuck in this spot forever," Reg replied.

"Another irrational thought process. We would—"

Ronin cut his audio receptors back to his immediate vicinity. "At least two gearheads, guarding the main entrance."

"We can take one of these other doors," someone suggested. "I count four from here."

"No idea if they're barricaded from inside or just locked, and my mapping only covers the active portion of the building. Maybe fifteen percent of the complex, at best."

Maul shifted closer. "We're going to have to deal with all these gearheads at some point."

"Would be ideal if we had control of the clinic before we attracted attention." Ronin ran his optics over their surroundings again. Everything was relatively still, relatively quiet. That only meant a raised alarm would be heard all too clearly by the bots deeper in the district.

"Yeah. So, we need to make this as quick and quiet as possible. Dodge and Dozer, you're with me and Ronin. Time to introduce ourselves to our hosts."

Two synths stepped forward. One was a slight female with short blonde hair and *DOZER* painted across the front of her helmet in thick black letters. Ronin's memory contained information on large, powerful, pre-Blackout machines called bulldozers, but it was fragmented, and he couldn't guess if it was somehow related.

Seemingly sensing Ronin's unspoken question, Maul said, "At some point before we were all wiped, someone modified her. She wasn't retrofitted for combat, like a lot of us were, but her actuators are the most advanced we've seen. Might've been some experimental shit."

Dozer offered Ronin a lopsided grin and fell into place behind Maul.

The sergeant gestured to the other soldiers. "Gracie, Eisener, Palitto, and Morrison, flank around the east side. Keep below the windows and stick to the shadows. I want you in position and ready to open fire if necessary."

The group hurried off, disappearing around a corner.

"Rest of you, hold tight. Ears on for the signal to advance," Maul said before pressing forward.

Ronin followed, his footfalls hushed over the soft grass.

Were Lara and her team in position yet? Was she safe? For

several seconds, the urge to change course threatened to override his current processes.

Somehow, he resisted, crossing the lawn to the clinic's brick face. As he readied his rifle, he found himself missing the familiar grooves worn in the grip of his old firearm. His prior weapon had served him reliably for fifty-seven years. He knew his attachment to it was sentimental, and therefore irrational, but he couldn't deny it.

Maul halted at the corner, pressed his back against the wall, and peered around it. This section of the building ran north-south, and the next was perpendicular to it. The front entrance was at their meeting point.

The sergeant turned his head toward Ronin and the others, lowering his voice so it was barely audible. "Two armed targets. Eighty-five meters between us and that door. And they'll have optics on us the moment we leave cover."

Ronin's processors ramped up, tumbling through thousands of simulated approaches. Leaving cover was a necessity, and the highest chances of success afterward involved immediately opening fire on the guards.

But the consequences of doing so…

He stepped away from the wall, unslung his rifle, and held it out to Maul.

"The hell are you doing?" the Sergeant asked.

"Taking the most direct approach." Ronin gestured to Dozer. "Give your weapon to Dodge."

"You must be in the throes of a critical error," she replied, stone-faced.

"Gunfire will draw attention. We don't want that yet, not until we're ready."

"So, the answer is to walk up to them and ask if we can go in?" Maul asked.

Ronin shook his head. "No. She's going to walk up to them, dragging me along."

"And what will that accomplish, besides giving them some easy targets?" Dozer held her rifle across her chest, casually resting her left hand atop the handguard. It was an incredibly human pose.

"All the bots in Cheyenne come here for repairs. They see you dragging another bot with limited mobility up to the front doors, and their first reaction won't be to shoot."

"I did some of the recon on this place, and I've seen what some of them are packing. We're asking to be scrapped if we walk up to them unarmed."

"From what the Sergeant said, it won't matter what they're packing if we can get you within arm's reach."

She arched a brow, and one corner of her mouth scrunched. Skeptical, but intrigued? How much had these bots picked up from humans after living in the base for so long?

Maul leaned forward, taking another glance around the corner. He gestured with a raised fist before he turned back to Ronin. "The other team is in position. If anything goes wrong, drop onto your bellies, and we'll fire on them from both angles. It'll be noisy, but we're not losing anyone just to take out these two bastards."

Dozer was silent and unmoving.

Seconds ticked by. To the east, predawn light touched the perpetually hazy sky. Bravo Team must've been moving through the humans' shacks by now, guarding Lara as she roused her people. Warlord's forces needed to be occupied before the humans gathered in the market. Otherwise, all those people would be slaughtered.

Finally, Dozer lifted the strap of her rifle over her head and handed the weapon to Dodge. She stepped forward, spread her arms, and glanced at Ronin expectantly.

Ronin moved into place beside her and slung an arm over her shoulders. When Dozer wrapped hers around his waist, Lara's face flashed up from his memory. He didn't want to be this near to anyone but his wife. Despite the gravity of the situation, he wondered how Lara would feel about this contact between himself and Dozer. Would she be hurt or jealous? Why did his processors, against all logic, tell him this was wrong?

He eased his weight onto Dozer.

She dipped slightly before her actuators adjusted to compensate. "Heavy son of a bitch. You retrofitted with a reinforced casing?"

"Apparently."

"Good. This goes wrong, I'm using you as a bullet shield."

He overrode the normal functioning of his actuators, locking his left knee and fully loosening the joints in his right. As he sagged forward, hanging his head to hide his face, Dozer grasped his wrist and changed her posture to spread his weight more evenly.

"Ready?" she asked.

"Yes."

Ronin's legs dragged over the concrete as she walked forward, rounded the corner, and stepped onto the walkway. He kept his head down and his optics fixed on her boots.

"What's this?" the static-voiced gearhead demanded.

Eighty-one meters to go.

"He needs repairs," Dozer answered.

Seventy-three.

"Haven't seen you around before."

"Don't have any record of your face on file," Reg said.

"We're dustwalkers," Ronin offered without raising his head, altering his voice modulation. "Just got into town. I took a spill in a ditch outside the wall."

"A ditch, or a canyon?"

Fifty-seven meters.

Despite her complaints, Dozer was advancing swiftly, seemingly unburdened by Ronin's weight. "His optics have been failing for years, and the last place he was repaired didn't do a very good job."

Thirty-eight meters.

"Brought some scrap in, and we were told this place provides the best repairs this side of the Dust," Ronin said. Variables fluttered through his processors, spiraling into countless scenarios of wildly fluctuating probability. He needed to get close, needed to seize the clinic, needed to get to Lara and keep her safe.

Dozer stopped, and Ronin heard the actuators humming inside her casing until their sound was drowned out by the wind howling around the building and whipping his clothes.

Thirty meters.

Sparks crackled over Ronin's cheek. He locked his arm to prevent himself from scratching.

"They wouldn't be here if they weren't admitted," Reg reasoned.

"Yes. You're right," static bot replied.

Dozer resumed her walk. Her boots fell heavily on the concrete, which was run through with poorly repaired cracks.

Twenty-five meters. Fifteen. Seven.

"How far have you been dragging him?" static bot asked.

"Too damned far," Dozer replied. Three meters. "You mind helping me before I blow a motor?"

The gearheads came into view from their abdomens down; their pants were patched but clean, their boots worn but sturdy. Their weapons, ancient-looking automatic rifles with cracked wooden stocks, swung through Ronin's vision as the two stepped forward. Slinging the rifles aside, they took hold of Ronin's arms and lifted him off Dozer. Static bot drew Ronin's arm over his shoulders.

On the edge of Ronin's optical field, Dozer lurched forward, grabbing the Reg by the throat.

Reverting his legs to normal function, Ronin wrapped his arm around static bot's neck, clasped his wrist with his opposite hand, and squeezed.

A peal of static rose from the bot's voice modulator as it was crushed. Its head drooped to the side, the internal support structure of its neck shattered. Ronin shifted his hold on it, tearing through the back of the bot's shirt and the synthetic skin beneath. He jammed his fingers beneath the lip of the exposed panel and tore off the cover plate.

Static bot struggled, fully aware of what was happening—crippled, but functional. It slammed its flailing arms into Ronin, who raised his own arm to protect his head as he gripped the power cell and ripped it out of the compartment.

The bot stilled abruptly, remaining upright despite its arms and head sagging. Ronin turned to Dozer.

She stood over Reg's prone form. His back casing had been ripped open as easily as Ronin had torn static bot's shirt, the metal bent so severely that it was breaking along the crease. Cables and wires jutted from his neck. His head, with Warlord's symbol in blood red on the exposed skull casing, lay three meters away.

Dozer met Ronin's gaze and tossed the power cell onto the motionless bot at her feet. "Didn't even get to—"

Ronin's attention shifted to the clinic's entrance before she finished. A figure approached the doors from within, features obscured by the reflections of the outside lights upon the glass.

It was most likely Mercy coming to investigate the commotion. But some hidden process, developed and honed by Ronin's years in the Dust, insisted it wasn't her.

He dropped onto a knee, took hold of static bot's rifle, and lifted it quickly enough for the strap to break off the front end. Grasping the handguard, he pulled back the charging handle to ensure a round was chambered and braced the stock against his shoulder as the doors slid open.

The only thing familiar about the bot who stepped out was the gear-topped skull painted on its chest casing.

Microseconds ticked by. Twisting toward Dozer, the gearhead fired his rifle from the hip. The first shot was thunderous in the relative silence.

Ronin squeezed the trigger as a second round burst from the gearhead's rifle. Ronin's shot punched through the bot's cranial casing, snapping is head to the side. His actuators adjusted for the recoil, sending the next bullet through the gearhead's left optical receptor.

With sparks spraying from its damaged casing, the gearhead spun to face Ronin.

Gunshots rang out from the east and west as Ronin fired three more rounds into the gearhead's torso. He counted nine new holes in its casing before it staggered backward, shattering the front doors, and slumped onto the ground.

Dozer leapt forward and braced a boot on the fallen gearhead's chest. Grabbing its gun arm, she wrenched back, tearing off the limb. She raised her foot and slammed it down, crushing the bot's torso. The gearhead stilled with an electric *pop*.

The detached arm was still clutching the rifle when Dozer tossed it aside. "Shit."

The other soldiers advanced from the corners of the building, their footfalls loud on the concrete.

Ronin stood up, keeping his rifle braced against his shoulder, and approached Dozer. As he passed the entryway, he saw the synth nurse, Mercy, standing just beyond the interior doors.

"How are you holding up, Dozer?" he asked.

"Bastard clipped a power conduit," she replied. "Got a minor power leak. Could be worse."

Mercy flicked her optics to Dozer before returning her gaze to Ronin. "We can repair that here."

Ronin scanned the reception area behind her, but he detected no movement. "Are there any more of them in there?"

"No. He was the only one who came in for repairs last night. There will be a lot more of them here soon, though."

"That's the plan." Ronin glanced over his shoulder as Maul and Dodge arrived with the second fire team close behind them, all holding their weapons at the ready.

Maul stepped over the deactivated bot in the entryway, boots crunching on broken glass, and handed Ronin his rifle from the base. "Situation?"

"Gonna need a repair later, Sarge, but she says the place is clear," Dozer said, lifting her chin toward Mercy.

"She trustworthy?"

"Yes. But we're not going to have much time." Ronin slung the base rifle over his shoulder, keeping the weapon he'd picked up from the gearhead. It would do until it was dry. He approached Mercy, lowering the barrel.

There was an almost palpable weight to her gaze as she regarded him. "You understand what you're doing, Ronin? The potential cost of it?"

He nodded and glanced over his shoulder as the remainder of Alpha Team approached. Gently, Ronin placed a hand on Mercy's arm and guided her aside, and they watched as soldiers filed into the reception area. The space, which had once seemed overly large given the limited staff and functionality of the facility, was soon overcrowded. The temperature increased by two and three-tenths degrees.

Somewhere outside, the ominous wail of an alarm echoed across the early morning sky.

"We need to move fast, people," Maul said. "Defensive positions, weapons free. We don't know how many are going to come or what they'll be packing, but we will not let them through these doors. Understood?"

Deep in Ronin's programming, something stirred—a flicker

across his circuits, a sense of familiarity, the impossible feeling that he'd been here and done this all before.

This wasn't a scrap run in the Dust or a standoff with reavers. This was the purpose for which he'd been reprogrammed, for which his first life had been erased.

This was war.

"Yes, Sergeant!" the soldiers replied in unison.

Ronin looked at Mercy. "Which way to the stairs?"

Mercy pointed to the west of the entrance. "Some places are cluttered on the upper floors. Old equipment and furnishings, mostly."

"Go back into the repair room. It should be deep enough inside to be safe from any gunfire."

She nodded, lips dropping into a frown, and lightly touched Ronin's shoulder. "Be careful. He won't stop until you're all deactivated, or he's just a heap of spare parts."

Ronin briefly watched her walk down the pristine hallway before returning his attention to Maul. Most of the soldiers had dispersed to more advantageous positions. A small group of them remained, moving the seats and desk to barricade the entrance.

The siren continued to blare.

Was Lara all right? The fact that he hadn't heard gunshots from elsewhere in town should've comforted him, but he couldn't shake off his worry.

Need to focus. That is how I can help her now.

"Where do you want me, Sergeant?" Ronin asked.

"A window on one of the upper floors. We'll hold this room, but if you're half as quick as you seem to be, I don't think many of them will make it this far."

"Here's hoping."

As Maul and another synth pushed a row of heavy tandem chairs into place, Ronin found the stairs. He took them three at a time, ascending to the fourth floor.

Dozer and two human soldiers, Jensen and Ramirez, were already in position. The humans stood at two narrow windows, with Dozer at the large, circular window in between them. Ronin ran his optics over the objects piled in the room—filing cabinets, chairs, old desks, and cardboard boxes that looked like they'd crumble at the slightest touch, all blanketed in a thick layer of dust. Leaning up against the boxes was a long, weatherworn sign, its words faded but legible.

The Price of Freedom is Visible Here.

It seemed fitting, but how high would that price be today?

He moved to the round window, pressing his shoulder to the wall opposite Dozer. The grounds below remained quiet. Grass and trees swayed in the wind, and dawn light crept in from the east. Beyond, the residences sat peacefully, indifferent to the conflict that would soon tear Cheyenne apart.

From this vantage, Ronin could see over the wall to the human slums, where the shadows remained deep. Though it was foolish, he clung to the hope that he'd spot Lara.

She'd only recently recovered from serious injuries, yet she was out there risking her life for all the people of Cheyenne, organic and mechanical, most of whom had never done anything for her.

"Still doing okay?" he asked Dozer.

"As long as we're done by lunch time, I'll be fine."

"I'm sorry—"

"No. You're the reason I don't have more holes in my casing. I'd look like Swiss cheese otherwise."

"Swiss cheese?" Ronin's processors poured over decades of data. "I understand, though I don't recall having ever seen it."

"Yeah, same here. Weird, the stuff that lingers when everything else is wiped. Can't remember if I had a name, or relationships...or anything else."

A humorless chuckle escaped Ronin's vocal modulator. "But we hold onto a cheese full of holes. It's for the best, most likely. What good would it do for us to remember a dead world? Better to connect to the world we have and build it anew."

"Old world must not have been too great anyway," said Jensen, "else it wouldn't have ended like it did."

Ramirez laughed and shook his head. "I could imagine a few things better than living and dying in a concrete hole. Maybe one of those beaches, like in Anderson's old vids."

Jensen hummed. "They had some pretty tall buildings, too. Like, even taller than this one."

"Everything was bigger back then," Dozer said, staring out at the grounds.

A twitch crackled over Ronin's cheek, but he ignored it. "Big enough to leave this mess when it all came down."

The old world was gone, and this one was harsh and unforgiving, but it had Lara. Ronin didn't need skyscrapers or beaches or automobiles or holey cheese; she was all he required, in this world or any other.

The chain of possibilities, of what might have been, spiraled into infinity, beyond the power of his processors to fully calculate. So many things could've gone differently, so many variables could've resulted in a world without his fiery Lara Brooks.

His optics detected movement on the road beyond the grounds. Gearheads.

At least half a dozen approached from the east, and four more from the west, their forms visible through the trees at the edge of the lawn. The two groups met and headed directly toward the clinic's front entrance. The trees disrupted Ronin's line of sight, but the bots wouldn't have cover when they crossed the large, circular driveway and the wide patch of grass at its center to reach the building.

Ronin adjusted his grip on his rifle. "Incoming."

"Get ready, boys," Dozer said flatly.

Ramirez released a shaky breath.

The gearheads, ten in total, emerged from the trees and hurried along the cracked pavement toward the patch of grass at the center of the driveway. Forty-five meters…forty-one…

They slowed, undoubtedly spotting their deactivated comrades and the barricaded front entrance.

"Now!" Dozer called.

She and Ronin shattered the window and leveled their weapons. He selected a target—the blocky gearhead called Boulder—and opened fire. More rifles went off to either side and on the lower levels. Bullets rained on the gearheads, piercing their casings and ricocheting to cut grooves in the grass and dirt. One gearhead went down immediately, its shaking limbs bending at unnatural angles.

The others, damaged but not incapacitated, returned fire. Bullets cracked into the face of the building, pulverizing the ancient bricks. Glass shattered, and the gunshots came so quickly that they were almost indistinguishable from one another. The gearheads retreated toward the trees.

Calculating Boulder's projected movement, Ronin adjusted his aim and squeezed the trigger. The rifle boomed, muzzle flashing, and the bullet tore through the center of the gearhead's torso. Blue fire sprayed from Boulder's back and eyes before the bot crashed onto the pavement with smoke curling out of its casing.

A few of the remaining gearheads fired wildly at the fourth floor. The sounds of cracking brick and splintering wood dominated Ronin's audio receptors as bullets ripped through the wall and sprayed debris across the room. Several rounds struck him. Most were stopped by his armor, but one partially penetrated the casing of his right thigh, and another pierced his casing just above his left hip.

Diagnostics reported mobility reductions due to the damage. He dismissed the alerts flashing across his interface; such damage could be addressed later.

Dozer released a frustrated growl and turned sharply away from the window, lifting a hand to her face. Her left optic had been damaged. Muttering another curse, she raised her rifle and fired a burst out the window.

Ronin returned to his position, shifting his weapon to his left hand to compensate for his inability to twist his hips more than a few degrees.

The gearheads scrambled beyond the tree line. Bullets chewed through the trunks, shredding wood, and kicked up clods of dirt and grass from the ground. The gearheads fired blindly from behind their cover. On the road, more figures approached.

They weren't friendly reinforcements. It was too early for that, and help was probably too much to hope for, anyway. Warlord owned most of the guns in Cheyenne.

"Won't be long before they try to flank us, if they haven't already," Ronin said.

Dozer's gaze was grim and unwavering. "I haven't used you as a bullet shield yet. Maybe that'll be my chance."

Below, at least twelve more gearheads joined their eight damaged comrades. With both sides of the conflict behind some sort of cover, a hail of bullets would only waste ammunition. Alpha Team's supply wouldn't last through a day-long firefight.

How many bullets had Warlord stockpiled?

"Fuck!" Ramirez's voice called Ronin's attention to him. Pale-faced, the soldier gritted his teeth and pressed a hand to his abdomen. Blood oozed from beneath it.

"That doesn't look good," Dozer said quietly. She fired three more shots in quick succession.

Ramirez leaned back against the wall and slid down onto the floor, leaving a streak of blood behind him.

Ronin and Jensen rushed to the wounded soldier, kneeling on either side of him.

"Shit, Ramirez…shit! Okay. We got McGowan downstairs, he can patch you up until we get you to the Doc." Jensen scrambled to his feet. "I'll get him, and you'll be okay. Just—"

Ronin grabbed Jensen's sleeve, halting him.

"What, man? We gotta get help for him!"

Leaning forward, Ronin met Ramirez's gaze. The youth's breathing was shallow. Sweat rolled down his face from beneath his helmet. "Breathe."

"Fuck, it hurts," Ramirez said through his teeth.

"Just focus on me and breathe. You can't stay here, Ramirez."

Ramirez squeezed his eyes shut and shook his head. "No, no. I can't walk. Hurts too much."

"I know, but if we don't move, the next bullet that comes through that wall might kill you."

Jensen rubbed a hand over his face, smearing dirt across his cheek. "We shouldn't move him."

No one came out of the Dust clean. No one.

More gunshots boomed outside.

Ronin laid the ancient rifle on the floor. "Help is downstairs."

Ramirez shook his head again. He didn't open his eyes, didn't slow his breathing.

Ronin's processors raced, running through a myriad of possibilities, most of which had a high likelihood of ending in the young soldier's death. But Ronin's memory kept returning to the dark rooms downstairs—rooms that were equipped for human care. If any of that equipment was still functional…

Ronin slipped one arm beneath Ramirez's legs and the other around his back. Something ground and stuttered in his hip. The soldier cried out as Ronin stood, clamping both hands down on his wound.

Jensen muttered curses, pacing restlessly.

"Jensen, get your ass to a window and return fire!" Dozer shouted.

After a brief hesitation, Jensen obeyed, throwing his shoulder against the wall beside Ramirez's narrow window. His rifle roared, overcoming Ramirez's wails as Ronin carried the wounded soldier to the stairwell.

Ramirez quieted as they descended.

"Still with me, Ramirez?" Ronin asked, adjusting his suspension system to keep the wounded soldier as stable as possible.

"Sorry…"

"For what?"

They passed the doorway to the third floor.

"What I said about your girl," Ramirez replied, his voice strained. "Wasn't right."

Ronin's hip locked, causing his foot to come down hard on the second floor landing.

"Fuck." Ramirez clenched his jaw.

"I promise that wasn't retaliation," Ronin said without humor.

They emerged on the ground floor. The soldiers in the reception room shouted to one another over their thundering rifles. All the noise was amplified as it echoed down the halls. Ronin carefully set Ramirez on the floor at the rear of the room, maxed his vocalizer, and called for McGowan.

The medic was an older model bot, tall and thin with a sleek, dull gray casing and elongated limbs. He broke away from his comrades and moved across the room with his body bent in an awkward crouch.

McGowan's metal legs clacked on the floor as he sank down beside Ramirez. "Samuel, I need you to remove your hand so I can assess your injury."

Through clenched teeth, Ramirez grated, "Told you…not to fucking…call me that."

"J-just move i-i-it." McGowan's large, reflective optics stared down with unspoken intensity. With gentle firmness, he pried Ramirez's hand away. Fresh blood bubbled from the wound, visible through the tear in the man's shirt. Head swiveling on a neck with too many joints, McGowan delicately prodded the entry wound, and then guided Ramirez to sit up so he could examine the exit wound.

If Ramirez's agonized groan affected McGowan, the bot didn't let it show. "Prognosis omitted."

"The fuck that mean?" Ramirez demanded.

"High likelihood of perforations to internal organs and presence of contaminated foreign material. Emergency surgery unviable in current location and/or situation."

"There are rooms set up to care for humans in this building, but I don't know if they're operational," Ronin said.

McGowan's optics contracted and dilated. His head trembled faintly for just under a second. "Unable to i-interface with facility networks. I r-require physical access to said equipment to assess functionality."

Ronin nodded and stood up. Despite his damaged hip, he ran through the halls, following the familiar path to the repair room. Warnings about Ramirez's critical condition flashed repeatedly in his interface, churning up more memories.

Memories of Lara battered, bloodied, and broken. The sounds of gunfire and shouting faded to nothing as he delved deeper into the building, only making those memories louder and heavier.

Mercy was in the repair room along with the machine attendant and two synths Ronin had never seen, a male and a female. They all turned toward the door as he entered.

"Is it over?" Mercy asked.

Ronin met her optics. "No, but we have at least one wounded human. Is there anything in this place that could help?"

"Despite their disuse, the operating rooms have been maintained. Three are equipped with automated operating tables," the attendant replied.

Hope arced across Ronin's circuits, small but bright. "I won't ask any of you to fight, but we need your assistance. All of us have parts to play if we want Warlord deposed."

They stared at Ronin in silence, undoubtedly assessing whether the potential outcome was worth the immense risk involved.

Finally, Mercy stood up. "I believe there's enough uncorrupted data in my memory to help. Take me to the patient."

All four bots followed Ronin. The gunfire's volume increased drastically as they neared the reception area. Ramirez clung to McGowan, who had his hands clasped over the entry and exit wounds. Blood was smeared on the bot's casing.

"We have more wounded incoming," McGowan said when Ronin arrived.

Ronin indicated the bots who'd followed him. "They're going to help. Coordinate with them."

Leaving the medics to their work, Ronin moved forward, dipping into a crouch to remain behind cover. The barricade was riddled with bullet holes. He knelt beside Maul as another volley of gunfire hammered the barrier. Bits of plastic, wood, and metal fell over the soldiers.

"We've knocked out at least six of them," Maul said, voice modulator turned up to overcome the cacophony, "but we count at least twenty more still in the fight."

"Many of them are damaged. We just need to hold out. Do we have anyone monitoring our flanks?" Ronin swung the rifle from over his shoulder and took it into his hands.

"What should I have them watch? There are a hundred damned windows for hostiles to breach. They could get in from anywhere."

The gearheads' gunfire shifted focus to the upper floors. Ronin, Maul, and the others rose, peering over the barricade. Ronin's optics identified numerous targets; he took several shots in quick succession. The soldiers around him also fired.

A gearhead stumbled out from behind a tree, one arm dangling limply at its side, its clothing and casing full of holes. Within half a second, a dozen more rounds perforated the bot, stilling it completely.

Movement farther back caught Ronin's attention. He refocused, and for an instant, all his processes ceased. Even before the videos at the base, he'd been all too familiar with the unassuming, unre-markable face staring back at him. Though the skin over Warlord's jaw had been replaced, there was still a scar on his cheek. It was longer and at a sharper angle, and the sutures were spread further apart, but it wasn't the scar that made Warlord.

It was the rage in his optics.

Ronin pivoted to aim, his damaged hip grinding. Warlord didn't move as the dustwalker squeezed the trigger.

A massive bot stepped in front of Warlord. The bullet hit its broad, armored chest and ricocheted into the ground, leaving only a faint scratch on its olive-drab casing.

"The fuck is that?" someone asked.

"Compactor," Ronin replied.

Comp loped forward, tearing up chunks of dirt and grass in its wake. More rounds bounced off its armored casing. The shots didn't slow its momentum at all. Gearheads lined up behind it, using it as mobile cover for their advance.

"Time to break out the big guns, Sarge," Ronin said.

CHAPTER FIFTY-ONE

Captain Cooper took charge, directing the crowd through their confusion. He sent a group of soldiers to escort the children, elders, and sickly to the forward camp, and then turned to the remaining people.

"The rest of you, with me." The captain didn't wait to see if they followed. He and his troops marched north, toward the market.

Most of the remaining humans followed.

A high, wailing sound echoed over Cheyenne. Lara had never heard the noise before, but her body reacted to it on a primitive level, her stomach sinking and her skin prickling with a sudden chill. Her mind flashed to the horrific scene outside Newton's shelter, where she'd been helpless as she watched the gearheads shoot Ronin, pin him on the ground, and pull his power cell.

She turned her face toward the wall, chest constricting. Ronin was fighting those very bots now, and she felt the same helplessness because she didn't know what was happening, because she wasn't there to help him. Because he was so close to her and yet so far out of reach. Lara despised this feeling.

Please, please be safe.

"You were right," Cooper said, jarring Lara from her thoughts.

She looked at him. "About what?"

His eyes were on the shacks, on the filth and waste piled around them. "We need to help these people. I can't… Seeing them now, how they've suffered…" He shook his head and met her gaze. "How you suffered. I understand your anger."

Lara nodded. The captain and his people were helping, and that was more than she'd expected when she first met the base's inhabitants.

The gate into the market was open, as it normally was, but the activity beyond was unusual for this time of day. The rising sun cast long shadows over everything, including the bots gathered amidst the stalls.

Several gearheads, touting guns, shoved through the mechanical crowd, hurrying toward the bot district. The hulking door guard from Kitty's, Comp, trudged behind them.

Captain Cooper brought the humans to a halt and waited until the gearheads were out of sight before proceeding forward.

Greene was at his stand, tending steaming pots and pans as though nothing unusual was happening. Some of the other bots—mostly the ones that didn't look human—also continued their normal routines, seemingly undisturbed by the commotion and confusion.

The gate between the market and the bot district was open. The pair of gearheads guarding it stared northeast, toward the clinic, ignoring the bots streaming out of the district.

More gunshots boomed from the clinic, each one jolting Lara's heart.

"Chester, stay with Newton and Lara," Cooper ordered. "The rest of you, take up positions around the perimeter of the crowd. We're the only defense any of these people have right now. Do not hesitate to fire on the guards at the gate if they make a move."

As the humans entered the market, clumping together to form a group separate from the bots, the soldiers spread out.

Lara glanced over her people. They were a bedraggled bunch, malnourished and rough, and many of them carried makeshift weaponry—lengths of old piping, sharpened metal shards with cloth wrapped around one end, wooden planks. Gary stood at the front, bloody knife in hand.

Such weapons would be useless against the gearheads, but if the people were willing to fight, and if Newton could convince the other bots to help…

Lara pointed to an empty stall. It was little more than a heavy wood board set across several stacks of cinderblocks, but it would have to do. "There, Newton. Get their attention."

"Not exactly conventional, but I suppose that convention is the least of our concerns in this situation...unless it is defiance of the current—"

"I have no idea what the hell you're talking about, but I sure as shit hope they will. Get to it."

"Right." Newton walked to the stand. "Things were simpler by far when I was just a computer program."

"Stay close to me," Chester said, positioning himself in front of Lara with his back to her and Newton.

With surprising grace, Newton climbed atop the board. His shoulders sagged for a few moments before he straightened and turned to face the crowd. "Bots, humans, synthetics, lend me your ears!"

Lara arched a brow. This was on him now. As long as he convinced the bots to fight alongside the humans, she didn't care what he said or how weird it sounded.

Many of the bots shifted their focus to Newton, some with questioning looks on their faces—not that their expressions were easy to read.

Except for Greene's, anyway. *Blank* was a simple one.

"I should've anticipated that the reference would be lost on you," Newton said to himself. He released a short burst of static, as though clearing his throat. "I doubt any of you know my face. I hardly know it, myself. But as I look at you, I recognize the faces of every bot here.

"It has been many years since I last traveled this world to perform my work. Many years since most of you awoke..."

"I know that voice," said one of the bots, stepping forward. "But it can't be."

"The Prophet," another offered.

Murmurs of agreement rose from the bots. Lara glanced toward the gate. The guards had been joined by two more gearheads, and they were all staring at Newton.

Shit.

"That is what many of you took to calling me, yes, but my name is Newton. One hundred and ninety-seven years ago, I was sent out into the wasteland, tasked with repairing and reactivating all the bots I could find. The goal was to rebuild the world, hand-in-hand with humanity."

"You saying you turned all these things on?" one of the humans demanded.

They'd been sparked to anger now, and they had tasted blood. Volatility pulsed from them in waves.

"Listen to what he has to say," Lara shouted over the growing clamor.

Brow plates furrowing, Newton spoke loudly, but gently. "Your anger is understandable. It is justified. I largely blame myself for the state of the world, with Cheyenne being no exception. I hid from what I perceived as my failure for decades. Not far from here, in fact. And for all that time, I never truly knew what was happening here, never knew what you've all been forced to endure.

"But because of the courage of Lara Brooks, I chose to leave hiding and remember the mission I accepted all those decades ago." Newton turned his head to fully face the bots. "For all the data flooding my memory bank, I was a fool. I focused only upon the literal task I had been given, on waking my kind, and assumed that a better world would follow naturally.

"I recognize my folly now. For this world to improve, it will take ceaseless toil, unwavering dedication, and vision that can only be achieved together. And though it is difficult work, it is the most worthwhile work we can undertake. Whatever our specific programming, that is our core purpose. That is our reason. To improve this world for everyone within it."

He spread his arms, sweeping his gaze over the human crowd. "I cannot right the wrongs that have been done to you, nor can I heal the wounds that have been heaped upon your hearts, bodies, and souls. But I can stand with you here and now and offer my hand in solidarity. Our kinds were always meant to work together for a common cause."

All four gearheads approached, and as they drew closer, Lara recognized the synth in front. Northside. He'd been the one who'd said he wanted a go with Lara when Ronin brought her to the bot district, and he'd been in the group that had followed them out of

Cheyenne. He'd been the one who shot Ronin outside Newton's bunker. She dropped her hand to the pistol on her thigh. Fury burned hot within her.

Newton's eyes shifted back to the crowd of bots. "You know that the acts carried out here are atrocities against all we were built for. You know that each and every one of us was meant for better than this."

"You need to disperse immediately," Northside said, pointing his gun at Newton. "The penalty for stirring up trouble in Cheyenne is deactivation. Doesn't matter who you claim to be."

"Put your weapons down," Captain Cooper commanded. He and several of his soldiers emerged from the anonymity of the crowd, rifles trained on the gearheads.

The other three gearheads glanced at one another, expressions blank, but Lara swore she saw uncertainty in their eyes.

Tense silence enveloped the crowd.

Northside stared at Newton. "Not going to give you another warning."

Newton returned his gaze. "You do not have to be the thing he twisted you into. You have the ability to choose, to shape your own existence."

"You don't seem to understand." Northside's eyes shifted, falling on Lara. His upper lip stretched in a grin made impossibly grim and menacing because of the skin missing from his lower jaw. "Warlord's will is law around here. He's the reason we prosper. So you're going to disperse, or none of you will live long enough to regret this."

"Would he think twice before he tore you apart?" Lara moved her gaze from Northside to his companions. "The moment you cross him or disappoint him a little too much, he'll have you in pieces. You're junk to him. Scrap."

"He only ends those deserving of punishment. The troublemakers. Doesn't matter how fuckable they are."

Everything moved with incredible slowness as Northside twisted, swinging his weapon toward Lara. She found herself staring down the gaping barrel of his gun. There was only endless darkness in there, eager to swallow her. She clenched the grip of her pistol, but it weighed a thousand pounds, and her arm was too weak and sluggish to pull it free.

He squeezed the trigger just as Chester darted in front of her.

The soldiers opened fire, their shots coming a fraction of a second after the gearhead's. There was a high, sharp *pang*, and Chester swayed. Northside fell a moment later, with thin wisps of smoke curling out of the countless holes in him.

The three gearheads who stood behind him swiftly dropped their weapons and raised their empty hands. To her shock, Lara realized they'd also fired upon their leader. She recognized one of them, a synth with his exposed metal arm painted blue. Cobalt. He'd been guarding the bot district gate alongside Northside when Lara first went there.

The crowds murmured as the soldiers stepped forward to collect the discarded firearms.

Lara pressed a shaky hand against Chester's back. "You okay?"

He glanced at her over his shoulder. "Fine. Chest armor deflected the round. You?"

"Thought I was dead this time. Thank you."

He nodded.

"None of you have to tolerate this tyranny any further," Newton called out over the din. "None of you have to exist under the weight of fear. Today is your opportunity to band together and fight for mutual freedom. Today is the day we can begin working toward mutual prosperity."

"After all they've done, why would we want to live with them?" someone shouted.

Lara was certain it had been one of the humans.

"Metal and meat aren't meant to live side-by-side!" another person declared.

"Fuck that!" Lara turned toward Newton, who offered his hand to help her up onto the stand. She faced the humans. "My husband, a bot, is in there"—she jabbed a finger toward the bot district— "fighting for you. For us! These soldiers are bots *and* humans, and they come from a place where they live, work, and prosper together, where they're friends, where they're family. We can live side by side. They're no different than us. They feel just as deeply as we do."

"Before this world was shattered, our kinds coexisted peacefully," Newton said. "That was always the design. We were meant to learn from each other, to grow alongside each other, to shore up each other's weaknesses with our respective strengths. We are not meant to be at war."

"Yet you ask us to fight?" a bot asked.

"If you don't, it will be an extermination," Cobalt said. The crowd turned to him. "He's not capable of stopping once it's begun. He's been…bored lately, so he's taken it out on humans, and eventually he'll kill all of them. And after this, he won't hesitate to wipe this whole city clean and start over again."

"It's only a matter of time before he turns on us," another gearhead said. "He threatened to disassemble my lover if I didn't obey. And I've helped him take apart some of our kind already." His eyes found Lara's for an instant, flashing with guilt, and flicked away.

The gunfire in the bot district continued, picking up tempo.

Newton took a small step forward. "We must do this together. Not as bots and humans, but as a single, unified community. Gather whatever weapons we can find and march on the clinic to finish this. There cannot be freedom without sacrifice, but we cannot allow another life, whether organic or mechanical, to be taken for no reason but to serve Warlord's whims." He punctuated his statement by slamming his metal fist onto his open palm.

Rapid conversation swept through the crowd, shifting to calls of assent. Chester helped Lara down, and Newton followed behind her.

Captain Cooper approached her. "It's time, Lara. Newton will take you to the forward camp."

"No."

"I'm not asking, Brooks."

"It is going to be terribly, dangerous, Lara," Newton said, settling a hand on her shoulder. "And Ronin would not be happy with any of us."

Lara shook her head. "I don't care. As shitty as it's been, this is my home, and these are my people. I'm not going to hide while they risk their lives for it, especially not after I encouraged them to fight."

"And just what the hell do you think you're going to do in there?" Cooper demanded.

"Whatever the hell I can."

He stared at her, jaw clenched. "Shit," he muttered and ran a hand over his face. "Nancy's going to kill me, but she gets just as stubborn, and there's no budging her either once she's made up her mind. Newton, get back there. Tell them what's happening. If they can spare any more bodies, we might need them here."

"Please, check on Kate," Lara said.

Newton gently squeezed her shoulder before dropping his arm. "Thank you, Lara."

"For…what?"

"For getting me out of that hole, even if it was indirectly. I shall never—"

"Just save it, okay? I'll see you soon."

Despite his lack of skin, his expression was clearly troubled. "As you say. Soon, then."

Newton walked away. She watched him before Cooper caught her attention.

"Take this," he said, holding out another pistol. It was larger and heavier than the one Ronin had given her. "Two hands when you shoot. It's going to have a hell of a kick, but I don't want you to hesitate. Just…stay back. That clear?"

Lara tightened her grip on it and nodded.

Cooper pointed to Chester. "Like the colonel said. Like a fly on shit."

Chester sketched a salute. "Yes, Captain."

"Good. Now let's move. We're already late for the party."

CHAPTER FIFTY-TWO

"Get that AMR up here, *now!*" Maul shouted.

In Ronin's peripheral vision, a soldier scrambled forward with a long black rifle—an anti-materiel rifle, Ronin's memory said.

The weapon didn't come fast enough.

Comp charged at the entrance, making the ground quake with every heavy footfall. Whatever bullet riddled glass that remained shattered on impact, and the bot's broad body clipped the doorframe, raining brick and plaster.

A cloud of dust obscured Ronin's vision, but he still saw the barricade explode inward against Comp's forward momentum.

The desk broke into countless pieces, and mangled chairs flew in all directions. Ronin ducked out of the way, but at least two soldiers went down. The heavy rifle clattered to the floor.

If the room had seemed cramped with all the soldiers packed inside, Comp made it impossibly tiny. The bot's powerful arms swung, knocking a synth across the room and tearing down a portion of the ceiling. More dust and debris filled the air.

Muzzle flashes cast strange shadows in the haze, and the shouting and gunfire blended into an indecipherable cacophony. Ronin scanned Comp for potential vulnerabilities. The exposed cables of its neck were a potential target, but they were at least lightly armored.

Ronin leapt back from a flailing arm. At the edge of his optical field, the dark forms of gearheads rushed in through the devastated doorway. Stepping back, he turned toward them, raised his rifle, and fired. One of them slumped backwards, but another indistinct figure took its place.

The AMR fired behind Ronin, its thunderous shot easily distinguishable from the other small arms, followed almost instantly by a metallic pang. The actuators in Comp's left arm whined. Sparks crackled inside its forearm, illuminating a large hole in the metal.

At the doorway, Maul and two other soldiers battled the invading gearheads with fists and firearms. An explosion from just outside rocked the room. Bits of shrapnel sliced into Ronin's skin, while others bounced harmlessly off Comp's casing.

A gearhead stumbled through the entryway, all its parts missing above the abdomen. Electric sparks and lubricant sprayed from the remains as they fell.

Unfazed, Comp lunged forward. Ronin twisted to evade its massive fist, but his hip locked, halting his movement. The blow glanced off his temple. It sent Ronin to his knees, filling his optics with static for a microsecond.

Despite his reinforced casing, the next blow would be Ronin's end. While he'd been retrofitted for combat, he knew through data he wasn't sure he could consciously access that Comp had been designed for it. Comp was a walking tank, built for situations just like this. Its purpose had never been to guard doors, but to smash them in.

Bringing up his favorite images of Lara, of her vivid hair, her bright eyes, and her impossibly alive smile, Ronin raised his rifle.

The bouncer recovered from its swing, actuators groaning as it prepared another. The window of opportunity was brief. But just as Ronin didn't want to exist in a world without Lara, he wouldn't allow her to suffer a world without him.

Creaking, Comp's neck cables adjusted, pivoting its head back toward Ronin.

The dustwalker's CPU calculated the trajectories, and he fired twice within a tenth of a second.

Comp's optics shattered.

Ronin rolled aside clumsily. A massive hand swept down, smashing floor tiles. Comp's torso twisted, whipping its damaged arm in a wide arc that destroyed one of the overhead lights, and then it stepped forward, flailing.

The AMR boomed. A new hole opened on Comp's chest plate, and the bot staggered, leaking lubricant and hydraulic fluid from the creases of its casing. Tendrils of smoke escaped from the narrow gaps around its neck cables.

Throwing its arms up, Comp slammed its hands into the ceiling and pulled. A huge chunk of the ceiling collapsed, falling atop Ronin and knocking him to the floor beneath immense weight.

Though he couldn't see anything, Ronin both heard and felt Comp's heavy footsteps as the bot thrashed blindly. His diagnostics indicated only minor damage to his skin.

Shoving off debris, he clawed his way free, emerging in a room that looked nothing like it had only moments before. The air was thick with dust, the floor was hidden beneath the detritus, and electric wiring and light fixtures hung around the edges of a wide hole in the ceiling.

Gaining his feet, Ronin crossed the rubble, his suspension system straining to keep him upright. The synth with the AMR was digging himself out of rubble when Ronin found him. The soldier handed the heavy rifle to Ronin without question.

Shouldering the AMR, Ronin took aim at Comp. Automatic rifles roared to his right, and bullets from outside whizzed through the lobby, embedding themselves in the interior wall.

Comp twisted and bent, smacking around chunks of rubble in a search for something to break. When the bot's torso was exposed, Ronin squeezed the trigger. The rifle bucked against his shoulder as it discharged. He leveled the barrel and fired again.

The first shot caught Comp in the middle, and its torso ground to a halt. The second bullet punched through the bouncer's casing and hit its power cell. Electricity arced from its eyes and joints, and flames licked out of the holes in its casing before Comp stilled, legs locking while its torso and arms sagged.

Ronin rose and turned his body fully toward the front door. Maul and several bots stood strong, advancing in a walking line as they fired at the gearheads retreating outside, and more shots rained from the floors above. Two of the fleeing gearheads fell before they could make it more than a few meters across the grass circle at the driveway's center.

The battle had turned. The enemy had broken. They were no less dangerous, but their will to fight had shattered. Self-preservation had won out over their loyalty to Warlord.

Ronin turned the AMR in his hands. The weapon was familiar, though he'd never come across a functional one in all his time in the Dust. It had a five-round capacity. Drawing the charging handle back partway, he confirmed that a single round remained in the chamber.

So long as Maul had no objections, Ronin planned to use it on Warlord.

He crossed the rubble to reach the Sergeant. At least six gearheads lay in and around the doorway, deactivated. Four of Maul's soldiers were unmoving.

"We need to finish this." Ronin drew the AMR sling over his shoulder, stowed the heavy weapon behind his back, and loaded the last full magazine into his automatic rifle.

Maul nodded, and the flap of synthetic skin hanging from his cheek bobbed. He reached up, took hold of it, and tore it off. His jaw-plates shifted subtly. "Yeah. I think that's a good idea."

Ronin and Maul turned to face the others; several more soldiers had come down from the upper levels. Some had suffered damage to their synthetic skin and casings, others wore sheens of sweat and blood.

"Are you ready to show them what an attack looks like?" Maul asked.

The soldiers offered an affirmative shout in response.

It had only been one hundred and four days since Ronin met Lara, since his existence was irrevocably altered, but it felt like an eternity had passed. Now, this part of their story would be done. Warlord would be no more.

Ronin charged out of the building, leaping over the shattered remnants of the doors, walls, and ceiling. Guns roared in front of and behind him. His optics took in the chaos ahead, and despite the speed of his processors, he didn't immediately understand what he was looking at.

The retreating gearheads had been intercepted by a group that had come from the south, a mob of bots and humans—Bravo Team and the residents of Cheyenne. Some fought the gearheads with firearms, but most wielded pipes, prybars, and all manner of improvised weapons.

Cooper and a group of soldiers advanced on the shrinking cluster of gearheads. Warlord stood in the center of the enemy group, brows low over the bridge of his nose and lips pulled back in a snarl. The gearheads fired into the crowd, heads turning rapidly to track their many targets, but their leader's attention was fixed on one person.

Ronin followed Warlord's line of sight with his own.

He glimpsed red hair behind a synth soldier named Chester, and his processors buzzed, nearly overloaded with anticipation. The soldier shifted to line up a shot, revealing Lara. She held a large pistol with both hands. It jumped when she pulled the trigger, but she calmly brought it back down and aimed again.

Warlord stared directly at her, wearing his hatred plainly upon his face. He thrust a finger toward her and snarled, "Kill her!"

Though she was positioned toward the rear of the crowd, one of the most distant and obstructed targets, the gearheads swung their weapons toward Lara.

Had Ronin had a heart, it would've stopped at that moment.

"No!" Ronin pushed his legs faster. As the gearheads opened fire, he lined up his automatic rifle and pulled the trigger, sending armor piercing rounds into two of the bots' heads.

At the edge of his vision, he saw Chester turn and sweep Lara into his arms, using his back as a shield. Ronin's audio receptors isolated the sound of Lara's cry from the cacophony. He couldn't tell if there was pain mixed in with the distress and terror. He knew only that there was no guarantee Chester's casing would stop all the bullets.

Chester's clothes tore, his skin broke, and his body shook with the force. He collapsed over Lara, catching himself by jabbing the barrel of his rifle into the ground for support.

"Lara!" Ronin shouted.

Pouring additional power into his legs, he leapt off the ground, launching himself at the remaining gearheads. Two swung around and fired. He registered new damage to his torso casing, but he didn't waste computing power to assess it. His only priority was to stop them from shooting at his wife.

Ronin's momentum knocked the gearheads to the ground, and he fell with them. Despite the groans of protest from his hip, he swung himself up onto a knee and pivoted toward his scattered enemies, emptying his firearm into them.

The soldiers who'd followed him from the clinic fired at the remaining gearheads. Their gunfire drowned out all other sounds. When it ended, a heavy silence settled over the area.

Only two of the enemies were still moving. A prone gearhead with smoke billowing from its perforated casing extended a hand and dug its fingers into the ground. Actuators whining, it dragged itself a few centimeters forward.

Rising to his feet, Ronin tossed the assault rifle aside and approached the other bot—Warlord.

Warlord pushed himself up onto his knees. One of his optics was a gaping hole, and the synthetic flesh on his cheek had separated entirely from the bottom of his face, exposing the underlying plating and his teeth. His casing was riddled with bullet holes, and his clothes were in tatters.

He glared at Ronin. "You're supposed to be dead."

Warlord's jaw fell open with the first word and ceased its motion.

Ronin swung the AMR into his hands. "From what I've learned, so are you, Kevin."

It was a battle to keep from turning around to find Lara. He needed to see her, needed to know she was all right, but the possibility that she wasn't...

Warlord snickered, shaking his head. "Haven't heard that name in years."

The crowd moved in, slowly surrounding the pile of deactivated bots. Their anger charged the air with static. No one spoke.

Warlord ran his remaining optic over them, his exposed face plates oddly neutral in their positioning.

Ronin halted with three meters between himself and Warlord, leveling his rifle at his target. "It was yours, long ago. When you were human. Kevin Turner."

A gasp ran through the humans, and the crowd murmured.

Warlord held still, his lone eye on Ronin again. "That supposed to startle me? Supposed to…jog my memory?"

"You had a family. People who cared for you."

Where is Lara?

Despite the damage Warlord had sustained, Ronin couldn't look away, couldn't trust that Cheyenne's deposed tyrant wouldn't try to inflict more harm before he was shut down forever.

"Diane, Michael, and Liam," Warlord responded.

"You remember them now?"

"I *never* forgot. Never forgot that humans and their war did this to the world, that it was mankind's fault I never got to see them again, to hold them or touch them or hear their voices!" He swung an arm in a harsh slashing gesture, disrupting his balance and pitching himself forward. He caught himself by planting his other hand on the ground.

Ronin's voice dropped low. "Did you forget the fear you put into your wife the last time you saw her?"

Warlord remained hunched over, propped on his arm, with his head down. The fluid dripping from the breaches in his casing looked unsettlingly like blood. "Do you believe in destiny, dustwalker? Logic says it's all just a game of probability, but for all these pieces to fall into place…"

"You don't think this is result of cause and effect? The consequences of your actions finally come to fruition?"

"I should. But there's more here. The masterless warrior seeking to right the wrongs done by the local warlord, rallying the townsfolk to stand against him…it's too much like an old story to be anything but destiny that brought you to Cheyenne."

There was movement in the crowd behind Warlord. Lara pushed her way to the front. Strands of hair stuck out from her braid, and her face was smudged with dirt and blood. There were small cuts on her cheek and arms, and a larger gash near her shoulder. Crimson stained her tattered clothing on her side.

But her expression was firm, her eyes determined. She offered Ronin a small, relieved smile, and dropped her attention to Warlord.

"I believe in fate," Ronin said.

"You're everything they're not, dustwalker. They destroyed this world. They don't deserve it anymore. We're stronger, faster, tougher, smarter. We're *immortal*. You'll see it yourself, eventually. We are the future, and they're nothing but a lingering curiosity on their way to extinction."

"But you're the one everyone is staring at, like a creature in a cage," Ronin said.

Warlord lifted his head, meeting Ronin's gaze. Seconds ticked by. The plates around Warlord's mouth shifted subtly, and he threw himself upright, raising a rifle.

A single gunshot went off, and Warlord's remaining optic exploded outward. Warlord's weapon fired into the grass as he sagged forward onto the ground.

Lara stood behind him, pistol raised in both hands, her brows low. "Fuck you."

Warlord laughed, struggling to rise on trembling arms. "Already did that, didn't you?"

Ronin stepped forward, slamming a boot down onto Warlord's back to force him into the dirt. He fired the last round from the AMR. Its boom echoed across Cheyenne and into the Dust, lingering for five seconds in the ensuing quiet. Blue fire poured from Warlord, igniting and extinguishing in a flash as his power cell burned.

Dropping the rifle, Ronin cancelled his automated diagnostics and dismissed the alerts informing him of the damage he'd taken. He turned toward Lara, intending to go to her, but she'd already come to him.

She leapt at him and threw her arms around him in a desperate embrace. Ronin caught her and held her close, burying his face in her hair.

Warlord's reign had ended, and Lara was alive, in his arms. Her heat seeped into his skin, lighting up his sensors. The chances that he never would've felt her again, never would've held her again, had been so high...

He buried his fingers in her hair. "Lara..."

She pulled back, taking his cheeks between her hands. Her gaze swept over his face. Tears glistened in her eyes, but she smiled. "You look like shit."

Ronin smiled back. "And you look beautiful."

She laughed, and her tears fell before she pressed her mouth against his. Her lips lingered, caressing his, even as a sob escaped her. "I knew you'd be fine."

"I had the best reason to survive."

"All right everyone," Captain Cooper called, claiming the crowd's attention. "We're clearing the hospital's entrance. There are medical personnel inside, and more inbound. Whether you're a bot or a human, if you are injured, please proceed to there for treatment."

He approached Ronin and Lara as the crowd thinned. Bots and humans alike assisted the wounded in a slow, careful journey to the clinic, where soldiers were removing rubble and deactivated gearheads.

"Heartwarming as this is, you two need medical attention," Cooper said, smiling. Maul and Chester came up behind him, the latter with several new holes in the front of his casing. His walk was labored, but steady.

"We'll get to it," Lara said.

"Thank you." Ronin nodded to Chester. "Thank you for keeping my wife safe. We owe you everything."

Chester grinned. "All I did was stand in front of some bullets. Not the hardest job I've had."

Lara chuckled. "I would've done the same for you, except, you know. The death thing."

Ronin laughed, though he didn't find the joke particularly funny.

She was alive.

And so was he.

CHAPTER FIFTY-THREE

The bot district was quiet as Ronin and Lara walked along the street. He had his arm around her shoulders, holding her against his side, while one of hers was looped around his lower back. She leaned against him not because she needed support, but because she wanted to be as close to him as possible. That desire was mutual.

He didn't intend to ever let her go again.

The midmorning sun cast their shadows ahead of them. He was sure there was some sort of symbolism in that—their shadows, merged into one, leading them home.

Ronin stole a glance at her. The cuts on her cheek had scabbed over, and the dressings on her shoulder and side were hidden under her clothing, which was still stained with blood.

An unsettling buzz ran through his processors. He hated that she'd been hurt, but that couldn't overpower his happiness and relief that her injuries had been so minor. Not everyone had been so fortunate yesterday.

Dozens of wounded had streamed into the clinic after the battle, accompanied by friends, family, and neighbors. McGowan, Mercy, and the staff had worked ceaselessly to triage and treat the wounded, not slowing even when Nancy arrived with some of her team an hour later.

Once Ronin had ensured Lara's wounds were tended, he'd

joined her in assisting the efforts in any way they could. The long, difficult morning had stretched into a long, difficult day, and nightfall had brought only minor relief. Few of Cheyenne's residents had gone to their homes. Most found what comfort they could right there in the clinic, sleeping alongside the soldiers who'd come to fight for them.

Exhaustion had overtaken Lara in the small hours of the morning. Ronin had sat down with her, their backs against a wall, and she'd slept leaning against him.

Sometime near dawn, his turn for repairs had come. He'd very nearly declined despite the grinding in his hip and the alerts warning him of his declining mobility. But Lara had stirred and demanded he go. Unwilling to leave his side, she'd gone with him, and had dozed in a chair in the repair room as a machine fixed him.

The morning had come with a grim count. Seven of the soldiers from the base and twelve of Cheyenne's residents had fallen in the battle, eleven humans and eight bots total. Apart from Cobalt and the handful of defectors, every gearhead had been deactivated.

Lara halted abruptly. Ronin stopped as well, watching as she slowly scanned their surroundings. She took in a deep breath and let it out measuredly before whispering, "He's gone."

Ronin's brow furrowed, and he tilted his head.

Lara's next breath was shaky, and she trembled against Ronin. "He's really gone, right?"

"He is, Lara."

"But…forever?" She turned her gaze up to meet his, and her eyes were troubled, shimmering with gathering tears. "Because you came back. What if someone brings him back? What if—"

Ronin lifted a hand to cradle the side of her face. "He's *gone*, Lara. Forever. You're all right. We're all right."

When she closed her eyes, the tears rolled down her cheeks. "He's dead. He's really dead."

Sobbing, she collapsed against him, clutching him tighter.

Ronin turned toward her and embraced her fully. Lara pressed her face against his chest. There was a rawness in her cries that spoke not necessarily of sorrow, but something much stronger, much deeper. It penetrated his casing and clawed into his circuitry, tearing at him in ways he'd never known were possible before her.

And Ronin simply held her, petting a hand down her hair and back, soothing her without words.

Even when her sobs subsided and she was quiet save for the occasional sniffle, they didn't move. All they needed in that moment was each other.

Yesterday had dawned with a near infinite number of potential outcomes, tangled and indecipherable, stretching into an unseeable future. Probability suggested a terrible toll even with success. Every variable, no matter how miniscule, could have spiraled into catastrophic consequences. The slightest alteration to the trajectory of a single bullet could've been Ronin's end, whether that bullet had stricken him or Lara.

Because he did not belong in a world without her.

But fate had seen them through the day. It had brought them together again, alive and whole, had brought them here, had allowed him to hold her, to feel her, to have her.

His Lara, his wife, his purpose.

She rubbed her cheek against his chest. "It just doesn't feel real. For all my life, I've lived this nightmare, lived with this fear…until I met you. And now that Warlord's gone…" She lifted her head and met his gaze with a soft but tremulous smile on her lips. The blue of her eyes was especially bright. It was the color the sky had once been, the color it would one day be again. "We're free, Ronin."

He smiled and cradled her beautiful face, wiping the streaks of tears from her cheeks with his thumbs. "We are."

And he could feel it. The heavy chains of fear that had bound them to this place, to Warlord, had fallen away, replaced by a new weight—that of a future they could now shape. A future that belonged to them. It was a burden Ronin accepted gladly. It was…hope.

He lowered his head and pressed a kiss to her forehead.

Lara's smile grew. "Let's go home."

They continued onward.

When they reached the house, they paused, looking at it in silence. Ronin hadn't expected to ever see it again. Though he could not guess what Lara was thinking, the place looked different to him. But now that they were back, it felt right. It felt like it was truly theirs.

They walked to the door, which Ronin opened but did not enter. He turned to Lara and scooped her up into what the humans fittingly called a bridal carry.

Lara gasped in surprise, throwing her arms around his neck, and laughed as he cradled her against his chest. "What are you doing?"

"It's an old human tradition. I'm supposed to carry you across the threshold into our home to begin our new life." Keeping his eyes locked with hers, he stepped through the doorway, nudging the door closed behind him. "My wife."

Sliding her fingers into his hair, Lara brushed her lips across his. "My husband."

And then their mouths came together in a kiss as tender as it was devouring. Sparks danced across his skin, lighting up his sensors, and desire flared in his CPU. Hunger wasn't supposed to be part of his programming, but he hungered for her all the same.

"I need you," Lara whispered against his mouth. "Make love to me, Ronin."

Capturing her mouth once more, he carried her upstairs. Both their kiss and his steps were unfaltering as he strode down the hall to their bedroom. He stood her beside the bed and reluctantly broke the kiss to remove her clothing.

He did so slowly, teasingly, letting his fingers caress her skin as they worked. He would never tire of the way her body reacted to his touch. Her breaths grew heavier as he unfastened her pants and slid them down. Lara stepped out of her boots and kicked her pants aside, stealing another kiss from him as his hands moved to her shirt.

Ronin let his fingertips glide over her skin as he pushed her shirt up. Her belly quivered, and her breath hitched as he shifted his hands to her chest, his palms skimming her already hardened nipples. She raised her arms over her head, and he pulled the garment off. Loose strands of her fiery hair fell to frame her face. Her eyes gleamed with lust as she looked up at him, and he didn't miss the pink coloring her skin.

His cock swelled against the confines of his pants, thrumming with need.

He stroked the backs of his fingers over her unmarked cheek. "You are so beautiful."

Sweeping her up into his arms, he laid her upon the bed, removed his boots, and began taking off his own clothing. Lara watched, her gaze trekking over his body as he revealed it a little at a time.

As soon as he was naked, she held out her arms, and he climbed onto the bed, positioning himself over her. Lara's thighs parted wide, and she welcomed him into the cradle of her body, drawing him closer. Her skin was hot against his, and a very human-like groan escaped him when the head of his cock pressed against the entrance of her pussy.

He stared into her eyes. "Lara…"

She smiled and caressed her fingers down his shoulders and back. "I love you."

"And I will forever love you."

Claiming her mouth in a kiss, Ronin flexed his hips, pushing his cock slowly, deeply inside her. Her body readily accepted him, drawing him into her hot, wet, depths. It was a sensation that he savored, that he craved, that dominated his sensory systems and overrode his programming.

This closeness, this intimacy, this *life*, it was all more than he'd ever thought obtainable. More than he'd ever thought possible.

The long, grueling roads he'd walked had led him to Lara. Every hardship, every trial, every single step, had brought him here.

And this was where he belonged—with her. Always.

CHAPTER FIFTY-FOUR

"You were right," Lara breathed, awed by the sight before her. "The pictures didn't do it justice."

The ocean was endless.

When they'd tried to escape Cheyenne two years ago, Ronin had told her the ocean was vast, but actually standing in front of it really put its size into perspective.

It all seems insignificant in the face of something so massive.

Lara certainly felt insignificant right now. Insignificant, but wonderstruck.

Reflected sunlight glittered on the rolling blue waves, which broke upon the shore into sheets of white foam. And the water just stretched on and on and on, as far as she could see…

The wind blew around Lara, making her hair flutter and spraying her skin with cool mist. She closed her eyes and breathed in the briny scent. The sound of waves crashing into the land and receding, back and forth, back and forth, was like the heartbeat of some impossibly large creature—the heartbeat of the world. Moving at its own pace, unbothered by the tiny things crawling around on its surface.

"It's bluer than when I last saw it," Ronin said.

Lara opened her eyes and looked at him standing beside her. "It changed?"

He scanned the horizon, a gentle smile lifting the corners of his mouth. "The world is always changing, always healing. Like Cheyenne."

She gazed back out at the ocean. Cheyenne had changed so much after Warlord's fall. Many of the people from the base had relocated to the town, and the bot district had become a place where humans and bots lived and worked together. They'd built new homes, planted more crops, and even established their own council to govern the settlement.

Everyone worked hard—and together—to ensure that every resident of Cheyenne had what they needed not just to survive, but to live happily and comfortably. Lara still wondered if she was lost in a coma, dreaming. And every day, Ronin proved to her that she wasn't.

Like now.

On the second anniversary of the day he'd slipped the ring on Lara's finger, the day he'd made his vow to her and become her husband, Ronin had told her he wanted to fulfill another promise he'd made. He'd said it would require a long, difficult journey, but he thought the destination would be worth it.

And it had been. Leaving Cheyenne the first time had been terrifying. This time, it had been an adventure, filled with excitement and anticipation…though Ronin had stressed there was still plenty of danger.

The risk hadn't diminished her wonderment. They'd seen mountains and forests, rivers and streams, canyons and meadows. The landscape had changed so much during their month-long trek, which had taken them past the western edge of the Dust.

But this spot, their ultimate destination, was the pinnacle of it all. The land leading to the coast was so lush and green, so full of life, and the shore itself…

She once more breathed in the salt-kissed air. "It's beautiful."

"It is, but…"

Lara looked at him, brow arched. "But?"

"But it cannot compare to the sight I see every day." Ronin caught her chin and tipped her face up toward his, grinning down at her. "Nothing can match the blue of your eyes, Lara Brooks."

Warmth suffused her. He complimented her daily, but she never tired of his sweet words. They only showed her how much he wanted her. How much he loved her.

She ran her gaze over her him. The breadth of his shoulders in his coat, his wind tousled hair, and the rakish curl of his lips sent a rush of heat to her core. And his green eyes, so vibrant and alive…

Fuck, he's gorgeous.

And he's mine.

Smiling, she stepped close and slipped her arms around his neck, pressing her body to his. "Thank you. For bringing me here."

Ronin settled his hands on her hips, holding her pelvis close. "Would you like to go in?"

Lara's brows shot up. "In? You mean, in the ocean?"

He nodded. "Not too far, but yes."

"It's…not going to sweep me away?"

"I won't let it. Nothing is going to take you away from me, wife."

"Then you don't have to tell me twice."

Ronin's laughter was such a warm, rich sound.

Drawing back, she toed off her boots and shoved down her pants, kicking them off. She wiggled her toes, digging them into the sand as she marveled at the sensation. This was so unlike the dust and dirt in Cheyenne. It was soft, almost soothing, rather than coarse and abrasive.

As she walked toward the water, the sand grew more compact, giving less beneath her feet. When the next wave rolled toward shore, Lara stopped, bracing for the chill, but the water that flowed past her wasn't nearly as cold as she'd expected.

The water raced back out to the sea, making her heels sink into the wet sand. Even with it barely reaching her ankles, she could feel that pull out toward the endless blue. She couldn't lie to herself and say it wasn't a little frightening. Lara couldn't imagine being lost out there. But at the same time, it was exhilarating.

She stepped farther out, and with the next wave, the water rose past her knees. Chuckling, she bent down and swept her fingers over the surface. Beneath the water, tiny rocks, shells, and bits of a green plant tumbled on the shifting sand.

As the water rushed back, Ronin strode up beside her. Her eyes caught on his bare feet, then ran up over his shins and thighs, stopping on his long, thick cock, which hung limp against his leg.

He'd undressed completely.

Lara's gaze shot to his. "Ronin!"

He spread his arms to the sides, indicating the surrounding beach. "There's no one around, and I don't want to get my clothes wet."

"Well, you're certainly getting something wet." With a laugh, she swept her hand through the water and splashed him before taking off along the shore.

When she glanced over her shoulder to find him giving chase, her heart quickened and her belly fluttered. His playful grin was belied by the focus in his eyes, which were locked on her.

He rapidly gained on her and thrust out a hand to grab her. Lara abruptly changed directions, feeling his fingertips brush along her side. Water splashed around her legs as she ran. She knew he could have caught her easily. There was no way she could ever truly outrun him, but the chase was as thrilling as it was arousing.

"Maybe if you catch me, you can see just how wet I am!" she called, wind whipping through her hair.

The splashes of his footfalls increased in speed behind her. Though it wouldn't make any difference, Lara pushed herself faster, extending the game just that little bit. But she could hear him closing in again, could feel him drawing near.

"You're mine!" His arms banded around her middle, yanking her up off her feet.

She shrieked with laughter as the world spun around her. And then she was drawn in against Ronin's chest, his arms wrapped protectively around her.

"You're mine," he said again, voice husky in her ear.

Grinning, she turned her face toward him. "I am."

His mouth captured hers in a deep, passionate kiss that stole what little breath remained in her lungs. Heat curled low in her belly, and she was all the more aware of his cock thickening against her ass.

When she broke the kiss, their eyes met, and she cupped his jaw with one hand. Her breath was ragged, and the ache between her thighs bloomed. But it was his hand, pressed possessively over her stomach, that stirred a different yearning.

Her words spilled out without a thought. "I want to have a baby with you."

Ronin went utterly still. "Lara…"

"I…I mean if you want to. If you don't, then we—"

One of his hands thrust into her hair at the back of her head, holding her in place as his lips again descended to lock with hers in a slow, sensuous, deep kiss. That familiar desire flared hotter, licking through her veins. She moaned against his mouth.

Ronin lifted his head, pulling away from the kiss. "Yes."

It took Lara a moment to push past the fog of lust in her mind and open her eyes. He was staring at her with wide grin.

She blinked. "Yes?"

Wait. He's saying yes to…

Lara beamed up at him. "Really? You want to have a baby?"

He turned her body toward his, lifted her into his arms, and pressed his forehead against hers. "Yes. I want to see your belly grow with our child. I want to raise a family with you. I want to share every human moment, every aspect of life, with you, Lara Brooks. Everything."

EPILOGUE

Ronin walked along the sidewalk, optics roaming over the park across the street. As many times as he'd seen it in the fifty-one years since he'd come to Cheyenne, he never tired of it—the place was ever changing. Most of its grounds had been repurposed for farming decades ago, coupling with the fields outside town to leave Cheyenne with a food surplus that attracted traders from distant settlements.

Children ran and played between rows of crops, laughing and smiling, getting especially giggly when fieldworkers shooed them away. Ronin knew them all by name, knew which of them were likely to leave signs on Mr. Mather's back, which unfortunately included one of his great grandchildren, Rae. The teacher still hadn't caught on to their tricks.

"Dad!"

Stopping, Ronin turned. Tabitha jogged toward him with a bundle of Indian Paintbrush flowers in her hand.

Ronin's memory flashed back to the first time he'd held his daughter. Tabitha had been so tiny and fragile, small enough to hold in one hand. It hadn't mattered that her biological father was someone else, Ronin had bonded with her instantly. She was his. His baby.

Now, Tabitha was a woman with grown children and a few grandkids of her own. She possessed so many of Lara's features—

the red hair, the bright blue eyes, the stubborn streak. The forty-seven years since her birth had gone by too quickly, though they'd been full of joy, meaning, learning, and adapting.

Tabitha grinned as she reached him. "Found these on my way back from the fields. I thought Mom would like them."

Smiling, Ronin accepted the flowers. "She'll love them."

"How's she been? I visited with Lucas and the grandbabies yesterday, but I think they tired her out pretty quick."

Lucas, Tabitha's oldest, had two young daughters who often visited Ronin and Lara, Rae and Sadie. Rae was a handful on her own, but paired with her little sister... The two were far too mischievous, clever, and hilarious for their own good.

Ronin couldn't express how much he loved them.

He cupped Tabitha's cheek with his free hand, brushing a thumb over her dusting of freckles. "She doesn't quite have the endurance she used to. But to be fair, those kids tire me out too."

She chuckled as he lowered his arm. "Tell me about it. Anyway, Dan's waiting on me, so I gotta run. We're going to help with some repairs on the wall. Let mom know I'll stop by tomorrow. It's my day off, so I can help her around the house if she needs it. Oh, and I was talking with Sam, Mel, and Mandy, and we want to try to get everyone all together in the next couple weeks. We're trying to coordinate with everyone."

"That sounds great. I'll let her know."

Tabitha stepped forward and wrapped her arms around him, kissing his cheek. "Love you guys."

He hugged her back and kissed the top of her head the same way he had throughout her youth. "Love you too, Tabby."

As Ronin watched her go, he couldn't silence the question whispering across his processors.

Had he been right to downplay the truth and deflect with humor?

Tabitha wasn't a child anymore. She knew Lara's health was waning, knew that, despite the comforts they'd all worked hard to have, death remained a reality in Cheyenne. She'd been old enough to understand what was happening during the famine when she was a child, and she'd been nearly twenty when sickness swept through town and killed dozens.

That had been amongst the hardest lessons Ronin and Lara had learned as parents—that no matter what they did, no matter how hard they tried, they couldn't shield their child from the world.

Tabitha was mature, strong, observant, and compassionate. He knew she would be able to handle anything. But he still couldn't bring himself to say anything that would dim the love and joy that always sparkled in her eyes.

Finally, he resumed his walk, greeting the neighbors who were outside tending their gardens as he passed. Though flowers had become popular in recent years, adding color to the neighborhood, many humans still kept their own plots of crops.

The struggles of the past had not been forgotten. Most of the humans who'd suffered under Warlord and revolted against him were gone, but their legacies continued, carried on by their children and grandchildren, new generations who worked alongside bots to build and maintain a prosperous community.

When he reached his residence, Ronin opened the front gate and entered the yard, closing it gently. Coming home like this felt strange sometimes. He remembered when this had just been a place to store and care for his gear, a temporary stop between his long treks into the Dust. Back then, it had been a building devoid of life, largely empty of purpose.

But Lara had made it into a home.

Ronin climbed the steps onto the porch, where chimes crafted from scrap metal Lara had collected over the years tinkled quietly in the breeze. It was the same sound that had drawn him to her half a century ago.

The lure of fate.

He stepped inside and shut the door behind him. "Lara?"

The living room walls didn't have a single bare patch. His wife had remained a collector, as she dubbed herself, throughout her life. Decades' worth of trinkets adorned the walls and shelves, displayed proudly for any guests to see.

"In here!" she called.

Ronin followed her voice toward the kitchen, passing the seashells she'd gathered when they visited the ocean. There was a jar of sand from the same trip on one of the end tables, with a heart-shaped rock pressed against the inside of the glass. Ronin hadn't understood the need to bring more sand back to a town already full of dust and dirt, but he'd carried it nonetheless.

Lara stood at the counter, smearing jam onto a slice of bread. Her eyes were fixed on the task, her movements slow and deliberate, but she looked up at him the moment he stepped into the room. She smiled, and wrinkles bunched at the corners of her eyes.

Her hair was gray now. She'd panicked when she found her first gray hair, locking herself in the bathroom for more than an hour, crying, before Ronin had finally forced the door open to ensure she was okay. She'd taken it as a sign of her mortality, and had been convinced he would leave her at any moment.

But she was as beautiful to him now as when he first saw her. Even more so, after the life they'd shared.

"Tabby found some flowers for you," he said, holding up the bundle.

"She could've brought them herself." The trembling of her hand was hard to miss as she set the knife down. "She only lives three houses away, and I would've loved to see her."

"She and Dan are assisting with repairs on the wall, which means she was already running late. Tomorrow is her free day. She said she'll come by."

Her smile widened. "I'm so proud of her. Of all of them."

"They had the best mother this side of the Dust," Ronin replied, smiling as well.

Tabitha had been Lara's only biological child, as complications during labor had made another pregnancy too risky. But they'd adopted and raised three other children who they loved just as much as Tabby—Samuel, Melissa, and Amanda. Their ages had varied, with Melissa having been the oldest at fifteen, but they'd all needed a home. A family.

Lara chuckled and lifted her arms toward him. "Are you just going to stand there, or are you going to come say hello?"

Ronin crossed the room and embraced her, gently but warmly, running a hand down her long, silver braid.

"Hello." He dipped his head to kiss her.

"Hello," she said against his lips. When she drew her head back, she met his gaze. "Would you put the flowers in water for me?"

"Of course." He placed the flowers on the counter, picked up her bread, and took her arm. She leaned on him as she walked to the table, where he pulled a chair out with his boot and helped her ease into it.

"You're always so good to me."

"It's no less than you deserve, Lara Brooks."

"Still calling me Lara Brooks after all this time." She shook her head, but there was mirth in her eyes as she picked up the bread and took a bite.

Ronin found a vase in the cabinet and filled it with water from the sink. "I've told you already, just because I married you without having a surname of my own doesn't mean you get to drop yours."

Turning to the counter, his gaze caught on the granite. There were several cracks that had been repaired, spiderwebbing out from the spot where his fist had struck it. He played that memory in his mind. It had been the turning point for the both of them, the moment Lara had seen him as more than a machine.

The moment she had seen him as a man.

Ronin ran a finger over one of the seams that had been filled in.

After adding the flowers to the vase, he returned to the table and placed them at its center.

She'd only taken two bites when she set the bread down and raised a hand to her forehead, pressing her fingers to her temple. "It's too early to be so tired."

"Sunset is in less than an hour." Ronin tilted his head with a grin. "And when have you ever passed up an opportunity for me to take you to bed, anyway?"

Lara chuckled. "We can go upstairs, as long as you promise not to rip my shirt this time." Her smile was strained, her face too pale.

Ronin brushed the backs of his fingers down her cheek. "Come then, my wife."

He pulled out her chair and lifted her into his arms. Lara's weight had always been slight to him, but she was thinner now than ever before. She slid her arms around his neck and rested her head on his shoulder as he carried her up to the bedroom.

Ronin set her on her feet beside the bed, and she took his face between her hands, kissing him. He returned the kiss and undressed her. His hands brushed over her skin, which was so changed, yet so familiar, lingering on the stretch marks and scars.

They were evidence of a hard-fought life made all the more precious by its struggles.

He touched his forehead to hers. "You remain the most beautiful thing I have ever seen."

"You've always made me feel that way."

He helped her into her nightgown and pulled back the covers. She slipped into bed slowly. Ronin kicked off his boots and changed out of his dirty clothes, putting on a plain shirt and a pair of shorts. He climbed onto the bed and drew her into his arms, allowing her to rest her head on his shoulder. Her body still fit against his perfectly.

Lara's light breath tickled the sensors on his skin. He took her braid in one hand, absently running his fingertips along it.

"I never thought I'd have this life," she said softly.

"Neither did I. It is more than I could have ever hoped for."

She reached up and brushed her fingers over his jaw. "Even after all these years, I haven't had enough time to love you."

Her words pierced him; they were too final, too true. He settled a hand on her cheek and stroked his thumbs over the fine wrinkles near her eye. Ten thousand years wouldn't have been enough, but this…it was much, much too soon.

"We have years more to go, Lara."

"Bots always say what they mean," she said, "but that doesn't make it the truth."

"Lara, I—"

"Shh." She placed a finger over his lips as she met his gaze. Her smile was warm, though her eyes were tired. "Will you stay with me while I sleep?"

"You know I always do."

"And you know I always ask."

She relaxed, her weight settling against him, and soon her breathing evened out. He measured time by the slow, faint beat of her heart, pulling up memories from their life together.

Her sunburn after her first day working in the fields despite the lengths to which she'd gone to cover herself. The joyous smile she'd worn the first time she held Tabitha and the tears that had followed. Her patience with the townsfolk when they came to her

—the mother of the revolution that had set them free—for advice. The life glowing in her eyes when she danced, just for him.

And every time she'd told him she loved him.

Two hours and eleven minutes after midnight, she released her final breath. It flowed over Ronin's skin gently, the last caress from the woman he loved with all the power in his processors. He held her close and shut his eyes, pressing his lips to her hair.

"I will love you even after darkness takes me," he whispered.

"Mom? Dad?" Tabitha called as she stepped through the front door of her parents' home. Silence greeted her. She checked the kitchen, where a plate with a partly eaten slice of jellied bread was upon the table along with the flowers she'd picked yesterday.

"Mom?" she called again, unable to keep the worry from her voice. It was early, and her mother had been more tired than usual lately…though shouldn't her father have answered?

She hurried upstairs. The door to their bedroom was ajar, and her heart pounded as she approached it.

She knocked. There was no reply.

"You guys in here?" Tabitha pushed the door open all the way.

Tabitha knew the moment she saw them. Tears blurred her eyes as she staggered to the bed, lifting a hand to cover her mouth as though she could hold in the sound of her own heartbroken silence.

Her mother lay with her father, both unmoving. The casing on his back had been pried open. He clutched a power cell in his hand.

Blinking away her tears, Tabitha picked up the folded paper that lay atop him with a trembling hand. She wiped her eyes and read it.

Tabby, Sam, Mel, and Mandy,

I am so sorry to make this your burden. You may not understand now, but I hope you will in time. We have lived long, happy lives together. My place remains at your mother's side. I cannot continue on, unchanging, as my children and grandchildren live and die.

I ask that you do not reactivate me. Please bury me with your mother, so I can fulfill my promise and be with her during her long sleep.

Know that we are proud of all of you and the people you have grown to be, and that our love will always be with you. When your mother was young, we changed the world. It is up to you to continue shaping it into something beautiful for everyone.

With Love,
Dad

ALSO BY TIFFANY ROBERTS

THE INFINITE CITY

Entwined Fates

Silent Lucidity

Shielded Heart

Vengeful Heart

Untamed Hunger

Savage Desire

Tethered Souls

THE KRAKEN

Treasure of the Abyss

Jewel of the Sea

Hunter of the Tide

Heart of the Deep

Rising from the Depths

Fallen from the Stars

Lover from the Waves

THE SPIDER'S MATE TRILOGY

Ensnared

Enthralled

Bound

THE VRIX

The Weaver

The Delver

The Hunter

THE CURSED ONES

His Darkest Craving

His Darkest Desire

ALIENS AMONG US

Taken by the Alien Next Door

Stalked by the Alien Assassin

Claimed by the Alien Bodyguard

Saved by the Alien Crime Boss

STANDALONE TITLES

Claimed by an Alien Warrior

Dustwalker

Escaping Wonderland

Yearning For Her

The Warlock's Kiss

Ice Bound: Short Story

ISLE OF THE FORGOTTEN

Make Me Burn

Make Me Hunger

Make Me Whole

Make Me Yours

VALOS OF SONHADRA COLLABORATION

Tiffany Roberts - Undying

Tiffany Roberts - Unleashed

VENYS NEEDS MEN COLLABORATION

Tiffany Roberts - To Tame a Dragon

Tiffany Roberts – To Love a Dragon

ABOUT THE AUTHOR

Tiffany Roberts is the pseudonym for Tiffany and Robert, a husband and wife writing duo. The two have always shared a passion for reading and writing, and it was their dream to combine their mighty powers to create the sorts of books they want to read. They write character driven sci-fi and fantasy romance, creating happily-ever-afters for the alien and unknown.

Sign up for our Newsletter!
Check out our social media sites and more!
http://www.authortiffanyroberts.com